WHITEWATER HONEYMOON

A SEDONA CHI MYSTERY

WHITEWATER HONEYMOON

A SEDONA CHI MYSTERY

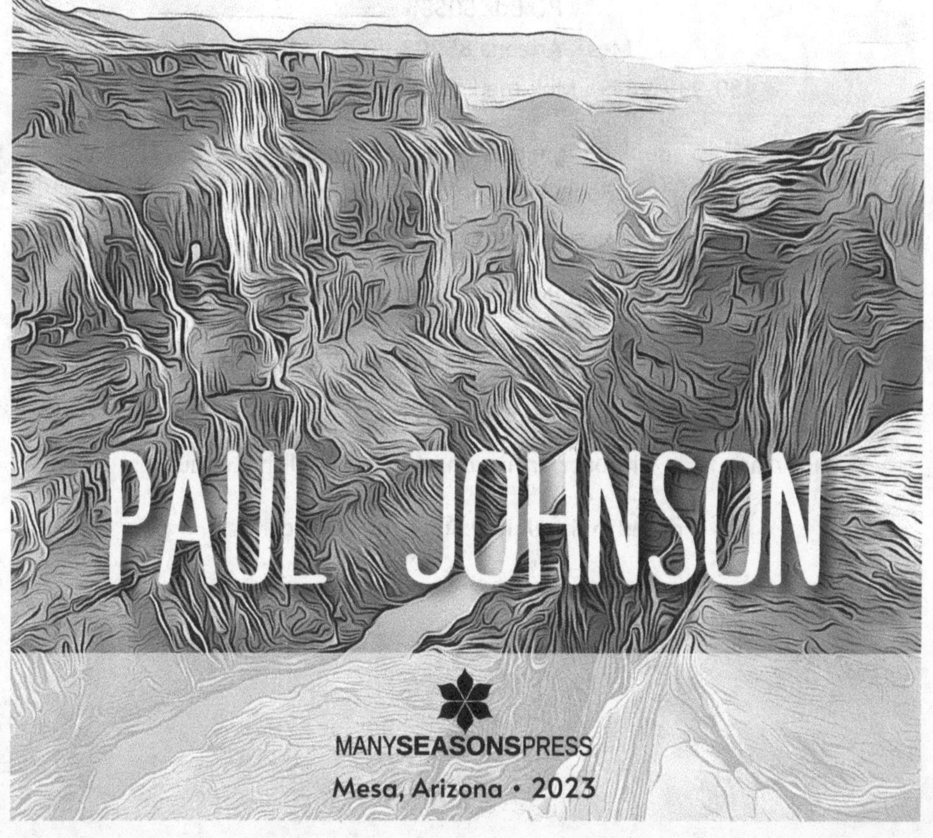

MANY**SEASONS**PRESS

Mesa, Arizona • 2023

FIRST EDITION

Whitewater Honeymoon
A Sedona Chi Mystery

Copyright © 2023 Paul Johnson

MANYSEASONSPRESS

Published by Many Seasons Press
an Imprint of Multimedia Publishing Project
PO Box 50553
Mesa, Arizona 85208-0028
480-939-9689 | MultimediaPublishingProject.com

Book designed by Yolie Hernandez
(AZBookDesigner@icloud.com)

Paperback ISBN: 978-1-956203-18-9
eBook ISBN: 978-1-956203-19-6

Library of Congress Control Number: 2022952347

Printed in the United States of America.

CONTENTS

1

COLORADO RIVER

SKIP RHODES POINTED ACROSS THE COLORADO RIVER TO THE dark, Precambrian, Vishnu schist that rose from its bank. Veins of pink mica and feldspar, from lava forcing its way into cracks millions of years ago, sparkled in the Arizona sunlight. Thick, brown water relentlessly rushing toward the Gulf of California sliced the ageless, black cliffs. Anything lost to the river would eventually end up there unless redirected by man.

"They're metamorphic, base rock, what's left of two-billion-year-old mountains, once higher than the Himalayas before being eroded by time. See how the rock face is vertically structured, not horizontal like the sedimentary layers compressing them from above."

He had driven his tour through the remote Hualapai Reservation, down a dusty, gravel road, to the bottom of the Grand Canyon. Few people, other than the Hualapai, even knew the road existed. They were a long way from Flagstaff or Vegas and a mile deep in the earth. Skip and Kulkulkan "Kuul" Balthazar, his friend and sidekick, were standing on Diamond Creek Beach explaining geology and Native history to the young couple he'd met in Sedona, where his private tour business, Sedona Chi, was located.

The four of them were alone except for the Hualapai River Runners who'd just taken out their blue-rubber pontoons up-stream. To the chagrin of the National Park Service, the Hualapai operated a river rafting business on the Colorado. It had taken years of court battles for the Native protectors of the land to prove their reservation boundary extended to the middle of the river – not to just the high-water mark as the federal government had argued. The Feds had never admitted it, but the fight was all about controlling water rights. In the end, the Hualapai had been patient and had won.

"The Hualapai call the river *Ha'yiđađa*," Kuul Balthazar explained. "The name refers not so much to the water but to its life-giving force. *Ha'yiđađa* is the backbone or spine of the river. Without it, the Hualapai would not survive. The river's canyons and eco-systems flow through their hearts. It's part of them; it's a sacred connection. Their first ancestors were molded from the clay of the riverbed," Kuul ended, scooping up a fistful of the sandy delta.

The River Runner guides and their adult rafters were busily unloading supplies and packs. After a few weeks of running rapids and camping under the stars, the distinctions between guides and customers blurred when it came to work. They were all connected now, all part of the river. The younger kids on the trip were splash-ing and playing in the shallow water. They'd become river rats but would soon be back home fingering video controllers and bemoan-ing the start of school.

Skip pointed to the layer of greenish, crumbling, shelf-rock above the schist. "That's Bright Angel shale, what's left of a five-hundred-million-year-old sea. It's where life began..."

"According to your origin story," Kuul interposed, grinning.

Skip was used to his Native friend's interjections. He'd come to count on them, and his sage-spun wit added color to his tours. They didn't have a set dialogue but bantered easily whenever there was an opening.

Kulkulkan Balthazar was an imposing figure. He had a heavy-weight build and stood a head taller than Skip, who wasn't short. When his clients first met Kuul there was always a nervous hesitancy, partly due to his stature, but mostly because they didn't know how they were supposed to act around a "real-live" Native. Except for kids, to them, it didn't matter. After five minutes, Kuul's big smiles and magical charm had them all peppering him with questions.

"True enough," Skip said.

He looked at his sweating clients, "It's hot down here, don't forget to drink your water." He bent over, wetting his bandana in the cool Diamond Creek stream, pushing it under his straw hat. The water was refreshing, running through his hair and down his neck. "Give or take a few degrees, it's the same temperature as Phoenix down here."

Skip and Kuul had been surprised at how receptive the couple had been to learn about geology and Native culture. Usually, it was his older clients who appreciated the history. Younger tourists to Arizona were always more into adventure hiking and Happy Hour. Not these two, they were both professors at the University of Colorado. He was a geologist working on his PhD, and she was an anthropology researcher. They were attentive and thankfully without internet, so unable to 'google' everything he said.

Skip was explaining the different strata of rock when they heard screams from upstream.

"LUKE. OH MY GOD, HE'S IN THE RIVER. LUKE!" a woman's panicking voice shrieked. *"SOMEONE SAVE MY SON. LUKE! OH MY GOD!"*

Skip, Kuul, and the professors were downstream from the rafters, where Diamond Creek fishtailed into the Colorado River. They were standing where the fault that created Diamond Creek Canyon merged with the Grand Canyon. Rocks, washed down the creek, had created a point out into the Colorado. Bigger boulders washed farther into the river, some submerged below the water's surface, had created Class III and IV rapids farther downstream. If Luke was caught in the main current, he was quickly heading their way.

"Help! Help me!" Skip heard the boy's low cry from the river.

He knew the kid was likely screaming at the top of his lungs. But from where they stood, the river's roar made his cry sound like a whisper. A stand of reeds and Apache arrow weed around a weeping Tamarisk tree kept Skip from seeing upstream to the rafters and Luke. If the boy was in the river, he'd float by them in a matter of seconds.

"Kuul!" Skip yelled over his shoulder to his friend, while stepping into the river.

Kuul was already running toward Skip's Bronco and the rope he knew was in the back for emergencies. Too bad his friend didn't carry a life preserver as well; it'd be on the list for their next trip. If he knew one thing, he knew his friend was the kind of man that would go in after the boy - current be damned. He grabbed the rope and sprinted, angling for a spot downstream. Maybe he'd get lucky and be in time to intercept Skip and the boy. He knew it was unlikely and his mind raced through other options. There were none.

Skip had waded thigh-deep into the Colorado. He could feel the force of the current growing with each step. He was solidly built, and his strong legs kept him upright...*for now*. The water ahead of him was moving swiftly but not yet violently. It was picking up pace before turning into the rapids that began after the confluence with the creek. He threw his hat Frisbee-style as far as he could into the current to visualize how fast. *Too fast*.

A few more steps...there, he saw Luke out past the arrow weed. The current had him. The boy was twenty feet farther into the river than Skip, but at least he was wearing a high-flotation life jacket and still had his helmet on. The jacket was keeping him above water. Skip knew from experience that rafting outfitters used extra buoyant jackets, rated for whitewater, and built tough. Most people would be shocked at how often they were needed. Even with the damming and controlled flow, the Colorado remained a wild, dangerous river.

The life jacket was the good news. The bad news was the river was running faster because it had rained yesterday. The brown color was sediment churned up by debris washed in from the banks, small streams, and cliff faces. The sediment could and had filled the clothes of people who fell into the river, weighing them down, making it impossible to swim, even sending them under never to be seen again. Old-timers used to run rapids naked because of that reason. The thought crossed Skip's mind, but he didn't have time to do any more than rip off his blousy, camp shirt.

Luke, still screaming for help, spotted Skip. Skip could see the terror in his face, but there was also fight in his eyes. He hadn't given up. The boy vainly tried swimming toward him, but the current had a different plan in mind.

"Hold on and keep swimming to me."

Skip knew it wouldn't make a difference, but he had to keep him fighting.

Luke nodded and tried even harder. The kid had spunk.

Skip waded in a few more feet, realizing if he went any farther, he'd lose his footing against the power of the river. Standing in place wasn't going to be an option for much longer either. He glanced over his shoulder looking for Kuul but didn't see him. Luke was coming fast. His choices were either watch the boy be swept into the whitewater downstream or dive in and swim to try to catch him. The latter meant they'd both head into the rapids. Luke was still trying to swim toward him, flailing one arm over the other. The boy's eyes were pleading with him – *Please don't leave me.*

Skip made up his mind. *No choice.*

He looked one more time for Kuul. This time he searched for him farther downstream. Maybe his friend was judging the current and headed that way to have an angle. There he was, scampering over rocks toward the bank, the young geology professor not far behind. They were aiming toward a spot at the head of the rapids. Past that they wouldn't have a chance; the current channeled everything toward the middle of the river. Skip signaled he saw them. He filled his lungs with air, and dove into the river toward Luke.

Skip's mind flashed to the combatant swimming course he'd endured in a past life. A life he didn't talk about. His trainers had thrown him into a life-or-death situation. You either succeeded, at least to the instructor's satisfaction, or you left the program. This time he knew he had to succeed. He prayed he'd judged the angle of his swim and the swiftness of the current correctly – and that there were no rocks waiting just ahead of him.

He broke water and continued swimming hard without opening his eyes. He could feel the waves breaking over him and the foam coating his face. His shoulders were already burning from the effort. He took another strong stroke. He was in a main current of the river now, and he felt it taking control. When he opened his eyes, Luke was a few feet to his right still fighting to reach him. The blind panic had left his face and he yelled something. The roar of the approaching rapids kept Skip from hearing. They were in the smaller riffles before the bigger whitewater. The boy was riding high in the water and moving fast.

Luke reached out, but Skip shook his head. He was still too far.

Skip took a deep breath and dipped into a wave, breast-stroking as strongly as he could. He tried going deeper, hoping the resistance would lessen and he could cut the distance. The current kept him just below the waterline. It seemed like he was under for an eternity. He surfaced, blindly lunging toward where he thought Luke should be.

"Right hand, REACH!" the boy yelled.

Skip stretched his shoulder. His fingers caught metal...a carabiner attached to Luke's life jacket. He pulled the hook toward him and reached with his left hand, getting hold of the jacket below Luke's armpit.

He had him if he could just hold on.

2

DIAMOND CREEK RAPIDS

THERE WERE TWO ROPES IN SKIP'S BRONCO. KUUL GRABBED both. They were old; twisted hemp with frayed fibers that looked and felt like yucca needles. The ropes had done some heavy lifting before his friend got hold of them. But they were still strong. Old didn't mean they couldn't work, it just meant he could respect and trust them.

Kuul scrambled across Diamond Creek, jumping from one rock to another and up the three-foot gravel bank on the far side. The Hualapai graded the channel to keep the beach from flooding. The rocks were bigger and the ground more uneven from there to the Colorado, slowing his progress. He still made good time, hopscotching across larger rocks and zigzagging between boulders. The trick to not twisting an ankle was being light on his feet and moving them forward the instant they landed. For a big man, his agility was amazing.

He was tracking Skip and the boy. Skip had reached the kid and latched an arm through his jacket. He could see his friend working to keep their feet forward so as not to lead with their heads. They looked like they were swimming side-by-side on their backs, the swirling water trying to spin and roll them.

Kuul was closing in from upstream, angling toward a point to throw the rope from...if he got there in time. They hadn't yet reached the start of the rapids.

"I don't know if you have enough rope," Kuul heard from behind.

He had reached the river. Skip and the boy were coming fast. The young geologist had followed him. Good, he'd need his help.

Kuul made a loop with the end of the shorter rope. It looked to be a twenty-foot length, and he used close to five feet. He slipped it over his head and shoulders, cinching it around his chest and under his arms. He threw the other end back to the geologist.

The man nodded, "There'll be a point, if you go too far, that I won't be able to hold you!"

Kuul nodded back, "Wrap the end around something and just keep feeding it!"

He headed into the current holding the other rope.

He'd only have one shot. Skip and the boy were coming even more quickly now. Kuul's feet found mud and pebbles. He felt more rocks the farther he waded out, some so big he stumbled. The current was strong, but he managed to stand against it. He just had to lean back into it and make sure his feet were braced flat on the bottom. Skip and the boy were still a little upstream from him, twenty feet farther out into the river.

The geologist yelled from shore, "That's it, there's no more."

Kuul felt the rope around his waist go tight. The geologist had tied it off.

He estimated they'd be straight out from him in two or three seconds. He wasn't sure how much rope he held, but it was a good length. Was it enough? He wanted to toss the rope in front of them, feed it out, and let Skip maneuver to it. But if it was too short the current would bring it back out of their reach. He knew the surest bet was to throw it directly to Skip. That would be the shortest distance. Skip was waving his free hand and yelling at him. That's what he was expecting.

Kuul swung the coil in circles over his head, letting it fly toward his friend. He prayed to his ancestors for their help in guiding the rope. It was a perfect toss and might even have gotten there if it had been one piece. It was two. Kuul was left holding one length, while the second length sailed worthlessly toward Skip.

Skip had known what was going to happen. He had remembered there were three ropes in the Bronco, and that none were over twenty feet. He'd been trying to wave Kuul back. There was no sense risking his life as well. He had already realized he and the boy would have to swim the rapids: one life jacket for the two of them.

"Are we going to die?" Luke asked. He was scared.

Skip knew Luke had seen Kuul try to rescue them and fail. His hopes had probably crashed. At least these rapids were just Class III. They should be okay as long as they stayed in a main chute away from any overhanging ledges and avoided submerged boulders. Past the rapids they'd be able to swim to shore.

For now, they were trapped, riding up and over cresting waves. Water cascaded down their faces, blinding them as they fell. It was like being in the bottom of a gigantic, front-loading washer, sloshing back and forth. They had just enough time between waves to catch their breath before suffering the same drenching all over again.

"No, we're just in for an exciting swim. We'll be past these rapids before you know it. Try leaning backwards and keeping your feet out in front. Pretend you're sitting in a recliner." They rode up and down two more waves. "That's it. If you feel your feet touch a rock, relax, bend your knees, and push off. I've got you."

"My dad doesn't let me sit in his chair," Luke said, gulping and spitting water.

"He will now. I promise."

They were riding lower than Skip would have liked. One child's jacket didn't support their combined weights. He thought about pulling his arm free and holding the jacket from outside. That would lighten the ballast by close to two-hundred pounds. He made a note to cut back on his landlady's pancakes. He decided against wiggling loose; there was no way he'd be able to hold onto the slick jacket in the heavier rapids ahead.

The waves were getting higher. They were being rocketed up and crashing over five-foot, brown crests, like a boat in rough seas. The biggest waves dropped them into holes before the current flushed them out and down the river. He knew each of those times they had been swept over a submerged rock. He'd heard of holes in some rapids so deep that they formed whirlpools and could sink a raft.

Silt and small debris were filling his khakis and dragging them down. It felt like bricks were in his hip pockets. The boy had to be suffering the same issue. If there was a silver lining, at least the river was running a little high, though he'd still twisted an ankle when his foot rammed a submerged rock. He was keeping his feet in front of the boy's to protect him.

Skip was wracking his brain, trying to remember the length of this set of rapids. An ex-girlfriend had brought him through here two years ago on a private trip she helped crew. He didn't think it was long, but it already felt like he and Luke had been riding a wet rollercoaster for hours. They crashed over another wave and Skip looked ahead...

Trouble.

"Luke, I need you to lean to your right and start backstroking. We don't want to spin though. Try to kick too. We need to move that way." Skip shouted, so the boy could hear over the roar.

He tried to keep his voice calm. They both leaned right and backstroked. Skip with only one arm, the other locked inside the boy's jacket.

"Why?" Luke yelled back.

Before Skip could answer, the boy saw their problem and began furiously splashing his arms. Each wave was now violently throwing them down. They'd both gone under several times, even with the jacket. It was becoming harder and harder to adjust their course.

Fifty feet ahead, directly in their path, two large boulders broke the surface of the water. There was a narrow gap between them where a log was jammed at water level, creating a dam. Other debris was being corralled and splintered against the rocks. At the top of the next wave, Skip swung his body hard to the right, throwing both of them in that direction. He prayed they wouldn't spin, but he had to try something. In a few seconds they would be smashed against the rocks.

He wasn't sure they were going to make it. It was going to be close.

He tried the same maneuver with the next wave, but they still weren't moving far enough to the right. It looked like they were going to hit.

"Relax your legs and don't let your head hit," Skip yelled.

At the last second, he threw his shoulder into Luke's, sending their upper bodies and heads spinning to the right. He braced himself and felt his right leg and hip smash the edge of the rock. Despite the pain, he pushed hard against the boulder. The circulating current sucked them in. They spiraled head-first around the side of the rock and dropped into a deep hole.

Water poured into the hole from around both boulders, churning the natural pot. Skip and Luke were being bashed in the bottom one moment and pushed up a wall of water toward the top the next. Each time they neared the crest, a wave coming around a boulder battered them back down. The crashing water sent them under and was sapping their strength. Skip knew they couldn't survive the vicious cycle much longer. Not with the beating their bodies were enduring. Not with the silt accumulating in his pants. Maybe he could throw the boy out - Luke would be on his own, but his chances would be better.

"I'm going to try throwing you out!" Skip shouted. Hard water, dead limbs, and loose debris were pelting them from above. "You'll be okay, just remember to keep your head back and feet out! Let the current do the work."

"What about you?" the boy screamed. "Please, don't leave me!"

"Get ready! We're rising again. Remember; keep your feet in front!"

"NO." Luke grabbed Skip's hair. It was all he could grasp. Their chins were barely above water.

"On three," Skip locked his elbows, using his arms as pedestals below the boy, and got ready to shove. "One...Two..." Luke had given up trying to hold on to him. His hands had kept slipping through Skip's sand-caked hair.

Skip hesitated. The boy was sobbing, and his eyes were lifeless for the first time. He shook him. "You're going to be okay. Stay strong." Luke looked at him and nodded.

"I'll get help and come back," he said, gamely.

Skip slapped the boy's helmet and smiled, "THREE..."

A yellow paddle with a blue handle burst through the wave in front of them before he could throw him. With the roar of the rapids and the waves crashing around the rocks, he hadn't heard the motor. A Hualapai raft had passed the boulders while they were trapped in the hole and motored back to them.

"The boy!" the Hualapai guide holding the paddle yelled.

Skip yelled, "Grab the paddle, they'll pull you in."

"You don't have a jacket," Luke yelled back. A life vest was thrown over the crest of the wave.

Skip laughed, "Grab the damned paddle. It's time to go."

•••

Past Diamond Creek Rapids, Jimmy Honga, the Hualapai guide who'd rescued them, pulled his raft over to give Luke a choice. They could continue downstream another thirty miles, run a few more rapids, take a helicopter from the bottom of the canyon up over the rim, and land to a hero's welcome in the Hualapai Lodge parking lot, or... Luke had stopped him there, happy with the first option. Skip grinned like a proud father.

The next few hours on the pontoon were a kiddie, roller coaster ride compared to Skip's and Luke's swim. Honga radioed back to Diamond Creek to tell Luke's frantic parents all was well. They'd meet them back at the hotel in Peach Springs. Skip's leg was sore, but nothing was broken. After getting into dry clothes, supplied by the rafters, and wrapped in warm blankets, they settled back against the soft rubber, Luke tight against his new friend.

"How about some famous river stories?" Honga asked when they reached a quiet stretch of river. "Those folks all decided to go by *boat*," he chided Luke.

Skip knew both stories. Honga lazily oared the raft from the back and asked the boy if he'd heard of John Wesley Powell. In 1868 Powell formed the first ever white man's expedition to chart the Colorado. He recruited a crew of Civil War veterans and mountain men. After months of near drownings and starving three men left the group at a side canyon, a spot later named Separation Point, choosing to climb out instead of continuing. Those three were never heard from again, while Powell's men reached safety in two days. Luke was captivated by the war-injured, one-armed Powell exploring the high red walls and being thrown out of his boat numerous times.

"Skip only had one arm to use, too," Luke said.

Honga's second story was about a 1928 honeymoon trip and tragic disappearance. In a particularly long rapid, he pointed out two fang-shaped rocks their boat might have hit, tossing the un-lucky bride and groom into the river. A little farther downstream, he stopped in quiet water, not far from the helicopter take-out, and showed the boy where their empty scow had been found.

Honga grinned, "My girlfriend plans on going to Hawaii after our wedding,"

Kuul was waiting at the Hualapai Lodge with the geologist and his girlfriend, having gotten the good news along with Luke's parents, Barry and Dani Hufflefinger from Tucson. The Hufflefingers had rented a motorhome and were on a month-long tour of their adopted state. They'd relocated from Sacramento to buy a bigger home for Luke and his sister, *'the Bun in the Oven'*. Their rafting trip was the first leg of a loop through northern Arizona. They planned on driving the Arizona Strip with stops on both rims of the Grand Canyon, to see it from the topside, with Page and Glen Canyon in between.

Luke ran to his mom as soon as he saw her. She hugged him so tight he thought he'd pop and then scolded him for playing too far out in the current. Barry Hufflefinger shook Skip's hand until his arm was numb, repeating over and over *'anything you need, anything you need.'*

Skip and Luke finally said their goodbyes, exchanging bear hugs and email addresses, promising to keep in touch. They even shook on swimming another river together when Luke was older. Dani Hufflefinger stood behind her son shaking her head.

"I'll be a stronger swimmer when I'm sixteen," Luke said.

"You better be," Skip laughed, tussling the kid's hair.

3

THE DONALDS

HREE SHORT HOURS BUT A WORLD AWAY FROM DIAMOND CREEK Canyon, Austin Donald sat on the sagging, plywood-floored porch beside his single-wide trailer. It was in a seedy RV park ten blocks from the Vegas strip. He took turns sucking on his Marlboro and from the oxygen tank beside his rocker. The losers across the street were hard at work, popping their trunk whenever an addicted client drove up. Like Donald, they'd probably come to 'Sin City' expecting to hit it big. That never happened. You either had money or you didn't. That's what Donald believed. If you didn't, you were no better than the dirty grit that blew through the city. That's how those who had made it, the fat cats, treated you.

"Fuck those bastards," Donald wheezed to the middle-aged man sitting across from him.

The street separating the rows of trailers was narrow, no more than an alley, and the kid sitting on the trunk smiled, flipping his scowling, old neighbor the finger.

Donald spat a gob of phlegm on the plywood floor and pushed it around with his cane, "In my day, we knew how to deal with dopers. They ruined it for everybody. Before them, the cops didn't care what we knocked off or who we beat up, as long as it happened off the strip. Guys like that we took out to the desert, and they never came back. It was a public service. But once the dopers started targeting tourists, they cracked down on all of us."

The old man evilly grinned at the kid, taking aim with his finger. His thumb, the imaginary pistol's hammer, was a stump below the knuckle. He'd lost it long ago. The kid just waved the gesture off. *Keep it up, smart guy*, Donald thought.

He looked at the man across from him, "There's a job you're going to do."

The man nodded and stroked his thick, black eyebrow. He did it unconsciously when he was thinking. The old man was fired up today, more than usual. He stared at him; ninety-four years old, one-hundred and ten pounds of failing flesh, a few wisps of yellowing hair above a deeply wrinkled face, a hunched back from a worn-out spine, and still the hate kept his mind sharp as a tack and a thing to be feared.

"I've got other irons in other fires," the younger man told Donald.

Donald glowered at him through devious eyes, his dry, purple lips opening then closing slowly as he rethought his rebuke. The man was a disappointment but all he had left. When he was younger, the man had determined he was smarter than his old man, but he was too afraid and weak to challenge him because deep down he knew he wasn't. Donald had made sure his son knew first-hand how violent his father could be. Some lessons last a lifetime, and Donald had known power once ceded from fear was never regained. So, he taught often and hard.

Austin Donald was the product of a tough childhood spent in a pre-war San Francisco orphanage with disinterested staff.

Beginning at age four, he'd been lent out for day labor on a farm. A sadistic foreman had abused and beaten him. Because he was small, he had been picked on at the orphanage by bored, bigger boys. He'd learned early in his brutal life to fight back, to *'get even'*. Otherwise, the abuse escalated. The most effective messages, he'd learned, were delivered extra violently. Acknowledging his small-ish stature, he exacted his revenge coldly, deliberately, and unexpectedly. He'd once attacked a bigger boy from behind with a ball bat, sending him to the hospital with a broken skull. The staff had punished and isolated him, locking him in a closet for weeks. That only made him more cunning - *better to work in the dark*. In time, they all feared him.

He became obsessively bitter watching other boys get adopted. The orphanage staff didn't even make an effort with him. Nobody wanted a damaged child with a dangerous record. They were just waiting for him to age-out or run away. Only once had Austin thought he had a chance. Now, over eighty-five years later, he still remembered the well-dressed, attractive woman that had come and talked with several other boys. He saw her watching him in the playground and later in the dining hall. He had been convinced she was asking about him. When she left empty-handed, he knew she was his mother and had decided to leave him again.

At age thirteen he finally ran away. No effort was made to find him. It was 1940 and there were bigger problems facing the State of California and the world. His first order of business had been settling the score with the foreman. The orphanage, its staff, and his mother could wait. He still delighted in remembering how he'd *'gotten even'* in the barn. He'd waited until the old foreman was drunk and passed out. He had woken quickly when Austin started cutting.

Donald's boys, including the surviving weasel sitting across from him, knew what he was capable of. Even now, with this damn tank of air and the cane that allowed him to stand, his boy was leery of him.

"Put your fires out, Earl. They aren't as important," Donald barked, swinging his cane toward his youngest son.

Earl started to object but thought better of it. "What job?" he said, stroking his eyebrow, smoothing the unruly hairs. He didn't like looking at the old man. He knew he was just a younger version with a tired face instead of his father's deeper wrinkles and brown spots. His own hair was thinning and turning gray, and they'd been the same size before his father had shrunk. Only Earl's black goatee was different. The old man had shaved with a straight razor every day of his life...*the damn strap*.

"That's better son. It's time our family luck changed. They've always kept us down, looked down their noses at us, making sure I fail. People with opportunities and money don't share." Donald stopped and spat again. "But they're too stupid to understand we got our own rulebook, and we get even until we have what we deserve. We live with a viciousness their world doesn't have. We don't let nobody get in our way."

Earl smirked. "Like Freddy?"

The old man's cane swung suddenly toward his son's head. Earl caught it, pulling it from his hand. Their eyes locked, the tension finally snapping when Austin held out his shaking hand. Earl laughed and handed his father his cane.

"You're getting slower...*Dad*."

"Your brother Fred never learned to keep his mouth shut!"

"What do you have in mind?"

The old man stubbed out his cigarette. He doused the butt in his glass and watched it settle to the bottom. He was deciding how much he could trust his son. If Fred were still here, he'd be a better choice. His older son hadn't been as smart and was always in some kind of trouble, but give him a job and he'd do it, no questions asked. But Fred had been dead for twenty-five years. Loose lips in prison weren't healthy. They'd pay for that too.

"My time's running out, and I got one more shot. Third time's the charm, right?"

Earl nodded. 'Charm' wasn't a word he'd use to describe the old man's luck. He was so filled with hate he hardly thought of anything else. The family code, *Getting Even*, was all that mattered to him now. It had kept him alive for ninety-four years.

"I want you to find Hyde. Drag him out of whatever whorehouse you find him in and bring him here. Keep him out of trouble. You're both going on a trip."

Earl started to rub his eyebrow but caught himself and scratched his goatee instead.

"He's out?"

Austin Donald, the family patriarch, grinned. "The salesclerk had a change of heart about testifying. He agreed the pistol-whipping might have confused him. His broken jaw and arms were healing, and the dizziness had gone away. He was mistaken about your nephew."

The old codger had sent someone, Earl thought.

It had been a while since he'd seen Freddy's boy, Hyde. They weren't exactly a close-knit family. Last he knew he'd been in Reno robbing liquor stores and living off a divorced hairdresser. The kid was shiftless and even meaner than his dad or the old man. Unpredictably mean, which never worked in the boy's favor, because he was also dumber than a frog in a frypan. He didn't learn, he just doubled down on his messes.

"Pretty Boy still in Reno with the hairdresser?"

Hyde was the only Donald that appealed to the fairer sex. At least until they felt his fist. And the kid knew it. He took after his mother and had a sort of rugged Orlando Bloom look. He was tanned, tall for their family, with long, brown hair he knotted in a man-bun.

"Last I knew and a nail specialist. I've got the address. Tell him he'll be gone a week or two. Not that I think he'll care, or she'd want him back. You know him; he's only gotten worse with the women. You'll have to keep an eye on him, keep him out of trouble," the old man said again.

Earl guessed he had been into more trouble than beating a clerk. But he knew better than to ask. He disliked dealing with him; Hyde had been a conceited brat, stealing candy, tying cat's tails and later chasing skirt, and he'd grown into a bigger headache than he was worth. The old man had raised him same as he raised his father – to be the aging man's muscle. Though simple as Hyde was, maybe he'd come in handy – if Earl needed a fall guy.

The kid across the street slammed his trunk after making another sale. The old man glanced that way and Earl stood up. It was time to leave. He'd find his nephew and bring him back. Then he'd listen to his father and decide if he wanted any part of what he was planning.

"Get me another pack of Marlboros and a cold beer from inside," the old man ordered, before taking another gulp of oxygen. "And Earl," he sneered, "Don't fuck it up."

Earl's temper flared, and he raised his fist, holding it in the air. His father glared at him, daring him. *So much hate in those black eyes. Why take the risk? He was sick and old, he'd die soon.* Earl stroked his eyebrow, sensing the old man trying to figure him out. They stared at each other for a few seconds before Earl went inside to do as he'd been told.

4

CAVERNS INN

SKIP'S ANTHROPOLOGIST CLIENT EYED THE SIGN WITH THE missing S and the old-time, gas pumps with glass containers. She and her geologist boyfriend were captivated with the Caverns Inn and its crazy, bygone-era collection. "This place is a slice of Americana, a part of our collective history."

"It's a piece of work, that's for sure," Kuul laughed.

"Seriously, it explains a lot about our sense of humanity, who we were as a people then, our patterns of behavior, our norms and values, even how we settled the land. It really is a fascinating reflection and record of our past."

"And what about the People here before Route 66?" Kuul couldn't help but add. "The People here before the railroad, the army, the priests, and the conquistadors?"

Kuul and Skip's Diamond Creek tour were spending the night at the funky motel before heading back to Sedona in the morning. Caverns Inn was a Route 66 staple, fifteen miles outside Hualapai

Nation. The place was rough around the edges, but billed by the owners as retro chic, ala Happy Days, which dated it even more. It was dark when they arrived, easing their first impression.

Fonzie's Triumph motorcycle was standing on its kickstand outside the first block of rooms, watched over by a life-size, emerald-green, Sinclair dinosaur. Only this Fonz was a sixty-year-old from Lake Havasu sitting at a picnic table drinking a Colt 45 with his club buddies. Their wives had probably gotten tired of them hanging around the house.

Kuul had parked the Bronco by the last block of rooms, across from a long line of junk Chevy Corvairs missing their rear engines. Somewhere Ralph Nader was saying, 'I told you so.' Skip had gone inside the office to get actual keys. They came attached to diamond-shaped hunks of green plastic, same color as Dino, with the room numbers hand-lettered in gold paint. *Fancy*.

Sixty years ago, the inn had been a busy stop servicing America's 'Byway to the West'. Now it was a long way from Interstate 40. To nervous tour customers, Skip always pointed out the *new* indoor-outdoor carpet in the wood-box, miniature golf holes - improvements were being made. In turn, his customers pointed to the rotting Chris-Craft dry-docked below the rusting swing. Recreational amenities aside, no other establishment better captured the rugged spirit of Route 66...and their rates were half those at Hualapai Lodge, the only other hotel within fifty miles of Diamond Creek.

Skip patronized the Caverns because the owner, Master Sergeant Bud Wisner, had sunk his life savings into making a go of it. They had history, and the Master Sergeant still *had a lot of work to do*. It didn't hurt that after a hot day by the river, Buddy's Bar was always open. Drinking was strictly prohibited back in town on Hualapai Nation.

Skip found his entourage encamped outside the Betty Boop dining room.

"Where are the *caverns*?" the geologist was asking. "I have a professional interest."

Bud had just brought out four ice-cold Coronas. Skip would have preferred a prickly-pear margarita; he had an inexplicable passion for the sweet drink. But beer was more in vogue; the Master Sergeant hadn't gotten his nickname by picking flowers. Fonzie's gang was watching too.

Bud beamed at the question, "They're up the road half a klick, past the stables."

Skip rolled his eyes. The "stables" was a dilapidated, split-wood corral used fifty years ago for roundups.

Bud continued, "In 1927, a young fellow by the name of Walter Peck was on his way to a poker game and fell in a hole. The next morning, after he'd sobered up, his friends lowered him 150 feet by block and tackle into a huge cavern. Some friends, huh? Maybe he wasn't all that sober either. Anyway, the walls were sparkling, and he thought he'd found gold. Wasn't any...*of course*, but he started charging two bits to lower tourists holding a kerosene lamp into the dark cave. Called them 'Dopes on a Rope'. It's a dry cave, so no stalagmites, but they did discover the skeleton of a giant sloth."

"We have time to play dopes in the morning?" the geologist asked, looking at Skip.

"Probably not, and it's not that exciting now. There's an elevator."

"Tell you what," the Master Sergeant said, pushing back his slouch hat, "You two married?" He grinned at Skip and Kuul then back to the geologist and his girlfriend. Being a good hotelier, he could tell they weren't.

"*Not yet*," the anthropologist answered.

The geologist took a long sip of beer, "I want to finish my PhD first."

"Well, when you do," Bud laughed, "We have a honeymoon suite down there. Very private and we cater in a five-course meal.

We can arrange the wedding too, but you have to agree to leave the bridal bouquet with our collection. Roses last a long time down there; that's a good omen."

They all had a good laugh and the couple promised they'd be back.

Bud started a fire in the concrete pit and left to get another round of drinks. In Northern Arizona, the summer nights got cool at forty-five-hundred feet above sea level. They were well north of the Sonoran Desert, saguaro bandits, and the hot Valley of Sun. The wind had picked up too, with a slight bite, suggesting an early monsoon.

It wasn't long before Kuul slipped into storytelling. They'd settled in around the fire and began talking about the Colorado River and its relationship to Native customs, behaviors, and values – their anthropologies. Most tourists assumed Kuul was *Diné*, Navajo, especially those from back East. And he didn't do anything to correct those assumptions unless asked. He'd found the tips were better. He was actually part-Mayan, part-Yaqui, and had a German great-great-grandfather who'd been a foreign mercenary for Maximillian.

"According to legend, *Yé'ii*, the holy ones, were born at the intersection of the Colorado and San Juan Rivers. This was long before Glen Canyon Dam. Rainbows would rise from the mist of the two rivers as they became one. These marked the *Yé'ii* paths through the world," Kuul explained.

"*Yé'ii* came to maintain *hózhó*, a sort of natural balance to our lives, right?" the anthropologist half-asked half-commented. "It's not my field, but I've read of them."

"Close," Kuul smiled. "They exist to maintain *hózhó*, there's a subtle difference. And it's not only balance, but beauty, harmony, and well-being to all things, not just the People. Navajos feel a sacred connection to the land. Most indigenous people do. That spiritual connection is why you see weavers weaving *Yé'ii* in their rugs and artists recreating them in their sand paintings. Each part of the environment, including the mountains and the rivers, are related to a Holy One, a *Yéí*."

The geologist added, "So, the *Yé'ii* of the Colorado smiled at Skip and the boy today." While he appreciated the concept of a benevolent deity, in reality, it was the pressures and gases deep inside the earth that shaped their planet.

Skip cleared his throat before his Mayan friend brought up the small klotchkes he made from bobcat scat and sold to unsuspecting tourists as spiritual fetishes. That was typically how his stories ended. Getting money from a white person, a *bilagáana*, was reparation. Kuul had a bit of the wily coyote in him when it came to business. "Switching gears, one honeymoon couple visiting the Grand Canyon weren't blessed...Glen and Bessie Hyde. You two would be better off taking Bud up on the Caverns Suite."

The anthropologist liked changing the subject back to honeymoons and marriages. "Their story's tragic. They died, right? Drowned in the river?"

"Disappeared," Skip corrected. She'd clearly been reading up for their trip to the Colorado. "Their boat was found, but their bodies weren't. It was the 1920's, a mini-age of discovery, Lindbergh, Shackleton, the race up Everest, and Amelia Earhardt. The Hydes were newly married, young, adventuresome, and decided to raft the river from upper Utah to California in record time. There had been few men do it before them. Bessie would be the first woman. The river was wilder back then, and it changed with the season. When they tried in 1928, it was before Hoover or Glen Canyon Dams were built to regulate flows."

Skip stopped to rearrange the fire, carefully placing two more pine logs that Bud had stacked beside the pit. "It's a good fire," he said to Kuul.

Kuul smiled, his friend was getting better at storytelling. It had only been four years since he'd arrived in Sedona and began offering tours. He'd learned to add a dramatic pause. The couple was waiting to hear more.

Skip poked around the fire in a few more places before re-starting. "They built what's called a scow, a kind of boat that was used in Idaho where Glen had run the Snake River. The Snake has a more gradual elevation change than the Colorado, so propulsion isn't as much trouble. Get it pointed in the right direction and it goes where it's supposed to. The Colorado is more dramatic, bigger elevation change, with killer rapids, eddies, and currents that fight each other. Yet there are sections most rafters have to row or motor because of still water. In others you're freefalling through narrow gorges that restrict flows."

The geologist actually raised his hand and Skip pointed to him, "I've studied the Snake area. It's very different from what we saw today. It's volcanic residue pressing downward. The river plain was created when the North American Plate passed over a hotspot beneath Yellowstone. The way the land formed is the same as how the Hawaiian Islands were created."

Skip nodded and continued, "The Hydes left in late October from southern Wyoming on the Green River. The Green joins the Colorado in Utah. By mid-November they had reached the Grand Canyon, below the lodges. By most reports, everything had gone well. A few days later they reached Hermit's Camp, farther down-stream, and..." Skip paused to stir the fire.

"And that's the last anyone saw of them," the anthropologist said.

Skip grinned at Kuul. "Right. When they didn't show in Needles, California by early December, Glen's father started searching. Their scow was found, unscathed, everything still inside, floating in a quiet section of the river hung up by its bowline. The mattress and springs, rifle, even the food they carried still there. Everything the father had said they took was still there, just not Glen or Bessie."

"Mattress and springs?" the geologist laughed. "You're kidding, right?"

"It was their honeymoon. They'd haul them ashore at night."

"They must have been thrown out in a rapid?" the geologist mused.

Skip shrugged, "Maybe, but nothing else in the scow was. No one knows for sure what happened."

The logs Skip put on the fire had burned down. One broke, dropping into the embers, sending a shower of golden sparks harmlessly into the night air.

"Speaking of bed," the anthropologist said to the geologist. "It's been a long and interesting day, but I'm beat."

The couple smiled, thanked Skip and Kuul for a day they'd remember, and headed toward their room after taking their empties back into the bar and saying goodnight to Master Sergeant Bud.

Kuul chuckled after they'd left, "Good bedtime story, Kemo. That girl's tired of being a maiden. They'll be talking about sleeping arrangements *and* matrimony tonight. I brought some corn starch in my medicine bag if I need to perform a Wedding Blessing."

"You brought a backpack with a bag of trail mix," Skip laughed, tilting his empty bottle. "The bar's still open..."

"One more," Kuul said, standing. "It's hard to see *hózhó* in that story. There was no ending, no harmony. No bodies to wrap or mouths to put corn in for their after journey."

Kuul went inside for two more Coronas. Bud was still there, and Skip heard them talking. The fire was burning low, and the wood was gone. He scooted closer and propped his boots on the rim of the pit. The heat felt good. His leg was sore, and it had a lot of company. He'd be stiff tomorrow.

The Milky Way was overhead, a veil of gauze across the sky composed of billions of distant stars and universes. Beside the gauze was a void of black space with stars and planets closer to Earth, almost close enough to touch. Caverns Inn literally was the middle-of-nowhere, probably why Master Sergeant Bud Wisner found refuge here. Skip understood. His past couldn't find him here either and the future was a clean slate. Out here, he could just stare at the stars. No other worries.

A girl in Sedona, Sky (her Mormon parents had named her Clara), had tried teaching him new-age astrology and how to divine information from terrestrial events. He'd just missed being a Libra, which she said explained a lot. She'd also taught him, in her flower-girl way, to be comfortable with his karma, admit his mistakes, and to be at peace with them. He was still working on the last one. Sky worked for him now, running her own tours for Sedona Chi, and in her mind, managing the office. They were just friends. She'd decided the darker colors of his aura weren't a good match to hers, which ended his romantic imaginations. That was her excuse anyway.

"Heavens are bright tonight. It's a good sign," Kuul said, sitting a pink drink instead of a beer bottle in front of his friend. "Sergeant said he knew you'd want it."

"Thanks."

The big Mayan could sense Skip had drifted into one of his lonely moods. That's when he needed to watch him, keep his demons in check. His friend was yet to see the ghosts of his ancestors.

"Last time we were here, it was with Lilac," Kuul said, gingerly wading in.

Lilac Williams was a former Tucson police detective and Phoenix private investigator, now a yoga instructor and firearm trainer in Sedona. His friend's and Lilac's on-again off-again relationship had been rocky; she'd bounced more than a few off his thick head. Kuul knew the younger woman, Sky, had just been an interruption. No *hózhó*. There was, however, a harmony and beauty between the more mature Lilac and his enigmatic friend. Their spirits were balanced, except when one or the other stepped off the scale.

"Still just friends; she's seeing the cop from Phoenix," Skip said, stirring the pink, prickly-pear syrup at the bottom of his cup. "That changes, I'll let you know."

"The one she shot in the cajones? Accidents like that don't just happen, Kemo. I don't think she's serious. She's just waiting for you to get your *chąą'* together."

"You're driving back tomorrow. I'm already stiffening up," Skip said, ignoring the subject and groaning as he moved his boots to stand. "Maybe we can make time to rope-a-dope that couple in the morning."

5

BESSIE AND GLEN HYDE

October 20, 1928

THE DAY HAD FINALLY ARRIVED. BESSIE HYDE STOOD AT THE bank of the Green River admiring her husband, Glen, as he finished outfitting the scow he'd built by hand. As soon as Glen said it was okay, they'd shove off on a grand adventure, down the Green. They would raft for one-hundred-twenty miles to its confluence with the Colorado River, through the Grand Canyon, and on to golden California.

"It looks like a floating coffin. That's what the old-timer told me." Glen laughed. "He asked if we had life preservers. I said, *'No'*. He asked if we had enough drinkable water to hike out if we needed to. I said, *'Won't have to'*. And even after I told the old cuss I'd run the Salmon in the same kind of boat, he just kept shaking his head, thinking I'm foolhardy."

"I wish I'd seen his face when you loaded the mattress and springs," Bessie said, her eyebrows rising seductively.

Glen winked, "I said it was our honeymoon trip, and he never said a thing."

Bessie was watching the bowline as Glen climbed in and out of the scow with supplies. It was a fine boat, their scow. The lumber and nails had cost them fifty dollars, and it had only taken the mechanically inclined, outdoorsy Glen two days to mold the rough-sawn wood into a craft capable of running the Colorado rapids. She liked watching him work. Seven years older, he was confident in himself and his capabilities. He was strong too, from having done manual labor on his father's farm. When he held her, she knew she was with the right man. His big hands could master just about anything, including her short, petite body.

"Hand me the cook barrel and the kerosene," he said.

Bessie knew she'd be doing most of the cooking, though Glen was more than capable. The barrel was filled with sand and ash. The kerosene was to start a cook fire for whatever Glen was able to hunt with his Winchester. They'd already loaded the Idaho spuds and canned fruit and vegetables from the farm. If need be, they could even cook on board.

It had taken her a long and roundabout journey to reach this point. Bessie still couldn't believe that just four years ago she'd been posing for her yearbook picture at Parkersburg High in West Virginia. In between, she'd graduated, moved to Huntington to attend Marshall College, married her high school sweetheart, Earl Helmick, left Earl and West Virginia for San Francisco and the California School of Fine Arts, moved in with her Bohemian, actress friend, Greta, met the love of her life on an overnight steamer to Los Angeles, and spent the previous winter in Nevada awaiting a quickie divorce. On April 11 the divorce had been granted, and on April 12, 1928, she married the handsome, confident man loading their scow.

When she'd met Glen on the luxury steamer they'd spent the night dancing, laughing at the silly prohibition laws from international waters, and dining on the finest food she'd ever had. They had walked off the ship in love and promised to each other, even though she was married. Finally, now, she was happy. She had a new husband, new flapper hairdo, new coveralls, a new horse at Glen's farm, and new prospects.

"How soon?" Bessie asked.

"We should be on the river by four, maybe an hour."

Bessie was anxious to get underway. The locals in Green River were too nosey, and neither of them wanted to spend another nickel for an extra night in the only flea-bitten hotel. They were mostly a bunch of alfalfa farmers, leading exactly the kind of life she and Glen had spent the summer plotting an escape from. Her next night in a hotel would be in sunny California.

There hadn't been much to do on an Idaho bean farm other than work. She had loved listening to Glen's thrilling stories about rafting the Peach and Salmon Rivers. And they'd both followed two, well-publicized, whitewater excursions down the wild Colorado. She couldn't remember which of them had come up with the idea first, probably Glen. They were young, daring, romantic, and desperate for some excitement.

If Mallory could attempt climbing Everest because, 'It was there', Lucky Lindy cross the Atlantic, and Amelia fly off that summer in search of adventure and fortune...well, they could do the same. Every day the papers reported some amazing stunt or record being set. And Glen had the boating skills and know-how to float them into history. *Why not*? she'd thought.

Bessie looked at the easy flow of the Green River, thinking that with any luck they would be on a speaking tour by spring, lecturing crowds of admirers at fancy vaudeville houses and staying at grand old hotels for free. She'd be the first woman to raft the dangerous Colorado River through the depths and desolation of the Grand Canyon. Glen planned on setting a speed record as well as being the first to run it in a sweep scow.

"Bessie, I think we're ready."

The Magarrell brother who'd helped Glen build the scow had come down to see them off. A few other curious locals were standing around to wave goodbye. The rest of the old-timers expected they'd see them again soon enough. The honeymooners wouldn't get far, not with that contraption of a boat and the man's only crew being his wife, an inexperienced girl who couldn't have weighed a hundred pounds soaking wet.

"Hold the line while Bessie gets in," Glen said to the brother.

Glen was standing on a platform a foot below the center of the scow's top edge, holding the forward sweep, an eighteen-foot oar cast into the quiet water from the bow. There was a sweep in the front and back for keeping the scow running straight. It was unlike every other boat that attempted the river with shorter oars on the sides.

Bessie climbed over a side that was nearly as tall as she, up to the platform beside her husband. He was beaming with anticipation, looking proud and grand as a peacock. She gave him a quick kiss.

"Just hold the stern sweep up out of the water until we get going. I'll maneuver us from the front."

Glen knew Bessie was in over her head, but this was his dream. They had a few days of quiet water and easy riffles for her to learn on before their first small rapids. She looked like a porcelain doll standing beside him, not like his sister Jeanne who had been on his Snake trip. But his wife was game and would catch on quickly.

The Magarrell brother pushed, and the lumbering scow slid into the current with Glen turning it to face downstream. Bessie waved goodbye to the few people there and hauled in the bowline. They were underway, tackling the river on their own terms, ready to master what few men had attempted before. Five minutes later, civilization was out of sight.

SEDONA CHI

SKIP STAYED WITH HER FOR THE FIRST MILE. BUT PAST THAT, Lilac William's long strides pulled her ahead. At least he got to watch her run the hill from behind, her red ponytail swinging back and forth setting their pace.

He was still stiff from swimming the rapids the week before. His knee was loosening with each step, but there was still pain every time he landed. That adventure had made him face getting back in shape. He wasn't in bad condition for a tour guide, but he'd neglected his old standards. Life had gotten too easy. Letting his hair hit his collar was one thing, adding ten pounds another.

Running from his cabin to Red Rock Crossing, skipping across Oak Creek on steppingstones, and racing up the rocky, back-side of Sedona's Baldwin Trail wasn't the workout he'd had in mind. And that was just halfway. Breathing was fine, but he was burning too many carbs keeping up. Lactic acid buildup was cramping his sides. She was torturing him on purpose.

"Different than the Zumba and low-impact wellness exercising you've been doing with Sky," Lilac yelled over her shoulder. "Forty-two is about the age men start losing muscle mass and stamina. Two more miles!"

"I thought we were doing Tai Chi?"

"We'll cool down back at the river. Drink some water."

Skip shook his head and soldiered on. He could lose a leg to a chainsaw accident and Lilac's answer would be *Drink Water*. The sweat was dripping down his back soaking his cutoff jeans. He was wet enough. He'd already shed his t-shirt with the sporty javelina serving steaming tamales. Lilac looked like she was in the midst of a light workout at Snap Fitness. He noticed a few shiny beads of perspiration on the sides of her long neck. Otherwise, her auburn hair and spandex were as dry as when they started.

He caught up going downhill. Her longer stride wasn't the advantage it had been climbing uphill. She even had to stop to rest at the bottom. It felt good to recapture a bit of his male pride.

"Let's cut over to Verde Valley School Road before you explode," Lilac said, jogging in place, waiting for him to recover. She'd slowed down not wanting to kill him too soon. Carrying him back from this far out wasn't part of her plan.

"I've got my second wind," Skip gasped.

He leapt off-trail beside her to pass, brushing a prickly pear paddle with his leg. He thought he'd easily land past it. He kept running, ignoring the stings. He heard Lilac's fleet feet hitting the path behind him and picked up his pace.

"Maybe we'll skip the Tai Chi," she laughed. "You'll be busy with tweezers."

They came to the end of the trail in fifteen minutes and jogged onto the road. The last mile was dirt and easier on the knees. At the turnaround, he sidestepped down the road bank to the sandstone shelves lining Oak Creek. Cathedral Rock with its twin spires and centered chapel loomed ahead. Its red reflection and the brilliant, blue sky were perfectly painted in a pool of shelf water. He found his usual boulder with the cupped seat and gulped from the nearly empty orange juice bottle he'd filled with water.

"Sip it, don't guzzle." Lilac said, sitting on the rock beside him, sucking from the plastic straw attached to the top of her bottle. She finished and replaced it in the mesh side pocket of her leggings. "You'll feel better in five minutes."

Her brown eyes were studying him over the strip of rosy freckles that always broke out across her nose and the top of her cheeks in the heat. With her height and long, toned legs that seemed to end just below her chin, she could have been a supermodel, Skip thought, except for her temperament; she could definitely stand-in for bad-ass Charlize in the Mad Max movie.

"Still glad you called?" she asked.

"I need to start working out and wanted to be pushed. You came to mind. You enjoyed this didn't you?"

"We're not back to your cabin yet. Tai Chi here or back there?"

"Maybe next time. How about we hike back, shower, and then see if Zula has coffee on?" The shower was a vague suggestion meant to give her options.

Lilac stared at him for a moment and undid her hair, shaking it loose, finger-combing and flipping it back in shape. Then she gathered it behind her tight neck to re-tie. Her teddy bear eyes softened. She sighed. Skip could see his offer hadn't been immediately tossed out. She was calculating whether to take a familiar road that hadn't led anywhere before. Another shower wouldn't be their first, but it had been a while.

It hadn't been long ago when she'd saved his life at a remote Sinagua ruin. He'd been dangling from a seventy-foot cliff. Any other woman, and most men, would have dropped him. In fact, he'd told her to do just that to keep from being pulled over. She'd gripped him tighter and refused. And then there was Kuul's opinion of their relationship.

"We'll hike back to Zula's. She'll have coffee at the bar. Maybe Sky will have the morning shift," Lilac said with an edge. "I saw her Volvo wagon when I parked at the lodge."

Skip had grown close to Sky, but not in the way Lilac assumed. Sky had come to Sedona with a conman as part of a spiritual scheme to bilk retirees. She'd been as innocent and gullible as anyone the dude had taken money from. When Skip ran him out of town, she stayed. They had a few fun months, but nothing more. She was unusually pragmatic for a double-jointed millennial. The girl had diagnosed that he had 'existential tensions' he needed to sort through before getting serious. He knew she placed Lilac near the top of that list.

Sky was helping Zula around the Sands Retreat and Lazy *SOB*, an old lodge and small bar. The two made an odd pair, zany enough in their own ways to hit it off. Sapphire Sky: the free spirit who was certain alien abductors had bestowed her with hyper-mobility, and Zula Ballsy, past Vegas showgirl and mob-boss widow who ran with the Rat Pack in the 60's. She had been Dean's personal hair stylist before his wife had run her off. She'd eventually married Tony "Two Balls" Ballsy, who was axed by the Jersey mob for skimming off the top. The Sands, then a run-down resort, she'd bought with his insurance money.

Skip wheezed, "Can I at least stop and change clothes?"

"You can do whatever you want," Lilac sweetly smiled.

The stop had been quick. He left Lilac on the porch, grabbed a blue t-shirt sporting a Kiltlifter Beer bottle in the hand of a Highlander playing bagpipes and traded his cut-offs for cargo shorts. He tried combing his hair. It was definitely getting too long, a far cry from the buzz cut he'd had for so many years. He'd let Sky cut it; she'd been joking about the unruly, gray wires.

The Sands Retreat had once been a working ranch and Skip's cabin had originally been the foreman's. It was a half-mile hike along the creek to the main lodge and *SOB*. Quiet, private, and remote – Lilac said the isolated cabin fit him. It had been the perfect place when he'd answered the old showgirl's ad. Skip could sit on his porch watching wildlife visit the creek each morning and again in the evening. That's when he and his close friend Don Julio, *tequila, lime juice, and Zula's homemade prickly pear syrup*, would toast the changing colors of the sunset and the shadows dropping down the face of the nearby red mountains. His existential tensions eased a little every night.

"You clean up well," Lilac panned. "Maybe you should try it some time." She had been watching dive-bombing hummingbirds and quick stepping Gambel quail in the open area between the porch and Oak Creek.

"Not before coffee. You ready?"

Lilac rolled her eyes. *What did she see in him?*

They didn't say much walking along the creek. The sound of water bubbling and washing over river rock was hypnotic. The wind was rustling through the mottled-trunk sycamores and the sun highlighting the fluorescent green leaves of the cottonwoods. There was a natural silence neither of them cared to break. Sonny O'Bryan, the old foreman and *SOB* namesake, had been right to build his cabin so far from the ranch and bunkhouse.

The path eventually turned left, taking them up the bank of the creek and into a large, green, grassy field. The Sands was a few hundred feet straight ahead. Zula was on the porch feeding bacon to her pet javelina, Spike. His big head atop his dark, spiky coat bobbed in the air for another piece. Spike had rescued her and Skip not long ago. At just the right moment, the pig had jumped an unscrupulous archeologist who'd been caught looting artifacts. His ego, and bacon expectations, had been heroically expanding ever since. Zula saw them and waved. Spike must have thought it was a game and jumped, taking the bacon from her hand.

"Damn pig thinks he's entitled now," Zula said as they got closer.

"He's not a pig, he's a peccary," Lilac winked.

The javelina's ancestry was a running joke at the Sands. They look like wild pigs, act like wild pigs, smell like wild pigs, but they're actually peccaries, which made Spike more related to a big rodent than a pig - hence his non-issue with bacon.

"Sky!" Zula shouted back into the lodge.

The screen door to the lodge swung open and Sky backed out with a tray of cups and a Mr. Coffee carafe. "I saw them coming," she smiled, sitting the tray on a rustic table made from juniper logs. The lodge looked like the Ponderosa ranch house on Bonanza. The porch had roughhewn, two-by-six planks for its floor and a juniper limb railing. Seating was either old church pews lined below the windows or the more popular Kennedy rockers.

"Boss, we got an email request for another Grand Canyon trip." Sky said, pouring black coffee into three cups and dipping an herbal tea bag into hers.

She was working part-time for Zula and living in a spare room. Since Sedona Chi's address was the lodge, she'd gradually assumed handling most of its correspondence and, with Skip's approval, started a new line of tours for Sedona Chi, focusing on spiritual mysticism, vortexes, and extraterrestrial voyeurism; none of which Skip bought into, but sorcerers and aliens were good business in their quirky town.

"Diamond Creek or the South Rim?" Skip asked. He offered two different trips. He blew in his coffee, sat in a rocker, and propped his boots on the railing.

"Both. And Desert View."

"It's a good thing you have a Girl Friday...*Boss*," Lilac said.

At least she smiled at Sky after she said it. The two got along, or rather co-existed in the same space when they had to. But there was a smack of competition complicated by nearly a ten-year age difference.

"Oh, I'm pretty much available all week," Sky smiled back.

"Your turn Don Juan," Zula grinned at Skip.

As far as he was concerned, they were all just having a nice conversation, the climate wasn't changing, Sedona's tourism was sustainable, world peace was just around the corner, and the Chicago Bears were winning the Super Bowl. Thankfully, Spike farted in a sign of male support, shifting the awkwardness.

"When?" Skip asked Sky, ignoring Zula's jest.

"They wanted October, but I told them we were booked. They were okay with the end of September. I know you and Kuul plan on going to Chaco and Mesa Verde after Labor Day."

"Good call, thanks."

"I'm still hoping you let me tag along…to Chaco. A culture that advanced, that aligned with the sun and stars, has to have had alien contact," Sky said, pleasantly glancing at Lilac.

Lilac ignored her, pouring another cup of coffee and petting Spike, who was rubbing his butt against her leg. She was used to smelly pigs.

"Chaco's up to Kuul. How big a group? We can take five in the Bronco, otherwise we need to rent a van and we have to charge more."

Sky understood their transportation resources but gave the manspeak a pass. "Only two, mother and daughter. Name is Chandler, both from California. In their comment section, Mom expressed interest in the Glen and Bessie Hyde story and the '56 TWA-United Airlines crash. I'd heard of the Hydes but had to look up the crash. They're both sad stories."

Zula chuckled, "People like rumors and mysteries. The Hydes are like Elvis, one of those two has shown up every few years just to give tour guides something to gossip about. Georgie White, Liz Cutler – over the years there's been ten or twenty Bessies that left poor Glen to drown and climbed out of the canyon."

Skip thought of the anthropologist and her boyfriend, "Part of our anthropology is to make up answers to things we don't understand. Rumors were bound to arise when the Hydes' bodies were never recovered. Cut through them and they're just statements about who we are and what we believe in. But the interest in the crash is unusual. A mid-air collision over the Grand Canyon is pretty much a matter of fact: maybe there's a family connection."

"Anthropology?" Lilac mocked. "Well, I'm sure the Sedona Chi staff can make them happy."

"We aim to please," Sky said.

7

CATARACT WHITEWATER

"**I**T SEEMED A GOOD IDEA TO LEARN MORE ABOUT THE RIVER and rafting it before the Chandler tour," Skip said defensively. "You didn't have to come."

Skip, Kuul, and Lilac were on their way to Flagstaff to meet with Chuck Prosser of Cataract Whitewater Rafting. Chuck was an old friend of Lilac's, and she'd set it up. It was a Saturday and traffic on the winding, two-lane highway through Oak Creek Canyon had been brutal. For the last forty-five minutes, all the way through the switchbacks on Arizona 89a, Lilac had been quizzing him about Sky's plans now that she was part of his business.

"Where's she staying?"

"Zula rented her half the duplex cabin, the one nearest the lodge. It was more convenient than her staying in town. Sometimes she works late at the *SOB*."

"It sounds *very* convenient."

"You know better than me that Zula needs the help."

By the time they pulled into Flag she'd exhausted the subject. Lilac was pretty sure whatever had been brewing between Skip and Sky had cooled off. Of course, it could warm up again, especially with their newfound proximity. *Two lonely souls in the woods*...she'd have to ask Zula about any nocturnal walkabouts. She was well acquainted with the passions ignited by the romantic isolation of Skip's cabin. A hypnotic blaze from the fireplace, the dreamy shadows on the log walls, and a warm Pendleton blanket had worked their magic on her multiple times.

"Park over there," she said, pointing to an open spot.

Cataract Whitewater was located in a storefront on Aspen Street in the historic district. They parallel parked the Bronco on Route 66 and walked two blocks past restored, sandstone-brick buildings built in the booming 90's, the 1890's. Prosser ushered them into a small conference room/training center that looked out at the Babbitt Brothers Building. The mural advertising the brothers as merchants, ranchers, and Indian traders was still in place. Skip's plan was to chat with Prosser and stop for a sandwich afterwards at the new Pita Pit next door. Like most historic districts, Flagstaff's had turned hipsterville.

"So, Lilac told me you have an upcoming tour with ladies interested in the Glen and Bessie Hyde story," Prosser said.

Chuck Prosser looked like a river rat: dishwater blond hair, streaked by the sun, sprouted below a worn, bucket hat. He had a lanky frame like he hadn't eaten for a week. The jeans were faded and his stretched-out t-shirt, the collar hung halfway down his chest, advertised his business. His Tewa sandals looked like they'd be more comfortable hanging over the side of a pontoon. The big smile was genuine and likely served him well with nervous tourists.

Skip explained, "I know the Hyde story pretty well. What I'm lacking is context on the Colorado around their time, late fall, early winter, late 1920s. I don't know how much detail my group will expect. I know the Hyde's trip was before the dams, so the level of the water changed by season and with different weather conditions. At least more than it does now."

Prosser smiled and glanced conspiratorially at Lilac.

"You ever rafted the river, Skip?"

Lilac was grinning like the cat that swallowed the canary. Skip guessed she'd told him about his rescue at Diamond Creek.

"Class III, maybe IV, but not in a boat and without a life jacket."

"Yeah, I heard. We do it differently at Cataract Whitewater," he laughed. "Though, it was a brave thing to do. I give you credit; not a lot of people have tried that."

"That would be my recommendation," Skip chuckled.

Prosser had been a river junkie since he'd worked as an assistant guide while in graduate school at Northern Arizona University. His career plans changed when he ran his first rapid. Ten years later he'd bought out his boss when he retired, and the rest was history. If anyone knew about the river's past, it was Prosser. He'd been on it most every week for over thirty years.

"First thing you need to understand is that the river wasn't mapped, let alone surveyed, until the 1870's. The section through the Grand Canyon was the last section of the continental U.S. to be explored. Except for Indians, most people considered it a hellish place that was totally worthless. It was to be avoided, not admired."

"Ancestral Puebloans had farmed the deltas for centuries," Kuul threw in.

Prosser nodded, "As did their descendants, the Hopi. Indian Gardens, halfway down Bright Angel Trail, was farmed into the twentieth century thanks to the spring that's there. The thermal currents rising out of the Canyon even allowed them to plant winter crops on the rim. The river wasn't even always called the Colorado back then. When the Hydes rafted it, it was still being referred to as the Grand River by many locals. Congress had just officially changed the name in 1921, seven years before their trip."

"Grand actually makes more sense than Colorado," Lilac said.

"I can see your point, but its headwaters are in Colorado. When the Hydes attempted running it in 1928, there had only been a handful of men who'd done the whole trip. Most notable were John Wesley Powell and the Kolb Brothers, who were the first to film it. You have to remember that there was no social media, cell phones, or television, and a lot of people didn't even have radios. Maps were pieces of paper, not something you pulled up on a tablet, and around Northern Arizona, not very accurate. At most, people had maybe seen still photos of the canyon and river or grainy, black-and-white snippets of the Kolb videos…if they had visited the South Rim, which the Hydes hadn't. Glen probably poured over Powell's 1868 and 1872 journals, not as histories, but as the best and most accurate accounts of the day. He didn't have a clue what he was in for."

"What about the time of year they chose? Late October?" Skip asked.

"Well, back then, the river dropped six-thousand feet in elevation from where they started to where they were heading; nothing held the water back that wasn't natural. How fast it ran depended on the water level. Unlike Powell, the Hydes did have a general idea of how and where those elevation changes occurred. They knew the river ran lower later in the year because the snow melt wasn't until spring and the summer monsoons were past. And lower means slower. Slow usually equates to safer conditions because you have more time to react. Glen had to know his scow was not a craft that maneuvered well, so reaction time was extra critical."

"So, he chose a safer time?" Skip asked.

"There is no 'safe' time. In low water there are more surface obstructions to deal with."

"The rocks you and Luke almost smashed into, Kemo," Kuul said.

"Right," Prosser confirmed. "In the fall and winter, the current might be slower because of the lower water level, but boulders that were submerged are exposed as jagged spikes just waiting to break up a raft."

"So why wouldn't they go in the summer if Glen was trying to break a speed record? That would seem to be a better time if your goal is to go fast and you are confident in your skills," Skip asked.

Prosser smiled, "He did want to set a speed record, and if your plan is to become famous, then do something nobody's done, right? But remember, there hadn't been many people do that trip summer or fall, and none in a scow, which he felt was better in whitewater. Also, this is just a guess, but it makes sense - he had a farm, and they were likely busy during the summer - and as fast as Glen and Bessie got married, they probably needed time to catch their breath and adjust to each other. You don't want to run rapids with someone you don't truly know."

"So, the sixty-four-million-dollar question is should they have made it?" Kuul asked.

Prosser didn't hesitate, "In my opinion, they were doomed the moment they pushed off from Green River. It was just a question of where it would happen. Bessie was untried...the scow was a bad choice for the Colorado...the time of year with more obstructions... no life preservers...Glen's overconfidence...I could go on and on. Death was waiting for them under the best of conditions."

"But you've been doing it for thirty years," Skip said.

"It's different now. The river has a more consistent year-round flow because of the dams, so there are fewer variables. It's also been charted and surveyed. After fifty years of commercial rafting, there isn't much we don't know. Our equipment is more modern and ideally suited to the conditions. In short, we've learned. Heck, old-timers used inner tubes and empty five-gallon cans as life jackets. That's how far we've come. The only real problems now are a rogue wave now and again, newly fallen debris, and rafters doing something they shouldn't be doing. Human error, passengers, not guides, is the overwhelmingly biggest cause of mishaps. The Grand

Canyon averages only about a dozen deaths each year. That's out of five to seven million people who visit the park annually. And very few of those occur on the river. They're falls, heart attacks, car accidents, murders, suicides, or a muscled-up kid stroking out from dehydration because he thinks he's invulnerable. I feel safer in a raft than at Flagstaff Mall."

"But there are still accidents, a foot in a propeller, a flipped pontoon…" Skip said.

"Yes, there are, and they get reported in sensational fashion, which isn't fair but that's life."

They heard the outside door open, and Prosser glanced over his shoulder and waved. "Be right there." A group had arrived to check in.

"Looks like you have business, Chuck. Thanks for taking the time," Lilac said.

"And the info," Skip added, standing and shaking his hand.

"Any time, if you ever want to get some first-hand knowledge, we can always use volunteer crew hands. Especially those that swim well," he grinned.

Skip pocketed the offer, but he felt much more comfortable on land. Hiking down a mountain might be more dangerous, but he'd rather trust his boots and solid rock than a plastic oar and unpredictable water. Besides, his last trip on the Colorado hadn't been all that fun.

"Lunch?" Skip asked Lilac and Kuul after they were outside. "I'm buying."

"You feeling okay, Kemo?"

"Coming was my idea. We can eat here in Flag or at the South Rim, our next stop."

Skip and Kuul planned on heading to Grand Canyon Village for the afternoon. He wanted to poke around the exhibit on the Hydes at Kolb Studio, and Kuul wanted to visit with the pretty Navajo cashier. Since her tagging along to Flag had been Lilac's idea, Skip just assumed she'd be okay with tagging along to the canyon. She loved the place as much as he did.

"Not me," Lilac said. "Cooper's up here consulting with the FPD, and we're meeting at the Lotus Lounge when he's done. I'd planned on shopping until he calls."

John Cooper was a detective for the Phoenix PD that Lilac dated off and on. Behind her, Skip saw him come out of the historic Hotel Monte Vista and put a keycard in his pocket. Lilac didn't know he was there. He was wearing an Aloha shirt, yellow with red hibiscuses, neatly pressed, fashion jeans, and an out-of-place fedora for cowboy-rich Flagstaff...not exactly proper attire to meet with his brothers in blue.

"I thought you were bored with him. Didn't you say he was too short and kind of dull," Skip said with PPD's finest now within earshot, frowning.

"Not yet and so are you," Lilac said, still not seeing Cooper.

Touched a nerve, Skip thought. *'Not yet' wasn't exactly a ringing endorsement and she had called them both dull, him as an insult.*

"Lilac," Cooper called, stepping onto the curb after jaywalking across the street.

Her eyes narrowed and she icily glared at Skip before turning. He shrugged back.

"Coop, I thought you were still in the meeting with the FPD."

Cooper hesitated for an instant, reading her lead, then gave her a quick kiss. "We finished early; the captain had a deposition. I thought maybe we could do drinks at the Lotus before an early dinner. I saw you leave the rafting office from a window. You guys want to join us?" he said, nodding to Skip and Kuul.

Skip started to answer, "Why not, we're...,"

"On our way to the South Rim, Kemo," Kuul interrupted. "You said something about margaritas and chili at El Tovar's lounge." Watching Lilac, he was glad she wasn't carrying her Glock. The daggers she was shooting were bad enough.

"Well, the Lotus can't compete with that," Coop said.

"Dinner will make you late getting back to Phoenix," Skip said, recalling the keycard and wondering about their plans after dinner.

"Drinks and a nice meal, something better than beans and stewed tomatoes, sound wonderful, Coop. Have I ever showed you what I can do with a cherry stem?" Lilac teased. She put her arm through Coop's, seductively playing with the hairs on his bare arm, her taunting eyes locked with the big dope's.

8

KOLB STUDIO

THE BRONCO COUGHED TWICE GOING AROUND GRAY MOUNTAIN but caught its breath heading downhill. Skip and Kuul had taken U.S. 80 north out of Flagstaff thru the red dirt of Navajo Nation and Cameron. It was the long way, but Skip preferred the scenic drive along the Little Colorado River Gorge. Rickety, wooden Navajo stalls lined the remote highway overlooking the distant crack in the land that wound its way to its more renowned and older cousin, the Grand Canyon.

At the east entrance, he showed his National Park Pass to a ranger with thick, black-framed glasses. His stiff-brimmed hat was too big, and it rested on the frames. After studying the pass for a full minute, as if he'd been handed a subpoena for Forest Service records, he waved them through.

"I used to think it was because he was new, but he's been here for a year now," Skip complained.

"Your card's picture of the polar bear on the melting ice flow probably bothered him," Kuul quipped. "He's at the east entrance for a reason - less traffic, less personal interaction."

"You buy they were there *just* for dinner?" Skip asked his friend. His mind had been on Lilac and Cooper since getting out of Flagstaff traffic.

"I believe they will have dinner, yes."

Skip glanced across the bench seat to the stoic Mayan, "You know what I mean."

"No."

"No, you don't think it was just dinner, or no, you don't know what I mean."

"Yes."

"Thanks."

They drove past Desert View, the first stop with vistas of the canyon. The spot overlooked the confluence of the Colorado and Little Colorado from a distance. Across from there was Chuar Butte, where United 718 had crash-landed in 1956 after colliding mid-air with the TWA plane. There was a plaque at Desert View's observation deck. Skip thought about stopping, but, as many times as he'd been there, there wasn't anything new to learn before the Chandler tour.

Thirty minutes later they were at Grand Canyon Village, parking in a small, hidden, gravel lot behind Verkamp's Visitor Center. The Verkamps had been three generations of merchants who ran a general store and raised their families on the rim of the canyon, only a hundred yards from the famous El Tovar Hotel.

"You want to see if we can get a room at Maswik Lodge or go home tonight?" Skip asked, walking down the paved, rim trail past the 1905 El Tovar. The hotel loomed as a testament to 20th Century National Park grandiosity, resembling a Bavarian-hunting-lodge in the Black Forest of Germany. Hopi House, which sat across the drive, was the true masterpiece of southwest-inspired architecture.

The Grand Canyon train had left a half-hour earlier, reducing the crowds to mostly those who were spending the night. It was late afternoon and nearly four hours until sunset. The sun was still high, but long shadows were already filling the side canyons, cracks, and dry washes, giving dimension to the canyon. Turkey vultures were soaring on the late afternoon thermal currents, which rose from the heat escaping the depths of the canyon.

"I've got a breakfast date in the morning, so back tonight," Kuul said.

He was quite the popular player. Skip had lost count of his ex-girlfriends and ex-wives. One or another was always popping up. None of them held their breakups against him. Kuul considered them all to be sharing each other's journeys. Their paths crossed, separated, and then crossed again. It was 'Great Spirit's plan'.

"Sandy Littlefoot?"

Kuul had been seeing Littlefoot, a pretty, sand-painting artist from Clarkdale, Arizona, for the past few months. Being Hopi, she got a kick out of his Navajo shtick. The two tribes had a long history of not playing well together. She appreciated Kuul's making a buck off their popularity with tourists.

Kuul grinned, "Dinner is with Littlefoot. I'm having breakfast at Red Rock Café with Toni Wathetewa. She's fed up with Yavapai and Apache men; they're ignoring their matriarchal laws. You know Toni, she won't put up with any male nonsense."

Skip silently wished him luck. Wathatewa was a handful and a tough nut. He had a hard time seeing the polished tribal council rep with his less serious friend.

"Let's stop at Kolb Studio and at least catch the West Rim shuttle to Powell Point for sunset. We haven't been there in a while, and we'll want to take the Chandlers to both."

Kuul agreed, "You remember Chooli Nez? She works part-time at Kolb Studio for Xanterra. Her grandmother was a weaver at Hopi House long time ago. I can catch up."

"Not that I recall. Past girlfriend or another ex-wife I haven't met?"

"One never knows where their journey takes them."

Kolb Studio was the former home of Emery and Ellsworth Kolb. They were two enterprising brothers who showed up at the Grand Canyon in 1901 and began taking pictures of tourists for Ralph Cameron. Cameron operated a lodge and, at that time, owned the Bright Angel Trail. That was before the park or El Tovar. In the early days, the brothers collected tolls as well as took pictures. Emery had even hosted the Hydes during their fateful trip, and, with Ellsworth, located their empty scow after they disappeared.

The Studio proved what a suspension of sound mind and lack of engineering could accomplish. Cameron had given the brothers a spit of land at the very edge of the canyon. They built a ramshackle house and photography studio, adding an addition from time to time, out over the rim, clinging to nothing but bare rock. Skip had never understood how the daredevil brothers kept their knees from shaking while working off thrown-together scaffolding cantilevered over thin air. The studio eventually included a theater to show their famous film of running the Colorado River. Thanks to the Historic Preservation Act, the persnickety Park Service was forced to restore it after Emery died. Otherwise, it would have been lost to time, along with the brother's three-quarter-century legacy.

"Chooli!" Kuul exclaimed on entering the studio, now gift shop.

The barrel-shaped Navajo woman stood behind the counter. Turquoise and silver bracelets jingled as she clapped her hands. Her almond-shaped eyes sparkled, and her lips curled slightly, which for a Navajo equated to a beaming smile, especially with *bilagáana* around. She came around the counter and gave him a bear hug, lifting the big man off the floor. "Kuul Balthazar! Long time, no see."

Kuul introduced Skip. From the reception, Skip guessed Chooli was another partner in his journey. Skip explained he was a guide and had a tour scheduled. The group was interested in the Glen and Bessie Hyde story. He wanted to reacquaint himself with the exhibit in the studio's basement.

"We have a good book on those two, *Sunk Without a Sound*. If I'm here, I'll show it to them. We also have *Death in Grand Canyon*, which has a section on that couple. Nowadays the river's much safer for white people. They spend big money to go there."

Skip had both histories. *Death in the Canyon* was over four-hundred pages and updated every other year. People never stopped inventing new ways to harm themselves. The Hyde's weren't the first nor the last to die mysteriously deep in the canyon.

"You know the Kolbs' river video is always playing in the projection room around the corner?" Chooli added. "We sell copies."

"We'll look for you. Thanks," he said, smiling at the Navajo saleswoman. "Kuul, I'm heading downstairs, be back in about fifteen minutes."

The brothers' video was playing on a pull-down screen at the head of the theater, above the stage from which Emery had lectured to tourists. The film held a Guinness record for being the world's longest-running movie. The picture was grainy, but Emery and Ellsworth could easily be seen scampering over boulders along the bank, setting up their boxy, black camera and tripod to shoot one or the other of them, usually Ellsworth, running rapids. Their rickety rowboat would be momentarily lost in towering sprays of foam and water, only to pop through on the other side.

The Hydes' exhibit was on a sidewall. Skip stared at the portrait Emery had taken during the visit. The honeymooners were standing outside against a stone chimney; the rocks likely hauled up from the bottom of the canyon by the brothers. Glen was a full head-and-a-half taller than Bessie, his hair neatly slicked back. He had a firm, simple smile and held his Stetson in his right hand, confident and ready to tackle the world. Bessie was beside him, wearing a leather aviator jacket with fur collar, her hands in its pockets.

Her bold and penetrating gaze stared straight into the camera. In the lower corner of the photo, Kolb had scrawled the date, *Nov. 16-28.*

They didn't look like a couple in over their head, or worried. The bulk of their trip was behind them. Part of the exhibit was a letter from Glen to his father Rollin Hyde, posted from Grand Canyon Village; *'at any rate, we are over all the worst rapids, so will go on'.* Skip thought about the phrasing, *At Any Rate...So Will Go On.* The sentence read like a man trying to convince himself of something he doubted.

• • •

Skip and Kuul hung onto the overhead handrail in a West Rim shuttle bus. Chooli was seated. Her shift had ended, and Kuul invited her to join them for sunset. "Next stop, Powell Point. Transfer stop to the eastbound shuttle," the bus driver announced. "Powell Point has a memorial to John Wesley Powell and the men who joined him in 1868 to survey the Colorado River. They were the first."

"First Europeans," Kuul leaned in and whispered to Chooli. She shrugged; she was used to their heritage being ignored.

They exited with other riders and walked several hundred yards along an asphalt path to the pyramid-shaped monument with the engraved names of Powell's men. There were thirty to forty people already there. Kids were running around, arguing with their parents, who feared their falling. At least a dozen millennials had earbuds; a girl had let one bud slip out and he could hear Katy Perry from a few feet away. Enjoying a sunset or sunrise, alone at the park, was a thing of the past.

Kuul and Chooli paid their respects to the Paiute in the picture with John Wesley Powell. He had led the explorer on several, precursory expeditions throughout the southwest and accompanied him on his second river trip. Without him, Powell probably would never have succeeded and would have passed into history as just another wounded, Civil War veteran.

The Mayan and Navajo headed out the rim trail to find a private spot for sunset and Skip began reading a story board with a picture of Powell's boat. He listened in to another guide escorting a family. They looked to be three generations; grandfather, grandmother, father, mother, and two arguing twins, that Skip judged to be about thirteen. "I wouldn't want to raft the Rio Grande in that boat, let alone the Colorado," the guide said. "That wooden chair lashed to the front bench was where Powell sat. Before every rapid, he'd call out if they were running it, lining it, or portaging. They usually pulled in and portaged, carrying the boat downstream past the whitewater. He'd come through Shiloh alive because he was a cautious, organized man."

"He'd lost an arm in the war, right?" the grandpa asked. Grandpas always knew their history.

"Which arm?" the twin who'd lost the fight over their shared tablet asked.

"Left," the guide answered absently. He was likely tired of the boys' inane questions. Skip had once had a bored teenager ask him if the Grand Canyon was red because of sunburn. Kids that age didn't have filters.

"Might rethink that answer," the boy's grandmother said. She was looking at the photo of Powell and the Paiute. Powell was pointing in the distance with his left hand.

Skip chuckled and walked around the monument to the overlook in front. Maybe he'd get lucky and there would be an empty bench to sit on and watch the light show from. Another shuttle had arrived and most of the crowd had scuttled off toward the pickup. Hopi and Mohave Points were more popular at sunset.

It wasn't much farther, by river miles, to Separation Point, where Powell's beleaguered and starving group of veterans and mountain men had fallen out. After months of exhausting work, near drownings, and hauling heavy, topographical equipment down the Colorado, three of his men were done. They'd been lucky, but luck only got a man so far, and they were past that point. Bad rapids were thundering around the next bend, and they knew they'd die there. The Grand had won, beaten them; to go farther was suicide.

Gazing a mile below, Skip wondered if Glen and Bessie had ever reached their breaking point. They'd gotten farther than Powell, but not much. It was uncanny how the two parties, sixty years apart, after so many months and miles on the river, having negotiated rapid after rapid, had met their fate so near the same spot. But they had. The Hydes chose to stay together and disappeared in the canyon. Powell's men hiked out to the plateau and vanished. Fate, destiny, karma; whatever it was had been waiting for them.

The two benches were taken, so Skip stood at the railing. The sun was slipping below the far horizon. The sky above the canyon glowed bright yellow with tinges of pink; the hues changing, morphing each minute. Without clouds, the heavens became big brushstrokes of blended color; vivid gold where the distant buttes met the sky, orange turning red higher up, and finally blues and purples. On the wind, he could hear Chooli and Kuul chanting somewhere along the rim.

He wished Lilac was here.

9

BESSIE AND GLEN HYDE

October 27-28, 1928

BESSIE BALANCED THE HUNDRED-POUND SWEEP-OAR, ADMIRING the gentle water of the Green River as it cut deeper into the earth, forming a land filled with canyons. She loved the river's romanticism, its rhythm. She thought of Longfellow's poem in Hiawatha:

> *Half in rest, and half in strife;*
> *I have seen thy waters stealing;*
> *Onward, like the stream of life.*

They had been on the river a week, through still water and small rapids. The sweep was getting easier to manage. She was learning. Glen had tied logs near the handle to act as a counterweight. Try as she might, she hadn't been able to hold it out of the water. Working it was still hard; the sweep weighed more than she did even before the extra twenty pounds. But the balance was better. Glen, on the other hand, looked like he was born with an oar in each hand. What a fine man she'd married. He was in his element here, in the wild, relying on his strength and skill.

There had been a few rough spots, but nothing serious. The water had been lower than expected and slow from lack of rain. They'd floated through Labyrinth Canyon, admiring the sandstone cliffs that rose and fell on both sides. They'd stopped and taken turns carving their names into a rock face next to several other inscriptions. "See, we've already made a name for ourselves," Glen had said, laughing.

On their fourth day, they beached the scow in a beautiful spot after a quiet day. The current was slow, and they were able to hear the sweet, liquid notes of canyon wrens. Glen hauled the mattress and springs onto the sand below a graceful willow. That night, they laid in bed listening to night sounds. Glen wrapped her in his strong arms, both of them naked under the quilts like all of God's other creatures sharing the canyons. They made love twice, and she rested her head on his stomach, playing with him with her hand. She'd tucked her bare feet beneath his to keep them warm.

"I could stay here forever, just like this," Glen said, moving his hand up and down her back. "The river fits me, and having you here makes it heaven. That was a fine meal you fixed, Bessie."

Bessie grasped him tighter and felt some life rise in him. "That's all I'm good for, skinning ducks you shoot and frying Idaho spuds?"

Glen laughed and slid his hand down to her hip, rolling her on top of him. "In a few days, we'll hit the Colorado, and then, Cataract Canyon. I've studied Powell's notes and I wrote Emery Kolb about it; it'll be a tough test."

"The graveyard of the Colorado," Bessie sighed.

She could tell his mind had changed to the river. Glen had told her that Cataract was the first dangerous spot for inexperienced river runners. Other rafters had died there, but they didn't have

Glen's know-how or his boat. He'd said they'd be fine. Laying there in the dark, she thought she detected his first bit of hesitation.

She kissed him and they made love again, Orion bashfully hiding overhead, the river rushing a few feet away, matching their rhythm.

The next day, they floated into a section where the cliffs spread wide, as if they'd been pushed back from the river. Fertile land on both sides was dotted in the distance with low, red buttes and lonely, rock spires. Glen called it Tower Park. Bessie found the openness comforting. It made her feel more connected to the rest of the world, not so alone. The feeling didn't last long though; the current carried them through the green vistas and into Stillwater Canyon, where the walls closed in again. The closer they got to the confluence with the Colorado the deeper the canyon seemed to become.

"It's like we're floating down into the earth," Bessie said.

Bessie did her best using the rear sweep in the calm, green-blue water of the Green River. She raised the oar out of the water by half-jumping and leaning her chest hard onto the handle. She turned her head to see Glen judging her method.

"It's good you're getting the hang of the sweep," Glen grinned, watching Bessie dip the oar into a wave as she was lifted a few inches off the floor.

Bessie smiled at his encouragement. "Is that the Colorado?" She was struck by how suddenly the pretty, green water changed to muddy brown, as if a line had been painted. Above the river, burnt orange rock appeared to be stacked layer after layer atop crumbling, sandstone slopes.

"Yup," Glen said, working his sweep to guide them right of center. "In a few miles we'll hit our first real whitewater. Are you ready?"

From where the two rivers joined, the flow steadily increased, taking them into Cataract Canyon. The current seemed twice as strong against Bessie's sweep. The Colorado was loud too, a lot louder. They rounded a bend, and she heard a roar ahead, the ferocious sound echoing off the canyon walls.

"Keep her straight and hang on," Glen yelled as they entered a rapid.

He was standing right beside her on the platform, and she could barely hear his instructions. The roar came from big waves breaking over submerged boulders. Bessie could not focus on what lay ahead of them now; she was desperately holding onto her sweep, battling the river's fury each time she dipped it into a swelling wave, trying not to lower it on a rock. She hesitated once, sneaking a glance to her left and right. Something was wrong! They were racing downstream, but beside them the river was moving upstream! Had they gotten turned somehow?

"Yahoo!" she heard Glen yell in glee. "Hang on Bessie! There are some big ones ahead!"

Bessie could feel the scow surge beneath her whenever Glen sunk his forward sweep into the water. She could feel him leveraging the river's force, pushing them one way or the other, just enough to keep them out of the bigger holes.

"We want to stay toward the center, or we'll get caught in those eddies by the walls!" he yelled.

Bessie was fighting the rear sweep. She knew if she lost control, it would violently swing on its pivot and could knock her or Glen into the rapid. Every time she dipped the oar, she tried keeping her knees bent and feet flat against the platform. She pushed down on the handle as hard as she could to raise it back out of the river. With every crest, the choppy waves sprayed water higher than the scow. She was soaked and cold. Muddy water was covering the bottom of the boat. The violence she felt below her was terrifying, but that was why they'd decided on the Colorado. No one had promised it was going to be easy. Bessie understood that a gentle, safe float wouldn't get them headlining the better vaudeville theaters with the best paying crowds. Adventure and danger would be what packed them in. And here it was, no longer an imaginary foe.

Adrenalin soaring, she plunged her sweep into the next wave. Suddenly, her arms and shoulders uncontrollably jerked to her left. The current had wrenched the handle in her hands as the oar hit the end of its arc and vaulted out of the wave. Her feet whiplashed from under her, and she lost her grip. Everything went topsy-turvy and Bessie flew above the platform. She stared down, airborne, in horror, at the frothing river below her.

"GLEN!"

10

THE CHANDLERS

WINONNA CHANDLER WAS BLINDED BY THE SUN SHINING through the gap in her bedroom curtains. A rude jolt of nature waking her up wasn't what she needed. If she wanted to see a sunrise, she'd have set an alarm. She stretched and grabbed the cell phone vibrating on the nightstand. She'd lost count, was this the fourth or fifth time it had interrupted her sleep? The smooth, satin sheets and thick, goose-feathered comforter had kept her from reaching it each time. Her bloodshot eyes tried reading the screen, *11 AM!*

No doubt it was Percy, her agent, panicking about last night. Winonna knocked two empty wine glasses over before finding her reading glasses, which she refused to wear in public. They made her look like Diane Keaton. She was only thirty-four. Maybe Doctor Tuck could do something about it; he'd improved everything else. She focused on her phone's caller ID - Percy.

"Please, Winonna, no more bad publicity! You'll end up on the Hallmark Channel as the lead's best friend!"

Winonna guessed the story had hit the morning L.A. Times. Even though she hadn't starred in anything for over a year, the paparazzi still followed her from club to club. Sleazy pests!

"It's one thing to get drunk and run around without a bra but flopping the girls around at Victoria's Secret! Jesus, how am I supposed to spin this? I got you out of that sticky situation in Miami with a few thousand and a promised screen test for the bellboy. But this, I don't know. Your little errs in judgement are about to end your career."

"Good morning, Percy. When do I deposit your next retainer?" Winonna answered, reminding her nervous agent who worked for whom. For what she paid him, he needed to fix this. "How bad is it this time?"

"How bad! How bad! There are pictures of you fighting with the clerk over a red teddy. The article mentions nipple holes and crotchless, matching panties. But that's not the worst. Please tell me you didn't shoplift it! Please!"

A hundred reasons ran through Winonna's mind, all of which she was paying a pricy Beverly Hills therapist to sort through. Whatever Percy laid on her wouldn't be half of what she'd heard from her mother. She'd shoplifted for kicks since being old enough to drive to the malls. Back then, her dead grandfather's money had been enough to make those troubles go away. He'd been a well-known movie director. She was a legacy in this lousy city. That used to mean something.

"I tried it on and forgot to take it off before leaving the store. The clerk over-reacted. I tried giving it back."

"There are pictures of that too. And there's video from another customer; you stripping off your blouse in front of the counter, dropping the f-bomb, and ripping the teddy off before throwing it at the poor girl. Thank God, the security guard covered most of the lens, but not all…maybe I can get you a role on late night Cinemax. On second thought, probably not, you're too short and too *OLD!*"

Winonna ordered him to make it go away, buy the video and maybe offer the clerk something to recant. Whatever, why did *she* have to do *his* work? She punched the call end button while Percy was still wailing about her prospects. If only Grandpa hadn't died when he did; he'd have taken care of problems like this. He'd had so many connections from the golden age of Hollywood. His father, great grandfather Bockner, was an influential real estate developer and close friend of Cecil B. DeMille. C.B. had gotten his friend's son into the business. In those early days, everybody still knew everybody. And stars could be bad and not see online videos of their indiscretions five minutes later.

Winonna checked her phone. She had several missed calls and voicemails from Hollywood Reporter, National Enquirer, and a blogger from some rag called White Lies and Soiled Bedsheets. But it was the chastisement from her mother she dreaded most. The woman set standards Winonna had never been interested in following.

After her mother's parents died in a plane crash, she had been raised by great grandmother Bockner, Nana Louise. Mom had never learned how a mother was supposed to deal with a rebellious daughter. The grandmother-granddaughter relationship was just a different dynamic, especially when it was overshadowed by tragedy. Raised by Nana Lou, her mother had become an 'old soul' by the time Winonna was five. Well, Winonna was no old soul.

Winonna had never met great grandfather Bockner. She barely remembered Nana Lou who'd lived with them her last few years. All Winonna really remembered was coming home one day from kindergarten to find out she was gone. Mom had gotten her quiet, dignified bearing from Nana Lou though. By all accounts, great grandmother had been a stoic easterner with a soft heart. With her husband's connections, she could also have easily become a star.

But she shied away from the limelight. Mom had told her, more than once, that Nana Lou preferred the business side, working behind the scenes, supporting struggling artists. No wonder her mom had grown up so sensible. *With all their money and good fortune, came responsibility*, Winonna had heard it over and over again.

Now her mother wanted to finally visit the Grand Canyon, where her parents had died so tragically before she could even talk. And she wanted her only daughter to go with her. Winonna couldn't understand why. Mom couldn't even remember them; the crash had been over sixty years ago. It wasn't like visiting her great grandparents' graves, which they dutifully did twice each year.

Winonna was smart enough to understand she'd grown up rebelling against her mother. If Mom liked a white dress, she liked the black one. She didn't want to be boring like her. She wanted to have fun, go to parties, and flirt with as many boys as she could. That hadn't changed as she gained her independence, which happened earlier than with most girls. Once she'd begun acting, she had her own money, and her mother couldn't stop her. According to her shrink, she'd been too young when she cut the apron strings.

Now that she was older, she wished she'd listened more. Acting bad had worked early in her career. But at thirty-four, she was realizing her misbehaviors were no longer impetuously cute. According to Percy, they were boorish, exactly what she didn't want to be. Maybe it was time to try modeling herself after Mom and Nana Lou, reserved and refined. She'd told her mom she'd go on the trip, but no guarantees.

• • •

For the fifth time, Charlotte "Lottie" Chandler listened as her daughter's phone went directly to voicemail. Obviously, she had turned it off. Not surprising with what she'd seen in the morning paper.

Maybe she'd grow up some day, but she was beginning to doubt it. 'Spoiled' didn't begin to describe her. Winonna hadn't changed her act since she was thirteen.

Lottie would always regret agreeing to let her young daughter audition for the part in that short-lived sitcom. That's where her problems had started. She should have known how it'd turn out. As a child, Winonna had been adorable, cutely audacious, and, unfortunately, a hit from the moment the camera light turned green. One small part had led to another and before long she had starred as the teenage girlfriend of a high school quarterback in a long-running CBS sports drama. They'd made her the bad girl that was always tempting the squeaky-clean boy, keeping him out late before the big game. That was before the movie roles, the cosmetic enhancements, and three failed marriages.

Lottie stared at the reflection in her vanity mirror. How many times had she been told her daughter looked just like her? About as many times as she'd been told she was the spitting image of her Nana Lou. All three were petite, with lively, dark, penetrating eyes. Just like Nana Lou, their hair was dark brown, and Lottie kept hers similarly short. They were all girl-next-door pretty. With their shape and narrow hips, they could have passed for boys. At least she could. Nana Lou and Winonna had a quiet sexuality about them. Even as Nana aged, men, especially strong men, had been attracted to her. Winonna had the same quality, just with different types of men.

Lottie inherited her grandmother's love of art. Maybe, unconsciously, her daughter saw acting as her art. Lottie could remember sitting on her grandmother's lap drawing pictures with crayons. She'd done the same with Winonna. If there had been any frivolity to Nana Lou it had been expressed in her love of aesthetics. Going to museums and gallery openings had been an escape. Nana had written poetry too, jotting lines and thoughts into her journal.

After graduating college, Lottie had become a children's book author. Nana Lou, before she passed away, had even contributed a few sketches. Lottie eventually married her publisher. They became wealthy from their incomes, and with the money she'd inherited from her grandparents - wealthy was enough to spoil Winonna. At a critical time in her daughter's development, her husband had died unexpectedly. He'd always played the role of disciplinarian. Because of the loss of her parents, she didn't have it in her.

At least her daughter agreed to accompany her to the Grand Canyon. Lottie was sixty-three and it was time. She'd put it off her entire adult life. So much of her family's history and who she'd become was the result of that harsh, isolated place. Her parents, Glenda and Norman Carson, had died there on United Airlines flight 718.

The mid-air accident had happened in 1956 when Lottie was two. Both planes had diverted off their course to sightsee. The 50's were still the dawn of passenger air service. Sheared of one wing, the airliner had crashed on a remote butte in the Grand Canyon. It had taken days to spot the wreckage and a week for mountain climbers from Colorado and Switzerland to reach the site and recover what charred remains were recoverable. Very few victims were identifiable. The desecrated bodies were buried en masse at the Grand Canyon.

Nana Lou had often told her, with tears in her eyes, how she and Grandpa Harold had stood behind the chain-link fence at the old Los Angeles International Airport waving goodbye to her only child while holding her baby. That was the last place both pair of mothers and daughters had been together.

Lottie had always resisted visiting the memorial. Her grandmother had only gone once, for the service. They'd often talked about going back but never did. Now that Lottie was older, she felt increasingly drawn to where her parents' story had ended. And in a way only she appreciated, where her family had begun. There were other secrets about the canyon she'd never shared with Winonna. Secrets her daughter would inevitably discover on her own someday. Having a tour guide tell the stories might make it easier for Lottie to lead Winonna down that path, to help her uncover all that really happened. Maybe knowing the truth would finally bring them closer.

Lottie tried calling her daughter again. She'd have to answer sooner or later. To her surprise, Winonna answered on the fifth ring.

"Mom, I don't want or need a lecture."

"Okay, okay. I'm only calling about the trip. We need to plan what to take."

This trip would change things, Lottie hoped. The beauty, the emotions, the stories, their experiencing them together - she'd try hard to get through to her, to build a bridge. The Grand Canyon owed her. It owed her family.

11

FORSAKEN SOULS

"**G**ET ON THE FLOOR!" HYDE DONALD MUMBLED.

"What? Don't shoot me, man. I have a family," the Forsaken Souls Liquor clerk said shakily, holding his hands up. He couldn't understand the man. The idiot had pulled pantyhose all the way down his face and then doubled and redoubled it back over his chin and mouth.

"On the floor!" Hyde screamed, rolling the stinky nylon above his mouth.

Gloria only had two pair and she was wearing the cleaner one. She was waiting in the car. They planned to celebrate at The Pickled Goose Buffet after he finished.

"That's better, man," the clerk said from the floor. "You gonna rob someone you need to make sure they can hear you. Otherwise, it's just confusing."

"Open the register."

"I'm face down on the floor, man. My arms are too short. Don't shoot me, man."

"Get up!" Hyde yelled. Just his luck he'd run into a comedian. The guy probably had a floor show at some cheap casino way off the strip. You never knew in Reno, it wasn't Vegas. It attracted a lot of stupid people.

"I'm going to fucking shoot you, you asshole."

"Don't do it, man. Do you still want me to open the register?"

Hyde shot a pint of Fireball behind him instead. Like magic, the clerk shut up and the register opened. Hyde reached across the counter with his pistol and hit Cedric the Entertainer as hard as he could. There...the asshole was finally quiet and on the floor. *Shit, that's a lot of blood! The old man, his grandfather Austin Donald, had taught him guys like that had thicker skulls, so you have to hit'em harder.*

"Hey! Romeo! What'd you do that for?"

Hyde turned with the gun in his hand. The voice had come from the door. *Damn!*

"We don't get there soon they'll be out of prime rib," Gloria said, stomping her five-inch heel. It snapped and she almost fell. "Shit!"

"Jesus, Baby. I told you to stay in the car with the engine running. You're supposed to be my lookout!"

"I asked the kid on the bike to keep an eye on the Mazda."

"What kid? Fuck Gloria. I'm robbing a liquor store here, for Christ's sake!" He raised the back of his hand to slap her, and she flinched.

Hyde ran to the door, shoving Gloria aside. There was a teenager standing next to a battered Schwinn by their car. He saw Hyde and waved. No one else was in the dark lot. He'd picked this store because the only overhead light was above the door, and it was flickering on and off.

"You said you were getting us a bottle of sweet Riesling," Gloria grumbled. "I told the kid we'd get him a six-pack. I think he's underage." She wasn't particularly upset about Hyde's change in plans, but she stepped out of arms' reach anyway. His not being a choir boy was nothing new.

"What did you think the hose was for? Stupid bitch."

"I don't judge, baby."

"Damnit Gloria. Now I've got to shoot the kid or at least hurt him bad enough he won't tell anyone what he saw. How many times do I have to tell you to stop and think? Go out there and tell him to wait."

Gloria stuck out her studded tongue, "You can forget about the pipe massage later tonight."

"Gloria," Hyde said, softening his voice. "What kind of beer does he want?"

"Bud light. He's got no class, you know. Not like you, baby."

Hyde shook his head. The kid should have at least asked for an import, Sam Adams or Fat Tire or something. If you don't demand much, that's exactly what you get. The old man had taught him that too.

"What kind of Riesling?"

"Whatever's cheapest, honey."

• • •

Hyde and Gloria were sopping blood juice from the prime rib with Hawaiian sweet rolls. Hyde had made the carver cut off fresh slices instead of accepting dryer pieces from the platter. The Pickled Goose was a nice place; there was a real candle at each table and extra forks. He'd sprung for two unlimited buffets and paid an extra buck for the desert table. That bought all the prime rib, lasagna, catfish, and fried okra they could eat. And Gloria would finally get the strawberry pie she'd been chattering about all day.

Out of nowhere, Earl Donald pulled up an extra chair.

"Who the hell are you?" Gloria asked, her mouth stuffed with candied sweet potatoes. There was something familiar about the man's eyes. He was gently pulling a straggly gray hair in his eyebrow.

"He's my uncle, baby. I've told you about him."

Hyde was being nice to Gloria, trying to make up for the liquor store. He'd paid the extra dollar just for her. Her massages were extra special when she was in a good mood and had a full stomach. She'd been mad ever since he'd kicked the shit out of her teenage lookout at the liquor store. She'd yelled at him from her Mazda, complaining the kid's puking made her queasy. It didn't look like the beating had ruined her appetite, however. Which was good, because Hyde was counting on her affections. *They were costing him enough.* She was a professional, when she wasn't doing nails, but Earl showing up put the pipe polishing job in doubt. He knew his uncle wouldn't be here if the old man hadn't sent him.

"Send the bimbo back to the no-tell motel she came from. It looks like she's had more than enough to eat."

"Hey!" Gloria cried, wiping lasagna sauce off her nose. "Are you going to let him talk to me like that? I don't care if he is your uncle."

"Baby, take the key," Hyde said, fishing around in his pocket. "Go home and wait up for me. Maybe warm the rose oils?"

"Not before the dessert table? You promised."

Earl stared at Hyde in disgust. What the old man saw in his grandson was beyond him. He'd followed him most of the evening. After the liquor store, Earl had been ready to walk. It was a mistake including this dumbass. He was pretty sure the unlucky teenager and the clerk at the store were both dead. Forsaken Souls was a low-life place, in a bad neighborhood, and the Reno cops likely couldn't care less about a Black dude and street junkie, but a double homicide would get the politicians' attention. With the 7-Eleven already on his record, it could get hot here for pretty boy.

Earl had called his father, Austin Donald, after the beating, suggesting they leave Hyde to fix his own bad decisions. The old man had insisted he pack him back to Vegas. "Bring him or don't come back yourself," he'd threatened. That was the second time Earl had thought about walking.

Hyde played it cool, and lazily forked another bite of meat. Earl was smart and dangerous in his own way. Not like the old man, but clever enough. He'd have to take him on sometime, but not yet, not if the old man needed him back.

"Leave, Gloria." Hyde tossed her the keys. She raised her hand to slap him, but he caught her wrist and twisted it tightly until she got the message. "I'll bring you some fucking apple pie and a lemon square."

He let go as she stood up. She picked up the keys and pushed his arm away as he tried patting her butt. Oil my ass, she thought. He'd be lucky to cop a feel. She found her heels she'd kicked off under the table and stormed out.

"Is there anything at her place you need?" Earl asked.

"No, she bought most of it anyway. My gun's tucked in my jeans."

"A car?"

"Fuckers repossessed it while we were at a movie."

"Fine, the old man wants us at his place in a few hours. You and I might be going on a trip tomorrow."

"Might be?"

"Depends on his plan and if I agree," Earl said, stroking his eyebrow and picking dead skin from under his fingernails. "So, the apple pie here any good?"

* * *

Austin Donald inhaled a long drag of oxygen and exhaled into a coughing fit. He wiped the yellow phlegm leaching down his chin with the rag he kept handy. His shrewd son was trying his patience and Hyde had been up to his old tricks, getting in trouble and trusting another slut. He'd send someone to take care of the girl.

They were sitting in his dingy living room. It was too cold on the porch. Donald rubbed his hands together to ease the numbness. He was freezing. His fingers stung like icicles when he touched his cheek. The bastard, Earl, had turned the heat down twice. Just to make a point – his father couldn't stop him. It would have been nice if he had spawned just one shithead who gave a rat's ass about making his life easier. But he'd raised self-interested brats only concerned with what their 'old man' could do for them.

"Get me a beer, Hyde. And don't be thinkin' they're communal property."

Earl laughed as Hyde trotted into the kitchen like a good dog. "You've trained him well."

"Better than you."

"Then let him do it"

Earl wasn't enamored with his father's plan, mostly because he questioned his motive. Hyde didn't know who the Chandlers were, but Earl did, and that colored everything as far as he was concerned. The old man had instructed him to blackmail the Hollywood star, Winonna Chandler. Earl had been a kid when his father had tried the same with her mother. All he had to show for it, or more accurately, not show for it, was a missing thumb. That's what the Chandler woman's grandfather had taken instead of paying up. The plan hadn't worked then, and a slightly different version probably wouldn't work now.

"Hyde's got his job, but I need you to be in charge. The kid doesn't have your instincts, and the smell of a pretty skirt will distract him. You saw it in Reno. I want someone smart enough to play a part and improvise when needed. You've worked this kind of deal before."

The old man wanted Earl to explain their history to Winonna Chandler…if she didn't already know. If she did, well, that's where improvising came in. He was to make it clear what she had to lose. And what the old man expected to gain. What he considered he was entitled to. The plan was for Earl to follow the mother and daughter on their trip, working his way into their circle with the girl's help, then pinch the family when the time was right. Hyde would be in the shadows. As the old man said, information has value and either she pays or else we'll make her wish she had.

Earl studied his father. Dried spittle stained the skin beside his mouth. He'd been coughing more and more. Hyde had returned with a cold bottle of Pabst. The old man's swollen, arthritic fingers were struggling to grasp and twist the cap. Hyde reached over and did it for him.

"Thanks."

"So, if they don't cough up?" Earl questioned.

"We get even," Donald sneered. His yellowed eyes lit up at the thought and his cracked, lips spread into a sinister smile.

There was the problem with the plan, Earl knew. Getting even was what this was all about. It wasn't about the money. The old man would be dead in a year; what did he need with money? He wanted revenge for a lifetime of being snubbed and forgotten. He wanted the satisfaction of seeing both Chandlers hurt and questioning who they were, just like he had suffered in the orphanage.

He'd play along…for now. But it was the money Earl wanted. Everything else was secondary. He'd contact the starlet and make her understand working with them was her best option. As sensitive as movie stars are about bad press, it shouldn't be hard. There was a good payday here if he played *his* cards right. He'd never seen the Grand Canyon; maybe this would be a working vacation, one that paid for itself.

Donald guessed what his son was thinking. The boy was scratching his eyebrow again. He'd always thought too much. He would have to make sure Earl didn't go freelancing. His son couldn't care less about retribution. That's why he needed Hyde backing him up, giving him another option if Earl weaseled out.

"Earl, make sure Hyde doesn't fuck this up. Use him how you want, just keep him on a leash."

Earl laughed. Hyde was sitting right there, grinning, proud to be included in the old man's manipulations.

"You can trust me, just like dad," Hyde said.

"Just like Freddy," Earl chuckled.

Hyde started to say something, but Earl waved the back of his hand at him, like he was shooing away a fly.

"You can trust me," Hyde repeated to his grandfather. "Another beer?"

Austin Donald wondered if it was a mistake using his grandson. *Just Like Dad*. His dad had had a big mouth and started talking as soon as the first tatted up Nazi cornered him in the prison shower. He'd run straight to the warden, who called the District Attorney's office, telling them one of the Donalds was prepared to sing. Donald hadn't had a choice. Freddy's accident happened the next day; it wasn't supposed to have killed him.

The old man scoffed at his worthless offspring. He remembered how the rich psychiatrists at the orphanage and in juvie had labeled him a psychopath, a danger to society with no feelings. They hadn't known the half of it.

12

TEQUILA MOON

"SPIKE! GET OUT OF THERE!" SKIP YELLED. THE PET JAVELINA was in his yard, rooting around the butterfly bushes he'd planted. Skip was on his porch with a strong Don Julio Anejo margarita. An extra finger and a dash of pink, prickly-pear syrup was giving him a head start on Tequila Moon, his landlady's monthly party for locals.

He was filling the hummingbird feeder hanging from a rafter with clear liquid. He'd nixed the manufactured, red dye mixture. If it wasn't good for him, it wasn't good for them. The color might attract them, but it wasn't necessary once they got hooked on the sweet juice. The flowering butterfly bush would be a natural attractor if it survived Spike's investigation. He nodded at the rufous hummer watching him from a nearby limb. The bird was on the lookout for less aggressive Anna flappers trying to steal a drink.

Birds were lucky, Skip thought. They lived in the present, unlike humans who were never able to discard their pasts. Skip had found the Sands Retreat almost four years ago. He'd been alone, burnt out, and needed to disappear. There had been a handwritten, index card tacked on the bulletin board outside Basha's Grocery advertising a permanent rental. Part of the listing read: *Prerequisite: Applicants must be reliable, sober, employed, and not a PAIN-IN-THE-ASS.* He had been reliable, had been sober, and he was planning to start a business. Three out of four wasn't bad. When Zula Ballsy showed him the O'Bryan cabin, it had been perfect, off by itself, a half-mile, densely-wooded hike from the main lodge – *secluded: his prerequisite.*

Over the past four years, Zula had become more than his landlady. She was family now, as much as he'd ever known. One of the few people he'd die for, which he almost had if not for Spike.

The Sands was outside Sedona proper, off Red Rock Loop Road, away from the touristy strip that out-of-towners flocked to on weekends. Whether or not Zula received the property as a severance package from the New Jersey mob after they whacked her husband, Tony "Two Balls," depended on perspective. Some gossiped it was pay-off for setting Tony up, and some said she bought it with the insurance money. Skip didn't care, he'd learned to judge people by who they were not who they'd been. Zula extended him the same courtesy.

It was an hour before sunset, which was the time Tequila Moon started. The hour when the rocks show prettiest in the late afternoon light, the lazy time of day. Zula's parties were low-key affairs; he knew most of the locals that got an invite. They eventually ended up around a bonfire sipping beer and chasing Tequila shots. At first, he'd stayed away, afraid he could have been traced after the job he'd done in Istanbul. But after a while, enough time had passed that he figured he was safe.

He considered napping in the Mexican hammock stretched between the porch's kiva poles; the hummers had enough food now to keep them happy. It was good to know he could close his eyes and sleep. Thanks to Sky's cosmic ministrations, the nightmares were fewer. It had been months since he'd jolted awake, sweating, remembering the blond hair and bloody mist floating above him, helpless to stop the man running toward him. She had helped him with his anger too - the rage that had always gotten him in trouble, and that, to be honest, had saved his skin many times in many places. He was under no illusions though; Istanbul, Bangkok, Warsaw, Quito, Montenegro – they'd find him if he stayed too long. The present is what he had.

The sun had set by the time Skip arrived at the lodge. He could hear people outside and see Kuul building a fire. Toni Wathetewa, the Yavapai Nation Cultural Director, was handing him kindling and pointing where to place it. Skip smiled, pondering Kuul and Toni together. They weren't exactly the perfect pair; she the protector of her People's past, and his friend, part Mayan, part Yaqui, and part German, who was okay with being mistaken for Navajo. Opposites attract, he guessed.

There were a few other locals standing around the fire. Kuul and Toni had managed, despite their differences, to get a good blaze going. In the cool, night air, it was the place to be. On the porch, he saw Lilac, Sky, and a stranger, probably a new guest who'd checked into the lodge. No way was he getting in the middle there.

He would have headed toward Kuul, but Zula was gesturing with a margarita in a plastic glass; it was pink and had his name written all over it. She was in her usual spot, holding court in a camp chair below a cottonwood. Sitting with her were Mustang Timmy, a colorful, octogenarian local, and his date, Agnes the loquacious librarian. A few more steps and Skip saw it wasn't Agnes but her sister Gladys. Maybe Agnes was stacking books?

"1800 Silver, not Don Julio," Zula said, handing him the glass. "I made enough for everybody. You'll have to slum it."

"1800 works," Skip said, taking a long drink.

He said hello to Mustang and Gladys and decided he might as well open a can of worms. "Mustang, where's Agnes? I was at the library yesterday and she was reading about the Spanish Franciscans around Tucson - said you were taking her to Tubac and San Xavier to visit the missions.”

The old rounder looked at Skip sheepishly.

“Oh, we take turns with him,” Gladys said. “I get tired of sitting at home, listening to Agnes all the time. She talks too much. Just like mom. Something pops in her head and out it comes like diarrhea. My husband, God rest his soul, sold suppositories to prisons. He always said, ‘lest said the better, you never want to poke the wrong hole.’ With Agnes working at the library, I never know if I’m going to hear about Bucky O’Neil and the Rough Riders, desert wildflowers, or Georgia O’Keefe and her poisonous plants. Lately it’s been the Indians and the Spaniards. When we were kids, our teachers used to set her out in the hall; we could still hear her talking to herself. I love her, but sometimes a person just needs quiet. You know? Rattling on and on, it drives most people nuts. I’m not sure where she got it from.”

“Not from you,” Mustang said, grinning and taking a sip of his beer.

“Nice night,” Zula said. The sky had turned dark purple, the colorful red rocks replaced by black silhouettes. A thumping noise by the closest guest cabin caught her attention, “Spike! Get out of the trash! That javelina is the one that drives me nuts. Wish he’d go bother someone else.”

“Who’s that with Lilac and Sky?” Skip asked.

“New guest, from St. Louis. Nice guy. He wants to talk to you about a tour.”

“Which tour?”

“Grand Canyon, I think. Says he’s in the business and here for a few days.”

“In the business?”

Zula shrugged her shoulders and sipped her margarita, smacking her lips. “I shouldn’t have emptied the lime bottle. Go talk to him, he looks outnumbered.”

Skip frowned.

"Neither one of them bite," Zula said. "Well, on second thought, maybe one of them."

"I took Lilac's firearm training workshop," Gladys offered. They all knew Sky wasn't the biting kind. "She's a good shot, hits what she's aiming for. We followed it up with a yoga session by the creek. That's quite a business she has going. Imagine, 357 Magnums and cow poses? I didn't know these old bones and joints could move so many ways. By the time we'd finished, I felt twenty years younger and capable of defending myself. Agnes is taking it next week. We're thinking about adding the devotional warrior pose to our morning routine, right after coffee and jalapeno bismarks at Sedonuts."

Mustang winked at Skip, "The girls are pretty limber."

"They know how to shoot too," Zula added.

After listening to Gladys explain how mixing fiber and chia seeds with bourbon kept her ligaments loose, Skip excused himself to go meet Zula's guest. By the looks of things, the man was keeping both Lilac and Sky well entertained. Whenever Lilac got bored, it showed. She'd get fidgety and eventually just walk away. He'd already watched her fill the stranger's glass twice. Sky was demonstrating her hypermobility, the gift from her alien abductors that kept on giving. Neither of them had so much as glanced his way.

Skip decided to detour to Kuul and Toni first. Toni saw him coming and waved...*that was different*. He had taken her daughter out twice, sort of – the 'sort of' hadn't gone over well with her mom. Lilac had suggested she was jealous. In her late forties, Toni didn't look like the mother of a twenty-eight-year-old. She was taller than most Native women and had a lithe, Marvel-action-movie figure. Her fashionable jeans had to have a forty-inch inseam at least. Impeccably brushed hair hung to the Concho belts she was fond of wearing. The sharp looks were matched by an even sharper brain and wit.

"Toni, Kuul," he said, greeting both.

"*Ya'at'eeh*, Kemosabe," Kuul said, laughing at Wathetewa. She rolled her eyes and jokingly pushed him. "We bet on whether you'd come here or go to the porch. She said you were more scared of Lilac than her. She won."

Toni was disconcertingly good at reading him. Her grandmother had been a seer. The Yavapai woman had once told him she felt he was a good, white man, but that she saw a dark side to his inner being that endangered those around him. *Not far off.*

"Kuul said you and he were..." he searched for the right word. Dating seemed rather juvenile.

"Call it cultural curiosity," Toni smiled.

"Kuul, I'm leading a small tour to Jerome tomorrow." Jerome was an old mining town turned artist colony halfway up a nearby mountain. "Mother and daughter from California. You'll recognize the daughter, some kind of star according to Sky."

"Tempting, but sorry, brother. I'm scheduled to install a bidet for the French Lieutenant's woman. Probably take all day." Kuul owned a plumbing company, AAA Plumber to the Stars. The business specialized in blessing the pipes of Hollywood stars, who he never referred to by name, with second homes in Sedona. "After that I've got to service a hot tub. National Treasure's back in town and crazy as ever."

"You're on for the Canyon, though, right?"

"*Aoo,*" Kuul said, meaning 'yes' in Navajo. Toni punched him again.

"Trouble at six o'clock Kemo," Kuul warned.

Lilac and Zula's guest were walking toward them. The man was thin and short, his lack of height exaggerated by being next to the taller Lilac. He was maybe early fifties, graying hair, alert eyes taking everything in. As he got closer, a little more wear showed around the edges, deeper creases in the forehead and a scar below one ear, probably late fifties on second guess. Skip's first impression was a friendly but tired Midwestern businessman on vacation.

"Jack Webster," he said, holding out his hand.

"He's a new guest," Lilac added.

"Zula pointed you out," Skip said, shaking hands.

"I'm glad the shuttle driver from Phoenix recommended her. This place is great. I have a lot of points I could have used at the Marriott, but I like scouting out local lodging options."

"Then how'd you get all the points?" Toni asked.

Webster smiled, but his eyes did a quick, studied appraisal of Wathatewa.

"On the road a lot. I work for a company that sells customized trips to people who can afford them. Like I said, I'm in Sedona doing a bit of scouting. We like to use local vendors and operators whenever we can. Our customers expect unique experiences."

Toni nodded. She stepped back toward the fire and crossed her arms. It was clear something bothered her. Skip wondered what she was seeing.

"Jack's interested in a Grand Canyon tour," Lilac said. "Sky told him you had one scheduled for day after tomorrow. She said it was a private tour, but he could talk to you to see if joining it was possible. I told him I was going too."

Skip was surprised. He'd asked Lilac to go along, and she'd said no; too busy. Apparently, she'd changed her mind. "All right," he said without thinking, trying to figure out her sudden switch in plans.

"Excellent!" Webster said, happy the trip had been so easily arranged. "I know its last minute, so I appreciate your making room. I was planning to find a guide and then she and the younger girl said you ran Sedona Chi tours. We're always interested in vendors with local expertise. If the trip goes well, maybe we can throw some work your way?"

"Huh..." *Damn*, the man mistook his saying *all right*. He'd meant Lilac. Webster seemed like a nice enough guy, and his offer of more work wasn't unwelcome. But he couldn't just add another person to a private tour.

"I meant it was okay for Lilac to join us. A mother and daughter booked the tour and there's Kuul and me. Any more than five and I have to rent a van, which changes my pricing. Maybe we can set something up for another time?"

"Oh, well, hmmm, that might not work" Webster said. "What if you ask the other party? My company can cover the cost of the rental and we'll pay a per diem for your own vehicle as a bonus, even if we don't use it. I get along with everyone, promise. You can't be in this business and not, right?"

"That seems fair, you can at least ask," Lilac chimed in.

"More the merrier?" Webster said hopefully.

They were momentarily distracted by the fire. Wathetewa had been adding logs and rebuilding the tepee Kuul had constructed. She had finally given up and knocked it down. Sparks shot up, popping in the cold air. Black smoke shifted over Webster, and he started coughing. Skip gave Toni an annoyed, suspicious look: *What the hell? You know how to build a fire.*

"Tell you what," Skip said, after they had relocated to the other side of the fire. "The mother and daughter get in tomorrow morning. We're meeting at eleven and then heading to Jerome. It's an old copper town with a lot of history. I'll ask and see what they say. If it's okay with them, it's okay with me."

"That's all I can ask for. Thanks," Webster said.

"And Lilac, Kuul's not going, so there's room in the Bronco."

13

BESSIE AND GLEN

October 28, 1928

"**G**LEN!" BESSIE SCREAMED.

The force of the current against her sweep had thrown her into the air. For the first time, the thought flashed through her mind that they weren't wearing life jackets. They'd been warned by the old-timers at Green River but had laughed it off. Now, seconds from splashing into the violent river, that decision seemed foolhardy. Wearing the heavy flight jacket, she wouldn't have a chance.

"I've got you," she heard Glen say, feeling his steely hand grasp her foot.

"Where'd you think you were going?" he joked, depositing her back on the platform. Her head had just missed the lip of the scow. "Get ahold of the sweep before it hits you."

After retrieving Bessie, he refocused on the river ahead of them, and they soon got past the worst of the rapid. Bessie composed her nerves as best she could and grabbed her sweep. She'd learned a tough lesson. One she wasn't sure would help if it happened again. Knowing what not to do was one thing, not letting it happen again was another. All she could do, she thought, was try not to let Glen down. He'd been so good to her.

"How many more rapids today?" she asked.

"Not sure, maybe a half-dozen. We're through the worst though – for today. We'll have a couple of big drops tomorrow, but we'll be okay."

Great, Bessie cried to herself. Ever since being thrown, her stomach had been anxiously flip-flopping. "Why don't we stop to camp?"

"Few more hours," Glen said, not looking at her.

Bessie now understood why Cataract Canyon was nicknamed the Graveyard. John Wesley Powell had given it that dreadful moniker, and he wasn't wrong. She and Glen were rafting the same section where his expedition had realized they were no longer on a gentlemanly expedition. From here on, theirs had been a test of survival.

Cataract Canyon was a fractious, serpentine gash in the Colorado Plateau; a plateau covering an area the size of Montana that was once at sea level. Over millions of years, inland oceans had come and gone, flooding the region again and again, leaving a series of horizontally deposited rock layers. Some layers had been sea beds and some towering, sand dunes. Seventy- to eighty-million years ago, the crashing of continental plates uplifted the entire region. The river formed later, cutting through the rock layers and exposing them. It was a hauntingly beautiful and lonely place.

The sturdiness of the scow made a difference, especially when they couldn't avoid hitting submerged and protruding rocks. For miles, the shoreline looked like the Gods had crushed the towering, red buttes into bus-sized boulders and rolled them down to the river. But the weight of their boat also meant they couldn't pull over and portage past the bad rapids like Powell and everyone before them. Powell had portaged as many as six or seven times some days. The waterlogged scow was just too heavy to get out of the river, let alone carry over a boulder-strewn bank. She and Glen would have to run every rapid, a feat never before accomplished.

"We're in for some more!" Glen yelled.

Bessie heard another roar up ahead. It seemed they'd been teasing an angry lion that stalked them all day. Working the rear sweep, her eyes were always trained toward where they'd been. It was up to Glen, looking downstream, to set their course. She snuck a peak while her oar was out of the water. Oh, God! The river, as far as she could see, was a maze of frothing waves, crashing higher than their scow.

"If you can't hang on, lock the sweep and dive into the bottom!" Glen yelled. There was no fear in his voice, just boyish excitement.

Bessie was determined to do her part.

They entered the rapid. After cresting several high waves and being tossed around like driftwood, the scow hit an even taller whitecap. It shot skyward, thru the foam and mist, before gravity slammed its nose down into a deep hole. In the hole, they spun and twisted, before being spit out and launched up again. They rode the same terrifying sequence over a dozen more waves. She could feel and hear the boat thumping against rocks and sliding past them. *If they hit a big one...*with each wave the scow groaned and bucked. Whenever Glen lost control, the scow angled against the current, resulting in t-boning blows that threatened to push them over. The river had them and would take them where it wanted.

"There's a tail wave pushing us!" Glen yelled, furiously working his sweep. "We need to stay straight, down the middle."

Bessie saw why. She couldn't believe what she saw. It had to be another optical trick. On both sides of the whitewater, they were fighting through, the river flowed backwards. It was like they were driving down a road in one direction while lanes on either side were going the opposite way.

"The eddy has us!" Glen yelled.

They were near the end of the rapids on the far-right side of the main channel. The scow had entered enough of the eddying water to be redirected toward the wall of the canyon. She was sure they were going to crash into the rocks. She tried working her sweep, but it wasn't designed to quickly move the craft sideways. It didn't matter. The eddy turned them back upstream before reaching the wall, into the outside lane heading in the wrong direction. They were safe but stuck in a watery roundabout.

"We've got to get back into the main current...We've got to get back into the main current!" Glen kept yelling.

Rapids are caused by debris and rocks obstructing the current. They constrict the flow, causing the river to rush violently past and over them. Past those constricted points, the current immediately widens out; the faster moving water in the center pushing peripheral, slower moving water to the sides. In places where the current keeps expanding downstream, the slower water has nowhere to go but back upstream.

"It's our third time through!" Bessie shouted. She was losing hope they'd ever get out of the eddy. No matter what they tried, once the upstream current weakened enough for Glen to get them back into the rapids heading downstream, they were slotted into the same path and redirected again. It was a never-ending merry-go-round.

"If I can get us stuck on that rock at the beginning of the eddy, I can pry us in the right direction and stay in the main channel. Get in the bottom, Bessie. I'm going to cast us on that rock."

Bessie started to object. "Now, Bessie!"

She crouched in the back, behind the platform, and felt the scow shudder as it rammed the partially submerged rock. Nothing broke apart and she saw Glen pushing with his sweep above her.

Finally, he sent them spinning in the right direction, downstream. Past the last rapid, the scow straightened and slowed down.

"We're free. Help me get to shore, I see a place to camp."

Bessie jumped back onto the platform. They were past the horrible rapids and in smaller riffles. They both worked their oars until they beached.

On shore, they made camp and Bessie started a fire. They were soaked. Glen decided to walk downstream. He wanted to reconnoiter the next rapids, which they could hear around a bend. After the fire was blazing, Bessie found a boulder by the water and sat. Her legs quaked like she was still standing in the scow. She pulled out her journal to make a few notes. *'No troubles,'* she wrote, chuckling to herself. She wasn't much for keeping a ship's log; when it came to writing, poetry was her forte. She put the journal down and opened her sketch book. Drawing she loved. Looking upstream, back at the rapids and the eddy they'd been stuck in, she drew a pencil sketch of jagged canyon walls with roiling, cresting waves. She made the waves look like the Japanese prints in the San Francisco museum she had visited with her friend Greta.

"Hopefully, that was the worst of it," Glen said, surprising her from behind. "That may have been the drops they told me about. We'll see tomorrow. At least I learned how to navigate eddies. There'll be more of those."

Bessie just nodded. He wasn't too convincing. What if they got trapped in an eddy without a handy rock to redirect them?

"Help me get the mattress out. I think it's an early night," he grinned.

They spent another quiet night under the stars. Bessie had trouble sleeping and woke early. By the time Glen got up, she had breakfast ready. The smell was what raised him. It had been the same in Idaho, the few times he slept in. A half-hour later they shoved off, still in Cataract Canyon, still in the graveyard.

By the time they pulled over to camp again, they'd run eleven more rapids. Each one had been as bruising as what they'd just been through. Bessie was exhausted. At least they hadn't been caught in any more eddies. They were too tired to bother hauling the springs across the rocky shore; they'd sleep on their blankets. When Bessie collapsed on the ground, making no move to prepare dinner, Glen fixed flapjacks.

"Get some rest. Tomorrow will be a big day. We should get past Cataract and it'll be easier then."

"We've been through the worst of it," Bessie said, parroting Glen. She groaned and rolled over, pulling the blanket over her head. "You can have my jacks; they'll just battle my nerves, and my stomach will lose."

14

GRAPES

"**J**UST MAKE THE BEST OF IT, HONEY."

"Genome...an old mining town? Mom, you sold me on a wine tour," Winonna Chandler protested.

"Jerome. And we can do both," Skip said. "Most of the valley wineries have tasting rooms there for thirsty tourists."

The Chandler's had arrived two hours earlier via private charter. Skip had picked them up at Sedona's small airport. They were sitting in the Lazy *S*OB having a mid-morning breakfast with Skip and Lilac. Lottie wanted to do something in the afternoon and Lilac had beaten him, suggesting Jerome. The choice of a ghost-town sliding down a mountain hadn't gone over well with her daughter. Nor had the Sands Retreat, which didn't have a spa or pool; Zula had pointed out the door, saying, 'The creek's that-a-way.'

The daughter was going to be a pain. He'd yet to meet anyone from California who wasn't. They just had a different lifestyle, especially the Hollywood crowd, which she was part of. Her mesh, turquoise, heeled sandals had confirmed it. *In the red dust of Sedona, really?* He tried not to judge her bejeweled appearance, the delicate, gold necklace with a ruby pendant and dangly, diamond earrings with sapphire mounts; after all, he was wearing a lava-pebble bracelet with copper knobs.

"Honey, I told you about Jerome. There are art galleries and bistros. No mines. You'll love it. And see, you can sample wine too," Lottie Chandler said, trying to cajole her temperamental daughter.

Skip had liked the mother immediately. She was short and petite, her lively, brown eyes seemed to have a million questions behind them – good questions. And she'd hit it off with Zula, who was a good judge of character. The old showgirl had even served Lottie her homemade prickly-pear syrup with the flapjacks. But when her daughter had asked for Greek yogurt, Zula had answered, 'the pass to Thermopylae was closed'. He didn't even object to Lottie's L.L Bean outfit, it seemed natural on her, as did the floral scarf loosely tucked in her shirt collar - *a classy bandana with a feminine touch.*

"Let's give it a shot, Honey," Lottie said.

"Okay, but the tasting rooms better have a decent chardonnay."

"I'll go get the Bronco," Skip said, happy to excuse himself.

Winonna looked at him suspiciously, "What bronco? Mom, I am NOT riding a horse. No way."

"Late model sports-utility-vehicle. Air conditioning, bench seats, and a stereo system," Skip clarified, overselling the comforts of the old war horse.

Lilac and Zula both snorted. His AC was hit and miss, the seats, to put it kindly, were *original*, and the stereo was a Delco AM radio.

Skip had Winonna sit on the driver's side of the rear seat. Salsa stains from spilled Tamaliza tamales were on the passenger side. Lottie rode upfront, shotgun. By the time he'd wound past the second switchback up to Jerome, he'd turned the AC off to stop the gaseous fog from rolling out the vents. It was cooler up the mountain.

"Jerome is perched on the side of Mingus Mountain, that big boy above us. It's part of the first 'range' in the basin-range country below the Colorado Plateau," Skip told them. "Millions of years ago, a fault created the Verde Valley below the mountains – all that flat basin we just drove through."

"The wasteland we sputtered through," Winonna snarked.

"The fault uplifted older, buried rock and a billion dollars of copper was made accessible. In the early 1900's, Jerome was the most populous town in Northern Arizona. And some said the wickedest too. Eventually, the mines played out and hippies discovered the abandoned bordellos and saloons in the late 60's. The early macramé and tie-dye crowd have become skilled artisans and gallery owners. There's still a quirky vibe though, much different than Sedona. Consequently, there's something here for everybody, history buffs, shoppers, oenophiles, and even food connoisseurs."

Everyone except spoiled movie stars, Lilac thought as they pulled into town.

"There are some great dinner spots," Skip said, downshifting from fourth to second. It must have been transmission fluid he'd seen as they'd driven away.

"They don't have bulldozers in Arizona?" Winonna cracked, noting the crooked buildings with leaning porch pillars.

"The whole town is on the National Register," Lilac sharply answered.

Skip hitched the Bronco in the lot above town, and they rode the shuttle down the hill to the historic fire station. He planned on touring them past the old hotels, saloons, and bordellos, all tourist shops now. Most visitors had heard of the sliding jail, half the town had slipped off their foundations after a mine explosion. He'd end at Pura Vida Gallery where he'd bought his lava bracelet. Vaqueros next door had Top Shelf margarita specials. Maybe early burritos there or head up to Haunted Hamburger for the views, their choice.

They got as far as Cadaceous Cellars, one stop past the Four Eight Wineworks. The daughter was having her way. "We're inside, you can take those awful sunglasses off," Lottie said.

"They keep me from being recognized."

"Smart," Lilac said.

Amelia, the server at the counter, was boxing four bottles of Queen B Sparkling Rosé and rolled her eyes. She'd sold a case to an Academy Award winner just last week. The Godfather star hadn't been nearly so pretentious. They'd even shared a joint out back.

Skip was already carrying a box from Four Eight. He'd need a wheelbarrow if they went any farther. "Let's grab a bite across the street at Grape's. We can snag an outside table and talk through the rest of their trip," Skip suggested.

They ended up inside, in a corner booth against the front windows. Winonna hadn't liked the metal seats on the patio. A waitress with ice-blue hair and a fancy belt and buckle tattooed around her arm came to take their order. "Hey, girl, it's been a while. Last we saw each other was at PJ's, right?"

"Sloppy taco and dollar beer night," Lilac smiled, recognizing her. The girl's name was Scarlet and at PJ's she'd been dancing on a table to Willie Nelson, *Mamas Don't Let Your Babies Grow Up to be Cowboys*. Lilac guessed her mama hadn't warned her about cowboys, hence the tattoo.

"Do you have anything from California?" Winonna interrupted. She hadn't found a wine list. "Grapes has to mean you have wine, surely." The sunglasses were off, and she was smiling nastily.

"Just broken dreams and a divorce decree," Scarlet joked.

"Anything white will be fine. Same for me," Lottie said, stopping her daughter from whatever offensive remark she intended.

"You got it, Honey. Root beers for you two?" Scarlet said, smiling at Skip and Lilac.

After Scarlet had left, Skip said, "Let's go over our schedule. It's your tour, so we can adjust it any way you like. We usually do

Sedona highlights on the first full day; the Chapel of Holy Cross, Uptown, Airport Mesa Overlook, and a hike if you'd like." Winonna glared at him; he should have guessed she wasn't a hiker. "Next day we'll head to Desert View in the Grand Canyon. It's downriver from where the United flight…" he stopped, at a loss for the right word.

"Crashed," Lottie said, a tear forming on her eyelash. Winonna put her arm around her mom's shoulder. Lilac was touched by the daughter's sudden empathy.

"I know you asked specifically about the…accident…and about Glen and Bessie Hyde." Skip paused, seeing the sudden emotion in her eyes and hoping she would explain her interest. She didn't. "We'll spend that night at a lodge on the Grand Canyon's south rim and explore the village."

"And Kolb Brothers Studio?" Lottie asked. "My parents rode the mules down Bright Angel Trail on their honeymoon and Emery Kolb took their picture. This trip is really about their memory."

Skip nodded, wondering if her parents might be connected to the crash. "You'll have time to go part way down the trail if you want. After that, you asked about going to Peach Springs in Hualapai Nation, west of the National Park, and taking the scenic road to Diamond Creek and the Colorado River…"

"I might stay at the hotel," Winonna said. She was sipping liberally on a Page Springs chardonnay and had put the gaudy glasses back on.

"That's fine," Lilac said, smiling. Wearing the darkly tinted glasses was probably a habit when she drank in public.

"Up to you. And then it's back to Sedona and the Sands, and the airport the next day."

"You said we can make changes?" Lottie asked. "Can we not do the Sedona tour tomorrow and go to Navajo Bridge and Lee's Ferry instead? And stay at Cameron tomorrow night? If there's an extra cost, that's okay. Same goes with cancelling a night with

Zula. I thought I'd like to start at one end of the Canyon and end at Diamond Creek. Kind of closes the loop."

"That's doable," Skip said, thinking out loud. "Would you be okay with still leaving day after tomorrow though? You can rest up at the Sands tomorrow and spend time on your own in town."

The change was workable, but he still needed a day to get everything ready to go, same for Kuul, and to make reservations at Cameron Lodge. He had to admit, the change was a good one. He hadn't been to Lee's Ferry in a while. The old ferry site was part of the Glen Canyon National Recreation Area and the launch spot for most commercial rafting expeditions through the Grand Canyon. Just downstream was one of the roughest sections of the Colorado, Marble Canyon.

"Thank you. Winonna and I can visit some of the art galleries and jewelry shops," Lottie said, placating her daughter. "I have a silver Navajo ring my grandmother gave me. Maybe we can find a matching necklace or earrings. I appreciate you being so amenable, Mr. Rhodes."

"Let's make it Skip. We'll be spending a lot of time together."

Lilac loosely followed their conversation, not particularly interested in the details. She hadn't made up her mind about going yet. She was, however, observing the daughter. Winonna had been paying more attention to tourists passing by the window than to her mother's new plan. Something was wrong about the girl, and it bothered her. She couldn't put a finger on it. Something more than with other California celebrities who spent time 'slumming' in Sedona. Lilac had met a few of those. Maybe it was being with her mother; that'd mess up most women their age. Winonna wasn't as ditsy as she acted either. Then again, she lives in Los Angeles, Lilac thought, the place breeds weirdness.

"Can I ask if there's a connection with the United crash?" Lilac asked Lottie, tired of watching her daughter who was waving to Scarlet for another wine.

Winonna abruptly stopped at the question. "Mom, you don't have to tell them. We don't even have to go. Let's go home."

"It's time, Honey," Lottie said, patting her daughter's hand. "I haven't visited their gravesite since the memorial. I was two. I barely remember. I should have come before but talking about it always upset Nana Lou. After her...well, the years just got away. Don't you think I owe it to them? Winonna worries about me. I should have told you upfront. In 1956, my parents were on the United plane that collided with the TWA flight over the Grand Canyon. It was the first commercial-passenger mid-air collision in aviation history and led to the creation of the F.A.A. I'm sure you know everyone died, there were no survivors. They're buried at Pioneer Cemetery on the South Rim of the National Park."

"I'm sorry," Lilac offered.

"It was a long time ago but thank you. The pilot had detoured to sightsee over the Grand Canyon. They flew around a big cloud not far from Desert View and Lee's Ferry. Once the pilots saw each other it was too late."

Skip wanted to be sensitive, but he had to ask, "How much history do you want during our trip? We can just stop and reflect wherever and whenever you choose? I don't want to say something I shouldn't."

"It's okay. You should probably err on the side of reflection. If we have questions, we'll ask. There's not much about the accident I don't know."

"Of course."

"Their dying in the canyon is what led me to the Glen and Bessie Hyde story. They are the two most tragic events in Grand Canyon history. The Hydes, I would like to hear more about. My daughter knows very little about their story."

"I can do that," Skip said.

"They were also your grandparents in the plane," Lilac said sympathetically to the younger woman.

"Yes, but I never knew them. Their loss affected mom and Nana Lou, her grandmother, more than me. The empty settings at the holiday tables, that's usually when we talked about them and the accident. Their absence was what was real to me."

Lottie had tears welling in her eyes again and Winonna handed her a tissue. They hugged. Skip imagined it had been a while since they'd shared their feelings. It was a touching moment. Even Lilac was sniffling. Mothers and daughters...

"One more thing," he said, their surprising disclosure had made him forget Jack Webster, "then I'll carry these packages back to my car, and you can have some free-time to explore Jerome. There's another guest staying at the Sands, Jack Webster, who asked if he could join our tour. I didn't know the purpose of your visit when we spoke. He seems like a friendly, respectful, guy, and he offered to cover some of the costs. I'd need to rent a van. After hearing your story, I'll let him know it's a no. But I promised to ask."

"I don't know," Lottie said. "This is very private for us."

"Understandable and not a problem. This is your family's trip. I'll let him know."

"Mom, maybe having someone else will lighten the mood? Keep us from becoming so God awful morbid. It could be a good thing," Winonna suggested. "Would the van have air conditioning and USB ports?"

Mother and daughter shared a silent exchange: *You really think so? - I think so - You sure? - I'm sure - Okay.* "Let Mr. Webster know why we're here and that we can't promise to be the cheeriest of travel companions. But if he wants to join us, he can."

"You're absolutely sure?"

"Yes." Winonna said. "I'm done riding Broncos!"

15

DOUGLAS MANSION

EARL AND HYDE DONALD WATCHED FROM ACROSS THE STREET. The girl had done well getting a table by the windows. From their spot outside the historic Connor Hotel, they couldn't hear what the Chandler's were saying, but they could see they were still there and would know when they left.

Hyde was guzzling a cold Corona from the Spirit Room Lounge, and Earl nursing an orange concoction with streaks of grenadine. Hyde had watched the chick at the bar pour two shots of rum in his uncle's glass. He had been flirting with her when Earl walked in. The girl was wearing a black tank top and had hair dyed to match. Her make-up was even darker. A heavy dog chain passed through the loops of her skin-tight cutoffs.

Belle had rested both elbows on the bar, leaning over so he could get a good look. That was after he'd paid for the drinks with a hundred-dollar bill and tipped her twenty. The Forsaken Soul cash had been burning a hole in his pocket, and Belle was a definite upgrade over Gloria.

"You any relation to those high-kicking, saloon girls," Hyde had asked, pointing at the mural of painted ladies above the bar.

That was when his shifty uncle had put his hand on his shoulder and said, "Later Romeo, we've got business."

"Shit, Earl, I was getting somewhere," Hyde said after Belle had left to wait on a trio of leather-clad bikers. They were comparing chains.

"Grab your beer, they've gone inside a restaurant."

The old man had told them to watch the Chandlers and for him to keep Hyde from being distracted. Those instructions suited Earl, for now. He wanted to see, but not be seen, so he had donned dark, aviator sunglasses and a non-descript ball cap.

From an outside bench, he glanced up and down the street. Cars and Harleys were parked everywhere; a few RVs stuck out into the road. There was another group of rough-looking bikers across the street smoking and sitting on what looked to have been a tiered amphitheater, now just rows of wide, concrete steps. Above the bikers, on another layer of this crazy hill town, there were locals picnicking in a park, their kids playing on swings. Tourists strolled along the sidewalk outside the nineteenth-century buildings, holding plastic cups of wine and beer and showing each other their crystal purchases.

"Where'd you get that damn hat?" he asked Hyde. His nephew was wearing a straw, cowboy hat with bent sides. A blue, paisley bandana was tied above the brim, held in place by a fake, silver dollar. It looked like something a bimbo would wear on a beach.

"Belle liked it. Especially the way the back rests on my bun and tilts the brim over my eyes. She said I looked cool."

Hyde tipped the hat back to take a swig of Corona. He liked watching the beer bubbles inside the clear glass. They reminded him of the aquarium his father had taken him to when he was young.

"I guess it hides your face. You found a place to stay?"

"Andante Inn, in town, but not far from where you're at. The rooms are separate from the lobby, so we can come and go without staff noticing."

"Good, we shouldn't be here more than a couple of days," Earl said, gazing at the fake, red feather sticking out of Hyde's hat band. His nephew looked like a Ralph Lauren model for Chaps. "Just keep following them. I'll be around. Once I talk to her, that little actress will keep us informed."

"What's the old man want with them?" Hyde asked, swirling his beer. "You want another drink? I'm getting another Corona."

"No, and you're done drinking. And leave the bitch alone. It's not what you're here for, and I don't need you in a bar fight with Easy Rider. You heard the old man." Earl frowned at his simple-minded nephew...*fucking hat*. "He wants to get even for some slight he's imagined. You saw how sick he is. Me, I'm in it for the money, which I'm guessing is what you're after too. I imagine Belle rewards full wallets, same as Gloria."

"How much are we talking? If we're going against the old man, it better be worth it. And enough to take care of him too. That trailer's a shitty place to end up."

"More than enough. Both Chandlers have secrets they'll pay big to keep that way. If the old man quizzes you, make sure he believes we're in on his plan. He's not a fool," Earl said. Hyde opened his mouth to ask, 'what secrets', but Earl stopped him. "Don't ask, you don't need to know, and if the old man wanted you to, he'd have already told you."

"What do I do now?"

The bikers at the amphitheater revved their Harleys. Earl and Hyde watched as they rumbled past, leaned into the corner by the old Fire Hall, and roared along the switchback road above them.

"Lay low. Head back to your hotel...*alone*...and watch a movie. Stay out of trouble. No drinking, no girls, and no masked visits to liquor stores. You need money, let me know. I'll take care of the Chandlers from here. If the daughter needs further convincing, I'll tell you how and when."

Earl rolled his eyes. The dumbass was staring into his beer bottle. Worthless.

• • •

Skip had packed the wine boxes back to the Bronco and driven down the hill to pick up the Chandlers and Lilac. Lottie wanted to stop at the mining museum. Skip had told them about the horse buggy used by Gordon MacRae and Shirley Jones in the musical *Oklahoma, the surrey with the fringe on top*. It was displayed in the museum's carriage house, and he'd thought, stupidly, Winonna might be interested in movie memorabilia. She couldn't have cared less.

"Oklahoma? God, that'd be worse than Arizona."

The museum exhibits were displayed in the first and second floors of the Douglas Mansion. In 1912, fresh from successes in Nacozari, New Mexico, James "Rawhide" Douglas began developing the Little Daisy Mine in Jerome. His timing was perfect. His crews uncovered a rich vein of copper just in time for the soaring prices of World War I. Rawhide built his mansion in the height of the boom, overlooking the entrance to his bonanza. He designed the house to double as a luxurious hotel for mining officials and investors. It was meant to impress, and the pearl-white adobe against the Arizona blue sky did just that. Jerome hadn't seen anything like it. There was a wine cellar, billiard room for the gentlemen, a fancy marble shower, and, much ahead of their time, steam heat to ward off the desert chill and a central vacuum system. Rawhide was a proud man - until the bottom fell out. By 1962, the Little Daisy was long abandoned. Rawhide's two sons sold the property and the mansion to the State. The museum opened in 1965, and admission was, as

Rawhide would have said, two-bits. Rooms were filled with mining equipment, pictures of the town and mine in their heyday, the original billiard table, and a fascinating model of the miles and miles of underground tunnels.

Skip had retold the history to Lottie and Winonna while strolling room to room. Lottie was absorbed, her daughter not so much. She'd wandered outside onto the back patio, overlooking the valley. She'd come on this trip to support her mom, not to learn about forged, double-headed pickaxes. A man with aviator sunglasses followed her outside. Surely, the paparazzi wouldn't bother trailing her this far, out to the middle of nowhere. She'd teach the Peeping-Tom a lesson. She reached into her bag for her stun gun.

"Have you considered what I said? On our call," the man asked. Winonna left the gun in her purse.

"That was you?" She'd been heading to the airport yesterday when a man called claiming to have damaging information on her. She'd told him to take a number but kept listening. He'd hung up before she could ask questions. "If it's about the Victoria Secret episode, it's already been in the papers. Here's the name of my lawyer," she said, pretending to rummage in her bag.

"It's about your family. What do you know?"

Winonna had no idea what he was talking about. Maybe Great Grandpa Harold had been involved in some shady studio deals? There was mob money flowing into Hollywood back in the day. She thought about her grandparents and the crash, wondering if it somehow involved them. Neither was what she would consider 'damaging'.

"Have you ever heard the name *Donald*?"

Winonna shook her head. "Wait - do you mean Sutherland? That old letch!" She'd guest starred on his show about a degenerate, rich family. That screen kiss had seemed a little too real, and one thing had led to another. Sure, there was the age difference, and she'd been married at the time, but still...*damaging*?

"Never mind for now. You and I are going to get to know each other very well. We know all about that romantic trip to Hawaii you took with the talk show host - that *woman*. Pictures too."

Shit, Winonna thought. She'd been depressed and sworn off men. The trip had been a short experiment between her second and third husbands. *It was okay to be bisexual now, right? Who in Hollywood wasn't?* She needed to talk to Percy. He'd know how to spin this. It hadn't hurt the Twilight girl.

"What do you want?"

"Nothing right now. We'll get specific later."

They heard footsteps crunching on the gravel walkway. Whoever was coming was out of sight; they couldn't have overheard.

"I thought I recognized you back in town," Skip called out as he turned a corner. He and Lottie had come outside to see the Oklahoma buggy. Lilac lagged behind them, stopping to study a hunk of green malachite and blue azurite rock beside the walkway.

The guide was off his rocker, Winonna thought. Of course he recognized her. They'd lumbered up the mountain in his crappy car and had lunch together. Maybe it was this thin Arizona air, hypoxia of the brain – that's all she needed.

"This is the man who wants to join us, Jack Webster," Skip said to Lottie. "Looks like Winonna met him first."

"Mr. Webster," Lottie said, introducing herself. "It looks like you've already met my daughter."

"We just bumped into each other," Winonna confirmed. "Two visitors, admiring the view. He hadn't mentioned his name or joining us."

"I didn't know who you were," Webster said. *Good, the daughter was keeping her mouth shut.* "I'd heard about Jerome and decided to check it out."

"We're both glad to meet you, Mr. Webster. We told Mr. Rhodes, Skip, that it's fine if you come along," Lottie said. "But we may not be the best company. Our visiting is in memory of my parents, Winonna's grandparents. They died at the Canyon."

"I'm sorry about your loss, but thank you, and please call me Jack. Family's important, I respect that. My dad always said, family is worth more than all the money in the world."

16

BESSIE AND GLEN HYDE

October 30, 1928

BESSIE AWOKE FEELING AWFUL, TOO SICK TO ADMIRE THE morning shadows dancing against the canyon's colorful walls. Last night's dinner was still rolling in her stomach. Curled in the quilts with her knees pulled to her chest, all she could think about was what would have happened if she had gone in the river. Or worse, what if Glen had gone in? She wouldn't be able to catch him like he had her. She'd be all alone in the graveyard of the Colorado.

Glen stirred and rolled over, rubbing his eyes. "Morning Bessie. How're you feeling?"

She leaned in and kissed him lightly. There was no use trying to explain a woman's fears to a man. He'd think she was being silly. "Ready to fix you breakfast and get going."

"Not yet."

He grasped her waist, pulling her on top of him. His kissing was deeper now. She pushed the pains from yesterday aside, forgetting about her stomach, and undid the wide buckle on his pants, sliding on top of him. Let him feel the hard ground for a change. They made love and groaned as loud as their urges commanded. There was no one to hear their cries.

She collapsed on top of him, and Glen held her tightly. They'd both used each other like it might be their last time. With the journey they faced, who knew what was around the next bend? For a few stolen minutes, she'd forgotten the low roar from downstream.

Bessie pushed herself up, "I think we have a little more bacon left. We need to use it. Hopefully, we can resupply at Lee's Ferry. If not, then at Verkamp's Store at Grand Canyon Village."

"Sound's good," Glen said, trying to pull her back down.

She smiled and teasingly slapped his hands away. "Pull your pants on and get the scow ready."

Bessie set about restarting last night's fire and slicing the bacon. Glen rolled up their bedding and carried it to the scow. As he did each morning, he waded into the river, walking around the scow and checking for any damage. He could see a splintered gash where they'd hit the rock yesterday, but nothing that needed repairing. The smell of the bacon cooking drew him back to camp.

"Only one thing better than bacon in the morning," he winked. Bessie handed him a cup of coffee. He blew the steam away and warmed his hands on the hot metal. "Fifteen minutes?"

Ten minutes later, Bessie stood on the platform holding her sweep while Glen pushed the scow into the river. She was feeling better, and the sex had bolstered her confidence in her husband. He'd keep her safe. She just had to take care of him.

By mid-day, they'd passed through a maze of rocky rapids. She'd counted ten. Glen was quickly learning how to move the scow just enough to keep them off the larger boulders. She'd only had to dive onto the floor of the scow twice. The few times she'd been really scared, Glen had been yelling, "Yahoo!" or, "We're shooting them now, Bess!" or, "We have to be setting the record!"

The more rapids they ran, the more she realized it didn't seem to matter how hard she worked her sweep. Trying to maneuver in the bigger whitewater seemed to make little difference. The scow stubbornly refused to alter the course *it* set. Luck was their chief contribution.

"The drops are up ahead!" Glen shouted over the growing roar.

They had just slashed their way through a mile-long series of smaller rapids. Ahead, the churning waves looked as large as the haystacks on Glen's farm. Higher and angrier than any they'd been through so far.

"They're huge! How are we going to miss them?

"We won't, we'll crash right through. Get in the bottom, empty out the cook barrel, and keep bailing!"

"Here we go, Bess!" Glen shouted, as they entered the first swell. The bow of the scow slammed into an enormous wave and popped out on the other side. Water and spray had poured over the sides and across the top, soaking them head to toe in one blast. "Another one! BAIL!"

Bessie felt like she'd been tossed into the ocean during a storm, the canyon walls, the sky, everything had been replaced by a sheet of raging water. She wiped her face, locked her sweep, and furiously started bailing.

"There's a narrow channel of passable water between the bigger waves and the canyon wall. If I can get us in that current, we'll slide through!"

Bessie peeked over the edge of the scow as she emptied another barrel. All she could see was brown, muddy chaos exploding all around them. They were dropping into the mouth of a chomping, spitting tiger. She ducked and hugged the bottom of the scow as it plunged onto the cat's rabid tongue, swallowed with a rush of water that drenched her and coated her hair with sludge.

"Sweet Jesus! Hold on!" Glen screamed.

Hold on to what, Bessie thought. She grabbed the springs that were wedged in the aft and prayed. The scow was hurtling downstream, gaining momentum. She knew Glen had little control, but he was still standing on the platform working both sweeps, trying to keep them straight.

"Get down here with me!" she yelled. Glen glanced down at her and smiled.

They slammed into a wave and Bessie felt the scow spin. The current had twisted them, forcing them back toward the middle of the river, out of the channel they were running. Back to where they didn't want to be. An enormous, tail-wave crashed over the side of the scow, pushing them sideways into another. Glen fell to his knees, but he jumped back up. They ran through another wall of water and foam. They were in the middle now. Glen was feverishly working the sweeps, trying to use the current to straighten the scow. It seemed to be working. Bessie prayed their momentum would carry them through. They were on a runaway train and had jumped the tracks.

"We're going in!" Glen yelled, dropping to his knees, but keeping hold of both sweeps.

Bessie dared looking up and could see nothing but a horizon of water on both sides of the scow. They were careening down, down, down. Crashing into the bottom of the hole, a tidal wave of soupy, torrid water collapsed on top of them, and everything went dark.

17

BESSIE AND GLEN

October 30 - November 1, 1928

MIRACULOUSLY, THE SCOW PASSED THROUGH THE WAVE WITHout sinking. Bessie wiped her face, her vision clearing in time to see Glen jump up and dip both sweeps into the furious froth, one in front and one in back extending over her head. The river thundered, fuming that they still survived.

She bailed frantically, but it was useless. Far more water rushed in than she could remove.

"I see quieter water!" Glen yelled. The earlier enthusiasm in his voice was muted now. "There's an eddy I can edge into. It's milder than yesterday's. I can hold us there until we catch our breath."

The water pouring in over the side had lessened. Bessie quit bailing and took her station on the platform.

"We'll find a place to pull in before long," Glen said, directing the scow into the milder current. "I thought we were goners in that last one," he grinned. They went up and over several smaller waves before entering a long series of riffles that ended in calm water.

They both slept well that night. Glen dragged the bedsprings and mattress ashore at a quiet spot, and they'd fallen asleep minutes after the sun dropped below the western rim. The demands of the river were taking a physical toll. In the morning, Bessie helped Glen with a few repairs to the scow, nothing major, but it'd taken a couple of big hits and one of the sweep paddles needed fixing. He also retightened the counterweight on Bessie's handle. 'For it to be that loose', he joshed, 'you must have been pushing it harder than the current was pushing us.'

Bessie made sandwiches and then they shoved off. Glen was determined to keep pushing the pace.

"I think I felt a raindrop," Bessie said, before they'd gone far. "Yup, see it hitting the water?"

"Just a sprinkle. We're past the rainy season. We're used to being wet down here, right?"

Bessie didn't feel like arguing. He was certainly chipper. As far as he was concerned, they'd come through yesterday fine. They only had a few small rapids left before they were out of Cataract Canyon - *if* that had been the Drops they passed yesterday.

"We're about through Cataract."

"Good," Bessie said, as the first drips of rainwater fell from her hat.

The rain turned into more than a sprinkle. It was soon steady and unrelenting. They ran one last rapid with a slight drop and Glen began working the scow toward a beach he saw a quarter mile ahead. The sky had gotten darker, blotting out the sun, except for a hole where it shone into a side canyon. The temperature was nosediving. Lightning suddenly lit up the walls; brilliant, jagged streaks shot out of the clouds, striking the red rocks up high.

"There are a few mesquite bushes by that beach. Maybe we can stretch the tarp over..." Thunder echoed through the canyon. "Over a couple of limbs," Glen said.

They tugged the scow as far onto the beach as they could. Glen sunk a short oar into the sand and tied the bowline. The rain was coming down in buckets. "Get the tarp," he barked to Bessie. He went into the mesquite and came back with a thick, dead limb. He dug a hole by the anchored oar, working the limb even deeper, tamping sand around the base, and retied the loose end of the bowline just above the ground.

Bessie struggled with the tarp against the wind. The steep walls of the canyon made a perfect wind tunnel. She got it to the mesquite and spread it open. She didn't dare try lifting it in the gale. Glen finished with the scow, and they both held onto a side. He slid his side over several low-hanging limbs three feet above the sand. "Hold it and watch out for thorns." 'Right,' Bessie thought. He threw a rope across the top, tied his end, ran around the mesquite and tied the end beside Bessie. Bessie broke branches above it, careful to avoid thorns, letting them rest atop the makeshift tent, to keep it from flapping in the wind.

"Boom, Boom, Boom!" The thunder sounded like fireworks on the Fourth of July. They both dove under the tarp as the canyon lit up with more lightning. The iron ore in the cliffs drew lightning like the pole on their barn. On the other side of the river, a rockslide gave way, debris disappearing with splashes into the Colorado.

"Let's get the mattress, my rifle, and some food. Everything else should be fine under the oil skins," Glen said, after several minutes and no lightning. "We'll make it fast. Ready?"

Bessie nodded and they ran into the downpour. She steadied the scow as Glen jumped in.

"Take the rifle and the food. I've got the mattress," he said, throwing it over his shoulder. "Go. *Go!*"

They ran back to the tarp, but neither of them was hungry. They huddled together, Bessie shivering, while the canyon shouted and echoed at them like the devil had let loose hell's fury. The thunderstorm lasted all night, never letting up.

Bessie slept poorly, awakening every few minutes to Glen swearing and vainly trying to adjust the tarp. It seemed to have a leak every square foot. In the middle of the night, she'd helped him dig a trench with the butt of his rifle along both sides of the tarp, channeling some of the storm runoff away from their bed. The rockslide they'd witnessed wasn't the only one they heard that night. Several more happened on the slopes above them; there was nothing they could have done if an avalanche had come.

It was dawn when Bessie opened her eyes, having finally gotten some sleep. Her husband's coat was covering her head and shoulders. The thunder and lightning were still in syncopation but playing at a slower beat than when she'd last been awake. She peered out from Glen's coat and could see the river in the early light. It was running high, twice as fast, with lots of woody debris. She could smell the muddy silt; it looked thick enough to plow.

"Morning Sunshine," Glen said, ducking back under the tarp. He was soaked and his wide-brimmed hat sagged over his ears and forehead. He put an armload of wet sticks and logs on a larger pile beside where he'd slept. "Not yet, but once this stops, we'll need some dry wood."

Bessie sat up and reached for the bag she'd brought from the scow. She was so cold. Her hands were crinkled from moisture and shaking. Glen had grabbed two cans of beans and she started opening them. "These'll have to do for breakfast, unless the rain stops."

"I like cold beans," Glen said, taking the cans and opener from her.

"Tha-tha-that makes one of us," she said, her teeth chattering.

Bessie picked at the beans, giving most of them to Glen. He wolfed them down and rummaged through the bag for some elk jerky, offering a slice to Bessie.

"Go ahead, my stomach can't handle it."

For most of the morning, they stayed in the tent, trying to keep warm and talking about the rest of the trip, dreaming about how they'd sell their adventure once they reached California. Glen figured with any luck, they would reach Needles and a warm, dry bed by the week after Thanksgiving. That wasn't that long; they could put up with a little rain.

In between downpours, he rushed outside and collected firewood. "It's clearing a bit to the west," he said after his last dash and piling in still more wood. Bessie thought they had enough logs for a community bonfire.

"Thank God," Bessie exclaimed an hour later when the sun hit the tarp and floodlights seemed to turn on. She'd stripped off her wet clothes and was shivering naked under the wet quilts. She stuck her feet in the sunshine outside the tarp, feeling a touch of heat for the first time in nearly twenty hours.

"How's the fire coming?" she yelled from inside. Glen was outside trying to ignite the damp wood. She heard it spark, begin to crackle, and then go whoosh.

"I used a little kerosene from the stove. The rain's over. It feels good - c'mon out."

Bessie raised the tarp to crawl out. She gathered her and Glen's wet clothes; she didn't see any sense putting anything on until they were dry.

"Don't!" Glen yelled.

It was too late, and a bucket-sized pool of cold water poured from the tarp onto her head. They both laughed, their moods buoyed by the improving weather. Bessie winked as she caught Glen staring at her chilled, wet breasts.

She strung a line between bushes by the fire to hang their clothes up to dry. Glen had stripped down to his drawers. Hopefully with the sun and the heat from the fire, everything, except maybe their heavy coats, would be dry and warm in a few minutes. Bessie felt Glen keenly watching her bend over to pick up their clothes and hang them on the line.

Bessie finished and stood beside him, rubbing her skin and feeling the fire warm her body. Glen pulled her to him, and they kissed. It was a good kiss, long and deep, their lips melding together from memory and passion. He lifted her and she wrapped her legs above his hips. Glen nibbled her neck, and, below, she could feel what he wanted. He put her down and she was pulling him on top, when the rain started again. A sudden gust of wind blew through their camp.

"We need to get our clothes," she said, laughing, half-slipping and half-running through wet sand to the clothesline. "The other can wait."

The rain began blowing sideways. The fire sizzled as cold drops hit the hot flames. Dark, gray clouds rolled over the canyon rim.

"Come on," she yelled.

Glen was just standing there, probably a little embarrassed and unsure what to do in his...aroused predicament. He grabbed his hat, which had been drying on a stick by the fire and ran to join her.

Upstream, a window was open to the sky and rays of sunshine fanned into the canyon. Whitecaps shined as if they were under a spotlight. A rainbow spread from rim to rim, moody blues and purples appearing first and then brighter bands of reds and yellows. The couple stood transfixed in the rain, admiring nature's different faces. A second rainbow faintly formed above the first.

"It's so beautiful," Bessie gasped.

Glen hugged his wife. "It's a sign of good luck."

The rain intensified and began pelting them in their faces. They crawled back under the tarp just as marble-sized hail fell. When the hail stopped, rain pounded the tarp, slapping the water-logged canvas, never taking a break thru the evening and all night. The Flagstaff papers would report it as the storm of the century. All Bessie would remember was her husband's stamina and how beautiful he'd looked when the lightning captured his ecstasy.

In the early morning, when the night was darkest, they stuck their heads out to check on conditions. The rain gusted against their faces.

Lightning flashed against the canyon wall and they both jumped. "That bolt looked like a lance with feathers dangling below the point." Glen said, pulling the tarp closed. He chuckled, "I have a name for the scow. What if we call it *Rain-in-the-Face?*"

"Rain-in-the-Face?"

"He was a ferocious Lakota war chief credited with killing Custer."

"Rain-in-the-Face, Rain-in-the-Face," Bessie repeated, trying it out. "I like it. Certainly beats *scow*, which sounds more like an angry, old cow. *Rain-in-the-Face* sounds like something that doesn't give up - despite the difficulties."

At the river, Rain-in-the-Face strained against the bowline Glen had neglected to check, while its namesake continued throwing lances, ice, and rain against all who dared to invade its land.

18

WUPATKI

LILAC STARED OUT THE WINDSHIELD. THE TOP THIRD OF THE SAN Francisco Peaks, north of Flagstaff, were lost in clouds. *Rain - Great!* She hoped she hadn't made another mistake joining Skip's tour.

After they had returned from Jerome and finished a pitcher of Zula's famous Blackberry Sangria, Lottie Chandler had asked her to join them. They were taking a van now and there was room, she'd said. The woman had appreciated the respectful interest Lilac had shown regarding her parents. She'd also taken Lilac aside, confiding that her irreverent daughter could use a positive influence, one nearer her own age.

"We spoiled her. We should have made her fix her own troubles instead of bailing her out every time. She didn't learn to deal with consequences. The callous nature she defaults to is my doing," Lottie had said.

From what Lilac had seen of Winonna Chandler, she was more than capable of causing trouble. Blaming the parents...no, that was too easy. If the actress had modeled her mother, she'd be a better person. It wasn't Lilac's influence she needed. But tagging along on the trip was a chance to spend some time with Skip. Maybe she'd see their potential more clearly. The Flagstaff date with Coop hadn't gone the way she'd planned. It wasn't his fault. Honestly, the problem was her indecision over the lunkhead across from her driving the van.

Skip stopped for gas at the Maverick station outside Flag. The sky was looking better, changing as it often did atop the plateau. The line of gray clouds was farther north than where they were heading. The Chandlers had gone inside, and Kuul and Webster were talking to an old Navajo sitting against a ponderosa pine. The man was usually there, living off the tips he got from telling stories. Skip was alone with Lilac at the pump.

"I thought you had plans with Coop?"

"Obviously not."

"Fine, don't bite my head off. Whatever Detective PPD did is on him, not me. I *was* glad you're here."

"Why?"

Lilac accepted that he probably was glad but questioned his reasons...and her own. She'd been too tempted by his veiled invitation to soap each other's backs after their workout. *Was that what made her shut Coop down?* Skip had changed since they'd been together. Maybe she just hadn't given him enough time to get past whatever it was he'd so obviously run from. He was angry less often. And Sky had told her his nightmares were fewer. *Clearly, the two were close enough for her to know about his bad dreams.*

Skip heard warning bells ringing from the Peaks and saw red flags unfurl from the sky; Why? What was it she wanted him to say? "That daughter's going to be hard to wrangle. She's not the kind to follow instructions. And the mother, as sweet as she is, is going to get emotional."

So, was that it? That was why he was glad she was here? Lilac felt like slapping herself. He just wanted an extra hand. He already had Kuul. *How many babysitters did this group need?*

"Besides," Skip added, noticing her frown...or was it disgust, "You seem interested in their story. That's why you're here, right?"

He finished pumping gas and saw the Chandlers coming back across the parking lot. *Who was he kidding?* He understood Lilac's question. He should have told her *why* after she'd refused to let him die at the ruins. How much he...surely, she knew how he felt.

"I'll ride in the third seat with Webster, Kuul can sit up front with you from here on," Lilac said, coolly. "I thought he was going to break a leg climbing back there."

Lilac slid into the back as the Chandlers, Webster, and Kuul walked up. The ladies took the second bench, and Webster, appreciating the switch in seating arrangements, joined the yoga instructor in the back.

Skip grabbed the receipt from the pump, jamming it into his pocket. "Guess you're shotgun," he said to Kuul.

"I'm not even going to ask what you said, Kemo. I've told you before; praise the moon in their skin and the stars in their eyes. And with her, it needs to be sincere."

Skip knew it wasn't the flawless texture of her skin, so smooth and perfect to the touch, or the intoxicating sparkle in her eyes that Lilac hoped to hear about. It was the things he hadn't said - for reasons he couldn't share.

Back on the noisy highway, he tested the rental van's audio system. An electronic toy he wished he had in his Bronco. "Today's a long day, Lee's Ferry and Navajo Bridge, but you did great getting away early and bought some extra time. If it's okay with everyone, we can also stop at Wupatki National Monument - a Sinagua pueblo just off the highway. The Sinagua were the people here before the Navajo and Apache, part of the ancient Ancestral Puebloan culture."

Skip scanned the rearview mirror. Lottie was listening and nodded in agreement. Webster was chatting up Lilac. Winonna was busy on her phone. "Okay then. Be prepared, we're about to lose service. It gets more remote the farther north we go."

Winonna sighed, "Of course it does."

Wupatki wasn't just one pueblo. It was actually dozens of different-sized, stone dwellings spread across thousands of acres in a seemingly dry, inhospitable environment. The land looked flat from a distance, all gray scrub with an occasional rock outcropping, under an endless, baking, blue sky. In its day, it had been a cultural crossroads; Puebloan people and Hopis to the east, Anasazi to the north and west, and the Hohokam and Mogollon peoples farther south. Today it was a barren area between Flagstaff and Navajo Nation, attracting few visitors.

Skip and his group poked around the visitor center before taking the short loop trail to an overlook above the largest pueblo ruin. The ruin was a five-story, apartment block the size of a football field that looked like irregularly stacked Legos. It sat on a ridge between two deep gulches.

"They picked this spot for reasons we can only guess, the nearest, permanent water-source is six miles away. Survival depended on a handful of seasonal seeps from snowmelt and rain off those tall mountains around Flagstaff. They fed themselves by dry-farming drought-tolerant crop species," Kuul explained. "Wupatki is the largest free-standing pueblo in Arizona. Meaning this was an important meeting place. The People here were far more advanced than nomadic hunters and gatherers. By 1100, the pueblo had over a hundred rooms and at least as many residents; thousands more lived within an easy day's walk. This was a thriving civilization well before the Spanish arrived. But something happened around 1400 to cause them to disappear – drought, over-farming, declining birth rates, religious conflict – no one knows for sure. Some modern-day Hopi who trace their ancestry here, claim this was just a stop on their clan's long journey."

"Is it all original?" Lottie asked.

"Not all, but most," Skip said. "The Park Service changed their policy in the 1950s. Before that, archeologists and rangers tried reconstructing the ruins. In the 30s, the first rangers even lived in some parts. But most of that has been removed. They realized it inaccurately depicted the past."

"The round, kiva-like, meeting room you see down there," Kuul added, pointing below the main pueblo, "and the ball court, farther down the trail, were both uncovered later. Their short walls are recreations on original foundations and partial wall fragments."

"Ball court? Weren't they all in Mexico and Central America," Webster said? He wanted to play his part.

"Not all, but this is the farthest north one has been uncovered. There have been dozens of courts discovered in Arizona alone." Kuul answered. "It's another reason why archeologists believe this was an important gathering place."

Winonna was pacing in a circle, holding up her phone, trying to find service. She finally gave up and stuffed it in the outside pocket of her shoulder bag.

"So, the ballgames are over. Is there anything else to do here?" the movie star asked sarcastically.

"Winonna!"

"Mom, I agreed to go to the Grand Canyon. Not, not... Wombattoo."

"Wupatki," Lilac corrected. "I'm sure if you wear those trashy sunglasses and wait in the parking lot, some solicitous cowboy in a pickup will offer you a ride back to Sedona."

The starlet's face reddened, and Skip quickly offered a couple of choices, "We don't have to all stay together." Best we don't, he thought, assessing the O.K. Corral standoff between Lilac and

Winonna. "I usually let folks explore on their own a bit. I'm heading to the ball court, but a shorter trail goes around the pueblo. There's a nice overlook on its backside and you can go inside a couple of the reconstructed rooms. Or you can check out the exhibits in the Visitor Center, which is air-conditioned. Let's meet back at the van in forty minutes."

Winonna and Webster stayed by the pueblo. Skip, Kuul, and Lottie, decided to see the ball court. With his Mayan heritage, Kuul had a special connection with the site. Lilac joined them part of the way, then turned off toward the kiva. "It's a good place to do a few yoga poses to ease the stress."

"Please, don't let her bother you," Lottie said.

"Oh...it's not her."

At the ball court, Skip, Kuul, and Lottie sat on the stone benches circling the base of the playing field, which was fifty or so feet across. "Is there a Mayan connection?" Lottie asked.

"Probably indirectly," Kuul said. "But the Maya empire was centuries older than the Sinagua. There were a few hundred years of overlap, but those were well before the Sinagua, and their Southwest contemporaries, settled into pueblos. Some academics believe the Sinagua were a northern branch of the Hohokam from around modern-day Phoenix, who were Toltecs from Mexico. This court's different from most others in Arizona though; it has stone walls, an opening, and benches. They haven't found balls here either, like at Casa Grande farther south. Some experts have theorized this was a trading plaza, not a ball court."

"Or both," Skip added.

Kuul shrugged, "Why not, we sell RVs at Cardinal Stadium. The Hohokam were big traders, in touch with Mesoamerican and Pacific Coast cultures. Customs travel."

"There's also a blowhole," Skip said, pointing Lottie to a rock shelf outside the ball court. "Someday that could yield a firmer connection with the Maya and Mesoamerica culture. It's a vent into the earth and blows hot or warm air depending on the relative air pressures above and below ground. The Sinagua would have seen this as a gateway to the underworld. They have found evidence and petroglyphs below suggesting rituals were held there, perhaps tied to their origin story. Mayans, it's believed, had similar beliefs about the underworld. As they uncover and explore more sites in the Southwest and Yucatan...who knows?"

Kuul nodded. "I've been thinking about major sites in the Yucatan, Uxmal, Ek Balam, Coba. My ancestors invited me in a dream. They have our answers."

"Maybe you'll want some company?" Skip said.

Kuul nodded again, "It will be a good journey."

"I've had so many dreams," Lottie said sadly. "When your ancestors die in a crash like mine - their bodies unrecovered - you're left to imagine what their final moments must have been like. Were they alive or unconscious when the plane crashed? Were they praying, crying, holding each other? Did they have hope until the very end or had they accepted their fate? I wish they could speak to me like yours do to you, Kuul. We were so shocked; it was all so sudden...like a...*horrible dream*. I remember my grandmother sitting me down and explaining the canyon had taken them both."

Skip understood that now was one of the moments it was best to say nothing.

A pair of ravens circled overhead, landing on the far wall of the court, breaking Lottie's silent reflection. "I'm glad you brought us here. The way the Sinagua and Hohokam suddenly disappeared, how little we know about them, all of the answers we may never get - it's like my parents."

• • •

Inside the kiva, a family with sack lunches was arguing over who got orange soda and who got water. The mother warned the father that he'd have to deal with Johnny Junior if he approved another sugar high. So much for yoga, Lilac thought. *Kids. Were they really what she wanted?* At least the knot in the back of her neck from a clueless tour guide and rude actress was manageable. She sat on a bench away from the carping and studied the pueblo from a distance, wondering if any of the Sinagua mothers and maidens had similar problems.

She watched Winonna follow the upper, loop trail around the south end of the pueblo. Lilac was surprised the spoiled girl hadn't hustled straight back to the center. Webster had taken the lower path, wandering across the front of the pueblo, stopping to read the story boards, and then looping north to explore the backside. The two would have to meet.

Twenty minutes later, Lilac's curiosity got the better of her. Neither Winonna nor Webster had reappeared. *Hmmm...maybe she'd remind them of the time.* She followed the route Webster had taken to the rear of the pueblo; expansive views spread across a wide gulch where there had once been Sinagua fields. The path ran along a ridgeline beside the pueblo. Webster and Winonna were nowhere in sight. *Maybe they rounded the south wall as she rounded the north wall?*

She heard muffled voices coming from the reconstructed rooms left by the Park Service. She also noticed a man, farther up the path, staring at the rooms. He was slim, athletically built, unshaven, and wearing a tacky cowboy hat. *Was that a man bun?* The man whistled when he saw her and disappeared around the far end of the pueblo. Lilac approached the roofless, reconstructed rooms, keeping an eye on the upper trail in case Bun Boy came back. She recognized the muffled voices.

"Look, it was a one-time fling, a girl's trip. I don't believe you even have any pictures," Winonna said. "Why don't you try bribing her, she's the popular one? Miss goody two-shoes on the early show."

"We can talk later," Webster said, ending their talk. He'd heard the whistle.

Lilac was standing ten feet away on a pebbled path that led into the rooms. Webster quickly said something else in a lowered voice.

"I don't care," Lilac heard Winonna say in a loud voice. "She's just here to keep the guide happy."

Winonna stalked out of the stone room; Webster appeared right behind her. Lilac glanced toward where the other man had been; he was still gone.

"Spying?" Winonna smirked, brushing red dust off her white sunglasses. "This dirt gets everywhere, just like snoops."

"No, just taking notes," Lilac said. She couldn't help but notice the pink mark of a handprint on her arm, above the elbow.

Webster seemed bothered but tried not to show it. He glanced up the path - then gave Winonna a quick, mean look. Lilac read it as a warning, but she couldn't be sure; the starlet wasn't exactly easy to get along with.

"We ran into each other inside. She slipped," he said. "It might be a reconstruction, but it gives a person a real feel for what it was like. First time I've been inside a pueblo."

"Did you get any pictures?"

"A few good ones," Webster said, ignoring the implication he'd been overheard. "I was showing her on the screen. Here," he said, flashing her a photo of the ruins on his phone.

"It's time to meet the others," Lilac said. There was no use questioning them about what she'd heard. "Skip's planning lunch at Lee's Ferry. It's time to get moving."

"Great, a boat ride in the desert!" Winonna said, brushing past both of them.

19

BESSIE AND GLEN

November 8, 1928

"WE'RE ABOUT TO LEE'S FERRY. THOSE DIRT TRACKS ON BOTH sides of the river are the old Honeymoon Trail, the Crossing of the Fathers," Glen announced. "Jump up here and help me with Rain-in-the-Face."

Bessie was sitting in the bottom of the scow catching up on journal entries, watching the cliffs rise and fall as the late-afternoon shadows played tricks on her perspective. The river had been calmer for days, mostly riffles and smaller rapids. Glen was worried about the time they kept losing. At one point, he turned the scow sideways and tried rowing. They hadn't gone fast enough to make it worth the effort. She'd counted three intersecting rivers: the Dirty Devil, Escalante, and the San Juan. The on-again off-again rains were filling their banks, pouring muddy runoff into the Colorado. Bessie thought it was the dirtiest place she'd ever seen.

Nothing like the crystal-clear, green and blue rivers she was used to back home.

The walls of the canyon were farther apart than in Cataract Canyon. And their faces were sloped; softer layers underneath had eroded faster, causing higher layers to unevenly collapse in diagonal runs. All along they'd seen Anasazi ruins; she'd convinced Glen to stop once and explore. Chiseled petroglyphs on the walls of blocked-in caves told their ancient history. She'd taken time to sketch the animal and human stick figures and the striking, geometric designs. How anyone could survive here for centuries, with how hard it must have been every day, and still find the time to draw such wonderful art, was beyond her imagination.

Glen Canyon had been a haunting, ghostly world of carved canyons. After what they'd been through in Cataract, it had been a needed respite. And a time to recapture their zeal for what Glen said was ahead - Marble Canyon and its feared rapids. Lee's Ferry would be their last 'civilized' stop before Marble and reaching Grand Canyon Village.

"That must be it," Bessie said. They'd rounded a bend and could see a few stone ruins and structures a mile ahead. A steel cable was stretched across the river and Glen directed the scow toward a sandy landing spot.

"Not many people here," Glen said, beaching the boat. A handful of interested locals near the buildings were watching them land. "I don't suppose they get a lot of business since the ferry was lost in June. Navajo Bridge being built downstream will replace it. We're witnesses to the end of an era, Bess."

"No sense driving down here on the backbone of a rocky road to ride a ferry when you can cross a bridge up top," Bessie added. "I wish it was still open though, so we could see more people." All she saw was three men waving, all tanned, wiry, and looking like they could be part of the landscape.

Lee's Ferry had been in continuous operation since 1873. John Lee had ventured to the desolate area to homestead a ranch and ferry his fellow Mormon settlers from southern Utah to new destinations along the Little Colorado and Southern Arizona. Mormons had been in Utah since the 1840's and had needed more land. The remoteness suited Lee, who was hiding out from his role in the infamous Mountain Meadows Massacre of gentile settlers. Four years after starting the ferry, he was arrested by the U.S. Government and executed by firing squad.

In 1879 the Latter Day Saints purchased the ferry service from Lee's widow and transferred it to Warren Johnson. It was Johnson's sons, Jeremiah and Price, and Price's son, Owen, who greeted Glen and Bessie.

"How do," Jeremiah called from shore. He and his brother had been born at Lee's Ferry and neither of them had seen a boat like the one they were eyeing. "You two must be the newlyweds we heard about. Kinda doubted you'd make it this far. But darn glad you did. My name's Jeremiah Johnson, this here's Owen, my nephew. The ugly guy is my brother Price. We run a ranch down here. Used to run the ferry, but no more."

"That's us. Glen and Bessie Hyde," Glen said. "I heard about the ferry - tough luck."

"Lost three good men too, one a cousin. They were taking the ferry across in highwater. Conditions pretty much just like this," Price Johnson said, sourly. Of the two brothers, he had the sterner face, even though he was younger.

"Where can we set up camp for the night? Sorry about the drownings, but I guess we proved our doubters wrong, now that we're through the worst."

"Hmmph, you've just been getting your ears wet," the younger Owen stated.

"You haven't proven anything yet, son. I've watched that devil my whole life and you're playing with death. That river takes everything," Price said.

Bessie judged him to be the practical brother. He was holding a wide, straw hat, rubbing his bare head; his face tanned like old leather from mid-forehead down. Calculating eyes shone beneath heavy brows, assessing their equipment.

Jeremiah Johnson smiled at the small woman whose dark, round eyes had been locked on what his brother was saying. Her husband might be confident, but he wasn't so sure about her. How someone so slight could hold one of those huge, heavy oars was beyond him. But she'd sure been working it on their way in; he had to give her that.

"Well, you come on up after you're settled and we'll talk," he said.

Bessie watched the Johnsons leave, lazily drifting back to a cabin where another man and a woman were sitting outside. It was clear Lee's Ferry was in decline. But it was good to see other people.

"Why don't we just stay in Rain-in-the-Face tonight? The river's quiet and it doesn't look like rain. I can fix us dinner in the cook barrel. We can let the water rock us to sleep."

Glen was wading around the scow, checking for any damage. He patted the scow like he would a horse after a good ride. "If those fellas had ever ridden a scow through here, they wouldn't be so quick to criticize. I doubt they've even ran Cataract. That Price is a character, isn't he?"

Bessie shook her head in agreement. They hadn't seen her husband in action and didn't know about all the experience he'd gained on the Snake. She was sad about the men who'd drowned, but they'd probably been trying to cross when they shouldn't have. Still, these men undoubtedly knew the river below the Ferry.

"I'm going to sit in the shade under that tree and write to Dad," Glen said. "Let him know we're past the Cataracts and at Lee's Ferry, having a great time and past the worst of it. Tell him to load up on groceries in California because you're eating us out of boat and home," he chuckled.

Bessie laughed and threw a scoop of sand at him. "Make sure to tell him how well I'm taking care of his son." She needed to write home too. Mom was worried about the trip, and she needed to assure her all was well.

Enough wood was left in the stove to get a fire started. Bessie considered walking up to the cabins to see if there was any meat they could buy. Since Glen had broken the sight on his rifle, his hunting skills had been hit and miss. On second thought, with what little cash they had, she'd wait until tomorrow when they got to the new Navajo Bridge and the trading post Glen had mentioned. These people were friendly, but she didn't see a store.

She watched Glen work on his letter and called him when dinner was ready. "It's stew. The last of the venison from that deer you shot," Bessie said, ladling a bowl for her hungry husband, who was sucking the fingers he'd stuck in the pot. She gave him a piece of hard bread to go with it.

"I'll post the letter from Lowrey Trading Post above the bridge," he said, stuffing the paper in his pocket.

They finished the basic meal and rinsed the metal plates in the river. Dish cleaning was an exercise in futility, smearing muddy water around until the dry air turned it to dust that she could brush off.

"Hey, in the boat," a man called out in a sociable voice. He had a high forehead and broad face and was dressed in a khaki shirt and pair of dusty work jeans. There was a patch on his sleeve Bessie couldn't read. Maybe in his forties, it was hard to tell on the river. There was a younger man with him wearing round, wire-rimmed glasses and a banded, felt fedora.

"Owen Clark," the first man said, introducing himself. "I'm the water gager here for the government. We make sure the states know the size of the pie they're cutting up. Lee's Ferry is the boundary between the lower and upper basins of the new River Compact. Saw you come in. Impressed with how you handled your boat."

"Government, huh," Glen said, suspiciously.

"Nothing to do with monitoring or patrolling river traffic, friend."

The younger man stayed quiet and pulled out a notepad and pencil. He licked the pencil and started scribbling on the paper. "I'm with the Flagstaff paper," he said, never looking up.

"Say, with those oars fixed at the stern and aft, how do you maneuver your boat?" Clark asked. "I was studying it and can't figure how you could move sideways to avoid the bigger drops."

"Have to know what you're doing," Glen said simply, making sure the man understood that he did. "Tell you what, let me show you." He leaned in and whispered to Bessie, "The other fella's with a newspaper. Let's give him a demonstration to write about. We need to get used to talking with reporters."

Glen jumped up on the platform and Bessie joined him, grabbing her sweep.

"Clark, just push us off, but hold the line and feed the scow out a bit."

The scow slid a few feet into the river, free of the sand, but languidly floating. Glen dipped the end of his sweep, made a short, lateral push, and Rain-in-the-Face straightened parallel to the bank. Bessie stuck her oar in from behind, gently moving it back and forth underwater, holding the scow steady. Glen raised his sweep, set it in the water to the left of the boat and pushed his handle. The scow returned to its original position.

"Pull us back in," he said, grinning.

The reporter had been furiously writing the whole time. "Last name with an *i* or *y*?"

"H-Y-D-E," Bessie spelled out, smiling from ear to ear.

Clark reattached the bowline and whistled, "Slick, but I rafted below here, through Marble Canyon last year. That's a different, hungry beast. A boat needs to move quickly in there, side to side to miss the worst of it."

"We'll make it fine," Glen said.

"We plan on setting a record," Bessie added for the reporter. "We're going all the way to Needles, California and running every rapid. It's a wonderful trip, and I look forward to being the first woman to do it."

"No doubt you will," Clark said to Glen, not wanting to start an argument. Maybe confidence and enthusiasm would see them through, he thought. "I went with the Pathe-Bray Movie Company - the trip last year. We had several boats, different than yours, the kind you see down here. Same time as now, but the flow was less, hadn't had the rains. We still almost lost one boat or another every day. And that was with thirteen men and an experienced guide who knew the river, recommended by Emery Kolb."

"We'll be fine," Glen repeated.

Clark could see that Hyde was getting defensive and that there was no changing his mind at this point. "Sure you will. It's just that with only one boat...all your eggs are in one basket, so to speak. We knew if we lost one, we wouldn't be stranded. You wouldn't want to get marooned in a remote section, and friend, it's all remote."

The reporter quit writing and looked at Glen over the top of his round glasses, "Would you call your ship a flatboat?"

"A scow," Glen said, trying to smile despite the stupid question. This could be the first of many articles about their trip. Explaining details to uninitiated correspondents would be part of his future.

"Well, good luck to you," Clark said. "I reckon our dinner's ready."

Bessie watched the friendly government man and the studious looking reporter head back to a cabin. Clark was talking the newspaperman's ear off, but she couldn't make out a word.

The next morning, they were in no hurry to get underway. Bessie wasn't ready to relinquish her land legs yet, so they hiked up a side canyon to see an Indian the Johnson's said sold moccasins. They weren't very practical for the rough planks of the scow, but it was a beautiful morning and seeing the Indian family at work tanning, cutting, and stitching the hides was a welcome change of pace.

Later, Glen spent time finishing his father's letter. While he was busy finding the right words, Bessie had wandered up to the settlement and was talking with Price Johnson, or more aptly, Johnson was probably haranguing her about continuing. Glen, seeing his wife getting increasingly frustrated and shaking her head, put the letter away and walked toward them. He could guess what the old coot was saying.

"If you lose the boat, you can forget about hiking out in these side canyons. From the riverbank you can't tell if they dead-end or not or which one to try. And the farther you go past here, the higher and steeper the walls become. Except for a few places that you'd have to know about, it's impossible to climb up top. We still haven't found the fellas that drowned in June."

Glen frowned and nodded a few times, but politely ignored him. The man was still upset from having lost a family member. "We need to ready Rain-in-the-Face," he said, taking Bessie's hand and leading her back toward the river.

"And what about food? You lose the boat, you lose your food and there won't be anybody coming down there looking for you," Johnson yelled, following them. "You can't climb out; you can't walk out. You'd be stuck for months. You'd starve."

"We'll be fine, old man," Glen said, untying the bowline. "Bessie, you ready?"

"You told your woman what she's in for?"

Glen lifted Bessie over the side and pushed the scow into deeper water. He jumped in and stood on the platform next to Bessie, giving her a quick kiss, before pulling his oar hard into the muddy current. Johnson stood on the bank, shaking his head with his hands on his hip.

"Never mind that old cuss, Bess. We're through the worst of it."

Four miles downstream they moored the scow below the Navajo Bridge construction site. They could see crews working hundreds of feet above them. There were letters to mail from the trading post and Bessie hoped to find a Navajo blanket to replace a quilt ruined in the bad storm. They met a surly Buck Lowrey who sold them supplies from his store. Like the Johnsons at Lee's Ferry and the old-timers at Green River, he tried talking them out of continuing, saying it was too dangerous and foolhardy. Glen had gotten mad and stormed off to talk with the workers pouring the concrete roadway.

Bessie paid for the supplies and the postage for their letters. Everyone was saying to give it up, except Glen. If not for Glen…well, if not for Glen she wouldn't be on this exciting trip, charting the next chapter of their lives. She had to trust him; he was her husband.

Bessie read Glen's letter home before sealing the envelope and handing it to Lowrey:

Dear Dad,

I don't think the cataracts are any worse than some places on the Salmon; that is, any more drop; but they are faster, and the waves dash higher… It was great sport…I'd quit the river here, not on my own account tho…But from what they tell us we are over all the worst water…Give my regards to my horse Barney,

Glen.

Were they really past the 'worst water', Bessie wondered? Not according to Price Johnson and Buck Lowrey, and who'd know better than them. And whose 'account' was he talking about - hers?

20

LEE'S FERRY

"**L**ISTEN TO ME!" LILAC HISSED UNDER HER BREATH.

"You're reading too much into it," Skip whispered.

The others were sitting in the van. Skip and Lilac were still outside. She'd told him about Winonna and Webster behind the Wupatki Pueblo.

"And the guy whistling a warning?"

"Come on Lilac. He and the girl just met. What could they be arguing about this soon? And lots of guys whistle outside. Maybe he had earbuds and was listening to Otis Redding."

Lilac reclaimed shotgun and the icy chill had Skip wanting to turn on the heater by the time they reached the highway. It was going to be a long trip to Lee's Ferry.

The 120-mile, two-hour drive past red mesas, naked buttes and parched gulches was as scenic as Arizona offered. Camel-looking humps of gray and purple-striped mounds of rock introduced the Chinle Formation. Navajo roadside stands, with black and red blankets flapping in the wind and worn, wooden boxes of shiny jewelry were festooned with flags and plywood signs. A herd of wild horses made an appearance. The turnoff to Lee's Ferry took them even deeper into the iconic sandstone cliffs. The road wound through colorful rock outcroppings and mountains sculpted by eons of wind and rain. Near the end of the drive, the lofty Vermilion Cliffs towered in the distance, on the far side of the Colorado River.

Lilac hadn't said a word the whole way.

"I thought we were stopping at Navajo Bridge?" Lottie asked as they crossed the single-arched, iron bridge and the visitor center entrance. Several tour vans were parked, and people were posing for pictures on the bridge abutment by the Navajo Reservation sign.

"Navajo are smart," Kuul noted. "Putting that sign west of the river stakes claim to the sacred water below."

"Lee's Ferry isn't far," Skip said. "A few miles past Cathedral Rock, the formation you see on the right." A skyscraper of red rock appeared to rise from the asphalt road they were turning onto. "We'll stop at the bridge on the way back. It won't be so busy, and the light and shadows are more dramatic later in the day."

"Late afternoon's a better time to see condors," Kuul added.

Most travelers bypassed Lee's Ferry. They were in a hurry, on their way to or from the North Rim of the Grand Canyon or touristy Kanab, Utah and Zion. The lonely Arizona Strip had never been a destination. Even the Franciscans, the first Europeans to visit the area, were only interested in finding quick passage between their missions in New Mexico and California.

Skip drove around Cathedral Rock and past curiously balanced boulders setting atop fluted, stone pillars. Two little boys were running circles underneath. He explained how millions of years ago the boulders had fallen from the top of the cliffs, compressing the earth they came to rest on. At first, they sat level with the ground, probably even cratered, like a golf ball plugged in a sand trap. Over time, the softer earth surrounding them eroded, but the compressed earth below held firm, except around the edges.

"Lonely Dell Ranch is up that dirt road. The original homestead of the Lee Family, who started the ferry service," Skip said, passing the ranger station before crossing a short bridge. "This is the Paria *River*. I know it looks more like a creek, but with the exceptions of the Colorado and Salt, it's the way most rivers look in Arizona. This flat area through here used to be farm fields and orchards. There was never enough ferry business to feed a large Mormon family."

"Looks like a rafting tour is preparing to head out," Lilac said. "Longer trips leave from here."

The boat launch was to their right. A hundred-foot-wide, concrete ramp provided their first good look at the Colorado. The river was calm and blue here, not yet the churning, dark rapids that began downstream. John Lee had chosen well.

"We'll park by the fort," Skip said. "Being the only settlers for hundreds of miles, the Lees were afraid of Navajo raids."

"Yeah, the unreasonable Indians were surprisingly unhappy about White settlements popping up in their favorite spots," Kuul said. "They never attacked though. Those early Mormons were too mean and too poor to bother with. The Navajo probably doubted they'd last long in such a harsh place."

Skip parked between two historical markers, at the end of a row of dusty pickups with empty boat trailers.

"Let's meet back here in fifteen," he said, pointing out the restrooms once they'd exited the van. "Everyone fill your water bottles from the cooler behind the backseat. We'll talk about the fort a bit and hike the path along the river. There are good views looking back downstream, more history to tell, and it's where they moved the ferry crossing to in 1899 - where it was when the Hydes came through."

The Chandlers and Webster walked toward the facilities. Kuul went with them, pointing out the rafters at the launch and Navajo fisherman casting from the bank. He was likely explaining how the explosion of commercial trips and Glen Canyon Damn affected spawning cycles. Lilac hung back with Skip, who was straightening up the van and rearranging suitcases that had shifted during the drive.

"Cooler leaked a bit. I forgot to bag it."

"I saw Cheyenne Roman with the rafters. She works for Cataract Whitewater, and I bet she's leading that group for Chuck. I think I'll go say hi."

Skip nodded as he slipped a black garbage bag around the orange igloo. A little space between them wouldn't hurt for an hour or so.

"This group's all yours. There's something off about Webster and I can't take much more of Winonna Chandler. I'll see when you get back from the hike...unless I've gone downriver."

"Wish Cheyenne luck for me."

Lilac left. Skip filled his bottle and toweled off the van floor. Fortunately, the suitcases were all hard-sided, except for his and Kuul's duffels. They'd have to use the Arizona air dryer tonight.

Ten minutes later, Kuul shepherded his flock to the fort, where he saw Skip waiting. Before starting the hike, he had run back to the van to get an extra hat for Winonna. She was bareheaded and complaining about the hot sun, threatening not to go.

"Why in the world would they live down here?" she whined, gingerly poking an old, wagon wheel leaning against the adobe ruins. Webster was peeking through a barred, partially collapsed opening that once was a fortified door.

"Well, John Lee was a practicing polygamist, like most Mormons then, and they'd been persecuted back East. Utah and Northern Arizona were their New Canaan. It was a place where they'd be free to practice their religious beliefs," Skip answered. "He brought two of his families here in early 1873 and built cabins by the Paria at a spot his first wife named the 'Lonely Dell'. They began ferrying Mormon settlers across the river to sites along the Little Colorado and farther south. The fort was built for protection. But with no attacks, it soon became a way station and trading post and finally living quarters as other families came."

"Glen and Bessie came through here, didn't they," Lottie commented.

"You've mentioned Lee was executed for his role in the Mountain Meadows Massacre. I wasn't sure what that was?" Webster asked.

"I'll get there," Skip smiled, holding up a finger to Webster. At least *they* were both paying attention. Winonna was twisting and bending his hat, worried about how it looked.

"After the execution, his wife sold the ferry rights to the LDS church, who sent Warren Johnson, another Mormon. For the most part, Johnson and his family operated the service until it closed in 1928. That was six months before the Hydes passed through. The ranch was still active, though. Lonely Dell's had a number of owners and uses since then - home, lodge, dude ranch, and now historic site," Skip finished.

He turned to Webster. "The Mountain Meadows Massacre happened in 1857 in Southern Utah. All 120 adult members of an emigrant wagon train traveling from Arkansas to California were killed. At the time, it was blamed on Indians. In actuality, it was the Nauvoo Legion, the Mormon Militia; they wanted it to look like an Indian attack and had recruited some Southern Paiute to join for the spoils."

"They also disguised themselves to look Native. But Arkansas people are hard scrabble, especially when protecting their little ones. The militia had bitten off more than they could chew," Kuul continued. "They battled for five days. By that time, the people in the wagon train knew there were *bilagáana*, white people, orchestrating the attack, even taking part."

"John Lee was one of the Mormon leaders?" Lottie asked.

Winonna had wandered farther ahead, uninterested in another old story. Why weren't these trails paved? The red dirt was already staining the white soles of her New Balances. She peaked into another old cabin and saw a piece of discarded equipment up a small hill. It looked like part of an old rusty furnace; no doubt the tour guide would jabber on about it. She glanced back at her mother and saw the group heading her way. Webster was watching her, she wasn't sure what he was after, but she'd just as soon stay out of his way and not give him a chance to catch her alone again.

"Yes, but he wasn't the only one," Skip answered Lottie. "And they were between a rock and a hard place. They'd originally feared the wagon train was the first wave of a government invasion. They didn't see this as part of the U.S. They saw it as their holy land. Once they figured out that wasn't what the train was, they realized how severely the outside world would condemn what they'd done. Ultimately, they convinced the emigrants who were running out of ammo and food that they'd be allowed to leave if they handed over their weapons. They did, and it was a mistake. A Militia man escorted each male and on signal, turned and shot them point-blank. The Paiutes and some of the Nauvoo zealots then turned their attention to the remaining witnesses, the women and older children."

"John Lee was involved in planning the murders, but he was also likely a scapegoat for Brigham Young, who, it's still debated, had ordered the attack," Kuul said, finishing the story.

"The belief is Lee was sent here not just to start the ferry, but partly to hide out from federal authorities. For a while it worked, but he was eventually hunted down, taken back to the site of his crime, and shot by firing squad. Mountain Meadows is a chapter of history that's always been, if not covered up, conveniently overlooked, because of the religious prejudices the truth would cause," Skip said.

He had been keeping an eye on Winonna. She was ascending the trail toward a rocky spot overlooking the Colorado and Lee's

Backbone, the hazardous road cut to the ferry across the river. On their side, the Vermilion Cliffs rose sharply above them. Their path crossed the base of a forty-foot landslide. The top of the slide had been flattened long ago by a mining operation, which had pushed larger boulders aside to make a separate trail into a side canyon. Winonna was on a less stable stretch where larger rocks above were supported by smaller rocks and loose gravel.

"Winonna, wait," Skip called. "Don't get too far from the group. It may look safe here, but it's still a wild place."

Winonna turned and waved. He wasn't sure how much she'd understood.

It began with small stones trickling down the slope above her. The girl was looking in the opposite direction, toward the river. A distracting motorboat carrying noisy sightseers had come around a far bend. By the time she looked back, she was in trouble.

"Winonna!" Lottie screamed as more rocks began to slide.

Skip was already leaping across rocky patches of the trail, running toward her daughter. The shower of small stones was harmless, but a large boulder teetered over her head, as if it were being rocked by an unseen hand, the gravel beneath it was giving way. Winonna saw the boulder shift and started to run but slipped in the path's loose dirt. The boulder wobbled backwards and stopped. She picked herself up and started dusting off her hiking shorts and turquoise sneakers. *Why didn't she at least run?*

"Forget your damn shoes and move! That rock could still fall!" Skip yelled, now only a few yards away.

"What kind of guide takes someone to a place like this?" Winonna said, continuing to wipe and straighten her dusty clothes.

The boulder reversed momentum, rolling back to the edge. More gravel gave way, and the rock came crashing down the slope. Skip saw panic in her eyes as she realized she should have listened. She started to jump away, but the smoother soles of her New Balance's slipped again.

Skip was only a few feet away now, the boulder bouncing straight for them. There was a narrow ledge halfway down the slope that slowed the boulder's descent but launched it into the air. *The trajectory gave him an extra split second...*

He dove for Winonna, his hands sliding inside the unbuttoned, linen blouse covering her silky midriff. Like a linebacker tackling a running back, he wrapped his arms around her waist, and they were airborne. They landed a few feet farther up the path in a patch of sand, Winonna on her back, Skip on top. He felt the edge of the boulder brush the bottoms of his feet as it cascaded harmlessly into the river.

Kuul had held Lottie back, and Webster was scanning the ridge from where the boulder had crested.

"Honey - Honey are you okay?" Lottie asked. Kuul had let her loose and she was leaning over them. Neither of them had moved yet.

"I will be if this sex maniac quits groping me," Winonna moaned, starting to wiggle free.

Skip braced himself against the ground. "If you'd stop pushing me, I'd already be free." His hands slid in the sand, ending up on her chest. It was a softer landing than he'd expected. Thankfully, nothing popped.

"Sweetheart, he risked his life!" Lottie scolded, seeing neither one of them were hurt, except for a few scratches.

Kuul grabbed his floundering friend by the back of his collar and pulled him off the girl. Skips flailing hands were caught inside Winonna's blouse and she rose right with him.

"Let go of me! Even Scottie Eastwood didn't grab me like that!"

Skip extricated his arms and she fell on her butt. "Whoops!"

He bent over to pick up his Stetson lying next to her and dusted it against his jeans, ignoring Winonna's outstretched arm. "Let's gather at that little overlook ahead. There are natural stone benches we can rest on."

"Never mind helping me up, I've got it," Winonna carped, brushing aside the hand that Kuul had offered.

Webster had been humorously watching the guide and movie star's entanglement. "Are you all finished?" he chuckled. "That rock falling was a freaky coincidence - bad timing. The recent rain must have wallowed out the gravel."

Kuul nodded. "That's how canyons widen. Rocks aren't all the same composition. Different layers erode at different speeds, and rocks up high fall."

At the overlook, Kuul unloaded the backpack with their lunches. Zula and Sky had packed six paper bags with a sandwich, chips and a homemade snickerdoodle cookie. They each found a rock to sit on, except for Winonna, who was worried about it rolling down the hill.

Winonna frowned at the pastrami. "It doesn't look cooked."

"Here," Skip said, rolling up his bag and tossing it to her. "It's ham." He kept the cookie. She owed him that much.

. . .

"Cheyenne," Lilac called out.

Her friend had just finished lecturing the rafters on everything from how to roll a dry bag to bagging their own poops like they would their labradoodles. She'd been standing on the tailgate of a 4x4 Ford 250, like Patton ordering his troops to battle from the back of a Willys jeep.

Cheyenne waved her over. Unlike Patton, Cheyenne was tiny, not the picture most people had of a female river-rat, except for the sculpted shoulders beneath her long-sleeved Cataract Whitewater tee. Her unconditioned, dirt-blond hair was braided into pig tails that fell halfway down her back. She was wearing knee-high, wading boots and a straw hat with a rawhide band. A paisley patterned bandana looped loosely around her neck.

"Load the Voodoo IPA in my cooler!" she yelled at another guide.

"Not exactly roughing it," Lilac laughed.

"You ought to see the filets wrapped in bacon and glazed with dijon mustard"

"Looks like you'll be off soon."

"Another hour. Jeremy left three cases of Merlot at the lodge. I told him twice to make sure he had everything before checking out. I sent him back, but that wine's probably halfway to Kanab by now."

"Marble Canyon lodge is only five minutes?" Lilac said, questioning the time to run back.

"Marble was full. We were at Cliff Dwellers, another twenty minutes. It's okay though. It gave me time to reemphasize what's up ahead to our guests. They're a bunch of rookies now, but in another twenty-one days...well, you know how it is. Wait until they get walloped at Soap Creek Rapids and Sockdolager. This river breaks newbies in quick."

"They get their first impression here and think it'll be easy," Lilac chuckled. "This concrete ramp looks like the boat ramp back home at their favorite lake."

"Better scenery," Cheyenne said, shaking her head in agreement.

Colorado whitewater trips start at Lee's Ferry, river-mile zero in the national park. The canyon walls are less than five-hundred feet high just downstream; they rise to nearly six thousand farther on. Softer deposits of sandstone, limestone, and shale face rafters in the beginning, but farther on, the river cuts into ancient schist - walls of hard granite. Once committed, they have no way out, fated to ride their rubber-membrane rafts through the worst rapids imaginable.

"Just last week, another company flipped a raft at Soap Creek. The guide said the wave came out of nowhere. They had eight passengers on board and all of them ended up swimming through the drop. Last summer, a lady fell off and got her foot caught in a propeller."

"That's why I like oars," Lilac said.

"I've always said this first section is the most dangerous. Sockdolager is a bear. It has some of the worst whitewater and our passengers are still green," Cheyenne said, packing jars of pitted olives filled with spiced cream cheese. "What brings you down here? It's a long way from Sedona's spas."

Lilac smiled, accepting the good-natured ribbing. Sedona was anathema to hardcore, adventure junkies, especially the rafting cadre that loved the solitude and roughness of the isolated river. They were explorers at heart, same as Father Escalante who'd been the first European to pass through Lee's Ferry or Major Powell who'd been the first to boat the river a hundred years later. Both parties had camped by the hill above the launch ramp.

"Tagging along on a private tour. Interesting group, mother and daughter whose parents and grandparents were in the 56' United crash. The mother's also interested in Glen and Bessie Hyde, which is why we're down here. Skip's created an itinerary that roughly traces their stops from here to Diamond Creek."

"Skip huh?" Cheyenne said, looking sideways at Lilac. "Thought that was over?"

"It is. I'm just here to help smooth the whole mother-daughter dynamic, not his wheelhouse. The daughter's a piece of work. Hollywood type, so superficial on the surface, you never know what she's really thinking. I'm probably making matters worse. Big reason why I wandered over here."

"Had a few of those," Cheyenne empathized.

Lilac grabbed a handle on the beat-up, metal cooler Cheyenne had loaded in the back of her pickup. They carried it down the concrete ramp to a heavily laden raft with a motor on back. The supply boat would follow the rafters, sometimes motoring ahead near the end of the day to set up camp.

Cheyenne looked up the hill, shielding her eyes against the sun.

"Jeremy should be showing up soon, everything else is onboard. I'll say a prayer when we pass Chaur Butte, where your friends' parents crashed. Every now and then we still see a flash of metal in the sunlight, up high, when we float past - a belt buckle or piece of jewelry for all we know. Not all those bodies were recovered. Some parts scattered down the cliff face where they couldn't be reached."

"Really," Lilac said. She was amazed since it'd been sixty-five years. Probably the same reason so many ancient sites were found so well preserved – the dry, arid climate.

"Not every trip, but I've seen the reflections. Not much else they could be. Marble Canyon's a tragic stretch of river. Not just that crash, the rapids in there have claimed more than their share of lives, especially in the early days, when the Hydes passed through. You know that Glen almost bought it in there? They say what happened there changed the whole tenor of their trip. Emery Kolb always said that Sockdolager Rapid badly spooked Bessie. You have to work as a team to get through. The stress of fighting all that power, outside your control, tests the best of us."

"You'll handle it," Lilac said.

"Better than the boys," Cheyenne laughed, spying Jeremy coming around the hill. "Well, I'm about to get real busy. Next time you're in Page let's do a girls night."

"Have a safe trip. Skip said good luck."

"It ain't luck."

• • •

The overlook where Skip's group picnicked was a bald spot where the Spencer trail branched off to an old mining site. The rusty relic Winonna had seen was a boiler that pumped water through hoses with high-pressure nozzles. Blasting the soft shale, miners sluiced the residue down a flume to an amalgamator by the river to separate any gold. Skip pointed to another rusting artifact submerged beside the bank.

"That's the smokestack from a paddle wheeler they built to carry coal from upstream to fire their boiler. Good plan, except the paddle wheeler ate most of the coal before they reached Lee's Ferry. Mining here didn't last long, not like the ferry operation or ranching."

He opened his bag of chips. *Barbecue. Sky knew what he liked.*

"That sandy area near the next bend, past the large rock with the flat face, that's where the ferry crossed. You can still see part of the cable on the other side. There's a stone ruin past that rock where passengers rested after crossing and waited for the ferry. Some of them carved their names in that flat face."

"We're not walking all that way, are we?" Winonna interrupted.

"It's only a quarter-mile, but I think we'll head back from here."

"Good. I'm looking forward to a hot bath and soaking my bruises," Winonna said, smiling for a change. *She was rethinking Skip - for big hands he had a light touch. She knew better than to accept his checking her girls out was totally innocent. Maybe the tub could fit two.*

"Sorry, just showers and we're under water conservation orders."

Lottie was staring downstream toward the launch, ignoring her food. "Is this where United staged the recovery after the accident? I know it was along the river, on a delta below the site. It was near where another river flowed in."

Winonna put her arm around her mother's back, pulling her closer. She knew what her mom was thinking – *they were still likely up there on the mountain.* This close to the actual site, the past seemed real, emotions more intensely felt.

"Mom, why don't you try eating something?"

"That site isn't easy to get to," said Kuul. "It's farther down-stream, near where the Little Colorado joins in."

"Oh," was all Lottie said, nibbling on the cookie her daughter had given her.

"This is a spot where Glen and Bessie Hyde stopped. They spent the night. The first newspaper report of their trip was from here," Skip said, hoping to lighten things up.

"The Coconino Sun, a Flagstaff paper. The reporter called their scow a flat boat. Glen didn't like that," Lottie said, wistfully.

She had researched their story. "Right. The Johnson's, who were running the ferry, and a handful of people at Grand Canyon Village and Hermit's Camp, met them during their trip. The records we have come from those stops and Bessie's journal, which has been lost."

"Buck Lowery and Adolph Sutro too," Lottie said, correcting Skip.

"Lowery was really part of the Lee's Ferry crowd," Kuul chimed in. "He was living down here then and made the ferry cross-ing twice a day to his trading post on the east side. Once the bridge was finished, he built Marble Lodge and a new trading post on this side."

"They met Sutro at the end of their Village stop," Skip added. "He was down at Phantom Ranch, on the river. I planned to talk about his role tomorrow...you have a good grasp of their story."

Lottie nodded. "I've always been interested by the parallels between my parents and the Hydes, both having been lost in the canyon. Both young, in their twenties."

"They're both part of canyon folklore," Skip said, hesitantly, not wanting to seem insensitive. *Where are the boundaries?* He glanced at Winonna for guidance and got a coy smile and wink in return. *Best to stick with the Hydes for now.* "They both wrote let-ters from here. Glen to his dad, Rollin, who was waiting for them in California, and Bessie to her mom, back east. She wanted to reassure her family that they were okay and update her younger brother, William - they were close."

"He went by Bill," Lottie smiled. "They both liked jazz, but it drove their father crazy. He talked her into cutting her curls and going with the new flapper hairstyle."

"And Bill later claimed that Bessie's first husband, Earl Helmick, told him that after she'd gone west, he'd sent her money for an operation. That she'd been pregnant when she left," Skip said. It wasn't just the river trip that made the Hyde's good storytelling fodder.

"Bill was never sure Earl told the truth," Lottie quickly added. "He was cuckolded, after all, and her leaving had hurt his pride. He would never talk about Bessie, not even after they were lost in the river. Years later, he'd still refuse interviews."

Skip chuckled at *cuckolded* - not a word heard very often. But back then, the term was a common, socially embarrassing description for a cheated-on husband. Lottie had a pretty good handle on Bessie's brief, but wild life.

Webster had been following the back-and-forth conversation, studying Lottie's gestures for any ticks or tells. She knew her story; that much was for sure. The sadness about her parents had seemed genuine. She'd pay to keep her daughter out of trouble when the time came. "Sounds like Bessie got around. Maybe old Earl Helmick wasn't the only one who took their secrets to the grave?" he said, stroking his unruly eyebrow.

Skip checked his watch, "We still have to hike back and stop at Navajo Bridge, then drive to our hotel in Cameron. The bridge is on the way; a few minutes to walk across and look for condors, then we'll get on the road again."

"Oh, don't worry, I have some in my purse," Winonna said, without thinking.

21

FOUL BIRDS

THE BLACK BIRDS SOARING OVERHEAD WERE THE UGLIEST animals Hyde Donald had ever seen - uglier than his wheezing, sick grandfather after a coughing spell. The old man had been a feisty shit-kicker before time caught him, though he'd been a scavenger, just like these red-headed vultures searching for their next meal.

Hyde could remember when he was five and the old man was seventy. Austin Donald hadn't seemed weak then, just mean. There'd been lots of visitors to their cheap apartment in Vegas. Scary visitors, but not because of anything they'd done; they knew better than to bother Donald's grandson. It had been the visitors' sunken eyes, bowed heads, dirty fingernails, and filthy clothes that scared him. Each one had begged for a bag of candy.

He'd hidden in his room the first time he'd watched the old man beat one of the dirty strangers. His grandfather hadn't just beaten him; he'd made Earl hold the dazed kid down after he'd collapsed. The boy had struggled to get up, but he had kept kicking him with his steel-tipped, alligator-skin boots until blood puddled on the carpet. The old man had dragged him to the front door by his belt and kicked him until the stranger tumbled off the stoop. The half-dead kid had lain outside Hyde's window, in a forsythia bush, bleeding and whimpering for help.

He could still hear the addict moaning when he closed his eyes. The old man had taught him to always hit harder than necessary. It was important to not get pushed around. *"Sometimes, people have to be encouraged to do the right thing,"* his grandfather had laughed. When Hyde turned fifteen, the old man was getting sick, and because Earl wasn't around as much, he began using Hyde to do his *encouraging*.

He gazed across the yellow hood of the rented Wrangler. The color reminded him of the forsythia from his childhood. There was even a bright red pinstripe down the side. Earl had bitched when he saw it; *"Why not just wear a fucking sign too?"* That was the problem with Earl; he preferred sneaking around, doing his dirty work in the dark, and then only as a last resort. That's why the old man didn't trust him. His uncle thought too much and acted too little.

He was sick of Earl making all the decisions. If the old man had taught him anything, other than to toe the line, it was to make up his own mind. Don't let anyone else order you around.

Fucking Earl. His uncle had called him stupid for renting the jeep. He'd even called him dumb, dumber than his father. He'd show him. Hyde was working for the old man anyway, not his scheming, slippery uncle. When Earl had said the Chandler girl was balking at the old man's plan, Hyde had taken it upon himself to 'encourage' her a bit. He was bored and could use a little fun.

They'd gone back and forth over how badly to scare her. Earl had grabbed his shirt and slapped him when he'd suggested rape. They'd stood toe-to-toe cursing each other before Earl had mockingly straightened his shirt, patted his shoulder, and promised his amorous nephew - 'Later, Romeo. For now, just scare her enough so she understands how serious we are.'

Hyde smiled as the van with his uncle and the pretty movie-star parked near the old Navajo Bridge. He'd been watching tourists come and go. The first thing they all did was walk across the bridge.

• • •

"You see it?" Skip said, whispering to Lilac.

"You think it's the same jeep?"

"Maybe, but there are a lot of yellow Wranglers in Arizona, not to mention from colorful California. I didn't notice the red stripe at Wupatki, but I wasn't really looking."

"Let's keep an eye on it. I can't see through the tinted windows. I'd like to go yank the door open to see who's in there, but it'd probably be an old couple day-tripping from Sedona."

Skip nodded. He was a little jumpy after the rockslide. Leaving Wupatki that morning, Lilac had pointed out a bright, yellow jeep with extra-big wheels and overhead spotlights parked in a handi-cap spot. She'd said it was the kind of idiot car the whistling man who'd spied on them would drive. He wasn't sure about the man spying, but it sure looked like the same vehicle.

The Chandlers and Webster had gathered outside the van. Webster was casually scanning the lot. "This is a short stop. There's not much to do here other than walk the pedestrian bridge," Skip said. "Kuul has a legend he'll share. It's best told while we're sur-rounded by the elements."

"Sky - Water - Earth," Kuul added, using his hands to point above, below, and to make a wide circle. "Afterwards, you can visit the gift shop. Sound good?"

Winonna thought Kuul's gestures were like a Burbank traffic cop's. She didn't much care to hear another story and made up her mind to not go far onto the bridge. It was the same old rocks anyway. If the red head went across, she'd beat her back and scoop the passenger seat next to the guide.

"Keep your eyes open for condors," Kuul said, looking high above the bridge.

Skip scanned the parking lot as they left – *no movement from the jeep*. The only other vehicles were a minivan, a small Winnebago, and a pickup missing its left fender that had seen better days. An older couple were the only other people on the pedestrian bridge. Skip guessed the Winnebago belonged to them and the pickup to whoever was working the shop counter. That left the yellow jeep and the minivan...*probably in buying souvenirs*.

Navajo Bridge was a scene straight from a John Ford western. Echo and Vermilion Cliffs loomed in the near distance, their plateau tops setting the horizon. Orange and red rock striations glowed in the late afternoon light. Deep side canyons disappeared into black shadows. Far below the bridge, the greenish Colorado River snaked between sheer walls of sandstone. A perfect reflection of the blue sky and canyon walls was painted on the water. Only the twin, single-span, metal bridges were forged by man.

"Built in 1928, it was the highest, steel-arch-construction bridge in the world," Skip said. "It's over eight-hundred feet long and a little less than five-hundred feet to the river. This roadbed is eighteen feet wide."

Two bridges, an old one and a new one, paralleled each other, roughly two-hundred feet apart. Crosshatched steel beams connected the roadway substructures to huge supporting arches. The railings were chest-high and constructed of smaller angle-beams with metal bands crossed at forty-five-degree angles in place of balusters. The metal bands threw checkered shadows over the road surface.

"How many steel-arch-construction bridges were there in 1928?" Webster cheekily asked.

"Good question," Skip said, laughing. He had no idea and shrugged. "I can tell you it only cost $390,000. Can you imagine that? That would, maybe, do a block of sidewalk today."

"Public infrastructure is expensive," Kuul quipped.

Skip pointed to two long gashes in the canyon wall below the new bridge across from them, "They blasted ledges to set the buttresses on. Most of the rock was captured in nets and transported away instead of being permitted to fall into the river. The new bridge opened in 1995 and was built to match. Standing here and leaning over, you can see both designs. They look the same, but the new one has a third more steel for heavier loads and has bolts instead of rivets, but otherwise..."

"Condor!" Lilac called out. They all looked up to see a huge, black bird floating above them. White stripes decorated its underbody. Long wing and shorter tail feathers were outlined by the cerulean-blue sky - a majestic creature in a majestic setting.

"He ties the earth to the heavens," Kuul said, bowing in respect. "The Mapuche in Chile believe the condor is the King of birds; that it symbolizes the four elements: earth, wind, fire, rain; that it embodies the virtues of wisdom and justice."

"That's a lot to carry on your shoulders," Webster joked.

"It's a big, ugly bird," chirped Winonna. "And I've seen prettier bridges."

"There is an ancient prophecy about the return of the condors," Kuul began. "The Aztec, Maya, and Inca all have similar legends about the journeys of condors and eagles. Long ago, human societies split into two paths, the paths of the eagle and the condor. The path of the condor is the way of the heart and intuition; that path is feminine. The path of the eagle is the way of the mind and industry; that path is masculine. Mapuche prophecy stated that over a five-hundred-year period, beginning around 1400, the Eagle People would become so powerful they would drive the Condor People to near extinction. But the condor would survive and return to fly in the same skies as the eagle, their two paths reuniting, creating a new, higher level of consciousness for humanity."

"Condors nearly became extinct in the Americas," Skip continued. "By the 1980's there were only twenty-two left in the world. Conservationists joined worldwide to capture, protect, and breed them in captivity to ensure the species survived. In the 1990's they were released back into the wild, some not far from here, deep inside the Vermilion Cliffs. Today, over three-hundred live in the wild; about a third of those are here in the southwest."

"Eagles have always been here," Lilac said, helping the boys with their story.

Kuul smiled, "Some cultures in the Americas believed the quetzal bird and the snake spirit joined, like in the prophecy. To the Aztec, Quetzalcoatl is a flying, feathered serpent that is the child of the reunited condor and eagle, the joining of what they both represent, and of the feminine and masculine. All the major Mesoamerican cultures worship a similar deity. Today, the legend represents adaptation of our ancient traditions to modern, technological advances. My Mayan ancestors called Quetzalcoatl - Kukulkan."

"Well, Kukuman, I think I'll wait back on land while you eagles and condors go on across the bridge," Winonna said.

"Kuul, doesn't the legend correspond with the arrival of the Spanish and their conquering Central and South America?" Lottie asked, frowning at her daughter as she left. "And five-hundred years roughly covers the growth of western civilization and the industrial revolution."

"The phoenix is kind of the same thing," Webster guessed.

Kuul and Skip both shrugged. "You can only project so far," Skip said. "Why don't you and Lottie enjoy the views on your own from here. Halfway is a great spot for pictures and to study the architecture."

After snapping pictures of Lottie with the gorgeous backdrop, Skip and Lilac decided to walk to the other side, leaving the others wandering back and forth across the roadway, looking down at the river and up at the mountains. The late afternoon air was pleasant, and no one seemed in a hurry to leave. A Navajo truck driver had parked his rig by a historical marker at the far end of the bridge. He was lining up a picture of his shiny, new, double-stacked truck with the bridges and cliffs in the background. Skip thought he might like a shot standing with his baby. They were nearly across, and he raised his hand to call out to the driver. But before he could call, screaming erupted from back on the bridge.

"Skip!" Lilac yelled, staring back over his shoulder.

Skip turned in time to see a man wearing a dumbass cowboy hat toss a squirming, screaming Winonna over the bridge railing. The man looked over the railing then bolted toward the parking lot. Another man, Barry Hufflefinger, Luke's dad, was running toward the site. They'd driven down from Page. "STOP!" Hufflefinger was yelling but froze in his tracks when Winonna disappeared. Cowboy Hat was charging straight at Hufflefinger now, the only way to get to his car.

Webster was sprinting from the center of the bridge back to where Winonna had gone over. Kuul wasn't far behind. Lottie had collapsed to her knees. She'd lost her parents not far downstream and now her only child. Her primal scream shattered the tranquil backdrop.

"*NOT HER TOO! PLEASE* God, not her too!"

22

NAVAJO BRIDGE

SHOULDER LOWERED, COWBOY HAT PLOWED INTO BARRY Hufflefinger, bowling him over like a sixteen-pound ball slamming the ten pin. Luke was running toward his dad from the gift shop, "Dad!" Hufflefinger jumped up, looking behind him as the man ran toward a yellow jeep. Recovered, he and Luke sprinted toward where the woman had been. A thin man with a goatee and bushy eyebrows was running toward the same spot. Skip and Kuul, who he recognized, were farther back.

Skip raced back across the bridge, knowing Hufflefinger and Webster would reach the spot first. Lilac was already ahead of him and stopped when she reached Lottie, who was holding her head, crying and screaming hysterically.

"SAVE HER! YOU HAVE TO SAVE HER!" the older woman shrieked as Skip ran past.

Lilac tried to calm the shattered woman. There wasn't much

chance of her daughter having survived the fall. Deep down, Lottie probably knew Winonna was dead. Skip slowed.

"GO!" he heard Lottie yell.

He was still several hundred feet from where Winonna had fallen. A sick joke inappropriately ran through his mind: he hadn't lost anyone yet on a tour. He told it to most of his customers after they inevitably asked if he'd ever left anyone behind. This was no joke.

Kuul was doing his best, but he wasn't the fleetest of foot and Skip flew by him like a Mazarati passing a Sherman tank. "She was still screaming until a second ago," his friend gasped.

"Winonna?"

"Yeah...you probably...couldn't hear her...because of the wind."

"I think I can hear her," Lilac said from behind. She'd caught up.

One hundred feet. Closing. Webster and Hufflefinger were leaning over the railing, yelling below. Webster began climbing over. *Shit,* Skip said to himself, *I might lose another one.*

"DON'T!" he yelled. Webster glanced his way and ignored him.

Luke was coming from the opposite direction, about the same distance from the spot as Skip.

Lilac beat them both there. She took a quick look and kept sprinting toward the parking lot. Cowboy Hat had stopped by his jeep to catch his breath. When he saw her coming, he realized she was after him. He jumped inside, firing up the engine.

She pulled her Glock 19 from the shoulder holster hidden inside her vest. She aimed at the front tire, just below the gaudy, sunflower paint and pulled the trigger twice. The first shot missed the tire, hitting the fender behind it. She was still breathing heavily from the run. The jeep rolled just enough, that the second bullet, arriving a millisecond later, shattered the passenger side window. The sharp booms echoed in the cliffs. The jeep accelerated and spun as her third and fourth shot took out the brake light above the spare tire and pinged off the rim. The jeep skidded around the stone entry sign onto 89a, and she watched it speed across the new bridge, out of range.

When Skip reached the railing, Webster was on the outside and hanging below the roadway. He had an arm locked through a diamond-shaped hole created by the metal bands. Hufflefinger had also climbed over, the toe of one sneaker in another cross brace and his armpit squeezed tight across the railing.

"Don't Luke, get down," Hufflefinger said. His son was leaning across the top, his stomach balanced on the railing, both feet off the road. "Run and get the bungees from the car. Now!"

Skip grabbed Luke and set him back on the pavement. The boy raced back toward their minivan. Skip leaned way over and saw Winonna, her arms and legs wrapped around a beam below the railing and angled back under the roadway. Webster had gotten a toe on it, but not solidly enough to support his weight and still hang on to the metal band. Little separated both of them from a five-hundred-foot drop into the Colorado.

"Grab my foot," Webster was saying. He had stretched his free hand toward Winonna as far as he could but was still short. The only way to get to her was to let go and slide down the beam like a firepole. Then the problem would be getting back up.

"I can't let go," Winonna wailed.

Hufflefinger started to climb farther down. Skip stopped him. "Get back here. We'll need your and Luke's help from up top when we get her loose!" Hufflefinger nodded and climbed back over the railing.

Skip swung over the railing, taking Hufflefinger's place above Webster, who was a few feet lower, his head just below Skip's knee. "Have you got her!" he yelled. He couldn't see Winonna from his new angle but could hear her crying. At least she hadn't fallen - yet!

"I can't convince her to let go and grab my hand. She's too far under to reach."

Skip climbed down until he was beside Webster and could see the panicked movie star, like Faye Wray clinging to the Empire State Building. "Climb back up but stay on this side of the railing. Get a better foothold." The man's toe had slipped off the post twice in the few seconds since Skip had arrived, each time leaving him dangling in the air. "I can get her, but I'll need your help."

"How?" Webster asked, wanting to understand the plan. If the girl died now the trip would end. Hyde's stunt might have just spoiled things.

"I'm going down there."

Kuul was up top with the Hufflefingers. "Kemo, is she okay?"

"Kuul, hook a belt on Webster. I don't want to lose him too. I plan to pass the girl up and he'll need both hands if I do."

"Here," he heard Hufflefinger say. Luke had raced back with a handful of thick bungees. Hufflefinger passed the strongest to Kuul.

Webster took Skip's hand and climbed up. Skip locked his fingers on a metal band level with his thigh and stepped down into thin air. His toe barely touched the beam that Winonna was clinging to. Seamlessly, he transferred his weight while finding the beam with his other foot. He released his right hand and dropped his shoulder until he was able to grasp an angle bar below the bridge. The only thing keeping him balanced was his tenuous hold on the metal band, now well above his head. To get to Winonna he had to get lower, since she wasn't moving.

He settled his footing, slid his left hand down across the metal bands, and let go to grab the angle bar. The hold with his right hand kept him from falling. He ducked below the bottom of the roadbed. There was a steel bar running underneath that crossed the width of the bridge. Holding onto the bar, he was able to inch his feet along the angle beam.

There was Winonna, not more than four feet away. She must have grabbed a post as she fell, and her momentum swung her under the bridge. She was belly down on the angle beam, the rocks and river her next stop if she let go.

"Look at me," Skip said. She shook her head. Her eyes were closed, and she was shaking. *"LOOK AT ME!"*

Winonna opened her eyes and quickly shut them.

"You need to slide toward me so I can get you. Can you do that?"

She opened her eyes again and Skip saw only terror. It was up to him to go get her. Even though it wasn't far, he'd have to let go of the bar and lie down like her to stay below the frame. He was figuring where best to put his hands when she started inching toward him, eyes closed.

"A little farther...almost there...gotch you!" He let go with one hand and grasped a handful of shirt between her shoulders. He found the back of her bra and held it tightly. "Keep coming...that's it..." She finally opened her eyes and grabbed his ankle.

"I'm going to inch my way to the end of this beam. It's only a few feet. You keep coming with me. I won't let go."

"Don't let me fall!"

"I won't. I promise."

Skip shuffled backward, slightly bent over, along the narrow beam. Holding on with only one hand, he had to go slow. "Okay, you're doing great. When I reach the end of the beam, I'll have to let go of you to stand. Don't let go of me." They reached the end of the beam and he leaned out past the post that angled up to the bottom of the railing. Winonna had a death grip but kept moving with him.

"Grab my hand," Webster shouted from above.

Skip reached and missed, but Webster grasped his shoulder. He had two bungees wrapped around him. Kuul, leaning over the top of the railing, had looped Barry Hufflefinger's belt through the straps and was making sure he couldn't fall.

"Winonna, grab my hand," Skip said, holding the post with one hand and reaching the other down to her. He could see she was too petrified to let go of his ankle.

"*GRAB MY HAND!* It's the only way. When you do, unclench your legs and I'll pull you up. Try to get your feet on the beam and stand beside me."

Winonna cautiously extended her hand, pulling it back twice. The third time, Skip grasped the underside of her wrist, before she could change her mind. "Grip my wrist!" She did and he swiftly pulled her upward.

With her other hand flapping in the air, Winonna grabbed for any part of Skip she could find. Her fingers found his belt, just as her feet slipped from beneath her. She swung off the beam, screaming hysterically. Skip was dangling her over the river.

Trying to hold her as she frantically tugged on his belt was making him lose his grip on the post. He couldn't hold her dead weight for more than a few seconds.

"Webster!"

"I've got you," Skip heard Kuul call out to Webster.

Webster grabbed his shoulders with both hands. The man had to be leaning forty-five-degrees out from the railing, held only by the springy bungees. Skip grunted and raised Winonna, while Webster kept him straight. He got his other arm around her waist, drawing her against him. Kuul pulled Webster back against the railing.

Winonna was hugging his chest with her legs wrapped around his hips. Her eyes were closed again. "I need you to reach and grab Webster's hand," Skip said. She opened her dazed eyes, squeezed him even tighter, and buried her face in his neck. "Get ready, I'm going to lift you." She raised her arms to around his neck. Her eyes opened and they were pleading with him. "I won't let you fall," he said.

"No, you won't," she answered, kissing him quickly.

"On three," Skip said. "*THREE!*" He raised her like a ballerina. Webster reached down and got her under an arm. Skip slid a hand under her rear and lifted. Webster pulled until she was holding him around his waist; her legs around Skip's face and hanging over his shoulders.

Barry Hufflefinger leaned over the railing as Webster lifted her to him. Luke braced his feet against the bottom of the railing as he held the back of his dad's beltless pants. Skip pushed her feet. Winona was able to get toeholds in the metal bands below the handrail as they pushed and pulled her over the top.

"You good?" Webster called down to Skip.

"I'm fine, get back onto the bridge."

By the time he scrambled up and over the railing, Winonna was crying in her mother's arms. Kuul was exchanging high-fives with Barry Hufflefinger and young Luke. Webster was sitting with his back against the railing, the bungees beside his outstretched legs. Lilac helped Skip down. His legs began cramping.

"You okay?" Lilac said, her eyes full of relief.

Skip nodded. She hugged him tightly. The tension in his body slowly released and he thought he might collapse, but she wasn't letting go.

"Don't do that again!" she finally said.

Winonna had partially recovered; nothing was broken or too badly bruised. But she was emotional – she'd cheated death. Seeing her savior's release, she ran to him, folding herself back in his arms. She kissed him again before he could stop her, this time longer with her lips slightly spread. Skip didn't know what to do or how to feel. In a strange way, they were bonded now. All he knew was he was happy they'd survived. As a reflex, he held her, patting her hair, as she nuzzled her head on his shoulder.

Lilac stalked off.

Kuul grinned at Luke, who had winked at him. "You'll learn soon enough. We can't live with them, and we can't live without them," he said, tousling the boy's hair.

• • •

"Did you get a good look at him?" Skip asked Lilac, fifteen minutes later.

"Same guy I saw at Wupatki. I guess I was wrong about Webster, the way *he* saved both of you. The risks he took surprised me."

"Pretty brave," Skip agreed.

"Marilyn Monroe should have kissed him."

Skip had thanked Barry Hufflefinger, recounting his heroism in front of his family. Luke had been beaming, seeing his father in a whole new light. They'd driven a big loop through Southern Utah after their Diamond Creek adventure and were onto Grand Canyon Village for the last few days of their trip. Lottie had been so grateful she'd insisted they meet in the park. Luke accepted her offer before his parents answered, excited to hook up again with his river buddy.

The ranger from the visitor center had heard the screaming and made them fill out an incident form. Winonna had been vague about the encounter and wasn't even sure she'd been intentionally pushed. The ranger wrote down Lilac's description, but she hadn't been that close to the man. Since everyone was okay, there wasn't much he could do except report the attack to the state and Navajo police, who would be hours arriving if he called. No one cared to wait that long.

Skip and Lilac were at an overlook between the two bridges. The others were resting on a picnic table beside the restrooms. They'd all agreed to take a few minutes to chill before leaving.

"From here, it looks impossible and incredibly stupid to climb down there," Lilac said. "It was dumb luck that she landed on a beam and didn't fall."

"Hopefully she'll stop wandering off," Skip said, looking across to the site. He'd been part of many daring rescues and extractions in his past life, but none that crazy.

"They might cancel."

"I don't think Lottie's a quitter, and this isn't a vacation for them. They're coming to terms with her family's past."

A shadow swept over them, moving stealthily over the canyon. Another condor was coasting on the late-afternoon thermals guarding its domain. It flew high above the river; a powerful, proud animal. The condor circled tightly and then swooped toward a dark spot on a ledge. It began picking at something.

"It could have been scavenging a broken, female carcass by the river," Skip said.

"She'd have made it sick."

23

BESSIE AND GLEN

November 9-13, 1928

"**I** DIDN'T SEE IT IN THE SHADOWS. WE WHACKED IT PRETTY good," Glen said, examining the bow of Rain-in-the-Face. "I shouldn't have run Badger Rapid that late."

After leaving Navajo Bridge, they were committed to Marble Canyon. It signaled the beginning of the Grand Canyon with over sixty miles of the worst whitewater. Glen knew from corresponding with Emery Kolb that he considered it impossible to run. In their 1911 trip, Ellsworth, Emery's brother, had twice tried running Soap Creek Rapid, which still lay ahead of Glen and Bessie. Once in his boat and once in Emery's, both times the powerful waves flipped the boats in the air, tossing Ellsworth into the deadly froth. Kolb had said he would have drowned if he hadn't been a strong swimmer and wearing a life jacket. The brothers ended up portaging and lining their way through Marble.

"Anything we need to fix?" Bessie asked.

By now, she knew there probably wouldn't be. Last night they had plowed into a group of rocks, getting hung up until Glen could pry them loose. The scow was a sound ship, and they'd been bouncing off boulders all along the way. None of them, so far, had done much damage to the scow's thick, waterlogged shell. The sweep oars, on the other hand, constantly needed repairs. They were solid, but not as sturdy as the body. Rain-in-the-Face would get them through Marble, she was sure of it.

"We're good. We should pick up time through Marble - make Grand Canyon Village in a week or less. Can't wait to tell Emery Kolb how we ran them all."

Marble Canyon was a treacherous stretch of whitewater between Lee's Ferry and the confluence with the Little Colorado River. In the lower half it narrowed and deepened into an eerie world of spectacular spires and jagged walls. The rim disappeared high above as the river cut deep into the black inner-gorge. In a matter of miles, the red walls rose over a thousand feet, leaving anyone on the river mentally as well as physically disconnected from life above. Bessie realized they were truly on their own here.

With few breaks, they ran rapid after rapid. The work had been hard, and she'd convinced Glen to pull over twice to bail and record their progress and the dangerous conditions with their new camera. She'd given Glen the camera and then scampered over slippery, cow-sized rocks to a boulder nearly surrounded by crashing whitewater. She imagined her perilous pose on a big screen in a Vaudeville theater, the crowd *oohing* and *aahing*. Price Johnson had been right, there was no way out of here; both banks were piles of impassable rubble at the base of unclimbable cliffs.

Soap Creek Rapids hadn't been the killer Kolb had warned them about. She'd been scared, sure. There were deep drops and few clear chutes to pass through. Plumes of angry whitewater had roared all around them. But Glen had stood tall on the platform and spotted a passable channel down the right side. He'd slid the scow through it like the expert Austrian bobsledders she'd seen in a moving-picture reel.

Soap Creek had just been the beginning. They spent two days and another morning battling the river's fury. It had thrown everything at them, but they were unscathed.

"Look up ahead, Bess!" Glen yelled. "The water's changing color, we're almost to the Little Colorado. We're through Marble Canyon!"

The river was calmer now, its brown color turning bluer. Rain-in-the-Face was floating peacefully, a few small riffles here and there. Sandbars had formed in the river bends. Grayish Tapeats limestone and green bright angel shale sloped gracefully down to the confluence. The never-ending red wall of sandstone still towered overhead.

"This part's not as fanciful as Cataract, but it's more majestic, so wide and high." Bessie commented. She lazily worked the sweep back and forth. They rounded a bend with a gravel bar and... "My God, it's beautiful! The Little Colorado water is so bright, almost luminescent. It's like He created a new color of paint, mixing the royal-blue sky with emerald-green grass, and then poured it into this ugly brown soup of the Colorado."

"Help me keep us to the right. It won't be too hard; the current's taking us that way. That crescent-shaped, sand bar where the Little Colorado enters looks like an island. See how the turquoise water goes around both sides before disappearing into this mud? Look ahead, how the walls keep rising. The east and west rims have to be miles apart. I've read they're as far as eighteen miles in some sections. The river looks straighter too, at least this next...Bess! Look at the mouth of that side canyon! They're staring at us!"

Two big horn sheep, a ram with huge, curled horns and a female ewe, stood not two-hundred feet away. The ram was warily watching them pass; the smaller female was scavenging in the grass. Typical, the woman doing all the work, Bessie thought, making a face at the stoic ram.

As beautiful as the scenery was, Rain-in-the-Face didn't slow down. In minutes, the tributary river was well behind them. Glen had been right about the canyon walls rising, but he'd been wrong about the Colorado's speed. It was running faster, and, in the distance, the inner gorge pinched back in. The rapids weren't bad yet, compared to Marble, but the wind was increasing, blowing into their faces. Their headway slowed considerably. Bessie's spirits fell as dark clouds began forming again. It'd be another miserable night.

Luckily, the canyon abruptly widened after they passed a series of riffles. They coasted into Furnace Flats, where Glen had promised they'd camp. The Flats was a unique feature in the Grand Canyon, a four-mile-wide valley with sandy, pebbled deltas lining the river. Lower sandstone bluffs flanked its perimeter. It was one of the few places where climbing to the rim was possible. The ancients had farmed the fertile, irrigated soil. Anasazi ruins were everywhere, tucked into ledges above the river and at the base of cliffs. Few white men had ever explored this deep in the canyon.

Glen steered the scow toward a small creek, studying the sky. The wind was picking up; feathery tamarisk and willow trees were doubling over in their fight. "We'll camp here. I'd go on, but we're not getting anywhere. The tarp's leaking, but it's the best we have."

They secured Rain-in-the-Face, set up camp, and hauled in the mattress. "How about ham, eggs, squash, and doe dads for dinner?" Bessie asked. She was starving. "We can stock up again in a few days at Grand Canyon Village."

Glen nodded. "I hope it doesn't rain, but hope don't pay a bill."

"When it does, it'll at least wet this dry sand that's blasting us. It's coated everything. This wind's the devil himself."

"If it's still blowing tomorrow, I may try rowing. It's worse here in the Flats, too open. We get out of here tomorrow and away from this valley, it'll be better."

Bessie thought about how steep-sided the inner gorge had been. Maybe Glen was wrong; *wouldn't the wider Flats disperse the wind?*

Dinner was quick and they spent the night huddled under the dripping tarp. Glen had fallen asleep fast and snored all night. She had punched his shoulder twice, but he'd just rolled over and started in again. By morning, the rain had stopped, but the wind was blowing even harder. Bessie fried more eggs and some spuds she'd sliced. If nothing else, they were eating well.

Everything in Rain-in-the-Face was coated with wet sand. They wiped what they could, but gusts of wind quickly deposited a new layer of grime. Downstream, they could see the spray from small riffles blowing back toward them.

"Let's give it a shot. I don't want to lose any more time," Glen said.

Bessie covered their supplies and then steadied Rain-in-the-Face as Glen shoved them off. At first, they fought against being blown back upstream. After a few minutes, she knew it was useless. Her moving the heavy, eight-foot oars through the wind was impossible. Glen, cursing their bad luck, took over both sweeps and managed to get them out into the main current. The scow was no longer being blown upstream but going downstream wasn't happening either. The gusts were too strong. Glen turned the long, heavy scow sideways and tried using the sweeps as oars, like a rowboat. Bessie knew that was just exposing more of the long scow to the wind, but she stayed quiet. They covered maybe a hundred yards, with Glen working harder than she'd ever seen him on the farm.

"We'll have to wait it out," he eventually said, giving up and heading ashore. The disgust on his face was clear.

"At least there's no more rain."

Glen gave her a sharp look and jumped into knee-deep water, dragging them onto another beach. Bessie hauled a few things across the sand and started setting up another camp. Glen grabbed his Winchester.

"I'll see what I can find," he grumbled.

Bessie understood he wasn't angry at her, just disappointed at losing another day. Wind and rain were frustrating to a man used to controlling his surroundings and bending nature to his will. To sit here twiddling his thumbs wasn't his way.

The next morning, the gusty gale had eased to a pleasant breeze. They shoved off, thinking that by nightfall, they'd be camped at Bright Angel Creek below the Grand Canyon Village. Glen had awoken in a far better mood and announced they had to be close, and that they were through the worst water, nothing ahead but smooth sailing.

A foreboding feeling swept over Bessie. Gloomy, granite walls hemmed in the river, not the soft sandstone and shale they'd gotten used to. This was the brooding, ancient schist, its black wall rising higher the farther they went, the river channeling its rushing water into ever tighter passageways. It seemed almost alive and evil, pulling them down into a dark underworld; a dark world where Hades ruled and decided fates.

Sockdolager Rapid was named by John Wesley Powell, the 1869 river explorer. The term was American slang for a knockout punch. The few who'd experienced it joked the root of the word was *doxology* – a hymn or praise to God - as in, *God, get me out of this mess.* Sockdolager didn't take prisoners. It accepted sacrifices.

"Glen, it's a brute!" Bessie screamed, seeing the first, huge waves.

The entire river rose in a single, crushing tsunami. Sadistic federations of boulders and deep drops were everywhere. And if Rain-in-the-Face didn't stay the course, into the mayhem, they'd be smashed against the granite walls. But to attempt navigating through the waves and rocks seemed suicidal.

The choice was made for them. The scow flew over the first wave, crashing down the backside into a deep hole. Tail and lateral waves drenched them from all sides, pouring over and into the bottom. Bessie somehow managed to stay crouched on the platform. Glen stood as they started rising again, climbing the next wave. He readjusted his grip on his sweep. Rain-in-the-Face slammed into the side of a boulder, bouncing and aligning them to be broadsided by a monstrous wave.

Bessie watched in horror as Glen's hand slipped off the handle and the end of the oar whiplashed out of the whitewater. The free-wheeling handle cracked him beneath the chin, like a Jack Dempsey uppercut, and he flew feet first out of the scow into the churning foam. It all happened in a split second. Bessie screamed as he vanished below the surface. She desperately wanted to reach for him but was afraid of losing her sweep.

Her mind was spinning. From nowhere, two hands appeared, grasping the lip of the scow, and she saw the top of Glen's hat as he tried pulling himself up the side. Then they crashed, spinning out of control, into another beastly wall of water. The hands and hat disappeared in the mist.

Bessie cried out as Glen went under again, *"GLEN! GLEN!"* Rain-in-the-Face continued hurtling downstream through the waves and spray.

Glen didn't come up.

24

CAMERON TRADING POST

A HAIRY WRIST WEARING A LAVA-BEAD BRACELET ROSE FROM beneath the table, beside Winonna.

"She dropped her fork," Skip said, on his knees, peaking over the edge.

"See anything you like down there?" Winonna said coyly. She had turned flirty after her brush with death and Skip's hero act.

Lilac rolled her eyes. She was a few minutes late to the restaurant and the others had already been seated. They were staying at the Grand Canyon Motel next door. Despite the name, the complex was located thirty miles from the east entrance to Grand Canyon National Park. The owners had figured out long before social media that the 'Grand' *nom de plume* on a billboard attracted more tourists.

The restaurant, motel, gas station, gallery, post office, and ubiquitous gift shop were collectively referred to as Cameron Trading Post. It had been since 1916, when two enterprising brothers, Hubert and C.D. Richardson, took advantage of the newly built suspension bridge over the Little Colorado, claimed a hundred acres, and threw up a tin shack to trade for Navajo and Hopi wool and livestock.

"So, it's not really part of the reservation?" Lottie asked, continuing the conversation that had started before Skip disappeared to retrieve her daughter's intentionally displaced fork.

"Technically, it isn't," Kuul answered. "Most people don't understand how much Navajo Nation has grown over time. The original reservation has been added to many times through acts of Congress and even purchases by the tribe. The trading post is, however, still owned by descendants of the brothers who founded the post.

"But we passed a sign saying we entered the Navajo Reservation?" Webster said.

He was sitting between Lottie and Winonna, Skip between Winonna and Lilac, and Kuul between Lilac and Lottie; a nice boy-girl-boy-girl arrangement. Two tables had been pulled together by picture windows overlooking a dusty wash that drained into the Little Colorado River. A river-rock fireplace with huge hearth rose from the carpeted floor. The tinned ceiling made the room seem older than it was. Dreamcatchers hung from everywhere. Every wall was covered by traditional red, black, gray, and white Navajo rugs made from handspun and plant-dyed wool. The rugs told *Diné* stories and legends through their geometric designs.

Kuul smiled, "In 1934, the Navajo acquired land south of the original treaty boundaries, but Congress deeded the plot the trading post sits on to the Richardson family. For years, this was where Navajo living nearby got their news about the outside world. The old traders, the ones who lived and stayed here a long time, were trusted far more than the government. But Native people are business savvy, they learned to play traders against each other; if one wasn't treating them fairly, they'd take their business to another post. Bad traders didn't last long. The Richardsons and their descendants treated them like family...well, almost."

"If you'd been here in the early days," Skip added, "you would have seen hogans where the gas pumps are today - built for the Native traders and their families when they came to visit. There could have been several thousand head of sheep awaiting transport to Flagstaff and the railroad. Trading posts were the start of the modern Navajo economy. Once people from back east started visiting the Grand Canyon via the Santa Fe, a market grew for Navajo and Hopi arts and crafts."

"What's a Navajo taco?" Winonna asked, studying the plastic-coated menu, not interested in the history lesson.

"More than you could eat," Lilac said. "Too many calories. You're watching those, right?"

Winonna grinned at her. "Skip, maybe we can share one? You feed me, I feed you." She scooted her chair closer to him, sliding her menu so he could see.

"Basically, deep-fried bread loaded with taco fixings. They can split it for us on two plates," Skip said, diplomatically.

"Sounds wonderful," Winonna cooed, resting an open hand on his arm and squeezing playfully while eyeing Lilac.

"'*I feed you?*' You get paid to lick *fingers* back in Hollywood?" Lilac asked.

Webster cleared his throat. "Rhodes, what do you know about the Hydes from before their trip? I understand Mrs. Chandler is interested in their story."

"Lottie, please," she said slowly. He had caught her studying him. He seemed so familiar. It nagged her. But at least he changed the subject. She'd have to talk with her daughter later.

"Well, Bessie Hyde was Bessie Louise Haley..." Skip began, stopping when a tall Navajo waitress in a traditional skirt approached their table.

She had to be close to six feet. Her long, black hair was carefully braided into knots every six inches. Pulled back, it highlighted a strong, high neck and an etched-in-stone, roman nose. Cocoa-colored skin and almond-shaped penetrating eyes demanded attention. A hundred-fifty years earlier she would have been a formidable female warrior.

"Kukulkan Balthazar. I thought that was you. You're not as handsome as my regular *Diné* customers," the waitress teased, her sculpted cheekbones rising high above her broad smile.

Kuul laughed, "*Yá'át'ééh*, Dezba Nez. We saw your sister Chooli at the Canyon. *Aq'*?"

"*T'áá íiyisíí ahéhee*. Chooli said you sang night songs with her," Dezba said, wagging a lengthy finger.

"Only to honor *Bidáá' Ha'azt'i' Tsékooh*. The canyon was special that night."

Dezba nodded. "What would everyone like?"

She took their orders, whispered something in Kuul's ear, and walked to the counter. The red skirt swayed a bit extra to keep the big Mayan's attention.

"She was from Ohio, right?" Webster asked.

"Shiprock, New Mexico, I think," Skip said, watching Dezba and looking at his friend for confirmation.

Winonna had changed her dirty sneakers for a pair of leather boots with heels and stomped the point of one into Skip's foot. As if to say, 'eyes on me, buster.' It hurt like hell, but not as bad as the quick jab to his ribs by Lilac.

"Ouch! I – I mean Pennsylvania."

"That was later," Lottie said. "She was born in Maryland. Or at least that's what I read."

"True, but the family moved when she was young. She grew up in Pittsburgh before moving on to West Virginia. The war years and the Spanish flu were tough times in the Steel city. Tough for working people. The Carnegies and other rich barons were at war with the unions."

"Parkersburg, West Virginia," Lottie said. "Oil was discovered. A lot of Pittsburgh money left the city for a gentler, get-rich life and to get away from the labor strife. She liked art in high school."

Lilac was mildly surprised by the details Lottie knew. Nothing you couldn't find out online in five minutes, but you had to take the time to do so. And not many people bothered. She tried catching Skip's eye to see if he had the same thought, but the lunkhead was distracted, making a face at Winonna. *In the middle of a conversation with her mother!*

While he'd been talking about Andrew Carnegie and the steel mills, Skip had felt a soft, bare leg press against his cargo shorts, followed by massaging fingers playing with the hair on the side of his knee. He sorted through his options for a few seconds, it wasn't really unpleasant, but then quietly shifted his chair toward Lilac. Winonna's meandering hand trailed behind.

"She and Glen married right after they graduated high school?" Webster asked. He smoothed his eyebrows and stared at Lottie, to whom he'd addressed his question. She seemed to have all the answers.

"No, she didn't meet Glen until later, in California. He was from Idaho," Skip answered. "There was, however, a short-lived marriage back east between Bessie and her high school sweetheart. We talked about him at Lee's Ferry. It didn't last a year. There's not much known about their time together. If she'd lived, maybe we'd know more, but, then again, without her and Glen's later notoriety, their past wouldn't have been studied like it has been."

"Right, Carl...Carl...What was his name?"

"Earl Helmick," Lottie added. "She was attending Marshall College and they snuck off one weekend to Kentucky. The only family she told was her brother Billy." Lottie paused to study Webster's face. "Billy's middle name was Austin."

"Hmm, I remember...he sent the money for the operation," Webster mused. "A hush-hush marriage and quickie divorce."

"They didn't call it the Roaring 20's for nothing," Winonna quipped, scooting closer to Skip. His hand caught hers as she traced circles up his leg. This was the most fun she'd had this trip. Maybe her mother was right; maybe she did need a steadier, more down-to-earth man.

Lilac noticed how Lottie stared at Webster, not quite angrily, rather curiously. Had something he said touched a nerve? She glanced at Skip. Had he noticed the same thing? No, the moron was playing patsy under the table.

Dezba and a young busboy in a white jacket arrived, balancing heavy trays piled with Navajo tacos and steaming bowls of mutton stew on porcelain plates. Another waitress stood behind with a tray of drinks, root beers and cokes, no liquor at the trading post.

"Your napkin belongs in your lap," Winonna said to Skip, patting it in place.

Skip nearly leapt out of his seat. He looked helplessly to Lilac, who just rolled her eyes.

25

BESSIE AND GLEN

November 14, 1928

BESSIE WAS ALONE ON THE PLATFORM, HOLDING ONTO HER OAR for dear life. Outmatched by the river, she'd helplessly watched Glen rise twice from the murky water only to be sucked back in with the next wave. When he'd gone under the second time, she was afraid that was it. Without her husband, she knew she didn't have a chance. It would just be a matter of time before the river took her as well. Sockdolager Rapid had landed an awful blow.

She desperately tried working both oars, hoping to keep Rain-in-the-Face from being too far downstream when Glen popped back up - if he came up. The thought of losing him screamed in her mind. But no matter how hard she braced her feet, the waves kept spitting the sweeps out. The scow was roiling through the rapids like a yo-yo.

"If I get out of this, I'm climbing the canyon wall no matter how steep it is!" Bessie swore out loud. *We're never going to be through the worst of it*, she thought.

She struggled on against the rapid, no longer trying to maneuver the scow for her husband. This was a fight for her life. She had to be careful, or the oars would do the same to her as they did to Glen. If he hadn't been able to hold them against the current, what chance did she have? The scow crashed out of control wave after wave after wave. God, Bessie prayed, please let it end, please bring Glen back.

At one point, her heart leapt when something white crested a whitecap, but it was just a chunk of driftwood plunging through the rapids. Twice she'd almost jumped down into the scow's hull; Rain-in-the-Face would get her through. But if she abandoned the platform and Glen resurfaced, she wouldn't see him. And if she didn't see him, she wouldn't be able to fish him back aboard. She crouched on the platform and rode the waves. Like a tightrope walker's pole, her sweep helped her balance, even if she didn't dare dip it in the water. *Where was Glen?*

Suddenly a hand appeared, clasping the side of the scow, then a second hand, clinging for dear life. No one could survive if they went under a third time. If she tried reaching him, she'd go over. Bessie swiveled her head downstream; she could see the end of Sockdologer. Somehow Glen hooked his elbows over the side and held on. She could hear his body pounding the side of the scow through more big waves and drops. Bessie was terrified he'd be crushed against a rock.

Glen was yelling, but the roar of the rapid muffled his voice. She thought she heard, "Don't lose a sweep!"

Bessie gambled and leapt down into the scow. She grabbed a rope and threw it to Glen, holding on to her end. The rapid wasn't as bad here, Rain had slotted into a swift channel. It was still a hellish ride, but not the nightmare they'd just pummeled through. Glen grabbed the rope with one hand, afraid to give up his grip on the scow. Bessie pulled as hard as she could as he climbed up over the side, falling into the bottom beside her.

He was grinning like a schoolboy who'd just bested his archrival at a game of marbles. Bessie had thought he had drowned, that she'd die alone in the Canyon, and here he was, in the flesh, smiling about it.

Glen kissed her and yelled brashly, "I thought I was a goner when I went under the second time." He laughed and leapt back onto the platform, grabbing a sweep in each hand.

Bessie watched in awe as he navigated them through the remainder of Sockdolager. After a while, she climbed back on the platform and manned her sweep. They'd gone several miles and rain began pelting her face. Gusts of wind from nowhere knocked her off her stance. In the thralls and spray of the deadly rapid, Bessie hadn't noticed the brewing storm. If it wasn't killer waves, it was something else on this River Styx.

"What a ride!" Glen said, finally reining Rain-in-the-Face over to shore. "Let's camp here tonight. Grab some grub. I'll set up the tarp." He took the beaten tarp and his soaked Winchester and ran for a sheltered spot against a group of boulders.

Bessie was shaking with emotion, not sure if it was the cold, fear, or the stress at nearly having lost her husband to this damn river. Every bone in her body ached. *Grab some grub!* – like nothing had happened.

Later that night, after Bessie's dinner, Glen managed to find some wood and start a roaring fire. The freezing rain had slowed to a drizzle and the wind slackened. They were no longer holding the tarp to keep it in place. It'd been a long day. Their longest yet, Bessie thought.

"Gawd, you ever seen anyplace this dark?" Glen asked. He'd already forgotten their ordeal.

The moon and stars were obscured by heavy clouds, leaving the depths of the canyon darker than anyplace Bessie had ever been. She could hear the river threatening them, but it was invisible in the thick mist and inky night. She scooted against Glen, nesting into his warm body.

"Do you think we should go on? We could try climbing out in the morning," Bessie whispered. She slid her hand below his stomach, squeezing softly. Glen tensed and held her tighter.

"We're fine, honey. That was the worst of it. In a day or two, we'll be soaking in a hot bath and sleeping in a soft bed. You'll feel different at the village."

"I was scared out of my wits. I thought you'd drowned and left me."

"You know I wouldn't do that. Not as far as we've come together. It's going to be a great life, Bessie, after we finish and sell our story. Come on, honey," he said, shaking her playfully. "What an adventure we're having. Don't tell me you're not enjoying it?" He squeezed her tightly, pulling her face to his and kissing her gently.

Bessie gazed at the flames rising from the fire and listened to the sizzle as raindrops hit the hot wood. Beyond the fire, the canyon was a dark void, eerily quiet except for the river's incessant howling. On the farm, they'd at least hear an animal from the barn or could turn on the radio, if it was a clear night. Without Glen, she'd go crazy here.

"I don't suppose we have a choice, really, but to make the best of it," she sighed. "It will be a great life, won't it? I was just so scared. I love you." She squeezed him harder where her hand rested, "Don't do it again, buster?"

Glen leaned back on the mattress, pulling Bessie and the quilt she'd wrapped around her on top of him. He slid his hands through her hair, brushing the tips of her ears, and kissed her deeply. Tracing his hands down the small of her back, he stopped at her hips and pulled her tight against him. She kissed him back, searching, trying to find a way to forget the awful day. She spread her fingers on his chest and raised her shoulders to look him in the eyes. His breathing was heavier. She could feel what he wanted and knew she'd give it to him.

"Promise me you'll keep us safe and never love anyone else. Promise," she said.

"Promise," he said, thickly.

She lowered herself, turning her face, letting him kiss her neck. He nipped her throat, his hot breath and the moisture from his lips awakening her desires. Bessie knew this magnificent, confidently naïve, strong man would die for her.

26

MOONLIGHT OVER NAVAJO GARDENS

"**S**HE WAS ALL OVER ME. WHAT WAS I SUPPOSED TO DO?" SKIP groaned. Lilac was busting his chops about Winonna. "It's a hero complex over my saving her. That'll go away."

Lilac rolled her eyes. "Just don't encourage her."

Dinner had ended with everyone stuffed and painfully waddling off to their rooms. The moon was bright and the cool night air on the plateau felt nice after the warmer Sedona evenings. Skip and Lilac wandered into Navajo Gardens; a green oasis hidden behind the trading post's gallery.

The gardens had been built in the 1930s. Ever since, they had been a pleasant surprise for travelers driving through the parched, cracked-earth reservation. A series of trellised terraces, with flagstone paths lined by stacked, rock walls, led to cloistered patios. Veiled benches rested beneath honeysuckle-vined arches. In season, roses and yellow daisies carpeted the red earth beside the walkways.

Winonna had tagged along until Lilac had bluntly stated three was a crowd. The actress sarcastically agreed and had stayed with them until her cell phone played the Twentieth-Century Fox movie theme. They'd laughed watching her run back toward the hotel, waving her phone in the air. Service was spotty.

"This is a curious little band you've collected," Lilac commented. They stepped out from under a trellis into a hidden patio shaded by tall cottonwoods and romantic willows. The tips of the cottonwood leaves were just beginning to turn gold from the chilly night air. They spied a stone bench that wrapped halfway around a lilac bush.

Skip sat next to her, their shoulders and legs comfortably touching. "More awkward than curious, people on group tours are out of their normal environments. They're thrown together in a place they know little about and asked to relinquish control to a guide they've barely met. That's not easy, even if they know each other. *And* they're from California. It would be strange if this trip wasn't strange."

Lilac shrugged, pressing closer against Skip. She hugged herself against the nippy air and wrapped her arm through his. She made sure her hair draped across his shoulder. Surely, he noticed the jasmine-scented shampoo from the hotel. *Nothing, nada, zippo...how many clues did lunkhead need? He was the awkward one.*

"So, are you going to tell me what happened with Coop?" Skip felt her tense and smelled flowers as she straightened her hair. She slid away from him.

"I told you I didn't want to talk about it."

They sat in silence for a few minutes. A gentle wind rustled the tops of the leafy cottonwoods. The garden's spring and summer flowers were gone, but the honeysuckle scent lingered. A lone coyote yelped from the river, and they could hear an occasional car cross the suspension bridge. Stars were appearing and the distant, orange speck that was Mars shone in the western sky.

"You want to walk across the bridge?" Skip asked, breaking the silence. "This time of year, the moonlight dances across the few pools of water left in the Little Colorado."

Lilac sighed. He certainly knew how to wax on about scenery. "We're not very lucky with bridges today." She scooted back against him and gently turned his face to hers, accepting who he was. He seemed to study her soft, teddy-bear eyes, trying to understand if she meant something other than the obvious. "Now would be the right time to kiss me," she said.

"Lilac, I'm the same man. I'm no different. There's still a past I won't share. You're better off with Coop."

"Shut up. Right now, tonight, I'm not asking for different. Either kiss me or don't. It's up to you. Don't use your 'past' as an excuse."

Neither of them noticed the man in the shadows on the top terrace. He had hidden in one of the few places with an unobstructed view down into the gardens.

• • •

Hyde Donald had made a mistake at the bridge. Things had gotten out of hand. If they'd only recognized the earlier warning with the boulder, it wouldn't have been necessary. Now he owed the bitch that shot at him; what the hell was he going to tell the rental company? Her wandering off with the guide was a golden opportunity. There were no tourists around to spoil things. Nor was his too-smart uncle here to keep him from proving himself to his grandfather.

The way the lovebirds were locked together they wouldn't hear a buffalo coming. After the man had kissed her, he'd held her face in his hands, whispered something, and then gone at her again. The woman had straddled his lap, letting his hands grab her tight ass. Except for his legs, extending from beneath her, the guide had disappeared in a mass of fiery, red hair. Hyde wished he was close enough to smell her scent.

"Fuck," he mumbled. He should have told his uncle to go screw himself when he'd ordered him to leave Gloria behind. And then he'd shut him down with the gothic chick in Jerome.

Hyde licked his lips. The swelling in his jeans grew as he anticipated their next moves. The guide was slow. The bitch was more aggressive. What a dope - she was there for the taking! Hyde decided - he'd give the woman a few more minutes to lather up. He wondered how far she'd go out here in the open. In his mind, he was already spreading her long legs. They made Gloria's look like stumps.

Five minutes of swapping spit and the dumbass hadn't even tried putting a hand where it didn't belong. If they were going to do more, it obviously wasn't going to be here. Time to make his move, Hyde thought. He'd sneak up and disable the guide. From the bridge episode, he knew the woman was a fighter. He'd have to be on her fast. He smiled to himself. Gloria wasn't much of a fighter...*facilitating*, yeah, that was the word for her. He'd give Red a taste of what she wanted. She'd struggle, but he guessed she'd like it rough.

Hyde surveyed all directions. Getting close was doable if they didn't notice him in the first set of steps. Not much chance of that; the guide had picked up his pace. The Indians had done a good job of camouflaging the paths with plants and trees. It was a far cry from the open bridge. Seconds later, he was steps from his prey, hiding behind a stone pillar. The buffalo could have ridden a dirt bike down the steps for all they'd known. The woman was moaning whenever they came up for air. He had no trouble getting within twenty feet of where they sat.

"Did you hear something?" the woman whispered.

Hyde froze in his tracks. *Shit!*

"No," the guide huskily answered.

Hyde grinned to himself and waited for the heavy breathing to resume, then crept behind the bench. Their seat was in front of a column bordered by a shrub with spent, purple blooms; a perfect place to attack. He slid his jackknife from his back pocket and quietly opened the six-inch blade.

This was going to be too easy - unless the bitch had a gun stuck in her panties. He stalked around the bush - more smacking sounds and moans. He'd learned from a Rambo movie how to clasp his hand over the mouth, jerk the head back, and slash the throat. He'd have to break their suction – Stallone hadn't had that problem. But by the time they knew what was happening...the guide would be dead, and he'd be on top of the woman.

Ready, Set, *GO TIME!*

*Bzzzz...bzzzz...bzzzz...bzzzz...*Hyde fumbled for his phone. *Not now! Fucking Gloria! Did they hear it?*

27

DAMN PHONES

"**W**HAT'S THE DAUGHTER SAYING ABOUT THE WHORE, anything new?" Austin Donald barked into his phone. He was angry at being stuck in Vegas inside a metal cage others called a mobile home. Away from the action meant a loss of power. There was no doubt in his twisted mind that his worthless offspring wouldn't fuck this up.

"Which whore?" Earl asked, knowing his feigned ignorance would further infuriate the old man.

"All of them. They're all bitches, generations of whores, especially the dead one, the one that fucked me over. They'll learn though, when I even the score." Donald raged.

Earl had taken wicked delight in getting his father worked up over his grandson's latest screw-ups. He'd told the old man about Hyde dislodging the rock and attacking the younger Chandler on the bridge, gleefully listening as he went ballistic. He chuckled, hearing the thump-thump-thump against the trailer walls; the old man's cane wasn't long enough to reach from Vegas to Navajo Nation.

"How's it left with Frank's boy? You set him straight?" Donald asked after regaining control of his temper. Whenever Hyde had fouled something up, he was always 'Frank's boy'.

Earl explained Hyde had been waiting in his room when he'd returned from dinner. "I was inches from taking a swing at his pretty face after the stupid stunt he'd pulled at Navajo bridge. I warned him if anything happened to anyone on the trip, our operation would be ruined. I even threatened him with the wrath of God." *The old man liked being compared to God.*

"That boy didn't get it did he?" Donald surmised. "I blame it on that damn junkie Frank bedded. That shit burnt his brain before he was born. Your warning him was like waving a red flag at a dumb bull. That wasn't smart, Earl."

Earl smiled to himself. The old man was denigrating him, trying to assert his dominance. It had been one of his go-to tricks when Earl was younger. He was losing it and he knew it.

"No, he hasn't," Earl answered. "Your brain-damaged bull looked me in the eye and said, 'You're too fucking soft. It was just to scare her. That's what the old man would do.'"

Earl had backhanded the younger man across the face and slammed his ears with the sides of his fists. Hyde had doubled over and almost vomited from the ringing in his head. '*Soft?*' Earl had asked, laughing in his nephew's tortured face. They both knew who had the upper hand. And Hyde knew what his uncle was capable of – he'd heard the stories.

That hadn't kept the stupid shit from taking a wild swing at his beloved uncle, which Earl had easily dodged. The kid had been unsteady on his feet and covered too late. Earl had punched him in the chest with the butt of his palm, sending him falling against a wall. Hyde had gamely risen, pulled a knife, and stumbled toward him. Earl had laughed again, "Try it. The old man may want you around, but I don't."

Austin Donald was furious with Earl; Hyde he could excuse. Quarreling offspring were going to blow what he'd waited a lifetime to accomplish. Fighting amongst themselves showed a lack of leadership from Earl and discipline from Frank's boy. Hyde was too stupid and Earl too much out for himself. He couldn't trust either of them.

"Where's he at now?"

"I dusted him off, gave him a few hundred, and told him to go to the south rim of the Grand Canyon, where our happy little group is headed tomorrow. Told him to get a room and lay low until he hears from me. Why don't you let me take care of him? He's nothing but trouble."

Donald ignored his suggestion. If he was ever forced to choose, he'd pick his malleable grandson over his dangerously sly son. "What about the girl? Is she playing along?"

"So far. If nothing else, Hyde put the fear of death in her. We're just lucky she survived. She and her mother aren't exactly Mrs. Brady and Marsha, Marsha, Marsha. Getting along just doesn't seem to run in the family. She's hesitant, but she'll do as I say when the time comes."

"Who?" the old man said, confused. "Is she, or isn't she?"

"She'll play along. The threat of busting her hot, all-girl luau got her attention," Earl said, knowing what the old man wanted to hear.

"I'm coming to the Canyon. Hyde will follow instructions if I'm in charge," Donald said. He didn't care if Earl's field demotion and the implied criticism of his handling his free-wheeling grandson ruffled feathers. "When you see me there, you don't know me. Got it?"

Earl wasn't keen on the old man muddying the waters. "What if the Chandler woman sees you?" His father's unhinged drive to get even could muck things up worse than Hyde. Everything was well in hand and going according to *his* plan.

Austin Donald snorted, "That bitch would stick her dainty nose in the air and refuse to acknowledge me. Hell, it's been so long she probably wouldn't even..."

The old man gasped and began sucking oxygen. A coughing frenzy ensued. How he'd handle the thinner air at Grand Canyon was a concern, Earl thought. It wouldn't do to have him croak in the middle of everything – afterwards, that would be okay.

Donald spat a diseased glob of yellow spittle on the floor. "Call Hyde, now," he wheezed. "I don't trust he won't do the opposite of what you ordered. Make sure he's left for..."

The old man began violently coughing again and hung up. Earl debated whether to call Hyde, he'd already made his orders crystal clear. Maybe it wasn't a bad idea to make sure his nephew had done as he'd been told.

• • •

Bzzzz...bzzzz...bzzzz...bzzzz...

"Is that your phone?" Lilac asked, breaking off their kiss. She felt for it in his pocket.

"No but keep checking."

Lilac jumped off his lap. She heard shuffling noises on the steps to the parking lot. A silhouette of a man ran under a security light. It was the man she'd seen at Wupatki and who had attacked them at the bridge. The outline of his silly cowboy hat identified him.

"It's the man from the bridge!" she yelled, already racing up the path toward the stairs. Skip was right behind her.

The steps led to a driveway that separated the gardens from the front of the trading post. They jumped them three at a time.

At the top, they stopped, scanning the drive in both directions. To the right was the hotel, to the left the commercial parking lot, their view blocked by the art gallery. They heard an engine turn over and ran left.

Lilac and Skip leapt, like competing hurdlers, over a stone wall bordering the lot. A Jeep with a red stripe peeled out of a space between two charter buses fifty feet ahead of them. It looked gold beneath the orange, sodium lighting. The passenger window was covered with plastic. They ran after it, hoping to cut it off before it reached the highway. It was no use; the driver gunned it and pulled farther away. They watched, out of breath, as the car accelerated past the gas pumps, turned, and fishtailed onto 89A.

"Did you get a plate number?" Skip gasped, bent over, hands on his knees. Running steps at this elevation, with an undigested Navajo taco, was physiologically reckless. Not to mention the probable waste of a good taco.

"Too dark," Lilac answered. "Damn!"

At the motel, Earl had heard the yelling and watched the chase from his window. He tried calling Hyde again, but no answer. The kid was on thin ice. The old man had been right about him and would not be happy.

28

DESERT VIEW

"**K**EEP YOUR EYES OPEN." SKIP WHISPERED THE NEXT MORNING to Lilac and Kuul, away from the Chandlers. They both knew he meant for a yellow jeep or the man in the stupid cowboy hat.

They had left Cameron Trading Post early and forty-five minutes later were at Desert View in the National Park. It was as close as they'd be to the actual United crash site. Through scattered, windblown trees, the edge of a deep, red canyon, the Grand Canyon, appeared to their left. A round, stone tower that architecturally blended into the harsh, rocky landscape lay ahead. The watchtower looked ancient; Skip usually joked that an Anasazi lookout, stationed atop, was flashing a signal toward the Painted Desert – *more tourists - hide silverware.*

"This will be an emotional place for both of you." Skip said. He was in the lead and began talking about the watchtower. "It's a re-creation. Made to look..."

From behind, Lilac caught his arm and stopped him. He turned and saw the strain in the Chandlers faces. A trickle of tears ran down Lottie's cheeks. Mother and daughter were holding hands; Winonna's knuckles white from her mother's squeeze. The actress's eyes pleaded with him, for what, he wasn't sure.

"Not the time for a history lesson, Kemo," Kuul said.

His friend was right. "The overlook behind the tower has views toward where the accident occurred. There's a plaque commemorating what happened. I wish I could say it will be quiet out there and you can be alone with your thoughts," he said, hesitating, "but this is a popular stop for charter buses. Let's take this at your pace."

Lilac released his arm; he'd gotten the message. He might be a dim bulb about feelings, but he'd realized he needed to slow down and give them time. In guide terms, don't push or pull your group, let them lead.

Winonna wrapped an arm around her mother, using her other hand to brace the older woman's elbow. She pulled her close, hugging her and kissing her wet cheek. Her own eyes watering. "It'll be okay Mom. I'm here. We can get through this together."

Lottie turned her face to Winonna, smiled, and gently patted her arm. The overlook was on an unobstructed point, and she smoothed her daughter's hair, which had been blown by the wind. "I'm so happy you're here, Honey."

It would be their first look at the majestic canyon. That alone floored most first-time visitors. Add their tragic connection with Chuar Butte, the spot of the United crash, and Skip knew they would be overwhelmed. No matter how prepared, no one, let alone these two, was ever ready for the flood of emotion.

The canyon was no longer a small, one-dimensional picture in a book or movie. People unconsciously measured themselves against nature's immense scale. Vivid colors, shadowy side canyons, sheer drops, the endless horizon, and the timeless river, all underscored the insignificance of a singular human. He'd witnessed crying, laughing, stunned silence, hyper-chattiness, humility, disorientation, and prayer. Imagine a response and Skip had seen it. What the Chandlers would see was the horror of a fathomless expanse, an expanse where planes could disappear.

"Lilac and I can take Webster inside the watchtower," Kuul suggested. "You three should go to the overlook alone. "*Hózhó*, the natural rhythm and balance to all life is out there, in the canyon. Peace will find you if you let it."

Webster agreed. "It's a moment for your family," he said to Lottie. She had already tuned her thoughts inward but gave him an oddly kind nod. She began to say something, but didn't, sliding back into her personal fog.

"Come on, Mom. We'll support each other," Winonna said, wiping her eyes with a finger.

"We have to. We're all we have." Lottie smiled and the two hugged again, each patting the other's back. Lottie fished in her bag for a tissue and gently blotted Winonna's tears like she was a child who'd skinned a knee.

Lilac was touched; even the insensitive movie star was crying. It was a good time to leave them alone. She signed to Skip, and, with Kuul, led Webster into the round watchtower.

"This was Mary Colter's building, right?" Lottie asked Skip. They were standing outside. "She also designed Union Station in Los Angeles."

Skip knew the question was her way of saying they weren't yet ready to go to the overlook.

"Colter did the interior design for the Harvey House Restaurant that was in Union Station. She was a Santa Fe Railroad architect who drew inspiration from the Southwest's past and indigenous culture. I think it's a brewery now. Part of the original Blade Runner, with Harrison Ford, was filmed there."

"I met him once," Winonna said. "At a premiere."

"*Witness* is my favorite," Skip said, glad to momentarily switch their focus away from the accident.

"The entrance to the watchtower is a large circular room. It's designed like a great kiva. There's a pole ladder to a second floor opening that's meant to mimic the ceremonial exit from one world to another. Colter studied area ruins, Spanish haciendas, Hopi villages, and old pueblos for her ideas. Those stones set in a diamond pattern above the door," Skip pointed, "The same details are at Pueblo Bonito in Chaco Canyon, which is over a thousand years old. She even incorporated real petroglyphs and Mesoamerican t-doors."

"It looks so old, ancient if you didn't know better," Lottie commented. Skip could see the dread etched into her weak smile. At least the tower was a temporary distraction.

"The railroad brought people to the Canyon and the Harvey Corporation fed them and showed them the sites. This watchtower was built to be a rest stop and gift shop. This was the end of the line for the day tour that left from El Tovar, the old hotel you're staying at tonight. At this late point in her career, it was 1933, Colter was probably thinking more of her legacy than selling trinkets. She drove construction foremen nuts with her exactness and unwillingness to compromise on the tower's authenticity. There are stories of her making workers change out stones she didn't like."

Lottie and Winonna both stared at the watchtower, never turning their heads toward the canyon. Skip realized they'd stopped listening, each lost in their thoughts. He doubted those were about ancient architecture or the tower's construction.

After several minutes of awkward silence and furtive glances between mother and daughter, Lottie took a deep breath and sighed, "Let's go pay our respects."

"You sure?" Winonna whispered, clutching her hand.

"I owe it to them, and I promised Nana Lou I'd come back. We should have made this trip together. But I know she's here with us. We're all here."

A plaque stood off to the side at the overlook. The worn sign was waist-high and angled so visitors could contemplate the meaning of its words and stare into the canyon at the same time. They were lucky. The crowd was gathered farther out, stacked three abreast behind the iron railing, selfie sticks extended skyward. Skip, Lottie, and Winonna were alone at the memorial.

Catastrophe can happen even in spectacular beauty. When technological advances and human actions fail, disasters may happen, Skip read silently. He'd read the words before, but they meant more now. They tried to explain to devastated families why 128 loved ones and crew onboard the United and TWA planes had suffered unthinkably horrific deaths. The third paragraph went further, giving them a noble reason - the crash led to the formation of the Federal Aviation Administration, *to ensure future accidents didn't happen in the same aimless way.*

Skip knew there was nothing he could add that Lottie didn't know. The plaque had a photo of the canyon from their vantage point, arrows pointing to the TWA crash site at Temple Butte and United's at Chuar Butte. Other photos showed a set of keys and a cigarette lighter found deep in the canyon.

Lottie hesitantly touched the keys. A living soul had once used them to lock a door and light a cigarette. They were far better reminders of the lost lives than words.

"They both smoked," Lottie murmured, "everyone did then."

She moved her hand to the photo of Chuar Butte, looked up, and found it in the distance; the morning sun highlighting its east side. Holding her daughter, she pointed to the spot. It seemed close, but it was so far that people at Desert View hadn't even noticed the smoke from the fires. Winonna buried her face in her mother's shoulder and cried.

Skip softly placed a hand on Lottie's back and whispered, "I'll be around when you're ready. Take all the time you want."

Skip retired to a quiet spot below the tower and behind a juniper tree. He'd waited there often, separate from the crowds. He could keep an eye on his people and reflect on the haunting beauty that surrounded them. The Hance Trail, named after an early miner and mule guide, switch-backed far below. They were kindred spirits, he and John Hance - lonely lives. He watched the Chandlers move to the end of the overlook, still holding each other. At least they weren't alone. When Lottie had told her daughter, *'I know she's here with us,'* it had reawakened his own memories, sad memories.

• • •

"She was a strong, motivated woman, Mary Elizabeth Jane Colter. She had to be," Lilac was explaining to Webster.

After his bridge heroics, she was ready to give him another chance. His being in the travel business didn't hurt either. She had her own yoga-and-firearm-training tour to promote. "It was the early 1900's and Mary Colter was a single woman, working in a man's world at a man's job, with a man for her boss. It wasn't easy."

Kuul smiled, "She could have been an Indian."

The three of them had climbed the circular stairway to the top of the watchtower and worked their way back down. Kuul had led, pointing out the colorful paintings and pictographs on each level and explaining their symbolism. Most were copied from ruins in the four corners area: Canyon De Chelly, Jemez, Betatakin, Keet Seel, and the Petrified Forest. The drawings covering the domed ceiling were copied from ancient rock paintings at Abo Caves in New Mexico. Colter had even had her artist replicate how the originals had faded and how later paintings, still centuries old, partially covered those in the worst condition. Somehow, her Hopi artist had captured it all without losing their vision of the overall aesthetic.

The famous Hopi room was where Kuul stopped the longest. He pointed to a circular painting divided into four quadrants. "It depicts the story of the first man to navigate the Grand Canyon and how he became the first Hopi snake priest," Kuul said. "The upper left quadrant tells of a chief's son who accompanied elders to gather salt near the confluence of the Colorado and Little Colorado Rivers. He is fascinated by the larger river, wondering where all the water goes. Wherever it ends, it must be very full. The chief encourages his son to build a boat and hands him a bundle of prayer sticks from their kiva for his journey.

"The upper right," Kuul continued, "shows the boy hollowing out a log to raft down the Colorado. Colorfully layered canyon walls are drawn on both sides. Symbols of friendly birds and turtles that help him along the way are in the sky and water. A rain cloud symbol is in the distance. The lower right quadrant illustrates the boy meeting the Snake People at the end of his trip. He's standing with the Snake chief and his daughter. The Snake People present him with several tests, all of which he uses his prayer sticks to pass. The chief presents him with a bow, the symbol of the Snake Clan, to take home, along with his beautiful daughter as a wife.

The last quadrant is the couple's journey back home. Thunderclouds are overhead and the Snake bow is dripping rain. These are blessings, he is bringing the water back," Kuul said, ending the story.

"The Hopi Snake Clan, one of the oldest and most secretive, grew from their offspring," Lilac added.

"So, it's just another river myth?" Webster asked.

"Like most legends," Lilac answered. "It's a story passed down orally from generation to generation. The Hopi didn't have an alphabet or leave a written historical record. But that doesn't mean there isn't some basis in fact."

"There are actually many more details and an epilogue to the story," Kuul said. "Academic papers have been written about this drawing, each with different interpretations as to its meaning. Personally, as long as the Hopi and other Natives have lived in this area, I'd bet they explored the river all the way to the Gulf of California. Tracking a water source in this dry environment would have been important."

"You're probably right. We Whites are a little Eurocentric in our beliefs. You ought to share the legend with Lottie, as knowledgeable as she is about the Hyde's story," Webster said. "If that Snake princess did come back to Hopiland, *she* would have been the first woman to raft the Colorado."

"The drawing doesn't actually show her on the river," Lilac said. "Their honeymoon trip would have been overland. I doubt even Hopi storytellers would suggest they boated upstream. Bessie's record would have been safe...if she'd made it."

Webster nodded thoughtfully. The red head was smart, and she'd obviously gotten close to Lottie. He hadn't forgotten the old man's missive to find out how much she and the guide knew. "Well, that would have made Lottie happy...if she'd made it. You don't think it's strange that she's so into a 1928 misadventure? It's like she knew them."

"Not particularly," Lilac answered. "As a woman, it's a story that captures your heart."

They stepped down from the Hopi Room to the watchtower's second-story terrace, the roof of the great kiva. The bend in the Colorado River as it turned west toward Grand Canyon Village was easily traced. Hance Rapids appeared as tiny, white brushstrokes on the thin ribbon of water. Except for Colter's tower and the concrete overlook, the view was the same as when the Hopi boy and the Hydes had both ridden through.

Webster's questions about the Chandler woman seemed out of place to Kuul. It wasn't the first time the man had tried to lead the conversation toward their past and the Hydes. That made him curious. Things out of place were almost always there for a reason. *Hózhó* - balance and harmony - everything fit somehow.

"Not strange," he said, agreeing with Lilac. "Maybe their spirits embraced in another world on their journeys."

· · ·

The Chandler's grief affected Skip more than he expected. Emotions that he worked to keep buried were rising in his chest. The anguish he sensed in Lottie brought it all back, the deep hurt, the pain of lost love, his anger over a life that could have been different.

He'd never been settled, the operations they'd sent him on hadn't allowed it. But there had been one time, seven years ago, before he'd even thought of Sedona or leaving the agency. Her exotic scent, olive skin, and intoxicating black eyes, had made him start planning a way out. In her arms, with her tender mouth mingling her life with his, his heart knew they belonged together. They'd met in Bangkok, though 'met' wasn't the right word. He was recuperating between assignments, and she had been following him. At first, he didn't know that she'd been part of a small team sent to find him after his escape from Tehran. Daria Ahmadi, Ministry of Intelligence of the Islamic Republic of Iran, VAJA for short, was the most beautiful agent he had ever tried to kill. She'd attempted the same solo, chasing him to Hong Kong after Thailand. They'd played cat and mouse for weeks across Southeast Asia.

Then, for two weeks, they'd barely left the rooms behind the Chinese shop where Skip had taken her. He'd killed there before. But he hadn't pulled the trigger and somehow, they'd fallen in love instead. Allegiances set aside and hidden off the grid in Singapore, they had given themselves fourteen days, no more. Then back. The last night they'd made promises. Skip had fallen asleep thinking that whatever time he had left would be spent running with the woman he loved. In the morning, Daria Ahmadi was gone. No note, no letter, no goodbye.

Four years ago, he'd learned she'd been assassinated by a VAJA team. The agency had showed him the intercept. The Islamic Ministry of Intelligence had discovered she'd lied about him; telling them she'd completed her assignment in a Hong Kong back alley. Her deception had worked, until he'd turned up, alive and well, against another VAJA team. The intercept had said that Daria Ahmadi, a high-ranking Iranian intelligence official, had been tortured in an Iranian oil barge and terminated by her own people. Not long after, Skip retired, and his agency created his cover in Sedona. His unfettered anger had made him unreliable in the field. An operative who'd lost his head and his heart was useless.

Skip stared into the canyon wondering about what might have been. Just like John Hance, he was hiding from life. Alone.

One pebble, then another, bounced off his back. He spun around, angry. Remembering Daria had put him on edge. It always did. Someone had to pay. It was a score he hadn't settled. God help whoever threw the rock.

"Hey, I called out to you three times. What is so interesting down there?" Lilac asked from above.

29

BESSIE AND GLEN HYDE

November 14, 1928

"HEY, STOP THROWING ROCKS!" GLEN EXCLAIMED.
They'd hit Bright Angel Trail sooner than expected and were hiking to the rim. Rain-in-the-Face was moored at the river. After nearly a month of living on the scow, they were in a hurry to reach Grand Canyon Village and the fancy El Tovar Hotel. Bessie was extra playful, happy to be off the dirty Colorado and on her way to a hot bath. She needed one.

"Oh, isn't it beautiful Glen? Look, those clouds drifting in the middle of the canyon are below us." Bessie was catching snowflakes with her outstretched hands. "The shadows are moving so fast across the north wall. The way the sun's popping thru makes the canyon look like a lighted checkerboard. Everything is so gorgeous."

Glen laughed and tossed a snowball at her. "Doesn't look like it will last long. Better enjoy it while you can," he said, eyeing her pretty clouds. He sure hoped this snow was short-lived. "Just watch your step while you're gawking. This is a fine new trail, but a little rougher than I expected."

"It's not bad," Bessie said, pulling her hat down to meet the sheepskin collar on her bomber jacket. The temperature was dropping. She wasn't about to complain though, not with a meal someone else cooked and a real bed only a few miles away.

"We've got a ways more to go."

As they climbed, the snow became heavier. The trail had been steep, until they reached a hogsback. There it was like walking on the spine of a dinosaur in a foggy, Jurassic world. Everything was coated in a soft white blanket. A thick, white veil hovered above, hiding the rim and sky. Tentacles of mist rained down the trail and fell into the canyon. Only fleeting, peekaboo views greeted them to the east and west. The snowcapped temples and buttes they'd admired on the north rim slowly disappeared with each foot they rose. They could still see stretches of the river, but the rim of the inner gorge blocked most of it.

"The river seems so tame from up here," Bessie said, stopping to take in the moody view.

"We're at least halfway," Glen said, scratching his head. The going was getting tougher, and he wanted to keep moving. Halfway was a guess, it was impossible to judge with the weather and being in such a big space.

"I'd like to take some pictures."

"Okay, but we need to get up top before dark." He knew Bessie needed a breather; she'd been sick again earlier. Glen sat his pack on a rock and fished the camera out. He had to admit, the view from inside the storm was dramatic. "Just a few, then we need to keep moving."

After the hogsback, the climb was steeper than before and slippery. Bessie kept searching above for a glimpse of the village. She expected to see the roof of El Tovar, but there was nothing other than dark, pine trees. The snow finally stopped but had accumulated more the closer they got to the rim. The air was icy cold by the time they reached the top, and wind blew through the pine trees, showering gobs of snow with every gust.

"I smell mules," Glen said, sniffing a foul smell. "I think we managed to miss the village. We should see Kolb's studio. It's at the top of the trail."

Bessie groaned. She was ready to collapse. The sun had set, and the chill cut through her jacket. The wind was brutal. Keeping her hat on was all she could manage. Her toes were tingling from the cold. For the last two hours, she'd imagined walking straight off the trail into the fancy hotel and flopping down by a roaring fireplace. The staff, maybe even rangers, would be there to congratulate them.

Instead, all she could see was an empty, stinky corral, more snow, and a forest of trees. She sat on a log and laid her pack on the ground. She felt like crying.

Glen walked past the ramshackle stables. "Hey, Bess, I see a road. We must have hiked the new Kaibab Trail instead of Bright Angel. We'll have to walk to town."

"I'm staying here!" Bessie wailed, knowing that wouldn't happen. She reluctantly shouldered her pack and joined her husband, resigning herself to a few more miles. "You're rubbing my feet when we get to a room!"

"Sure, and anything else you want," Glen grinned. "Give me your pack, Honey. At least the road will be level and easy."

"Easy if we hadn't just spent the afternoon traipsing out of the continent's deepest hole!"

She refused to give up her pack; the extra layer helped check the freezing wind blasting her backside. They should have stayed in Idaho, tucked inside their warm cabin. Now they were lost and walking toward who knows where. Her toes were rubbed raw. The tingling had transitioned to dull, throbbing pain with each step. She was ready to scream and give up when two dim lights appeared behind. *A car, thank God!*

"Get him to stop, Glen!" Bessie begged, moving to the side of the road.

"It can't be that much farther to the village."

"I'll hail him then! Far be it for a man to ask for help, even if his wife is dying from exposure."

Lou Barker was glad the snow had stopped. He'd borrowed the jalopy from his buddy to go see his girl at El Tovar. He'd spent the day driving from the ranch where he worked. The last thing he expected was hitchhikers in a storm, after dark, four miles from the closest cover. But there the little girl was, standing in the middle of the road, waving him down in his headlights. He slid to a stop, leaned sideways, and kicked the frozen passenger door open.

"You're a godsend!" the young woman cried. "Thanks for stopping. I'm Bessie Hyde and this is my husband Glen."

Lou nodded.

"We hiked up from the river, been rafting since October. Any chance you can give us a lift to town?"

Lou looked her over and studied the sober man standing next to her. The Winchester slung over his shoulder made him nervous, but it wasn't unusual. He couldn't just leave them here, but he wasn't buying a woman boating the Colorado.

"Climb in. I'm heading for El Tovar, the hotel. My gal works there."

Bessie scooted next to him before he finished his sentence. *Finally, out of the wind and snow.*

"Thanks for the ride. We won't bother you any," Glen said, sitting next to his wife and yanking the door shut. "We're up here to stock up on supplies. Say, was that the new Kaibab trail back there? I'd planned on coming up in town."

"It was if you hit the top a few miles back," Lou said, pointing over his shoulder. "You came up at Yaki Point. Pretty spot, but a long way from the lodge and railroad. We'll be there in a few minutes. You really came from the river?"

"All the way from Wyoming," Bessie said, shivering. Feeling was coming back to her feet and fingers, which just made them hurt more. "Down the Green River, past Lee's Ferry. We've each been knocked in for a swim. I'm sick of the mud and wet camps. Ready for a hot bath."

"And you're here getting supplies to go back?"

"We're past the worst of it," Glen added. He wished Bessie would keep her mouth shut about their misadventures. He'd have to talk to her; there'd likely be newspaper people at the hotel. They wanted to tell an exciting story, not a foolhardy one. Her being scared would make him look bad.

Lights appeared on a hill and Lou pulled to a stop below. "That's El Tovar. Bright Angel's farther down the rim path. I'll let you out here. I've got a buddy works as a wrangler at the mule barn who lets me park outside."

Bessie and Glen thanked him for the ride and waved as he drove away. They watched the headlights bounce across the railroad tracks and stop a few hundred yards farther at what had to be the stables. There were steps to their right leading to El Tovar. The lodge's heavy beams and turreted roof made a memorable impression as they climbed. Bessie couldn't wait to get inside.

"Let's see if they'll give us something to eat," she said.

The lights they'd seen were from rooms above the porch. As they got closer, she could see guests moving behind fancy curtains, wealthy sightseers delivered each day by the railroad. It was a grand place. "You think we can stay there?"

Glen snickered, "Too pricey for us, but dinner, sure. Let's pop a cork. We can get supplies and look up Emery Kolb in the morning."

El Tovar lobby looked like the hunting lodge of a Bavarian prince. Dark, log walls were capped with mounted trophies; glassy-eyed elk, deer, pronghorn, buffalo, and moose peered over the room. Piano music and laughing voices floated down from above. Bessie expected Dukes and Duchesses to waltz down the grand stairway in their festooned uniforms and sparkly dresses.

And here she was in the same smelly clothes she'd worn for days and washed in the muddy Colorado. The elk over the door seemed to turn up its nose.

She spied an overstuffed, leather sofa by a crackling fireplace. A painting of the Grand Canyon hung over the mantle. The artist's exaggeration of sharp peaks, soaring cliffs, and sinister shadows was terrifying. *How different it looked in oil.* Bessie shrugged off her wet coat and stood in front of the fire, warming her hands.

"Moose in Arizona?" Glen said, studying the taxidermist work. "Maybe it was *Rooooo*sevelt's."

Bessie turned her back to the fire. She dropped her dripping hat and ran warm fingers through her wet hair. The heat spread to her neck and scalp. She bent over, wiggling her bottom. A rush of warmth climbed her spine. The dampness she'd lived with for a month began ebbing away. She wished she could strip and hang each piece of clothing from the mantle. Better yet, she'd burn them.

"You stay here," Glen said. "I'll see about dinner and find out where we can stay."

When he returned, Bessie had taken up residence on the leather couch. It was fine with her if they spent the night right there.

"You'd need to be a Rockefeller to stay here," he grumbled. "But they offered to feed us when I told them about our trip. I promised to mention them in our book," he grinned, rubbing his big hands over the flames. "Fire feels good."

"I'm good on this couch," Bessie cooed, slipping deeper into the butter-soft cushion. "But I'd dearly love a hot bath?"

"They said there's room down at Bright Angel. It might be a tent cabin though...but with a stove and good bed. I'll get you a soak somewhere if I have to knock on doors."

"Come here," Bessie said, winking. "Get me warm before dinner." She curled her legs beneath her, making room. Glen settled next to her. She wrapped her arms around his neck, nuzzling her face into his shoulder. He needed a shave.

"I'm sorry we can't stay here. I know how much you hoped we could."

"A nice warm tent with a real bed is just fine. Next time they'll put us in the honeymoon suite for free – you just wait. But you better get me a bath; that elk up there has my scent."

30

EL TOVAR

"YOUR ROOMS ARE ON THE THIRD FLOOR WITH A PARTIAL VIEW of the canyon," Skip said, handing El Tovar keycards to Lottie and Webster. Lottie and her daughter were sitting in an ageless, leather sofa enjoying a fire in the lobby. Webster was admiring a bronze sculpture of a stagecoach on the mantle.

Kuul and Lilac were parking and checking in at Thunderbird Lodge, a cheaper and less atmospheric option. It had all the charm of a Soviet-era apartment building in post-war Budapest. He'd meet them after getting the others registered at the finer El Tovar, Grand Canyon's best-of-show.

"That stagecoach is a replica of how tourists got here before the railroad," Skip said. "Even that was for wealthy visitors. The pioneer operators, old timers like the Basses and Berrys, transported their customers in a buckboard. It would take a day of bouncing over rough roads on hard, spine-wrecking benches. If they were lucky, there was a tarp to keep the sun off."

"So, not much different from the back of a van," Webster quipped.

Skip shrugged.

"I made a reservation for you in the dining room at seven. If that doesn't work, feel free to change it with the maître de'." Skip said to Lottie. "The table seats four, so Jack can join you if you choose. Otherwise, Webster, you're on your own."

"I'll probably do room service," Webster said.

"Remember, we won't be joining you. This is your free night. El Tovar Restaurant is a real treat, one you'll long remember."

"We'll miss your stories," Winonna teased. "Are you available later?"

Skip ignored her. She was back to being her brash self. "I'll help with the luggage and make sure you're okay with the rooms. You can call me if you need anything the desk can't help with."

The actress winked from behind her mother's back and mimed using a phone.

"I can take Lottie's bag," Webster grinned, seeing Winonna's gesture. "I just have my duffle."

"Thanks."

Lottie's bag was a light, aluminum roller...her daughter's wasn't. Skip had already dragged Winonna's luggage from the van. She had the biggest four-wheeler Skip had ever seen, the expansion zipper straining like a tube top on Cardi B. There was also a smaller suitcase, a 'cosmetic bag' the size of a hamper, and a rolling 'toiletries bag' with a too-short Velcro strap.

"We'll have to take the Rotunda stairs, national parks don't come with elevators," Skip said, struggling to stack Winonna's pieces, while two bellboys disappeared down a hall.

"Don't drop anything," she warned him.

The Rotunda was a two-story room adjacent to the lobby. Split-log walls, lodgepole columns, beamed ceilings, and thick, wool carpet created a rustic chic. Classical paintings of the canyon adorned the walls. The front desk was on one side, the concierge table and lounge on the other. Wings to guest rooms ran in both directions. A stately staircase led to the original women's lounge. In the late Victorian age, the sexes mingling unchaperoned was frowned upon. To ensure compliance, a life-sized portrait of a stern Fred Harvey, El Tovar's original hotelier, towered over the landing.

Lottie stopped at a curio cabinet showcasing Native jewelry - turquoise necklaces, silver bracelets, and ornate concha belts. Carved figurines of indigenous animals filled one shelf; each creature embedded with intricately inlaid gems. "Beautiful." Winonna pointed out a three-layered turquoise and silver necklace. A repeating arrow motif was inlaid with rubies and bits of pink coral imported from India. A pendant with a bear hung below, its features flecks of turquoise and cobalt.

"What are these figurines?" Lottie asked.

Skip started to point to a coyote carved from onyx. Winonna's toiletry bag shifted, and he grabbed it instead. *Close.* "Fetishes," he said, pinning the bag of personal hygiene against his hip. "The animals embody characteristics their owners wish to emulate; bears for strength, cougars for stealth, eagles for vision, and so forth; not exactly religious, but close if you worship nature."

"And the coyote?"

"He was a complicated character. On one hand, noted for his intelligence and cunning. On the other, a renowned trickster, always working for himself and not the common good. Someone to be wary of."

Webster started to say something but was distracted by a commotion in the guest hallway. *Damn*, this wasn't the time or place, he thought, seeing the source.

"I like the owl better," Lottie said. "Has to be wisdom, right?"

"Uh-huh, the clerk can show it to you?" Skip nodded, hearing the commotion as well. An old man was being wheeled in from the accessible entrance. He was threatening the Navajo bellboy pushing him.

"Bump my knees again Geronimo and..," he cursed, shaking his cane.

Lottie's focus was still on the fetishes, but Winonna and Webster were closely watching the old man's antics.

"Skip," Lottie said, getting his attention. She'd have the clerk show her the owl later. They had a few hours before dinner, and she had another idea. "Could you take us to the Pioneer Cemetery? My parents are there. I promise not to be maudlin again. There's a monument, and I remember being there for the service."

Between the old man's antics and Lottie, Skip's attention to the toiletry case had faded. It slipped. He reached, catching the Velcro strap, ripping it open. A leopard-patterned thong fell into his hand. Winonna stormed away without a word, and he quickly shoved it in his pocket.

"Sure, give me an hour to get everyone settled and checked-in at Thunderbird. I can pick you up out front in the van."

"Thank you. And don't look so embarrassed...I did her laundry for years."

Webster watched the Navajo bellboy push the old man into the Rotunda. His father's eyes were riveted on Lottie Chandler, gleaming at the opportunity. She finished talking to Rhodes, chuckled, and turned back toward the stairs. The old man pulled slightly on his left wheel, veering the chair into her path. The bellboy tried straightening it, but not before it bumped into Lottie.

"I'm so sorry!" Lottie exclaimed. She'd seen the wheelchair too late. An oxygen mask clipped on the arm had fallen to the floor. She knelt to pick it up. "Are you okay? I didn't know you were..."

Lottie gasped as she looked up. The old man in the chair smiled evilly at her. His cruel eyes froze her to the spot. A shiver of fear ran down her spine, even with the shriveled body helplessly twisted into the seat. She felt panic rise from her stomach. He grabbed her hand and pulled her toward him. He exhaled and she smelled hate, the rancid escape of air making her gag. She tried freeing herself, but his grip was surprisingly tight.

Austin Donald whispered, *"Hello...Niece."*

. . .

An hour later, when his phone rang, Skip guessed the call was from Lottie to cancel the cemetery visit. Bumping into the old man had obviously upset her. She had hustled up the stairs, unlocked their room and disappeared into the bathroom, shutting the door without a word. Winonna had taken her mother's bag from Webster and strangely told him to just leave them alone. But instead of cancelling, Lottie was calling to say they were ready.

"The Pioneer Cemetery is beside the Shrine of the Ages," Skip said, as mother and daughter climbed into the van. "The Shrine is a church here at Grand Canyon Village." Skip glanced over his shoulder. Both women were quiet and staring out opposite windows. "It services both tourists and resident workers, and the rangers offer nightly programs there. Do you remember your parent's ceremony?"

"You should keep your eyes on the road," Lottie answered.

Nervous and probably a little depressed, another moment to keep his mouth shut, he thought. What she remembered was her business.

"I'm sorry," Lottie apologized, smiling at him in the rearview mirror. "Being here is affecting me more than I had anticipated."

"Understandable."

"Nana Lou was holding my hand. I had just turned three," she said, speaking more to her daughter. "That was the only birthday she didn't plan something special. I think she was always trying to make up for my mother being gone."

"I remember Nana a little," Winonna said.

The two women were sitting closer. The mother was holding her daughter's hand in her lap. He guessed Winonna had never been told all the details.

"The ceremony was weeks after the accident and funeral. Your grandparents had already been buried, and everyone agreed that was too soon to gather the families. They'd just been through weeks of hell with the search and recovery. The bodies they could identify had been sent to their hometowns. The unidentifiable remains were buried here."

She was sparing Winonna the grisliest details. Her daughter didn't need gory facts from a half-century ago. How the *'unidentifiable remains'* had fit into four coffins. How most victims had burned to ash in the intense fire or been thrown to places the rescuers couldn't reach, where they still rested.

They drove on in silence until Skip reached the Shrine. "Past those stone arches. It's a small place."

Mother and daughter walked to the cemetery holding hands. Skip followed respectfully behind. The memorial was the tallest headstone; a beacon beckoning them toward the tragedy's final chapter. A plain, granite slab with a plaque read: *In memory of those persons who lost their lives in the aircraft accident at Grand Canyon, Arizona, June 30, 1956.* Chiseled in the stone were thirty-one names. Lottie traced the list of names, stopping at the two she knew. She began to shake, and her daughter steadied her hand. They touched the names with their fingers intertwined. Their disagreements and differences were unimportant in that moment, replaced by the deeper bond of family.

"I remember standing with Nana under a huge canopy. Everyone was crying, except for her. She just stared off toward the canyon. I remember the flowers...so many flowers. A choir sang hymns and people joined in. I can't recall the sermons, but I can picture the speakers standing behind a pulpit."

"All my life they've been in the background," Winonna said, sniffling. "I never thought of them being...being someplace specific."

Skip left them alone with their memories and wandered over to another group of gravestones but was still within earshot.

"Nana Lou said that if I kept their story in my heart, they'd always be with me. That's one reason why we never came back. I've passed that sentiment on to you. Remember them that way when I'm gone, not their laying here in...not their laying buried here."

Pioneer Cemetery was the resting place for many Grand Canyon legends - men and women whose marks and stories are still remembered and told. John Hance, Ralph Cameron, Ada and William Bass, and others are buried close to the United Memorial. The thirty-one names on the memorial, however, found their peace elsewhere. Chuar Butte - that was their resting place.

Lauzon, William Francis, U.S. Army, Skip read on a gray tombstone - another old-timer. Bert Lauzon had come to the canyon to be a miner. He'd ended up a Coconino County constable, guide, and early ranger, with a career that spanned most of the last century. Skip envied those who'd seen the canyon before mass tourism, before the smog that floated in from L.A., before the National Park Service and their over-zealous regulations. Men like Lauzon, Hance, Cameron, and the Kolbs, they had been the true founders, the one's introducing a young America to its natural history.

"I remember the smell of pine," Lottie said from behind, surprising him. "I hope I'm not interrupting." She sniffed the air. "They say smell is the most enduring sense."

She seemed in a better mood. Skip looked back to the memorial. Winonna was still there, placing flowers. The movie star had appropriated them from a nearby grave.

"I wanted her to make her own connection. Someday she'll come back without me. Was Mr. Lauzon a friend of yours?" she smiled.

"In a way, I've talked about these old-timers enough that I feel like I know them. He was a ranger and constable here for many years. He was part of a lot of stories I tell. I'd bet he was at your parents' funeral. Before the memorial service you remember."

"It was a tight community then, wasn't it?"

"Yes, it was," Skip said. "Lauzon met Glen and Bessie when they stopped here during their trip. The Hydes journey interested him; he'd been with the Kolbs for the last few days of their river trip."

"You sure? I haven't heard of him."

Skip continued, "Years later, he claimed Bessie had said she was sick of the river. She wanted to quit, and the only reason she went on was because of her husband's ambition. According to Lauzon, Glen was fixated on setting records and on Bessie being the first woman through."

"Do you believe that?"

"I believe Lauzon did. They had definitely had some rough spots and were lucky to get this far, given the river conditions. Maybe she knew that. But, over years of retelling, stories tend to change. Lauzon wasn't alone in recalling her hesitancy twenty-thirty years after the fact. These old timers, keeping each other company and swapping yarns, probably sat around stoves, drinking coffee and theorizing about what happened. Like you said - tight community. It'd be only natural to try to outdo each other...then again, none of them suffered fools or lies."

Lottie nodded. "Without knowing them it's hard to understand the truth."

Skip wondered who she meant, Lauzon and his friends or the Hydes. Winonna joined them, and he didn't have a chance to follow up.

"I don't suppose Captain John Hance will mind my borrowing his flowers. I left his flag."

"Asbestos miner, cougar hunter, the canyon's first paid guide, and he led mule trains. Not the kind of man who'd miss daisies."

"Anyone here you don't know?" Winonna teased. "You should begin adding the cemetery to all your tours. I like it. It's peaceful here. The first stop on this trip I've appreciated. I'm glad we came."

It was nice to see her relaxed and not playing a drama queen, Skip thought. This new, polite, thoughtful Winonna he could get along with. Like she was revealing a personal side she seldom, if ever, let out. Then she checked her phone and the transformation suddenly ended.

"Time to vamoose the caboose." she said, tapping the digital display. "Aren't you supposed to keep us on track? I've got make-up and wardrobe to do before dinner. Spielberg comes here, doesn't he?"

Once a queen, always queen.

"Thanks for bringing us," Lottie added.

31

PRICKLY PEARS

"PLEASE, *PLEASE*, TELL ME YOU DIDN'T SHARE YOUR JOHN Hance tall tale about riding across the canyon on a cloud to the North Rim to hunt mountain lion," Lilac said.

Kuul and Lilac were nursing Summer Sunset ales in the Bright Angel Lounge. Skip was finishing the last of a prickly-pear margarita that had been over-packed with ice. He calculated he'd paid $3.50 a swallow. Catching the busy bartender's attention to argue over a refill wasn't happening. What'd the guy think, he was checking for wind with his finger?

Kuul had snagged the table atop the stairs by the only window. The bar didn't have the cachet of the more famous El Tovar Lounge, but El Tovar didn't have the humorous Fred Kabotie murals on its walls. The painting of dude tourists wearing funny hats and haphazardly riding mules down the Bright Angel trail was generally regarded as the famed Hopi artist's veiled social commentary on race relations.

"I left out how they fall through an opening in the clouds and Hance safely steps off his horse ten feet before hitting bottom," Skip joked, but neither of them laughed.

"Empathy Kemo, empathy. A story about crashing into the canyon isn't appropriate, brother."

"A little credit from both of you please. I didn't tell the Hance tale to the Chandlers. Now, let's go over the rest of the trip, unless you two critics want to keep judging my style?"

"It's not hard, Kemo."

"What style?" Lilac grinned.

They clinked glasses with a waitress in red-leather pants and fake cherries pinned in her hair. Her name tag said she was Carmen from Argentina, and she had brought Skip another margarita.

"You don't even know what they're toasting," he laughed, as Carmen sat his glass down.

She smiled, *"Sí, pero es regalmento con muy macho turistas y rosa bonita* cocktails."

Kuul and Lilac howled as she left.

"Speaking of *turistas*, I plan to walk them along the rim trail from El Tovar and do my usual history talk along the way. Hopi House, Bright Angel, and how Mary Colter's Lookout Studio was built to compete with the Kolbs. Maybe give them time inside Hopi and Kolb if they want to shop."

"That should excite them, Kemo, especially the girl."

"*Ohhh*, that girl will want to shop," Lilac added. "She's a bad actress, but I'm positive she knows her way around any store...especially with her mother's card."

Skip frowned. Any escalation of the cold war between his ex-girlfriend, or whoever Lilac was, and Lottie's daughter was bad business. There was already too much emotion on this trip.

"Maybe you should skip this one. Remember she's a client. They pay my bills."

Kuul cleared his throat, "With Lottie's interest in Glen and Bessie Hyde, are you planning to spend more time on the Kolb brothers than usual?"

"Yup, and out the west rim at Powell and Pima points. I want to talk about Hermit's Camp, the last place the Hydes were seen."

Lilac didn't like being dismissed. Lunkhead, even as blind as he was, had to know the movie star had set her sights on a new boy toy - him. Playing footsy under the table at Cameron and butting in on their garden stroll were just her first moves. Spoiled women like Winonna Chandler didn't take 'NO' for an answer.

"I don't like her!"

Here we go. Skip rolled his eyes without realizing it.

"I know that Lilac, you've made it very clear, but we've got her for a few more days."

"Don't patronize me and don't roll your eyes."

"Look, this whole trip is weird. Don't make it weirder. The rockslide at the ferry, the random attack at the bridge, the..."

"Random! It was the same guy at Wupatki. Twice isn't random. And what about Lottie's correcting you over and over about the Hyde story? You haven't found that odd? There are too many twists happening with this group."

Kuul added thoughtfully, "I would like to know what that old man in El Tovar whispered to her." Skip had told them about the run-in. Some of what Lilac was saying came from her green-monster spirit, but not that.

Skip knew they had a point, but what was he supposed to do? This job was different than his past. Yes, he'd been taught to trust his gut and keep his guard up when signs dictated doing so. And this trip had been full of signs. If one lesson had been hammered home, it was to never ignore or rationalize them. The old feeling that bits of intel were being withheld nagged him. If this had been an assignment, he'd have already aborted.

"I understand and don't disagree. But this isn't a normal tour, we understood that going in. I really need your extra eyes," he sighed, draining his drink and crunching an ice cube in his mouth. "I'm breaking my rule and getting another drink."

Carmen was busy insulting a group of German bikers in her pleasant-sounding Spanish. Their thick, dominating accents had carried across the room, at least to Skip's trained ears. "I'll be right back, and we can finish this," he said, deciding it'd be quicker to take his chances with the surly bartender.

Kuul joined him at the bar. "Once she starts on you, I'm next in line. Indians always get caught in the middle. That's how we lost a continent."

They heard a chair scrape across the concrete floor behind them.

"HEY! COWBOY! STOP!"

Skip turned in time to see Lilac leap down three stairs and disappear into the hall.

. . .

Lilac was nowhere in sight when Skip reached the hallway.

"Right! Go!" Skip shouted to Kuul. "I'll check the lobby."

Kuul ran toward the restaurant and Skip ran left, past the gift shop into the smoky-smelling lobby. A backpacker couple who looked as if they'd just hiked up Bright Angel trail sat on a bench beside the huge fireplace. Their boots and packs were tossed on the floor.

"Did you see a woman run through here?" Skip asked tersely.

The girl looked at the boy she was with; her eyebrows arching in expectation of his answering. The boy shrugged and she frowned back at him.

"We were just in the bar together. Did you see her?"

Skip aggressively stepped in front of them. He'd guessed who Lilac was chasing and there was no time to waste. The girl's anxious glance to her friend, *boyfriend, you need to man-up and take charge*, told Skip she was quickly forming an opinion: agitated stranger - been drinking - chasing girl. She was probably thinking they'd been fighting, and Lilac had run away.

Kuul ran into the lobby and saw his friend at the fireplace hovering over a nervous-looking young couple. He placed his hand on back of Skip's shoulder. "She wasn't in the restaurant. Did you see her?"

The girl eyed Kuul for a second, "She was yelling after another man who'd run into the museum," she said, pointing down the hall to the right.

"What did he look like?" Kuul asked calmly.

"Lot younger than your scary friend, six-foot maybe, thin, a crappy beard."

The boy added, "He had a girly, cowboy hat on and…"

Skip didn't wait for him to finish, "Kuul, check the terrace out back. I'll check the museum."

Skip ran into the museum, a one-room collection of Harvey Girl memorabilia. The room's showstopper was a Mary Colter designed geological fireplace built from rocks stacked in order from the bottom of the Grand Canyon through its top layer. During the day, crowds would be listening to their guides explain its history. At night, the room was empty. Exit doors, painted in Native geometric patterns, led from the museum to the rim. Skip raced through them to the sandstone terrace overlooking the canyon.

Kuul wasn't there. His eyes raked up and down the rim path in both directions. It was too dark to see anyone beyond the building. Sidewalk lamps from Bright Angel to El Tovar cast dim halos of light on the paved path every fifty feet. Between lamps it was as dark as a cave. The Park Service kept even ambient lighting low to showcase the stars. The edge of the canyon was just a black abyss.

Were they out here and which way did they go? His eyes were still adjusting when he heard yelling and Kuul.

"Kemo, this way!"

Skip tore along the path, in and out of the lamplights. A six-foot buffer and a knee-high, stone wall built in the 1930's by the Civilian Conservation Corps (CCC) were all that separated him from the canyon's rim. He saw Kuul run through a halo and disappear again in the dark. He thought he heard scuffling along the rim. But all he could see were the tiny circles of light and El Tovar's shaded windows atop the hill. After dark, the curtains were all drawn.

"I see her!" Kuul shouted. "Go left, Kemo."

The path split. Left ran directly against the CCC wall. Thick bushes in the area between the walks made it even darker; the lamps were on the other path. Two feet away, on the backside of the wall, Kaibab limestone cliffs plunged straight down for hundreds of feet. Every year a few tourists died here from falls, taking risky selfies, or grabbing for windblown caps.

He couldn't see Kuul, but he could hear his heavy footsteps. His friend couldn't be more than fifty feet ahead. The scuffling sounds were louder - a fight.

"KUUL! Where is she?"

"BITCH!" he heard a man's voice bark.

Kuul didn't answer and Skip heard Lilac scream, then falling noises as someone went over the wall. Kuul's heavy footsteps were just ahead, and a different, quicker set of feet began running away, escaping toward El Tovar.

"LILAC!!" he yelled, his voice choking back panic.

"KUUL!"

No answer. He should have caught him by now. Whoever the other person was, his steps were sounding fainter as he got farther away. Skip swore to himself, if he'd hurt Lilac, the man was dead already.

"Lilac!" he cried again, though not as loud. In his heart he knew what had happened. Raw, gut-wrenching fear and guilt flooded his brain.

He kept running, slowing to look over the wall as he went, continuing to call for his friends, hoping against hope. Ahead a bulky shadow carefully climbed over the wall and disappeared in the blackness - Kuul.

Skip knew then, beyond any doubt, that Lilac was gone. A wild howl of pain erupted from his throat. So many words had been left unsaid.

He compartmentalized the crippling fear inside him. There wasn't room for that and for what he had to do. He felt the familiar, cold fury build from the pit of his stomach. They'd taught him how to nurse his rage, how to let it consume him while still maintaining control. The anger was an old friend. Blood flushed through his veins as he forced open a closed door in his mind. From here on he was nothing more than reflexes and training. He hadn't exacted retribution for Daria Ahmadi, he would for Lilac Williams.

At the spot where Kuul had dropped over the wall there was a plaque commemorating the installation of the first rim-to-rim telephone service. The Mayan was standing on a lip of the wall's foundation, praying to his ancestors. Scrub sprouting from the edge of the cliff disappeared within a foot. Below - *Nothing*.

Kuul stopped chanting and stared blankly up at his friend. "She is gone. The Gods admired her battle and spirit, granting swift passage to the next world." Tears welled in his usually stoic eyes. "The jaguar inside me was too slow, brother."

32

HOPI HOUSE

HE'D KILL HIM, AND HIS WOULDN'T BE A QUICK PASSAGE.
Skip ran toward the dark, looming outline of El Tovar. The old hotel sat on the rim at the top of Grand Canyon Village. *There! Ahead!* A shadow with a cowboy hat ran through a halo beside the hotel's side porch. Skip guessed the man was either a guest or parked in the lot farther up the hill. A turnaround in front of the hotel separated it from the iconic Hopi House. A low, landscape light below several trees cast the only glow between the two buildings.

The man was stopped at the turnaround, checking to see if anyone was watching. No one was. Tired tourists were in bed and the train had long since left. His hesitation was a mistake. Skip hadn't stopped, closing in on his prey without being seen. This was his territory. He'd left the path twice, cutting across bare ground, running in a straighter line as the other man followed the path. The cowboy hat turned; the man heard him coming.

Skip expected him to run into the hotel. He didn't. He ran around the perimeter of the turnaround toward Hopi House, Mary Colter's masterpiece, her re-creation of a multi-storied pueblo. The cowboy hat kept turning, looking back over his shoulder. With each turn, Skip gained a few steps.

Southwest pueblos are called stacked apartments because each flat roof is a balcony for the room setback above. Hopi House had four stories of stacked rooms, each offset and at different heights as if they had been added over several centuries as the village grew. Kiva pole ladders rose from one balcony to the next. Originally, Native artisans had lived in the rooms at night and set up shop on their balconies during the day. Tourists would climb the ladders and camouflaged stone steps to view their work. The balconies were off-limits now, the ground floor steps guarded by a four-foot iron fence.

Skip was a cold assassin now, Lilac's loss buried deep inside. He was hunting and there was no room for emotion. He'd molded the fury in his belly into stony determination. His senses were sharpened and clicking at a heightened level. The musty scent of fear lingered in the man's wake. Prey was out there, a living being he planned to dispatch. *Dispatch*, that's what the agency had called it. It was cold-blooded murder, as necessary now as it was then. He wasn't Skip Rhodes any longer. He was what he had been.

Cowboy Hat finally spotted him. Skip dropped all ruse of trying to catch him unaware. The man had paused by the corner of Hopi House, near an iron protective fence, making up his mind whether to keep running or stand and fight. Skip hoped he chose the latter.

Skip didn't hesitate. He charged like a bull out of a chute, with the same intended violence. He'd catch him in the parking lot for the kill. That's when the man first surprised him. He vaulted over the iron fence and scrambled up the stone steps to the first balcony on Hopi House. Mary Colter had built the narrow stairway to look like the ruined sidewall of a long-gone room. The hat disappeared into the darkness; dim light from the hotel porch and beneath the landscaping didn't breach the black night.

Skip barely touched the top rail of the fence as he leapt over. He took the sandstone stairs two at a time, reaching the balcony just as Cowboy Hat climbed off the kiva ladder to the second story. The man was trapped now. He had two choices; fight him atop Hopi House or leap off the pueblo. Either way, Skip would catch him. Jumping would be a desperate move; from this height it'd be impossible to not twist an ankle at best.

The second balcony had been Nampeyo's workspace, a noted potter from the last century who was credited with saving ancient Hopi designs. The only addition to Colter's masterpiece was another adobe block room and open-air ramada on her balcony. Skip climbed the ladder to the balcony and crouched at its edge. Cowboy Hat was at her door, his head swiveling between looking for Skip and checking for any security measures. He'd made up his mind to kick the door in but changed it as Skip grunted and charged.

The only way past him was the way they'd come or a short ladder to his left leading up to another balcony. The man feinted to Skip's left and then jumped right toward the shorter ladder. Skip anticipated his move and blocked him, stationing himself at an angle between both ladders. Cowboy Hat no longer had a choice and squared himself, moving an arm behind his back. Skip heard the distinctive snap of a jackknife.

"You're dead and don't know it," Skip hissed.

The man foolishly stepped toward him and thrust the blade underhanded at Skip's stomach.

• • •

Lilac was cursing herself for letting the man get enough leverage to shove her over the wall. On her way down she'd felt sure she was dead. And she would have been if not for the advantageous decision of a CCC engineer, eighty years earlier.

Outside the wall from the CCC plaque, the ledge of limestone had crumbled. Lilac had gone over backwards, rolling and sliding toward the edge of the cliff, desperately grasping for anything she could find. Just as she'd accepted the inevitable, her hands found an old metal telephone pole. She was able to hook an elbow around the shaft, but her momentum whipped her lower body out over the canyon and back like a metronome, her feet swinging in midair.

The force of suddenly stopping had dislodged her elbow from the pole. At the last second, she'd caught it with one hand and quickly interlocked eight fingers around the base - her legs still dangling in space, her feet scrambling against the side of a cliff. Peeking down, she was unable to see any toeholds. Maybe there was another ledge below, but maybe there wasn't. She managed to work her arms back around the pole, so the immediate danger of falling was past.

Her mind kept picturing the fall into the dark abyss. The Park would probably never find her body, and if they did, they probably wouldn't attempt to recover it. She'd lay rotting, broken, food for vultures. Seconds seemed like hours. She fought to keep her elbows wrapped around the pole. Then she heard feet hitting ground and chanting begin from above. A moment later a man howled in pain and another set of feet ran away.

"Help me," she cried.

"Lilac?"

"Kuul, I'm down here, hanging onto a pole."

She heard rustling and his feet sliding in loose rocks. She thought she saw movement above her, but it was too dark to tell if it was Kuul or something he'd dislodged. That's all she needed, a rock shower.

"She's alive!" she heard him call out, assumingly to whomever she'd heard scream and run away. That had to be Skip. He was probably chasing her attacker.

"Can you climb up?" Kuul called down. "I can't see you."

"I can't get my feet under me. And I can't let go of this pole!"

"I'm coming to you."

Lilac didn't want the big Mayan trying. *"NO! Don't!* It's too dangerous. Let me figure this out." If he slipped, there'd be no stopping. And she knew if he slid past her, she'd try catching him, and they'd both go over the edge.

She heard his feet carefully start to move. A shower of pebbles rained down past her and over the edge. She listened and didn't hear them land. She still couldn't find any toeholds, and she couldn't brace her feet against the cliff without losing her grip on the pole. A dark shadow moved above her. She heard more rustling and then saw a small tree bend down. Kuul was moving laterally to her left, still skidding, but not falling.

"How far are you?" he called to her.

"Not far, can you see the pole. It's short, maybe waist high. I'm holding the bottom." She could see his outline now. He was a little farther away than she'd thought.

"Hold on, I can see you," Kuul said.

She couldn't do anything but watch as he crouched, centering his weight behind his feet in line with the slope. He let go of the tree he was holding. It wouldn't have done any good to tell him to stay put. He slid toward her, toward the canyon, controlling his skid until he grabbed a dead juniper. It was just to her left, its top leaning out over the cliff edge.

"Glad to see you're hanging in there," Kuul quipped.

"Now that you're here, give me a hand."

"How about a leg? My hands have a real affinity for this tree trunk."

Kuul kept hold of the juniper and sat on the ground. He wrapped his arms around the trunk like she had hold of the pole. Stretching his leg, he found her pole with his foot and braced his body.

"Can you grab my leg?"

Lilac let go of the telephone pole with one arm and grabbed his ankle. The shift let her raise her foot enough to find a crack. With that leverage, she was able to climb Kuul's leg until they were both holding onto the precariously rooted juniper. The trunk loosened with their weight but held.

"You first," Kuul said, pushing her up to another short tree.

Once she had a good hold, she helped him up. They worked that way until they'd climbed over the stone wall. Spent and breathing hard, they sat on solid ground with their backs against the wall.

"Where's Skip?" Lilac asked between gasps.

"Chasing your killer."

. . .

Skip let Cowboy Hat thrust the jackknife toward him. He hunched his back and leaned forward at the same time to create a pocket with his middle. The man overreached. Skip pushed his arm harmlessly aside and grasped his wrist. He drove his other fist hard into his ribs.

The man doubled over, and Skip yanked him closer, slamming his knee into his stomach. He heard air escape from Cowboy Hat's diaphragm. Skip laughed, taunting the disabled killer. With the man bent over, he planned to smash his knee into his face while slamming his head down. Two forces crashing together would double the impact. The man's jaw and skull would shatter. He loosened his grip on the man's limp knife hand to ensure his head didn't bounce as his knee struck home. He wanted the man's skull to crumble in his hands.

The younger man surprised him for the second time. Instead of leaning forward, he dropped to one knee. Skip had both hands on top of the man's head and was driving a leg toward his chin. The man reached and grabbed behind his raised leg. Skip staggered back off-balance. The slashing knife found his thigh and he felt the sting as the blade sliced through his khakis.

Cowboy Hat was quick. He had to give him that. The man was on the short ladder to the next balcony before Skip recovered. His leg was bleeding, but the cut wasn't deep.

He just missed grasping the man's foot as he jumped off the top rung. By the time Skip was up, the man had run across the balcony. It was smaller than Nampeyo's and he was climbing the last kiva ladder to the roof of Hopi House. Skip followed, under control. Their cat and mouse game hadn't changed; the man still had nowhere to go. The pain in his leg only refueled his anger.

On the rooftop, Cowboy Hat ran to the backside and looked down. *Shit!* It was too far to jump. He looked back and saw the guide standing in front of the ladder, smiling. He knew he'd been lucky to escape him once. The guide had a good thirty pounds on him and was out for blood. Whoever this fucker was, he wasn't a run-of-the-mill, tour guide. He raced from the back of the roof to the far side. Another faux wall of staggered steps led to a lower balcony on the canyon side of the pueblo.

Skip stalked him, telling the man in a cold voice what was going to happen. At the lower balcony the man jumped a short distance down to a larger balcony. There were no ladders or stone steps to flee from there to the ground. Skip smiled to himself. He couldn't pick a better spot, hidden from the hotel porch and windows.

The man was kicking an old, wooden door that led to an altar room, installed by a missionary who'd worked on the original design with Mary Colter. Cowboy turned to face him, knife in hand. Skip motioned with his hands to bring it. He'd kill him here, but not before he hurt him.

"You shouldn't have killed her asshole. Whatever pain she felt, I promise yours will be far worse."

"The bitch shouldn't have chased me. Did you hear her screaming as she fell?"

"Only the canyon will hear your screams," Skip growled.

The man stepped back, and Skip moved straight toward him. It was a different, better move than the wild lunge earlier. He made several sweeps with his blade trying to back him off. On the man's third swing, Skip stepped quickly to his side. As the man's knife hand swept back, he grabbed his arm, bent it behind him and twisted hard until Cowboy Hat screamed and dropped the knife.

He held Cowboy's bent arm tight, pinning it against his back and yanking it toward his shoulder. Using his free arm, Skip locked his elbow around the younger man's neck. He squeezed until the man stopped struggling. He released the man's arm and slid his hand to the side of his head.

"Listen for the snap," he whispered.

He didn't want the end to happen too fast, instead of one quick thrust and twist he steadily pushed the man's head to the side. When he couldn't push anymore, he spread his fingers over the man's cheek and hooked his thumb under his jaw. The asshole understood he could snap his neck at any time.

"You shouldn't have killed her. On your knees, *NOW!*"

He drove his knee into the man's kidney, and he screamed. Skip forced him down, keeping his hand tight against the asshole's face.

"Quit crying and listen. This is a sound you'll only hear once," Skip chuckled.

He raised his elbow and jabbed his thumb deep under Cowboy's jaw, pressing the palm of his hand against his cheek and leveraging his fingers hard against his temple. It was time to end this.

"On three, asshole. One...two..."

Suddenly everything went black. Skip's head exploded and his knees buckled. Then nothing. He was out cold when he hit the roof.

33

BESSIE AND GLEN

November 15, 1928

BESSIE RAISED HER FINGERS TO SHIELD HER EYES AND GAZED into the awakening canyon. The murky, pre-dawn colors acted as a tonic to her restlessness. Between the army cot in the old cabin and Glen's snoring, sleep had been impossible. On top of it, she'd been sick again. She'd made up her mind Glen could cook his own breakfast when he finally woke up. He needed to start getting used to it. No way could her stomach handle the greasy smell of bacon frying.

She had put her musty clothes back on and stole out to watch the sunrise. She'd heard about the splendor of Grand Canyon sunrises, especially from the terraces below the new Lookout Studio. The clothes could be washed later. The air was cold up top on the rim, and she'd wrapped two blankets around her shoulders. She had gone back in to get the second one after stepping outside.

The golden ball was hidden below a butte to the east. But the north rim was brightly lit because of the fall angles. There, white limestone shined like a spotlight was cast across it. And not just in one place; everywhere up and down the canyon where the rim was angled in the same direction. Successive layers of rock would be brilliantly painted as the light crawled downward. Eventually, the ball would rise higher in the blue-purple sky and the light would nip the tips of exotically named temples, Shiva, Isis, and others she couldn't remember.

Rays of light darted from the sun in all directions as it rose. It was like a diamond under a jeweler's lamp. The bottom rays streaked into the dark canyon. The glare made the inner gorge even more impenetrable to the naked eye. Green-black Moab limestone, below the already lit top layer of Kaibab limestone, made its first appearance. Where the angle had reached deeper, red Hermit Shale was turning fiery umber. A rainbow of rock, each layer a different color, slowly formed.

The canyon's unveiling was the most magnificent site Bessie had ever witnessed. How she wished Glen was here to share the glory...two hands softly grasped her shoulders from behind.

"Second prettiest thing I've ever seen."

Bessie smiled and pulled his arms around her. The warmth from his body added to her pleasures.

"I lined up a bath for you in the lodge. They understood how a gal whose been on the river for over a month might need scrubbing."

Bessie twisted his fingers in jest, just enough to make him say, "Ouch."

God, she looked forward to that bath though. Hot water, the grit out of her hair, no more nasty smells, warm feet - *Clean, Dry Toes!* Hopefully, he'd also lined one up for himself.

"What's our plan today...other than baths and getting supplies?" Bessie asked. "It'd be fine with me if we spent the day curled up in that big sofa at El Tovar."

"Kolb's expecting us. I'd written him. He'd mentioned a meal when we got here, and I'd like to catch his show on his trip down the river. He has a theatre and charges to see the film and hear his lecture. I wouldn't mind picking his brain about what's ahead of us either."

"Well," Bessie said, turning in his arms, "Let's go back to the cabin and you can warm me up before our baths. Then we can meet Emery Kolb."

The sunlight reached the terrace, and they were bathed in light. She wrapped her husband in her blankets and kissed him. This was going to be a good day, Bessie thought...for a change.

• • •

Kolb picked them up mid-morning. He'd driven them out the west rim route to Powell Point where they could see patches of the river. There was a plaque with the names of the Major's men, including the Howland brothers and another man who had left the group never to be seen again.

"The dedication ceremony was held here after Congress finally declared the canyon a National Park," Emery told them. "That wasn't until 1920. The high and mighty Park Service acted like they were the first ones here. Ellsworth and I got here in aught one and felt like *we* were late to the game. There were already lodges, camps, and tours down to the river."

On the way back to the village, the determined Kolb had tried convincing them to take life jackets for the rest of their trip. He'd even offered up a couple of tire tubes they could have for free. Bessie admitted to herself that Kolb had a point, especially when he'd pushed hard after hearing they'd both been tossed from the boat.

"A tube's better than nothing," he'd said.

Glen had just laughed, "You haven't seen our scow. Don't need any with Rain-in-the-Face."

Later she'd sat on the porch with Emery, while Glen paid for supplies at Verkamp's General Store. He'd again asked about the jackets and if she'd been scared when Glen almost drowned. She hadn't been able to meet his knowing eyes when she'd confessed, "a little."

They'd sat silently afterwards and watched the Vercamp children play hopscotch and ride their bikes along the rim. Bessie wondered what it would be like to live at the edge of a world wonder. She thought about the red-headed children's mother; what did she think every time she called her babies, and they didn't answer? After thirty years and two generations, the Verkamps were used to it, Bessie guessed. Everyone here was part mountain goat.

"We'll walk home," Emery said, taking one of Glen's sacks as he came out. "Blanche will have lunch ready by now. I get you two back any later and she'll throw my best camera out the back window."

"She wouldn't do that!" Bessie laughed.

"Maybe not, but Edith might, my daredevil daughter, as an excuse to go find it," he winked. "She'll join us. She doesn't often get to meet girls close to her age with the same sense of adventure."

Blanche had the table set by the time they arrived, and Edith was there, wearing new red shoes. Bessie left the men alone and joined the women in the kitchen.

"By God, Kolb," Glen said, "That's one helluva view you've got out that picture window."

"Put her in myself with Ellsworth."

Glen and Emery were in the living room, downstairs from his studio. Emery and his brother had built the house, room by death-defying room, on a spit of land given to them by Ralph Cameron. It was perched so precariously on the rim that Glen had had second thoughts about coming inside.

"Kinda like being a bird, only in an easy chair," Emery said. "If it weren't for Colter's ugly Lookout Studio, the view would be perfect. The Santa Fe and Park Service thought they could tank my photography business, but I beat'em. Tourists want their pictures taken by a genuine Kolb brother," he snickered. "All they have up there now are telescopes; a closer peek just spoils the grandeur."

Glen was admiring the framed photos on an end table. He shook his head at one shot of the brothers. Ellsworth Kolb was standing on a log spanning a crack in the rim, a deep chasm below. A rope was wound round the log to raise and lower Emery as he dangled below with a camera. *These boys were nuts!* But Glen felt proud to be welcomed into a living legend's home and to have joined the elite group of explorers who'd run the Colorado. Of course, Kolb had taken his brother on his trip, not Blanche.

Another picture showed a brother, Glen wasn't sure which, poised on a boulder beside the river with a coiled rope in his hand. The other brother was shooting a rapid. Glen guessed at the location, "Sockdolager?"

"Above that. Almost lost Ellsworth there. The fool kept trying and our boat kept quitting. You see he's got a jacket on," Kolb noted, deciding he'd give Glen one last chance. "I'm betting he's a stronger swimmer than your little wife."

Glen frowned. "For the fourth time...don't need preservers. Our scow's solid and we've shot every rapid after a quick study. Haven't lined once...or stopped to stage photo ops. We're setting a record and don't want to waste time. I had a lot of training up on the Snake."

Emery nodded and smiled. No sense beating a dead horse. The young man wasn't wanting for confidence. Best let him keep it. That and the unconventional boat he'd described was all he had.

"What happens when you scrape or hit a rock?" Emery asked. "That's gotta happen if you don't line, can't be helped I imagine."

"Rain-in-the-Face laughs and we bounce off. I built her myself at Green River. She's a tough ole warrior."

"Hmmm," Kolb mused, wishing he could see the floating contraption. It had to be huge not to flip. "How do you maneuver something that big? I've seen sweeps and never guessed they'd work here. You have to move side-to-side too quick."

"Just point her nose and say giddyup. She finds the right way with a nudge here and there. Bessie's even getting good at it."

"Lunch is served," Edith interrupted, poking her head into the room. "Your wife says she may not wait on you, says it's the best home-cooked meal she's seen in a long time. You better hurry. The way she's talking she might eat both your plates. Gosh, I like that hairdo she has. It's so cute on her."

After lunch, they all walked outside. Emery set up his latest camera and posed Bessie and Glen in front of the studio's stone chimney. "Take that hat off, Glen. This might be the picture to use on your book and the boards at the theaters," he teased. "Turn to face me a bit, Bessie."

She was standing angled toward her husband with both hands shoved in her pockets, staring into the camera lens like there was something hidden inside. Blanche and Edith laughed; they both looked so serious. Glen started to say something just as Emery took the picture.

"Let's take another," Kolb said.

"Smile, honey, you're such a pretty girl, and you're going to be famous." Blanche said. Bessie beamed. Blanche could count the girl's teeth. Even Glen had broken into a rakish grin.

"Much better," Emery said, snapping the shot. "Get back here next year and I'll give you a copy. Hope to see you both at my lecture later."

"Will do, Kolb," Glen said, tugging his hat back in place. "You ready, Bess?"

"And willing," she said, still smiling at Emery.

"Good luck talking to that reporter from the Denver Post," Kolb called out as they walked up the hill.

Glen had bumped into the journalist that morning while Bessie had been soaking in her bath. He had made a point of mentioning the records they were setting, and they'd agreed on a time for an interview. It was another lucky encounter and a chance for more publicity, like with the cub at Lee's Ferry. Flagstaff, Denver - both good starts. This time, Bessie thrilled him with her rescue of her twice drowned husband. She'd played it up like the Perils of Paulene. The reporter had promised it was front page news.

They'd returned later to see Kolb lecture to a packed house. He'd stood in his basement theater, beside a table covered with mood-setting Navajo rugs and canyon memorabilia and given a running commentary of his and Ellsworth's exciting river trip. The crowd had swooned and screamed as the grainy film captured their "amazing" exploits through "deadly" rapids.

Glen had leaned over and whispered to Bessie, "Notice how it's Ellsworth mostly running the bad ones. Emery's ashore manning the camera."

"We should take notes on how he's excited this audience though. The lady next to me has clung to her husband's arm through his whole talk."

Before going to bed, Glen finished a letter to his father about their stop at Grand Canyon Village: *"At any rate we are over all the worst rapids, so will go on."* Damn Kolb and his life jacket harangue. He hadn't helped ease Bessie's mind nor had the movie with his hair-brained escapades; she'd tossed and turned all night.

In the morning they walked to Kolb's. They'd agreed to meet them for breakfast. Afterwards, the Kolb's had taken them aside and tried convincing them to abandon their trip. Speaking to Bessie, Emery had offered their home for the winter if they didn't want to continue. He and Blanche were going to Phoenix and staying awhile to visit friends. He'd warned them there were worse rapids to come, worse than Sockdolager and Soap Creek.

"Wait 'til spring when the river's better. California ain't going anywhere," he'd said to a sulking Glen.

Bessie thanked him, but explained Glen was keen to see it through. There'd also be work to do at the farm come spring. They appreciated his concern, but they'd be fine.

"Well, you let us know if you get in trouble and need any help. If we're in Phoenix, I can always wire Ellsworth." Emery had said.

Blanche drove the honeymooners back to the Kaibab Trailhead, wishing they'd taken her husband up on his offer. At the trailhead, she watched them gather their overloaded bags and supplies. How they were going to carry all that down Kaibab she didn't know. A wrangler had already headed down with gallons of kerosene for their stove. More goods were being taken by mule to Phantom Ranch.

"Time to leave, Bess. It's a long hike and we still have to stop at Phantom."

Bessie retied her ugly, worn boots, double-knotting them so she wouldn't stumble going downhill. At least it wasn't snowing. She'd tucked the slouch hat in a pocket just in case. With her leather jacket and wool pants, she looked like a boy scout, only with cleaner, better smelling hair. She hugged the older woman, holding her a bit longer and tighter than normal.

"I wonder if I shall ever wear pretty shoes again like Edith's," Bessie whispered in her ear.

Blanche smiled sadly and handed Glen a bag with leftover sandwiches.

"Take care of her," she told him. "Good luck to both of you."

34

RECRIMINATION

"WAKE UP. RHODES! ARE YOU WITH ME?"
Skip forced his eyes open and sat up shakily. His mind swirled, reality still a blur. A man was kneeling beside him, jerking his shoulder and spitting in his face. His head was pounding. Confused, he grabbed him and rolled him over, pinning him with the weight of his body. He shook his head trying to remember what had happened. There'd been a chase and fight.

The man slapped him in the face. Skip felt a feverish surge of adrenalin and tightened his hold. The man was punching him and flapping his legs to buck him off. Skip stared at him, disoriented. He blinked hard trying to clear the fog.

An image of a cowboy hat pinged into his consciousness like a text. *This wasn't Cowboy Hat?* He'd been chasing a younger man. The reddening face in his hands was older. He looked around and didn't see the hat. Nothing made sense.

His head was still spinning, but he loosened his grip. Memories flooded back; *a soft touch, a sweet smell, red hair...man on a roof, choking sounds, killing again.* What had stopped him?

He glared at the man beneath him, trying to remember. The man was scared and trying to hit him again. Skip blocked his flailing fists and kept him pinned to the roof. *He knew this man.*

"What's wrong with you? Get off me!" the man yelled.

"Lilac, where's Lilac?" Skip mumbled.

"I was on the hotel porch and saw you fall. The man you were fighting ran into the parking lot and drove off."

Reality flooded back: the tour, the chase, the fight...*everything but what had happened to Lilac.* This was Jack Webster. He was scouting local tour operators for a St. Louis company. *Lilac, where was she?* Something broke inside him. He recognized the same sick feeling he had when he'd been blown, when he'd read the communique about Daria.

"Lilac?" he asked sharply.

He released Webster and tried to stand. His legs wobbled and he knelt back down. He shook his head and popped his neck side-to-side, gingerly standing again. The dizziness was better. He offered a hand to Webster who was sitting on the roof.

Webster angrily brushed it aside, rising and dusting himself off. "I'm rethinking our future collaboration. We can't afford to fall in with bad company."

'Fall in, fall in'...his words echoed. "LILAC?" Skip cried. The final, awful memory zapped him like lightning. *Scuffling sounds - her screams - Kuul's chanting and lamenting he'd been too slow...it all* poured in. Kuul wasn't to blame, this was on his head. She'd warned him something was off. *Everyone he loved...*

"She fell in the canyon," Skip moaned, falling to his knees, his hands rubbing his face harder and harder until he began punching himself.

"I didn't know...I...I don't know," Webster stuttered. He hadn't seen how the fight started, just how Rhodes had been about to end it. Something bad must have happened to his girlfriend. It wasn't hard to fit the pieces together. *Damnit Hyde! His father would have to let him deal with his nephew now!*

"Let's get down from here," Webster said, helping the guide up.

Climbing down Hopi House, Skip filled Webster in on his chase and Lilac's disappearance. And that it was the same man who attacked Winonna at Navajo Bridge. Webster's only question was if the man had said anything – maybe it would help identify him.

At the bottom, Skip shot ahead of him, racing toward where Kuul had been - rushing into an old nightmare. The halos of light from the lamps mirrored his life: a few dim, bright spots. No matter how far or how fast he ran, the path always led into the dark and ended in death. *Daria Ahmadi*. There was no processing Lilac's light being gone. Not yet. Despair descended over him like a shroud, suffocating his soul. His humanity had disappeared for years after Daria. It had been Lilac who rediscovered it. He couldn't go thru that abyss again.

Farther down the path, two figures appeared under a lamp. A large one and could it be... "Kuul!" Skip called, stepping up his pace. Both figures waved.

"Kemo, I have her," his friend called back.

He ran toward the light, toward Lilac. The big Mayan was supporting her; she had an arm over his shoulder. Skip gathered her and wrapped her in his arms. She melded into his embrace. "He drew a knife and I tripped over the wall, backing up," she said, crying. His hands smoothed her hair then raised her face to his. "You're a fighter, you survived." He kissed her tears before crushing her against him again. They held each other tight; he knew he could never live again without her, he didn't want to.

"I'm never letting you go," Skip whispered.

Lilac stiffened and pushed herself free.

"You left me, you ran away," she wept. "You couldn't have known whether I was dead or desperately needing your help. *WHO ARE YOU?*" she screamed.

Skip stepped away and was silent. It was the one question he couldn't face.

Lilac knew in her heart who he was. That he wasn't who he claimed to be. *Could she live with that?* Could she love a man capable of such emotionless, calculated assessments about life and death? A man who hid in plain sight, a man who wouldn't, or worse couldn't, be truthful with his friends. Her eyes pleaded with him to tell her she was wrong.

He didn't.

•••

"Shit for brains! That's who you are, crap instead of functioning cells," Donald swore at his grandson. "And your uncle had to clean up another of your messes." Fucking Frank's boy, maybe Earl was right about getting rid of him.

"He told me to disappear. He said you were here," Hyde meekly countered.

It hadn't been who Donald was expecting when he'd opened the door. Earl was supposed to bring the movie star to his room for a friendly *chat* about why she needed to cooperate. Instead of Winonna Chandler and his son, it had been his bruised grandson standing in the hall. He should have left him in Reno with his slut. The boy was like his father, weak-willed and always making bad decisions.

Donald swung his cane at boy genius. He was whimpering about how he hadn't started it; like every other time he'd gotten in trouble. Hyde dodged the blow, but the old man's follow-up smashed his ear.

"Could you be any stupider?" Donald hissed.

Hyde rubbed the side of his face and backed away. The old man was really pissed this time.

"We told you to leave them the *fuck* alone. Now you've killed one of them. You don't see the problem there, dipshit? Earl should have let the guide finish you. It would have saved us the fucking trouble."

"It wasn't my fault! That bitch recognized me and chased me along the rim. She's the one that shot at me. What was I supposed to do?"

Hyde had meant to follow their instructions, but he had to eat. How could he have known the red head would be in the bar sitting at the one table where she'd see him leave the Harvey Restaurant? Or that the woman could run him down. *Christ, she was fast!* He'd only done what he had to do. The old man needed to understand he could still be trusted.

"Let me go get the daughter and bring her here. I'll do it without any fuss."

How could anyone with his genes be so dumb? The damn apple didn't... Donald heaved with agitation and doubled-over hacking from the lack of air. Bile filled his mouth, which he spat in a trash can by the desk. He wiped his mouth on his sleeve, feeling old and tired. He grabbed the desk for balance and reached behind him for his wheelchair and oxygen. It was too far.

"Chair," he gagged.

Hyde rolled the chair to him, bumping the back of his legs. His knees buckled and he collapsed hard into the seat. The kid fumbled like a candy striper trying to fit his mask. Donald spit the last of the hacked-up phlegm on his girly, cowboy hat and pushed him away.

"Don't fucking help me anymore! You worthless shit," he yelled, delivering one last whack with his cane.

"Grandpa," Hyde moaned.

"Shut up and listen! I ought to kill you myself the way you're screwing things up for me. You're as useless as your fuckwit father."

"He wasn't useless!"

The insult changed Hyde's demeanor and he glared at the old man. He was sick of hearing him and Earl call his father names. They were the ones messing this deal up, pussyfooting around with the mother. The old man was dying, any fool could tell that. He took a step forward with his fists clenched.

The old man swung his cane again. "Anytime, dumbass. Anytime! I've put far better than you in the ground."

Hyde relaxed and grinned. "You know I don't like your bad-mouthing dad. Why push those buttons?"

Donald laughed at him. The kid was too scared to tackle a sick, old man. The years of browbeating had done their job. He could push the boy as far as he wanted, punch any buttons he chose.

"Listen up. Go to Peach Springs and put our plan in place on the road to Diamond Creek. That's where this will all end." Donald paused to catch his breath. "Keep your pretty face out of sight. And you better pray you don't fuck up again!"

35

RUMORS

A DULL, THROBBING REMINDER OF THE FIGHT BEAT INSIDE Skip's head. The capillary expansion from two cups of coffee in El Tovar's upstairs salon hadn't helped, nor had his restless sleeping. The Chandlers and Webster were due any moment to begin a morning tour. Hopefully Webster was in a forgiving mood, if he even showed. Kuul was sitting across from him, but Lilac had found somewhere better to be.

A young boy's voice rose from the stairs. It was better medicine than the caffeine or sleep. "They gave me a choice and I picked to spend the day with you and Skip."

"You don't want to hike down Bright Angel to Indian Gardens with your parents?" Skip heard Lottie ask.

"Nope."

"Okay Luke, but you might get bored. We're just visiting some old buildings and taking the park shuttle to a few stops along the west rim. You have to promise not to wear out these old legs?"

"Boring? Not! Being around Skip's better than playing Mortal Kombat."

Skip grinned, his head already feeling better. Lottie must have run into the Hufflefingers. Luke's joyful exuberance would be a welcome change of pace.

"Skipper!" Luke called, jumping the last step after seeing his friend.

Kuul chuckled, "Commanding a lifejacket's earned you a nautical title - *Skipper*."

"I've been called worse."

"She'll come around, Kemo."

Luke ran around the carved railing overlooking the Rotunda to give his Skipper a bear hug. Lottie and Webster topped the stairs and joined them; Webster casting a wary glance at Skip.

"I ran into them at breakfast and Luke reminded me of my invitation," Lottie said, tugging his cap. "He's a brave boy and deserves a reward."

Luke showed off his special, centennial-edition hat "Over one-hundred years, see, GC 1919. I know it was a few years ago but pretty cool, huh."

Skip tipped the hat's bill up the boy's forehead, "Pretty cool under there too."

"Winonna's sleeping in and won't be joining us. I thought Luke could take her place?"

"No problem," Skip smiled, elbowing Luke's shoulder. "We always have room for experienced canyon guides. Anyway, Lilac's made other plans too."

"So, she's still around?" Webster asked.

"Her business and he didn't say that," Kuul answered.

"Did something happen?" Lottie asked, picking up on the tension. On closer inspection, she noticed a bruise below Skip's eye.

Kuul recounted events for Lottie while Skip took Luke aside to make hot chocolate. He also drained the last, cold dregs from the coffee carafe. Lottie was deeply bothered by another attack and needed convincing not to cancel the rest of the trip.

"I'm confident we scared him off. Whoever he was, he'd be stupid to try anything else. Especially during the day with so many people around," Skip said. "It's your call, Lottie, but, given the special nature of your visit, maybe you want to reconsider."

"The way he tore out of here in his jeep, I agree," Webster added. "He seemed anxious to put some miles behind him. By the way, Rhodes - no hard feelings."

"If you both think it's okay," Lottie acquiesced.

"Good. And, Webster, I owe you for the assist last night," Skip said, "Well...since you've all had breakfast, how about we walk down the rim trail to Kolb Studio? We can talk about the brothers' role in the Glen and Bessie Hyde story."

Luke chimed in, "Jimmy Honga, the Hualapai guide, told us about them. They died in the river by the *fang* rocks. Unlike Skipper and me, they didn't have life jackets."

"Maybe that's what happened. Though there's more mystery surrounding their deaths than Honga let on," Skip said, lowering his voice conspiratorially and pausing dramatically. Luke's eyes went wide. "A skeleton was found years later at the studio."

"A skeleton! Cool! Let's go."

Skip had walked from El Tovar to Kolb Studio countless times, but it seemed different after last night's crazed chase. Running in the dark, believing Lilac was gone, it was all replaying in his head like an old black-and-white episode from the Twilight Zone. Reconciling that with the Crazy Rich Asians, on vacation, snapping posed selfies and feeding hungry rock squirrels, was not easy.

Past El Tovar he stopped to talk about the Civilian Conservation Corps, how in the 1930s they'd erected the south to north rim telephone line and built the stone wall; Lottie appreciated his romantic story about the lonely CCC worker and the Harvey Girl. After taking pictures of the worker's 'heart rock', he sent them ahead to the museum at Bright Angel Lodge and to refill water bottles. He and Kuul lagged behind to study the scene of Lilac's rescue in daylight.

"We both could have gone over. That was the pole that saved her," Kuul said, pointing and realizing how lucky they'd been. "Kemo, you were right to continue chasing the man. I thought she was gone too. At the time, I was mad at you, picking your revenging spirit over helping your friends. But he should be caught and punished - that is what your ancestors called you to do."

Skip stood beside his friend, struggling with his own thoughts. "The pole didn't save her, Kuul. You did. Things would be much different this morning if you hadn't. My anger made my decision and that was wrong."

Ahead, Luke was waving from the terrace behind the lodge. Outside the museum, Webster and Lottie were at the rim taking pictures of Mary Colter's Lookout Studio. Skip and Kuul waved back and joined them.

"They made me stay back here. Mrs. Chandler didn't want me near the edge without you. Where's the skeleton?"

"Wrong building, buddy. We'll get there, I promise."

Skip walked them through Lookout Studio, giving more details on Colter's natural, architectural style. How she had cast off the reigning Victorian vernacular in favor of a reimagined southwest design. They ended behind the studio, standing on its upper terrace, overlooking the canyon.

"See how irregular the stones are, they aren't cut and there are no straight mortar lines. From a distance it looks like a part of the mountain, but it's always been a gift shop, not a photography studio. Kolb's reputation as the premier Grand Canyon photographer was dominant by the time it was finished."

"This terrace is a special place to watch the sun god, *Kinich Ahau*, bless the day," Kuul said.

Leaving Lookout Studio, Skip led them farther down the path to a chocolate-brown, clapboard-sided house clinging to the edge of the canyon, the topmost floors cantilevered over the rim in death defying fashion. The fact it'd been hanging there for over a hundred years underscored the glacial pace of erosion.

"Whoa! Who lived there?" Luke exclaimed and they all laughed.

"Emery Kolb, but before we go inside, let's stand over there and talk a little history," Skip said, motioning to an iron railing that overlooked the canyon and the side of the house and studio. "The rumors behind the Hydes' disappearance all come back to the two days they spent here in the village and in this house. Many of the wild stories that surfaced in later years were tied to Emery Kolb."

Kuul saw Lottie subtly nod, like she knew what was coming and agreed. He also noticed Webster was watching Lottie.

"The Hydes stopped at Grand Canyon Village to resupply and meet Kolb, who they'd corresponded with before the start of their trip. They had lunch, here in his house, with him, his wife Blanche, and his daughter. He took their picture by that chimney. Two weeks later, Bessie made the last entry in her river journal. And a month after that entry, it was Emery and his brother who found their fully loaded scow floating in the Colorado, its line caught on something under water, *perhaps even someone*."

"Jimmy showed us where they found it!" Luke enthusiastically told Lottie and Webster.

"How'd the old man, Kolb, start the rumors about foul play?" Webster asked.

Kuul had the impression he already knew the answer. Had they ever even discussed 'foul play'?

"It wasn't until later," Skip said. "A sort of cottage industry sprung up about how Bessie, after they'd left here and on or about November 30, 1928, was too scared to go on. How she somehow overpowered and killed her stronger and much bigger husband."

"And then, by herself, hiked and climbed out of the canyon from a spot where it's impossible," Kuul added.

Skip smiled; their tag team was back in the saddle again. "Kind of doubtful, but Emery did a few things, beginning when he found their scow, which kept fueling alternative endings. First, instead of finding out what the scow's line was caught on below the surface... Emery cut it. He claimed it was to get the boat to the bank. That act led to theories that either Glen or Bessie had snagged a foot in the rope at their last stop and been dragged under when the scow accidentally entered the river. The survivor either jumped in to save their spouse and drowned, or they were left stranded in the canyon without any provisions. But we'll never know if that happened because..."

"Kolb cut the rope," Lottie said.

"Yes, he did. In later years, he kept changing his story about their lunch. It became how Bessie was worried because of their mishaps and how she wanted to stay at the village. He wrote to no less than Barry Goldwater with the same story. Goldwater considered himself a river historian and had reached out to Kolb."

"But that wasn't the end of it," Kuul said. "In 1960, when Emery was seventy-nine, he built a boat that looked amazingly like the Hydes' scow, only a whole lot bigger. He planned to raft the Colorado again but had to give it up when no one would go with him. And then there was the skeleton they found up in that attic after he died." Kuul pointed toward the top of the house. "The whole state, even the governor, thought it was Glen Hyde."

"The skeleton! I wondered when you'd get to that!" Luke yelped.

Skip smiled. "Positive identification took a few years. They'd put the poor guy on ice at the coroner's office and forgot about him. Eventually it was proven to *NOT* be Glen. But in the meantime, there was an older woman, traveling alone, on a rafting expedition in the early 1970's, who claimed to be Bessie. She said Glen had been beating her and she'd killed him with a knife when he tried forcing her to continue."

"And then that FBI man, Robert *Fucking* Stack, put that shame-less woman on his TV show, Unsolved Mysteries," Lottie exploded. Her swearing surprised everyone. Luke eyes grew saucer-sized at the f-word. "I'm so sorry," Lottie said, childishly slapping her hand over her mouth,

Skip cleared his throat, "It was definitely a hatchet job. But Stack went even further. His producers cobbled together a totally fictitious and libelous account of how Emery had offed Glen at the studio, hidden the body in his attic for all those years, somehow gotten the scow more than a hundred river miles downstream, and put Bessie on a train back east under a fake name. And then, she of course returned to the scene of her crime forty years later."

"Never mind people had seen both Glen and Bessie after their stay at the village, or that the skeleton in the attic had been proven to be a miner the brothers had found traipsing around the canyon, or that the imposter said she'd *knifed* him," Kuul finished.

"Stack said she'd made that part up to protect Kolb. Bob didn't know what he was talking about," Lottie said, quieter than before. "He said Glen had brow beat her from the start. He made him sound like an abusive, dangerous man, an ambitious 'good-ole-boy' who had crawled out from under a rock."

"I take it you've seen the episode?" Skip asked.

"Several times. I ran across it while researching my parents' accident."

Skip glanced at Kuul, who was studying Lottie. Kuul's gaze showed he was having the same thought; *this wasn't the first time Lottie had finished telling a story that Skip had started.* She'd done her homework.

"The rumors eventually died down after facts finally proved them as preposterous as they were," Skip said. "Stack's is the most imaginative, well-known reconstruction of their ending, but there's been no shortage of other reported Bessies and Glens who escaped the river and led lives under assumed identities. Every one of them has been proven false."

"They both drowned," Luke said, like a jury foreman announcing a verdict. "Heck, we could have."

"That's what most people think. Let's head to the shuttles and go out to the west rim," Skip said. "There's more to tell there."

"I think I'm going back to the hotel. A nap's in order," Webster yawned. "Last night's excitement kept me awake and I've seen the canyon before."

"You sure?" Skip asked. He'd been hoping to redeem himself.

Webster nodded. "Though before you leave, I have a question for Mrs. Chandler. Do you agree they drowned?"

Lottie stared at him for several seconds. "You don't know?"

• • •

After Webster left, Skip asked Kuul to show Lottie and Luke the inside of Kolb Studio, especially the small-screen video of their river trip that always played in the old projection room. Both brothers were filmed being lost time and again in the mists of the Colorado. He wanted to call Sky in Sedona and give her an assignment, which he didn't want them to hear.

She answered on the second ring, "What's up, Boss"

"I have a job for you."

"I have two already, I don't need three. I'm in Boynton Canyon with four geriatric yoga enthusiasts who don't have three good hips between them. They can't stop yammering about their Swami back in Miami. They flew in yesterday and called to book a vortex tour today. And I've promised Zula I'd varnish the *SOB* bar."

"Jeez, how many pepsis wasps are under your bonnet? I'm not the one who came up with the idea for 'enlightenment hikes'. If you were busy, you shouldn't have taken the booking."

"Sorry, the old farts are driving me nuts. What do you need?"

"Can they hear you?"

"Their hearing is worse than their joints."

Skip gave up. "I need you to research the Chandlers, especially Lottie...and Jack Webster too. I'm not sure what I'm looking for but see what background you can find."

"What's wrong?"

"Nothing. This has just been a weird trip." He didn't want to get into the attacks, Sky would just start in on the color of their auras and their core vibrations. "We're heading into a cell-service desert on Route 66 toward Hualapai tomorrow, so it'll probably be evening before you can get hold of me."

"No problem, I'll find out what I can when I get back. These geezers can't last much longer."

"They're customers Sky."

She moaned, "You should see them, they're on their hands and knees drawing circles in the dirt. Oh, for the love of Cat Stevens... Mrs. orange-dyed hair can't get upright! She's rolling toward a cholla. I gotta go Boss - call you later. *Hey! You! Dali Llama! Don't turn that rock over.*"

Skip laughed, "Find whatever you can and call me back. And good luck."

36

SPITTLE AND THREATS

"**I**'M NOT A NURSE," WINONNA CARPED TO THE WHEEZING OLD man in the wheelchair who opened the door. From the looks of him, that's who he needed.

"Shut up and get in here," he tried yelling, but ended up sputtering.

The door slammed shut after she entered the room. Webster had been standing behind it.

Winonna had spent the morning sleeping in, trying to relax in the short tub the hotel called a spa bath, and bartering, unsuccessfully, with the rude, Navajo salesgirl working in the second floor of Hopi House. The turquoise jewelry was exquisite, but nothing like Cartier yellow gold with diamonds. What made these Indians think gluing broken pieces of gems into a hammered, nickel-band bracelet was worth *sooooo* much? They probably made them sitting behind their tepees.

But it had been better than spending another day with her judgmental mother looking at rocks and old buildings. They'd already seen the memorials to her grandparents. For the life of her, she couldn't understand her mother's insistence on the rest of this trip. After the salesgirl had declined to use her Apple Pay, she'd made up her mind to make arrangements for a driver to take her to Vegas. Webster could do whatever he wanted with his pictures.

That plan had changed when she'd opened the note shoved under her door. It was from Webster, telling her to meet him here at eleven. If she didn't, the note warned, the consequences would be along the lines of what happened at Navajo Bridge. That threat had been enough to make her show up. If he hadn't helped save her, she'd have already flown the coop. Who the mean old man was, she didn't have a clue.

"Take a seat on the couch," Webster told her.

"I'll stand thanks. Whatever you want, make it quick. I'm leaving this godforsaken, dried-out crack as soon as the concierge can arrange a ride or flight back to the civilized world."

Webster smirked at the old man in the chair - *I told you so.*

Winonna recognized the look. She often used the same smug glare with her anxious agent. The last time was when directors began calling with juicy, bad-girl roles after the shoplifting charge. She knew her town; any publicity was good publicity.

The old man exploded, "Sit the fuck down...SLUT! You're no different than your arrogant, entitled mother. Either do what we say, or you'll get the same as her. Rotting apples don't fall far from the tree, and you're as spoiled a bitch as I've seen."

Winonna glanced around the room. An assortment of pill bottles and an extra oxygen tank sat on a side table. The window curtains and blackout liners were pulled tight – *not a good sign.* The sickly, yellow glows from rawhide-shaded bedside lamps were the only source of light. A stink permeated the room, old man smell - body odor and a faint whiff of urine, masked by too much Old Spice.

"My advice is to do as he says," Webster laughed.

"Shut up, Earl," the old man barked.

So, he was Earl, not Jack. Webster was probably made-up as well. Winonna studied both men - same size, the old man was just hunched more - same balding hairline, *Earl* just had more left on top – same eyes, both alert and calculating - *and the same exact sneer*. She guessed the resemblance meant they were related, maybe grandfather and grandson. Whatever their relationship, it was clear the old guy was in charge.

"Who are you and what do you want?" Winonna weakly demanded, dismayed her voice sounded so unsteady.

"Ask the one you slid out of. Though I doubt she'd tell you," Donald said acidly, rolling his chair close to her. She had to shift her knees to avoid the gray sweatpants that outlined the bones of his skinny legs. "What I want is her money, all of it, and you're going to help me get it."

"You need to talk with her lawyers, not me. I don't control her finances."

The old man raised his cane. Winonna recoiled and turned away, crossing her arms in front of her face. Then he began coughing uncontrollably. Spit flew all over. She wanted to yell at him to cover his mouth.

"Can," he choked. "Earl, the fucking can." Webster handed him a trash can, and he spat into it, hacked again, and then spit several more times before recovering.

"Care for a cocktail?" he hissed at her, stepping closer, offering the can while he wiped his chin and cracked, colorless lips with the back of his sleeve. "We know about the shoplifting, the fight with the store clerk, and your lesbian thrill ride."

"You don't know Hollywood if you think that hurts me. My agent can't keep up with the calls. You're as dumb as *Earl*."

The old man's ashen face reddened. His jaundiced, dehydrated eyes narrowed as a maniacal gleam lit them on fire. Brown teeth were bared like an animal before a kill.

Winonna had never seen that kind of raw savagery in any of her directors. He was like Jack Nicholson in *The Shining*, only older. His nostrils flared and he raised his cane, same as Jack had done with the axe. She screamed and raised an arm to block the expected blow. A vicious slap came from the side; he'd used the cane as a feint. The taste of iron filled her mouth. Tears of pain and fear raced down her cheeks.

The old man was slapping the arm of his wheelchair in glee. She glanced hopefully at Webster, who just shrugged - *I told you so*. She tried standing, but the old man pushed his cane against her throat, and with the sharp, metal tip he spread open her collar. She froze. He traced the tip down her neck and slid it into her cleavage. Dropping it below a button, he popped her blouse farther open, resting the tip on the top of her bra. His eyes were excited now. He laughed and pushed her back against the sofa. The cane retraced its path, and he pressed the tip under her chin, tilting her head to meet his eyes.

"Girl lover," he jeered. "What a waste. Maybe I'll let my grandson try to change your preference"

He finally lowered the cane and settled back in his chair, placing the plastic mask over his nose and mouth. Gulping for air, his lurid eyes never left hers.

"Gay doesn't hurt either. I'll probably get an Oscar," Winonna mumbled unconvincingly. There was no sense trying to convince him it was a one-time experiment. And admitting she preferred men didn't seem the best course of action.

"Your fucking family has far worse scandals. Scandals I can make public."

"What scandals?" she warily asked, bracing herself for another blast of venom.

The old man's hardened stare suddenly turned blank. He didn't snap back with a sharp answer. Confusion clouded his eyes and he looked at her with uncertainty. *Something had changed!*

Was it possible the old fart was having a stroke? Could she be that lucky?

"Ask mother. She's not just here to see where her child...her child..." he mumbled. His head slumped, "She'll...she'll pay for what she's done."

Webster cleared his throat and she listened as he spelled out the 'Oscar' worthy' role she would play. The story he told was beyond shocking, but how else could he and the old man know so much about her family. It gutted everything she thought she knew. She'd argued twice, unable to believe all he was saying. Both times Webster had threatened to go public. The pictures with her co-star were just prurient icing on the cake; they'd been following her for a while. He'd also been graphically clear about what the old man was capable of; the attacker at the bridge was his grandson. If she screwed them, he'd turn the boy loose.

The old man had rolled himself into the bathroom. The coughing, wheezing, and snorting were constant reminders of his evil presence. Winonna had found it impossible to ignore the sounds. Hopefully, he'd die in there. She heard water splash, choking, and the old man gagging, and then the door opened. His face and few wisps of hair were still damp, a trickle of pink saliva trailed from the corner of his mouth. But his clear eyes told her that whatever had stricken him had passed.

"She on board, Earl, or do I get to have some more fun? It's been a while since my last poke."

"She understands."

"Good." Donald wheeled his chair toward Winonna, licking the drool away with his tongue, the cane lying across his lap. "Look at me, sweetmeat."

Winonna met his gaze.

"Your family stole my past and I'm about to change their future."

37

BESSIE AND GLEN

November 16-18, 1928

BESSIE AND GLEN HAD BEACHED RAIN-IN-THE-FACE AT BRIGHT Angel Creek, where they were to pick up supplies trekked down the shorter and easier Bright Angel Trail. Construction workers from the Fred Harvey Corporation were building permanent tourist facilities upstream at Phantom Ranch and they'd hiked a quarter mile in from the river to see the work.

"It used to be Rust's Camp, but Harvey and the Santa Fe mowed his little operation over, just like they tried with Kolb's studio," Glen said on their walk back.

At the scow, a portly, middle-aged man with his hands on his hips was studying their gear. "Wonder what that fella's planning?" Glen said, as they approached the bespectacled man with the sporty English cap.

Adolph Gilbert Sutro wasn't just any tourist. He was from San Francisco and a true adventurer, despite his slightly frumpy look. Sutro was also rich - generationally rich. His namesake grandfather had built and profited from the Comstock tunnel in Nevada, charging the large, silver mining corporations a fee to drain their mines. Adolph senior had gone back to Frisco, made astute real estate investments during the city's early days, and eventually got himself elected mayor as an independent progressive.

The Sutro checking out Rain-in-the-Face was now head of the family's enterprises. He was an accomplished pioneer in his own right. It had been fifteen years, but he'd set a number of records in hydroplane aviation, risking life and limb in a pontoon biplane over San Francisco Bay. For his prowess, he'd earned the first Hydro-Aeroplane club license. Prior to that, he'd experimented with the Wright Brothers. He wasn't a man easily scared, although he prided himself on being cautious and prepared before accepting life-balancing risks.

"Back at camp they said you've come down the river all the way from Wyoming. Is this what you've done it in?" Sutro asked, skeptically. Their boat looked like a floating cargo box to him.

"True enough. We're half-way through a record setting trip. We've run every rapid and are setting a pace that won't be broken for a while. My wife here," Glen said, proudly pointing to Bessie, "will be the first woman to navigate the river. We're expecting to make some good money off it when we finish and tell our story."

Sutro smiled and said hello to Bessie, introducing himself to the bold couple. With the wife, he didn't sense the same bravado as in her husband. What a little thing she was, he thought. Hardly big enough to help manage the clunky looking boat. She looked a little pale and under the weather too.

"You always keep your boat tied up this way? A bowline looped around an oar pushed in the sand."

"It's a scow," Bessie said. "My husband knows what he's doing."

"Didn't mean to suggest otherwise," Sutro said, softening his tone. "You've made it this far, so you're obviously in good hands. How soon are you leaving?"

"Soon," Glen said.

"Well, if you can give me time to get a pack together, I've got a proposition for you. I'd like to join you for a way, catch a few rapids, and leave at the next trail to Hermit's Camp. I suspect you'll get there later today. Being down here, the river's got my interest piqued. How about it? Might be useful having an objective account of your record-breaking run."

Glen looked at Bessie. He wasn't sure he wanted the man's company, even for a day. The crack about their mooring didn't sit right. Bessie eyed the new camera Sutro had been taking pictures of Rain-in-the-Face with. He could take some great action shots from inside the scow. And she'd heard of the Sutros, they were famous in California. He might be a good contact to have later.

"Rapids won't be easy," she said. "But if my husband's okay with it, I am." She nodded at Glen to tell him it seemed a good idea.

Glen rubbed his chin, taking a few seconds to think over Sutro's offer. "Get your stuff, we'll wait here. No farther than Hermit's Camp though."

"Oh no, that's enough to give me a taste. I'll be back shortly, let me grab my pack and tell the wrangler I hired to haul the rest to Hermit's instead of El Tovar where I was staying."

Sutro was quick, and Glen pushed the scow into the current a half-hour later. In the meantime, Bessie had convinced him that the stranger seemed a good sort and that they could get added publicity later from having a celebrity along.

They were in trouble less than a mile downstream.

"Keep her out of that eddy!" Glen yelled over the roar of the river.

They'd run into another whirlpool, this one bigger than what they'd experienced in Cataract. Strong waves kept pushing

Rain-in-the Face into a large, circling eddy along the shoreline and sending them back upstream. No matter what they tried the scow kept repeating the same pattern, refusing to let them continue downstream. They'd been in the same frustrating loop for nearly an hour.

"Let's try beaching her upstream of the eddy and pushing off into the main current. We should clear the whirlpool if we can keep her in the center," Glen finally suggested, not knowing what else to try.

After beaching and laboring to get Rain in position, Glen shouted at Sutro to get inside. He and Bessie would push into the current at the right time and then leap in to join him. If they worked the sweep oars hard, they should slot into the main current and avoid getting caught in the whirlpool.

"Make sure you get in," Sutro warned Bessie.

"Now! Push!" Glen ordered, reading the swells.

Bessie pushed the scow and leapt inside. Glen was right behind her after giving the boat a final tug to straighten her out.

"I think we're good!"

Sutro wasn't sure; he could feel the tail wave sending them toward the swirling water. The scow was trying to turn again. Glen and Bessie were pulling and pushing furiously on their sweeps. *It was going to be close.* Just as Sutro thought they might slide by, Rain-in-the-Face's nose surged right, and the scow spun into the whirlpool. *Caught again.*

"We've got no choice but to try it again!" Glen hollered. "Nothing else we can do."

After several more attempts and tons of spent energy, the scow finally stayed in the main current and sailed past the whirlpool. Glen and Bessie were exhausted. They'd been repetitively using the same tired muscles.

At least they were safely headed to Hermit's Camp, Sutro thought. He'd had his taste of running rapids. When he flew, he had absolute control of his machine. As plucky as this pair were, they didn't control their scow, the river did.

It was only a matter of minutes before he saw the Colorado wasn't done with them yet. The inner gorge narrowed, and they kept gathering speed. He spied two boulders breaking the surface, like the devil's horns. Past them, the river dropped steeply into an endless series of frothing waves. Whatever lay hidden in the water was masked and waiting. Naked fear grabbed him for the first time. The whirlpool had been exhausting, but it'd basically just whipped them around. But these rapids...there was no way to avoid crashing into the granite walls.

"Kept her left, Bess!

Bessie saw jagged spires of brimstone rising out of the foam. The current was forcing them toward the meanest of the waves and drops. The angry water was cannon-firing any debris that dare enter its realm into the hard, cliff face.

"Glen, I'm scared!"

"Hang on aviator!" Glen yelled to Sutro, who was shivering in the scow's bottom. He chose his path and laughed nervously. "We're going in."

Rain-in-the-Face rode into the churning waves. Sutro wasn't sure what kept the oaring couple on the platform and in the boat as it flew up and over crests taller than cabins. They crashed down the back sides into deep, hellish holes. Water flooded over them, inundating the boat. Each wave twisted and turned them uncontrollably, and each time he was certain they were flipping. They were ice cubes in a cocktail shaker being shaken by a madman.

He'd given up all hope and was praying to Jehovah, when the current spit them from the last of the waves and into calmer water. Glen spied a sand bar and signaled Bessie to steer that way. He and Sutro jumped out as they got close and pulled the scow in as far as possible. Sutro collapsed on the beach and Glen rammed an oar into the sand, tying off the bowline. Bessie stumbled ashore, looking for a soft place to fall.

"I'll find some wood for a fire," Glen said. "This sand's soft enough for our bedrolls, I'm too tired to haul the bedsprings up here."

Sutro was fine with spending the night on the beach. He wanted to get to Hermit's Camp alive; taking an extra day was a distant, secondary consideration. Solid ground had never felt so good, even after his many aerial misadventures.

That night around the fire, Glen kept bragging about the money they were going to make playing vaudeville theaters. Sutro listened politely as he dreamed of striking his own Comstock Lode - getting away from the river in one piece.

"I was born for show biz," Bessie chirped.

Dry, warmly wrapped in quilts, and resting in her husband's arms, she was singing a different tune than earlier. While Glen had gathered wood, she'd confided that if it weren't for her husband, she'd quit the river. She'd even said she might not leave Hermit's Camp and hinted about enlisting his help. They'd had too many close calls, worse than today.

"The money will set us up. She may be bent on show biz, but I was born to run wild rivers and explore. Nowadays, there's a buck to be made doing just that."

Sutro wanted to point out the flaws in their dreams, but he didn't. He was counting on them to get him to Hermit's Camp. Glen was a decent enough guy, just a bit brash, over-confident, and unworldly. It came with being young; he hadn't learned his limitations. Sutro knew from experience that becoming famous through crazy exploits was a dangerous game. How many times had he almost died crashing planes? He'd been fished out of San Francisco Bay twice. Orville and Wilbur had nearly killed themselves learning to fly in homemade deathtraps - not much different than learning to run rapids in a poorly designed and cheaply crafted boat. You needed luck, and you either had it or you didn't. He hoped they did.

"Money aside, my guiding philosophy has always been I'd rather be a live coward than a dead hero. That conservative view has stopped me from wing walking and marriage," Sutro said, and they all laughed.

"Let's turn in," Glen said. "Heroes need rest."

· · ·

Sutro awoke to the sounds of vomiting. Bessie was having another rough morning. She was doubled over, heaving into a stand of tall grass. With the prospect of another wild day on the river, he felt like doing the same. Glen was packing the scow with the few items they'd brought to their camp, ignoring his wife's discomfort. Sutro decided to give Bessie her space and walked to the river.

"Strong headwind this morning," he said to Glen. "Your wife sick often?"

"Probably all the muddy water we ingested yesterday," Glen chuckled. "It's been a long, wet, cold trip. She'll be fine."

Sutro helped stow the blankets and cook stove, then wandered downstream behind a bush. When he came back from his morning constitution, Bessie was in the scow ready to go.

By the time they pulled in at Hermit's Creek, they were again exhausted after running one bad rapid after another. When they'd cast off from Phantom Ranch, he'd had the thought in the back of his mind to maybe finish the trip with them. A day and a half later, however, he realized his generous assessment of Glen's skills had been a mistake. He also didn't trust Glen's decision-making - prioritizing future payoffs ahead of staying alive. He'd been foolish to join them. Never again would he let his curiosity overcome his good sense.

"We'll hike to the Camp with you to say goodbye," Bessie said. She'd been nervously eyeing the fearsome set of rapids downstream while Glen secured Rain-in-the-Face. She shivered at the thought of running them. "Those are horrifying, Glen."

Glen stared at the rapids a long time. "Okay, I guess you can use a break. They're a rough set, that's for sure."

Hermit's Camp was another Fred Harvey concession. The rustic facilities were deep in the bottom of the canyon, managed by a married couple, the Pifer's. A trail led from the rim for visitors to ride mules down into the canyon to the Colorado. It was developed to compete with Ralph Cameron's privately-owned Bright Angel Trail. November was late in the season, and few people were around when they arrived. Sutro's man was there with mules outfitted for their ride back up.

Bessie and Glen signed the Pifer's guest book and enjoyed a quick lunch. Bessie was in no hurry to leave. She chatted with Mrs. Pifer and let her show her around their house and camp, taking time to examine each of the artifacts they'd collected from around their home. Glen wasn't stomping his boots, but impatience plastered his face. He was anxious to get back on the river and through the next rapids before stopping for the night.

Sutro posed the couple for a parting picture outside, and it was obvious from Glen's expression that he was holding in his anger at his wife's orchestrated delay.

"It's *Time to Go*, Bess."

When Sutro waved goodbye from his mount, Glen was already marching back toward the river. *Yep, I'd rather be a live coward than a dead hero*, he thought.

Bessie, Mr. Pifer, and another guest lagged behind Glen. As they approached the river, the rapids roared at her. She didn't want to disappoint Glen, not after they'd gotten this far, but the idea of careening through more whitewater, praying they would somehow avoid boulders and stay off granite walls, terrified her. But what choice did she have?

She took her time saying goodbye to Mr. Pifer and his guest, who had come to watch them launch into the churning, head-high waves; waves that seemed to never end. She desperately tried to steel her courage and join Glen, who had untied Rain-in-the-Face. He stood waiting, holding the scow in place against the current. Bessie felt each step was leading her toward total disaster. Why was he so hell-bent on leaving so soon?

"Let's go," he said, reaching his arm out to help her.

Bessie hesitated, stared at the shore, too afraid to look at the rapids, and kicked a few pebbles. Pifer and the other man had wandered downstream and were sitting on rocks overlooking the start of the whitewater. The constant roar of the river kept them out of earshot. *God, she wished the noise would stop.*

"Why don't we stay here tonight?" she timidly suggested. "I'm spooked right now, Honey. My stomach's still roiling. I'll feel better tomorrow."

Glen slammed the oar between two rocks and looped the bowline around its handle. Bessie saw his angry look and instinctively moved back. He stepped forward.

The river continued to scream. "Let's stay, please. We can talk about the trip tonight," she pleaded.

"Bess, it'll be fine. These rapids are bad, but they aren't any worse than what we've been through. We spent an extra day at the Village waiting on our supplies to get packed down. I don't want to lose any more time."

Bessie still hesitated. Something was telling her to not get into the scow.

"We'll get through okay. I promise," Glen said. "Come on now, it's time to go." He was reaching and motioning for her to join him.

Bessie stepped back, stumbling over a loose rock. Glen leapt forward and caught her as she leaned forward to regain her balance. He pulled her into his powerful arms and half-carried her back to the scow, lifting her over the side and setting her on the floor. Bessie pushed him away, "Please, let's stay. Something's going to happen! I can feel it!"

Glen gathered the rope and oar, pushed Rain-in-the-Face into the current, and leapt over the side and up onto the sweep platform.

"Honest to God, Bess, we have to be through the worst of it. You're just scared and not yourself. That damn Sutro talked too much. Now climb up here and man your sweep. You'll feel better with something to keep you busy."

They were already entering the first big waves. Bessie knew she had to help him. What choice did she have?

38

HERMIT'S AND ADMISSIONS

 KIP, KUUL, LOTTIE, AND LUKE WERE AT PIMA POINT ON THE west rim shuttle route. From their mile-high perch, they gazed down at a cascade of red buttes eroded into shapes styled as temples. Side canyons and draws carved from colorful, rock strata wound around them like a giant serpent trail left in the earth. Near the bottom, the eroding layer of green shale disappeared over an edge into the vertiginous inner gorge. The two-billion-year-old granite crack was separated by a harmless-looking, brown ribbon crisscrossed with wavy streaks of white rick-rack - the Colorado River.

"See those bald spots, where the side canyon bends away from us, below the red wall and above the draw going down to the river," Skip said, pointing Lottie deep into the canyon. "That was Hermit's Camp, the last place the Hydes were seen alive. There were reports that they'd argued there. Bessie was refusing to continue, and Glen grabbed her and physically threw her into their scow. It was that

episode that spawned the rumors about her murdering her husband, some with and some without Emery Kolb's help."

"What happened to the camp? Nothing's there," Webster
asked. He had changed his mind about the nap and been waiting
for them at the shuttle.

Kuul answered. "Once the Park Service took over Cameron's
operation and his privately run Bright Angel Trail, there wasn't a
need for it. They improved Bright Angel and turned an old camp at
its bottom into Phantom Ranch."

"Believe it or not, the Harvey Corporation had installed an
aerial tram from the rim to the camp to dismantle most of it to
use elsewhere. All those changes were still underway when the
Hydes rafted through," Skip added. "They picked up a passenger
at Phantom, Adolph Sutro, who rafted with them for two days and
later abetted the rumors with a first-hand account of Bessie being
scared and wanting to quit. He left them at what was left of Hermit's
Camp, the first trail heading out of the canyon."

Luke leaned over the rail, craning his neck, pointing west toward a squiggly, milk-chocolate line at the bottom of the canyon. "Is
that the river? I think I can hear it."

Everyone quieted, trying to hear the rush of water.

"You've got great ears, like the jackrabbit," Kuul finally said
to the boy, who beamed. "That rumble is the river's life rhythm.
Water, sky, matter - each is here in abundance and their balance
sustains us. Listen closer, can you hear grinding and splashing
sounds?"

Luke tried stepping to the lower crossbar of the railing, so he
could bend at the waist. Skip grasped his collar and pulled him back
down. "You can hear it fine from where you are."

"I can hear it," Lottie whispered, trying to focus on the sound.
"Those white streaks are Granite Rapids. They're what scared her.
She saw those when they stopped to let Sutro out, that's why she
was ready to quit."

"You're right. Those are rapids," Kuul confirmed, "They mark the beginning of the Upper Granite Gorge, miles of bad water gushing through evilly pinched points caused by small creeks dumping debris and rocks into the river."

"No wonder she wanted out," Lottie mused.

"Not badly enough," Webster said. "She should have killed him if he was making her go down those."

Lottie and Webster's eyes momentarily locked, then quickly they looked away. Skip had seen similar, clandestine glances between too many faces to not recognize their meanings. Lottie was curious, warily curious. Webster's look was taunting and cruel.

"Well, she didn't," Skip said. "Not at Hermit's Camp, anyway. There's too much proof they both left together. Of course, facts seldom stand in the way of a good conspiracy theory. One story, Pifer and his guest helped her do away with Glen after he flew into a rage when she refused to leave. Another rumor, Emery and Bessie prearranged his meeting them at the camp and waylaying Glen, throwing him in the river and setting the scow adrift. Both cases were fueled by there being so few witnesses. Decades later, when historians began checking stories and interviewing people, they couldn't find the Pifers or their guest. Emery, of course, denied any part. And Adolph Sutro was anything but forthcoming. His recollections were oddly vague and sketchy."

Luke had clung to every word of the mystery. "So, maybe she did kill him. Maybe she whacked him like Lizzie Borden!"

Skip and Kuul laughed at his joke. Lottie grimaced.

"But there's a record of them after Hermit's Camp," Skip said to Luke. "Remember what Jimmy Honga told us - they disappeared farther downstream, past Diamond Creek. Bessie's own journal takes them well past there. Rescuers found Glen's tracks and another campsite below Diamond. They even reportedly carved their initials in an old mining cabin at Diamond. There was also photographic evidence they made it farther - a picture in Bessie's camera.

No, if something happened between them, it was well past Hermit's Camp. But it's possible their disagreements grew after that point."

"All of that could have been faked," Webster suggested. "Her journal was copied by Ellsworth Kolb after they found the scow. His version is all that's left. The original was lost."

"We haven't mentioned that yet," Kuul said, eyeing Webster.

"It's an interesting story. You hooked me and I looked it up online."

Kuul nodded, he wasn't sure he accepted the man's explanation. And it wasn't just Webster, Lottie also seemed to know more than she was letting on. These people knew too many details about the Hyde's trip. He wondered if Skip was having the same thoughts.

"Well," Luke said, disappointed Skip's story hadn't ended in a video-game-styled death match, "Maybe she shot him past Diamond Creek with his Winchester?"

Skip admired his persistence. "How'd she get out of the canyon, buddy? You've been through there."

Luke frowned and shrugged, "Maybe she didn't. Maybe a wild animal got her."

A shadow cast from a lonely cloud in an otherwise blue sky settled over where Hermit's Camp had been. They could see the trail leading in and coming out, but the area where the buildings had been was shrouded in a dark haze. Kuul, Luke, and Webster started walking back to the shuttle stop. Lottie and Skip stayed a moment longer at the overlook; the woman lost in thought.

"She didn't want to go," Lottie stated. "She loved him, but she was scared and wanted to save her family."

"Glen was all she had," Skip answered. "You don't give up on someone you love."

• • •

Knock - knock - knock.

At first, Skip thought the knocking was at the room across the hall. He'd settled into his room for the night after dropping Lottie and Webster at El Tovar and reuniting Luke with his tired parents.

Knock - knock - knock. It was a quiet, hesitant rap on his door.

When he opened the door, Lilac was leaning in the archway. Her eyes were red, and she was staring at the floor. She seemed nervous. Not wringing hands, cracking knuckles nervous, although she was rubbing her fingers. They were pretty, long, sculpted fingers. She glanced up at him twice, both times quickly breaking eye contact.

"I want to talk before heading home."

She walked into his room and stood behind a side chair, holding its back – a classic defensive posture. It was a light chair; Skip knew she was capable of winging it across the room. After several, excruciating seconds of studying his face, she stepped toward him, back toward the door - without the chair. He was sure she had decided this was a mistake and to leave. She stopped and stared at him again, her usual strong, confident glare returning. *Maybe he was supposed to say something.*

She shook her head at his pitiful, confused expression.

"I won't call it love. You don't deserve that. But I don't know what else to call it. Whatever this *relationship* is, *I need to understand it*. I need to understand you and..."

"Lilac, I..."

She held her hand up stopping him.

"Not yet. Just shut up and let me finish. I'm going to tell you what I want. What I *need* if we have any chance of making this work. If you even want it to. I don't even know that," she said, holding his eyes with hers until he nodded.

She took a deep breath, "Usually, with men, they tell you upfront where they're from, what they do, who their families are, hell, even their favorite teams. They can't wait to tell you that easy stuff. But what women want to know is what they feel and what they're thinking, and what they believe in. That's how we decide if we can trust them. With you, it's just the opposite. Before last night, I thought I could trust you. Our problem is that you've never shared anything about Skip Rhodes. Everything with you is in the moment. Maybe you're more open with Kuul - I don't know and don't care. *But* if we're going to be more than what we are, and that's what I want, then you need to tell me...*Who You Are*."

"Are you sure you want to know? Maybe I'm not who you need me to be," Skip said, coldly.

"Maybe. But that's for me to decide."

From his stony tone and dead eyes, she could tell he'd flipped some internal switch. He wasn't her scarred, troubled, intriguing boyfriend any longer. Nor was he any normal tour guide. It was a hunter's eyes she stared into, a lone wolf that wanted to run alone, not a thing you wanted to back into a corner. This man was darker, scarier than the one she knew; she felt ripples of danger and the little voice in her brain yelled 'get ready to run, girl.' What door had she opened to his soul?

"There are things I can't tell you. I've told you that. Why do you have to push?"

"I tried," Lilac said, stepping toward the door.

"Wait - Please."

His body tensed and she could see he was fighting against himself.

"You shouldn't trust me," he started. "I'll tell you what I can... more than I should, and then you can't ask for more. No matter what Lilac, you can't ask for more."

She sat in the chair.

Skip struggled with where to begin. He knew this would forever change how she saw him. He wasn't some starved, stray, emotionally abused kitten she'd adopted - far from it.

"I've done ugly, awful things, Lilac. My only *relationships* have been fleeting, superficial retreats from a violent reality." He thought about Daria. "Only one was ever real, before our games and breaking of rules caught up with us. We'd made plans, we shared things, and it didn't work. Getting close only made things worse."

"Were you in love? Do you still love her?"

"I wanted to quit and be with her. When it was time to decide, she didn't. A shrink would say that's why I don't trust you enough to tell you everything."

"You can."

Skip's brain was processing how much information to give her. Telling her about Daria Ahmadi was only part of what she felt she deserved. He hadn't yet touched on her question of who he was. *Should he?* He could always disappear and start over again. Names and identities were easy. *Could she accept it?* As an ex-cop, she'd seen the world's underbelly, but nothing compared to what he'd witnessed – what he'd done. Underneath her tough shell, she was as innocent as Luke. Most people had no clue what was out there, gunning for them. Their worlds were small and safe. He had been a reason they could live those sheltered lives.

Skip inhaled and released the air slowly, like he'd been taught.

"I was recruited, not by any agency you've heard of, while at a small, midwestern university. That's how they did it, how they found their people. Other 'protective agencies' like Ivy Leaguers, they help with the politics, and they have contacts. The agency that employed me doesn't care; they're non-existent, deeply buried in a bureaucratic maze of rabbit holes. And they train that way; years pass before you're told who they are. They think they're patriots, and I did too for a long time, but their actions, while necessary, are coldblooded. Evil has a home in many places, Lilac, and there's no easy way to exorcise it. They need a certain kind of person; a person who can justify crossing boundaries."

Skip took another deliberately controlled breath, giving him a moment to think. He gave her a hard, calculating look. *She won't let it rest there.*

"The assignments were never clean," he said, looking straight into her eyes.

She looked away and he knew she understood.

"But you left, after the woman," Lilac whispered. She'd been holding her breath. Strangely, the sense of danger she'd felt from him was gone. An emotional numbness and the deep pain of loss had replaced it. The kind of pain that leaves a hollow in your stomach and that you can't hide from.

Skip icily repeated her words, "Who-Are-You. That's what you asked for. That's who I *was*. I don't apologize for any of it." He didn't tell her that's who a part of him would always be. No one could just leave that life.

"You're saying you killed...murdered for them...or...or worse? And *Skip Rhodes* - what's your real name?"

"Neither matters any longer."

Lilac wasn't sure what his answer meant. Had he put that life behind him? Was he saying they were through? Did it mean he viewed his soul as dead, his humanity irredeemable? What was inside him to have accepted that life, to have gone that far? She had to get away to think. Her heart felt deep sorrow for him...for her. Everything had changed. His face was expressionless, his blue eyes emotionlessly studying her reaction. He had to know he'd never be Skip Rhodes to her again. He was right; she shouldn't have pushed him.

Skip sadly saw she wanted to bolt. He'd been resigned to that ending from the start. Lilac's sense of right and wrong was strong. Lying would have been better. He sighed, accepting her unspoken judgement. Someone, somewhere, sometime had written you can't outrun your past. He understood and had long ago accepted it. Telling his story had been inevitable, but look at the damage he'd caused and to someone he...

Lilac's hand hesitantly reached out - fingertips softly touching his strained face. A face in which she read remorse. She kissed his cheek. Was it compassion, a spark of hope, or a wistful goodbye? She honestly didn't know. She smiled dimly and lightly pressed her lips against his, her hands still cradling his face. Skip started to put his arms around her, but she stopped him.

"We'll talk again. I need time."

Knock - knock - knock.

Not now. Skip ignored the door.

KNOCK - KNOCK - KNOCK. Whoever it was wasn't going away.

"Go ahead. I have to leave."

Skip opened the door, catching Winonna Chandler's fist as it came forward. She was leaning against the doorframe, one long heel raised behind her. Her breasts suggestively turned toward him. The same pose used in a million calendars pinned up in service stations.

"Mind some company?"

Skip thought he smelled jasmine or honeysuckle. It'd been a chilly walk from El Tovar and her sheer, silky blouse left little to the imagination. Her hair was swept to one side exposing a sexy neck he hadn't noticed before. The moist, seductive, movie-star lips were painted a pink shade to imitate...well, to imitate.

"Not at all," Lilac said from behind him.

Winonna was surprised but didn't miss a beat, "Am I early?" She winked at Skip and walked in.

"A little late," Lilac answered.

Winonna had guessed Rhodes and the red head were more than just tour buddies. Seeing her here this late, with wet eyes, albeit threatening ones at the moment...she'd read this manuscript before. The little smudge of lip gloss on Skip's lip suggested even more. She had to hand it to Annie Oakley. She wouldn't have thought crying was in her repertoire. And the man they both wanted was just standing there, not knowing what to say - *that was promising*.

Skip began stammering.

"It's okay," Lilac said, patting his arm. "Take care of her. Cruella de Vil is probably just out of toothpaste."

She brushed past the movie star into the hallway and turned.

"I know who he is. You'll be safe but don't expect much else."

39

FRICASSEED ROADRUNNER

"**R**OADKILL," WINONNA MOANED, PRETENDING TO GAG.

"Skunk's not half-bad so long as the anal gland's been removed," Kuul joked.

They'd left the Grand Canyon early on their way to Page Springs and Diamond Creek. Pulling into Seligman, Arizona, they stopped for lunch at the Roadkill Café, a true, local joint with a sign picturing a cartoon buzzard on a desert road pecking at a dead pile of fur.

"You can wait in the old jail out back if you aren't hungry," Skip added.

After her late-night stunt, he wished he had the key to throw away. She'd flashed more skin than a New Orleans tattoo artist saw during Mardi Gras. It had taken him an hour to wrap her up and herd her back to her room.

"Apparently, if your town is in the middle of nowhere Arizona on Route 66 you sell what you have," Webster said, eyeing the green, space alien sitting in the rusty Ford pickup without a motor. "Check out that stuffed dummy bathing in the claw-foot tub on top of the gas station."

"We aren't really eating here?" Winonna asked suspiciously. "This is a joke, PLEASE!"

"Kuul was kidding about the polecat, they actually serve a great burger and make excellent margaritas, or there's a large selection of craft brews," Skip said, hoping to mollify her. He didn't regret declining her offer last night, but there was no sense in not playing nice; her mother was a paying client. "Beef burger or..."

"Beef."

"We'll give it a shot," Lottie said. "Anyplace with this many motorcycles out front has to be good. It will at least be a story," she teased her daughter.

"If their menu says they're serving dead chicken like that ice cream place back there," Winonna said, pointing down main street, "I'm out of here."

"Would you want live chicken?" Kuul laughed, holding the restaurant door open.

A waitress outfitted like Betty Boop with curled, black bangs plastered to the side of her face smiled at Skip, "Welcome back stranger, main room or the bar?"

"Let's go all in," Skip grinned.

Betty Boop led them to a knotty-pine-paneled room, seating them on both sides of a counter, not the main bar, which leather-clad bikers lined shoulder to shoulder. Above the weekend, cycling enthusiasts were hundreds of dollar bills signed and tacked to the wall. The plaque next to the dozen beer taps read, 'Unaccompanied Children will be SOLD'. Betty dropped laminated, single-sheet menus in front of them, wiping a dried glob of red goop from Winonna's.

"It's just ketchup."

"Sure it's not from Bullwinkle up there?" Winonna sarcastically asked, nodding at the moose head on the wall.

"Or Bambi," Webster suggested. He was sitting across from the movie star, looking in the opposite direction.

Betty shrugged, "Blood dries darker."

Skip's phone began vibrating as Winonna and Lottie were disagreeing over the menu, whether the gourmet, baby swiss, bacon-avocado burger on brioche bun and the California cobb salad were jokes. It was Sky, he saw glancing at the screen. She'd likely found something on the Chandlers or Webster.

"I'm in Seligman at Roadkill," he said, answering the call and standing up. "I'll call you back in five, soon as I step outside."

"I'm still here, she's not," Winonna coyly said, assuming it had been Lilac.

"I've got to take this," he said to the group, ignoring her. "Kuul, order me a jalapeno and blue cheese..."

"Possum burger," Kuul grinned.

Skip excused himself and left the restaurant, but not without Winonna complaining he had tricked them and was bailing on the food. It hadn't helped when Kuul ordered the fricasseed roadrunner with glazed coyote gut. Betty Boop had asked if he wanted the calf-brain gravy on the side.

• • •

From the parking lot, he thumbed 2 on his phone, "Sky, it's me. What'd you find out?" Loud, muffled roars erupted behind him before she could answer. "Hold on," he shouted. Milwaukee 114 Fat Boy engines had fired simultaneously on several Harley's. He waited until they'd rumbled past the abandoned, black-and-white police cruiser with a cutout of Barney Fife.

"Go ahead."

"Sounds busy there, boss. Hope you aren't wearing your Bikers Suck Tailpipes t-shirt."

"Sky."

"Well, the Chandlers definitely have money and I verified Lottie's parents died in the 1956 crash. From what I could find, her grandfather, Harold Bockner, was quite a bit older than her grandmother – makes for a happy couple I've been told." Skip rolled his eyes...Lilac, Winonna, now Sky. "He made a fortune in the early days of L.A. real estate. Suburbs, you know. Lots of old newspaper clippings. Like most rich people in those days, he began bankrolling the movie studios. He hung with the DeMilles, Fairbanks, Barrymores - Hollywood royalty. Lottie's grandmother, Louise Bockner, I couldn't find anything on before their marriage, other than she was from back east before moving to California. Active in charities, especially the arts, but she kept a lower profile than her husband. Pretty common back then. They raised Lottie after the accident."

Interesting, but nothing unusual, other than the plane accident, Skip thought.

"What'd Lottie do?"

"She was - is an artist."

"Painting?"

"No, she wrote poems and illustrated children's books. Not much lately though. With a rather large inheritance, she's pretty active in philanthropic circles. Kind of picked up where grandmother left off. She married her publisher. Winonna is their only child. And she's been a wild one, if you believe the Hollywood reporters. She hasn't had a meaty role in a while - mid 30's is getting old. Glad I'm not there yet. From what I saw before you left, that fits, right?" Sky chuckled, "How's that going by the way? Lot to handle, I bet."

Skip wondered if Lilac had checked in with Zula and told her the story of the starlet's late night scantily dressed visit to his room. He could picture Zula bawdily retelling it to Sky.

"About what you'd imagine. Did you check on Webster?"

"I found a website for the tour company he claims to scout for."

"Claims?"

"There was no mention of him on the contact page and it list-ed a lot of staff. So, I called and asked for him." She made a drumroll sound, "They hadn't heard of him or so they say. Now it could be he'd caused some trouble and been fired, or, maybe, they just keep his role anonymous. But it sure didn't sound like that, and I couldn't find any other Jack or John Webster that might be a match. I'd keep an eye on him."

"Hmmm. Keep looking, you find anything else, let me know. Try searching for any connection with the Chandlers. Kuul and I have both been getting a weird vibe, especially between him and Lottie. It's probably nothing. We've only got a couple more days and we'll be back."

"Will do boss. Say hey to Lilac," Sky said and hung up.

Yep, she'd checked in.

• • •

"Time to hit the road," Skip declared after wolfing down his possum burger. The others had already finished when he returned. Except for Winonna, who was forking her last bite of homemade lemon pie. "We should have you in your rooms at Peach Springs within an hour."

"This is the Indian Hotel on the reservation?" Winonna asked, like she was anticipating a wigwam with a dirt floor and newly skinned hides for blankets.

"Hualapai Lodge," Kuul said.

Lottie mouthed a silent apology.

"I'll drop you at the lodge with Kuul and your baggage. I have to get our permit at the Hualapai Fish and Wildlife Office for the drive down Diamond Creek Road tomorrow. You never know when they'll be open or closed, so I want to get there early in case I have to go back. Kuul knows how to sweet-talk the desk clerk; their check-in procedures are rather quirky."

"They take great delight in confounding *bilagáana*, especially those with attitudes," Kuul said.

"I'll behave myself," Winonna said. "I know who you mean."

"*Bueno*. Just be cool when they ask what size of earplugs you need. They're serious and they're not for your iPod. The Burlington Northern runs a hundred feet out the back door and we're at a corner, which means train whistles."

"Sounds lovely," Winonna said.

They'd been cruising Route 66 for ten minutes when Lottie spotted the first string of red, Burma Shave signs - nostalgic throwbacks to when 66 ushered speeding Pontiacs westward from Chicago to L.A. Humorous and corny, they broke up the long, lonely stretches of road where radio waves hadn't penetrated. Most had hidden meanings or warnings. She read them off as they sped past.

Broken Romance...Stated Fully...She went Wild...When he went Wooly.

"Fitting," Webster said.

40

BESSIE AND GLEN

November 30, 1928

B Y THE TIME THEY REACHED DIAMOND CREEK, BESSIE WAS WILD with fear. The Colorado was tired of their trespassing and angry at its warnings being ignored. The romantic notions Bessie had harbored at the start of their honeymoon trip were long gone. They had been soaked in muddy water and beaten on the rocks.

Diamond Creek, however, was a godsend. Fine sand was blown into a wide beach and a clear stream ran beside it. At least she'd be able to take a bath and wash her hair. Bessie wiggled the warm, soft grains between her bare toes. If it wasn't for the dirty river and all the rocks, she'd have thought she was in California with her friend Greta. She stared up the deep side canyon. This was also the easiest spot to hike out.

A huge fault had created a side canyon from Peach Springs and the railroad to the river. Until two decades ago, a pioneer family, the Farleys, had run a rustic lodge a mile up the trail. Old man Farley had started bringing tourists to the river by buckboard soon after the Santa Fe crossed northern Arizona. What a rough ride that would have been, Bessie thought. A monsoon had flooded them out years ago and all that remained were several ruins and a dilapidated outhouse. Still, his old road offered a way out.

"Since we're camping here, we can hike up the road a way," Bessie suggested. Maybe she could convince Glen to keep walking to Peach Springs. He hadn't said as much, but the Upper Inner Gorge and its big rapids had spooked him too.

"Runoff has to come thru here something fierce," he said. "Look at the size of these boulders that have been moved. Wouldn't want to be here when that creek floods."

"What about the hike?"

Glen knew what she wanted. They'd hike to the old Farley place, to get her mind off the river, but no farther. "It's at least twenty miles to town and there's no shade or water, unless you can find a spring or seep."

"Aren't there ranches, they'd have water."

"Just Indians, this is a reservation," Glen said. "Good luck finding them. They'd have to want to find you. We're better saving our supplies and sticking to the river. Sightseeing we can do later. We'll spend the night here in those old mining cabins up on the shelf."

In for a penny, in for a pound, Bessie realized. Glen was right, the hike to town would be tough and probably take several days. And they'd be in a fix if they got lost.

"I'll take you to the Farley place, but no farther. Won't hurt to stretch our legs."

The road, or what was left of it, wound through a cut in the granite schist. It narrowed at one place to the width of a San Francisco trolley - maybe two. The black cliffs rose higher than the pictures she'd seen of the Eiffel Tower. The walls were so sheer and the canyon so narrow, the rock layers stacked above were out of sight. Around one bend, water cascading from a thick crack created a pretty waterfall and grotto.

They hiked until they found ruins, past where a creek entered to the left. Seasonal rains rushing down the main canyon had cleared most of the buildings. A boulder the size of Rain-in-the-Face rested not far from a dilapidated shed. "He should have known this was bound to happen," Glen said.

They poked around until Glen grew bored exploring and headed back. Bessie followed. The threatening roar of the river kept her from enjoying the lush, green scenery bordering the stream. Unlike their walk out, the angry roars got louder and louder with every step. Every turn, the rapids ahead shouted at her. Maybe they weren't shouting, she thought - maybe they were laughing at her and Glen for returning.

Two hundred yards from the river, the walls of the side canyon spread to meet the inner gorge. Left of Diamond Creek, the granite walls had crumbled, spilling into the Colorado, joining chunks of debris washed downstream to form more whitewater. Bessie saw a treacherous animal path leading up the slope, disappearing high around the next bend - *you'd have to be a mountain goat*.

Right, the canyon wall was steep and worn farther back. At the base, were sand dunes stabilized by riparian plants that had found soil instead of rock. On the highest dunes, old, mining shacks from a defunct, uranium operation languished; they hadn't found anything. Bessie could see where the miners had chiseled their names into the wall of rock.

"We'll sleep over there," Glen said. "I'll go get the springs and stove. You pick out a good spot."

Bessie chose a cabin that still had a semblance of walls but a holey roof. The sky was clear, and she wouldn't mind going to sleep looking at the stars. Maybe Glen would point out more constellations. He knew them better than she did.

Later that night, lying in bed, Glen pointed out Cassiopeia and Andromeda in the western sky. The Milky Way filled their entire view through the hole in the roof. Neither of them felt like talking. Their minds were on what they'd face tomorrow.

"Let's leave a mark. Let folks know we were here, that we got this far," Glen said, pulling out his pocketknife. He carved their initials in the solidest piece of wood he could find. "There, this place won't forget us now."

Bessie almost told him to add +1 but decided against it. He'd find out soon enough. She didn't need him worrying any more than he already was. She kissed him and rolled over, snuggling into the quilts, his warm body spooned against hers. It was getting cold.

• • •

They were back on the river early the next morning. Bessie stared longingly at the Diamond Creek beach as Rain-in-the-Face drifted into the riffles heading downstream. There'd be no going back. The roar of new rapids was already reverberating through the dark cliffs. They were like the call of the sirens to Odysseus.

"We get through today and we'll be home free!" Glen said. His excitement betraying how happy he was to be on the river, fighting nature and winning every battle.

By late morning, they both realized how badly the day was going to challenge them. They hadn't gotten through the worst of it as Glen promised. They'd been in a constant run of rapids, bad rapids, all morning, with no safe place to stop and rest. Scouting ahead had been impossible. Bessie had lost count of the times she'd been sure they were crashing into the canyon's unforgiving wall.

The last rapid had been an extra-long run of mean whitewater. Entering it, they couldn't see the end. Rain-in-the-Face had followed the main channel easily enough, but it had been a hair-raising, lightning-fast ride. Wicked, sharp boulders had threatened them on both sides, and they could feel the scow buck as it slid over others. Any other kind of boat would have been dashed to pieces.

Belched out of the last waves they could already see the next set. Two huge, fang-shaped rocks jutted skyward on the right side near the end of a long series of rapids. Debris from upstream flowed toward them like moths to a flame. Strong, swirling eddies tossed anything caught in the wrong current into the two jagged daggers.

Bessie's heart sunk; they'd smash on the fangs in minutes. "Glen!" Bessie screamed, "We can't go in there!"

Both banks were solid rock, slippery, wet, and polished by the constant rub of water. Glen desperately searched for a spot, any spot, where they could tie up the scow. He needed to scout a way through and past those two rocks.

"Over there," he yelled. He pushed his sweep as hard and fast as he could against the current. "If we can get there and hold it, I think I can get us tied."

He guided the scow into a small eddy to slow their speed. Maneuvering the bow left, he found a tight spot where they could nose Rain-in-the-Face into a V-shaped crack in the rocky bank. He jumped out, jammed the short oar in between rocks and looped the line. Bessie hadn't wasted any time getting out of the scow and clambering up onto a ledge above the river. Glen made sure the scow would stay put and joined her.

"Whew. What do you think? I don't like the look of how the current throws everything into those rocks," he said, pointing downstream, waving his hand from one trouble spot to another. "It's those two fangs, near the end, I'm most worried about."

"We need to go back to Diamond Creek," Bessie yelled at him.

Glen didn't answer. The river was so loud she wasn't sure he heard her. She'd been following his motions more than his words. She could see he hadn't understood her and emphatically pointed back upstream. *Diamond*, she mouthed.

Glen frowned and cupped his hand over her ear, "It's too far and there's no trail. Rain-in-the-Face wouldn't stay here long if we went off and left her. If we got stuck and had to come back..." He shrugged his shoulders. "Let me work my way upstream and scout a way through. You stay here."

Bessie shook her head *No* and yelled in his ear, "If Rain goes, I won't be able to hold her. We need to take what we can now and try to make our way back. I saw a goat trail high in the rocks at Diamond. We can find another one here. I bet there is."

Glen held up ten fingers, "Give me ten minutes, Bess. I've gotten us this far."

Bessie thought it over. He deserved the chance. She held up ten fingers and nodded. Glen smiled and headed downstream, scampering over rocks.

She honestly didn't know what she'd do when he came back saying he saw a way through. And he would, she knew he would. He wasn't going to give up on the river. He wouldn't be able to admit he wasn't right. She knew that. That confidence was one of the things she loved about him, but here, now, it might be the thing that would get them killed. His hollow words kept ringing in her brain - *We're through the worst of them, Bess.* They weren't, they never would be, she knew that in her heart.

She watched him climb to a point and study the flow. His head was nodding up and down and a hand was moving in front of him. She'd seen that so many times; he was tracing in his mind the path he planned to take. He turned, waved, and started coming back, believing he'd found a way through, but Bessie knew better. He was going to get them killed. *Pride, damn pride.* It was up to her to stop him. *But how?*

Bessie made up her mind in an instant.

She had to act now if she was going to act at all. Glen was moving fast across the rocks, like he was in a hurry to die - *the fool, couldn't he see what would happen.* It was just a matter of seconds before he'd be back and wanting to shove off. *You have to do it. He hasn't given you a choice,* she swore to herself.

Bessie climbed from the ledge down to the scow. She glanced back. Glen was on the ledge, screaming; he could see what she planned and was mad as hell. The river's ever-menacing roar drowned him out.

She slipped the line from the oar and shoved the scow into the current. *They'd have to find a way back to Diamond now.*

"Good luck, Rain," Bessie cried.

41

PEACH SPRINGS

"**I**T'S 19.4 MILES TO THE RIVER. FROM HERE ON, DIAMOND CREEK Road is all gravel and rock, sand in a few places farther down," Skip said. "Rollin Hyde, Glen's father, eventually determined the beach might have been their last campsite. It's also over this part of the canyon that the TWA flight likely diverted from its flight plan. It's close to the end of both stories."

Skip had stopped where the pavement ended. Past the cattle guard, the road headed down into a wide canyon. Far in the distance were cliffs of Redwall limestone. Up ahead they could see an old, splintered scaffold across a wash that had carried water lines to town from springs a mile farther down. The railroad needed water for their steam engines. Access to it had been fought over ever since.

"It gets bumpier the farther we go," Skip said. "This first section is like an interstate compared to what we'll finish on before reaching the river. We'll make several stops to stretch our legs and talk. But this is your tour, you see any place you want us to pull over - let me know."

"There's an overlook into the lower canyon where I must stop," Lottie said.

Skip had given up trying to figure her out. They couldn't be in a more remote place, and she had a specific spot in mind. Nothing down this road was marked on any map.

"I know it," he said. "It's usually our second stop. There's some interesting geology there and you get your first look at the ancient Vishnu Schist from where a fault raised it up. After that the road descends faster. You're the first person I've had who has known about it."

"There was a Hualapai rancheria in the flat above there," she said, as if he should know.

"That was after the reservation boundaries were settled and the white ranchers had given up their claims," Kuul stated.

He was in the wingman seat and looked at Skip, then shrugged. He was having the same thoughts about Lottie.

They drove past two strange, saucer-shaped, storage bins that Webster joked looked like spaceships. The road disappeared into a grove of cottonwood trees. Another curve and they saw two mule deer skittering across the road into clumps of cattail a hundred yards ahead. Skip pulled the van over, parking on the side of the road. Kuul hopped out and opened the side doors.

"What's out there?" Winonna whined.

She and Lottie were in the middle seat, Webster in the back. Until she moved, the other two weren't getting out.

"Nothing that won't sting you, scratch you, or bite you," Kuul teased.

"Great!"

"Winonna," Lottie said, nudging her daughter.

Skip was in the road waiting, studying the sky, and watching for other vehicles. He doubted there would be any; the drive was so remote. Usually, the only other traffic was the Hualapai rafting buses, which would have already gone down. They got an early start downstream, unless they were picking up a longer trip that had left from Lee's Ferry.

The other four gathered around him.

"If anything bites me, I hope your liability insurance is paid up," Winonna smirked.

"If you hear a rattle, move away," Kuul said.

Winonna didn't even want to be here, and the Indian was playing Seinfeld. She had balked at leaving, but Webster had not-so-kindly and quietly reminded her that she needed to stay with her mother, 'until it was time'.

Trickles of water ran in a graded ditch and cut across the roadbed farther down. Low hills full of scrub gradually rose beside them. Between the hills and the road was a wet area with large cottonwood and willow trees. Cattails sprouted alongside the ditch, and a broad-leafed plant with huge white flowers grew among them. The scene always reminded Skip of a desert oasis in an Arabian movie.

"These are the Peach Springs the town is named after. They're why the railroad put a stop in town. Controlling the water for their engines and the white ranchers using it for cattle are why the Hualapai were forcibly removed. Even after they were finally granted a reservation and allowed back, the government continued leasing water rights and the best land out from under them."

"That was a sad part of our national history; how we treated the people who were here," Lottie said. "They were our friends."

Kuul said, "It wasn't until the 1940s that they gave up those rights, and then, only after railroad technology had replaced steam and the need for water. The government still had to pay the railroad extra to carry their freight in order to seal the deal. With the white ranchers, the government just canceled the leases. Until then, the People had refused to live in their own town. They had battled in court for years. That Hualapai rancher you mentioned scraped a living off pretty dry land, though they knew of secret springs the *bilagáana* didn't."

Skip spent a few minutes pointing out different flora, while keeping a nervous eye on the overcasting sky, and explaining they were entering a transition zone between the high and low desert zones. Shortly, the scrub pine, mesquite, and barbed acacia would disappear, and they'd be surrounded by truer desert plants - cacti, ocotillo, and yucca.

"The pretty white flower, what's that?" Winonna said, bending over, thinking about picking it.

"Don't touch it," Skip cautioned, and she stepped away. "That's a sacred datura and every part of it is poisonous. Some people get a skin irritation from just brushing it."

"God! You can't even pick the flowers in this place. I'd hate to be lost here," Winonna moaned.

Kuul had also been eyeing the sky and didn't like what he saw. It was a rule here that if rain was coming you should turn around, especially this time of year at the end of the monsoons. Getting caught in a flash flood would be bad. Canyons were just bigger, older versions of smaller arroyos and washes that filled with raging storm surges during heavy downbursts.

Skip helped Lottie and Winonna into the van and shut the door.

"What do you think?" he asked Kuul.

"*Ix Chel*, Little Rainbow - could go either way," he answered. "Those gray clouds get worse; you might need to make a tough call."

"I defer to your Mayan Gods, but I think we're good to the overlook. We can decide then."

Kuul nodded.

The overlook was at mile twelve on the drive. Not far, unless the road was bumpy gravel and the scenery caused someone to ask to stop every mile to take pictures. There wasn't much color in the fall except for the red, blooming spikes atop random ocotillo and an occasional dusty Datura. The moody, heather-colored clouds and their shadows provided a sense of drama.

By Bright Angel Pass, Winonna was complaining about needing a bathroom break, despite Skip's earlier warnings about coffee. The canyon sides pinched at the pass and a low saddle sat between the two. The road rose into the saddle and the green, Bright Angel shale they'd looked down on yesterday from the rim. To their right was the overlook. Past the overlook, the canyon narrowed, snaking through an eroded fault line that led to the river.

"You should look for a bush at least this high," Kuul said to Winonna, hashing a line across his waist. "Pick one with leaves and shake a limb." The Mayan was enjoying himself.

"Ha ha," Winonna said. "I can wait."

"The Hualapai homestead must have been in that side canyon," Lottie said, pointing to her left. "They came from there."

"That's Lost Man's Canyon. There's a small spring there. No one lives down here any longer though," Skip answered.

"Who was he, I wonder?" Lottie muttered, almost to herself.

"My guess would be a uranium prospector. He was probably dreaming of a mother lode raised by the fault."

Kuul added, "Lots of accidents happen in the side canyons. They are good places to get lost or hide. There's a tale Geronimo had a hideout near here. You're not supposed to hike there without a permit and Hualapai guide – lots of sacred places to be protected."

"You ever hike down here instead of drive?" Webster asked.

He was standing where the overlook crested, watching Winonna. She had decided to find a bush after all and wandered down the hill.

"No," Skip answered. "It's a long way and you'd need to carry a lot of water. There are no refill stations like on Grand Canyon Park trails. And coming back would be all uphill. Not an easy trek. The road suits me fine."

Skip had lost sight of the movie star; she'd gone around the bend in the road in her search for modesty. Not having a visual on all of his clients here in the desert made him nervous. There was too much that could happen. That went double for non-outdoorsy types. He'd give her another five minutes and then send Kuul.

"Kemo, look who's coming!" The big Mayan was behind the van and quick stepping back up the road, carrying a brown, paper bag.

Skip grinned. "Lottie, follow me." Maybe this would lighten her mood.

Trotting up the road were three hairy burros. When the largest spotted Kuul's bag, she picked up her pace. She was the mother of the other two. Momma was cocoa brown; her colts were white and gray. The white one was the smallest and lagged behind, more interested in what it could find in the ditch. Kuul was quartering an apple he'd pulled from his bag.

"Are they wild?" Lottie asked, catching up with Skip. "They seem to know Kuul."

"Yes, but we see them every other trip or so. They look for us, I think. We didn't see them at all last year and were afraid a mountain lion might have gotten them. But they showed up again this spring."

Kuul had placed a slice of apple on the back of his hand and held it out. Momma hesitantly shook her head a few times, then spread her lips revealing her big front teeth and gently plucked the piece clean without touching his hand. Skip and Lottie joined him. Momma was staying put, anticipating the rest of the apple. The bigger of her two offspring was close, but held back, still deferring to its elder. Kuul cut another slice and tossed it to the gray colt. The smaller, white burro was standing in the middle of the road twenty feet away.

"I've never gotten that little colt to come any closer," Kuul said, lobbing a piece at its feet. "But Momma here doesn't have that problem," he said, brushing her head back. "She can get rather insistent." He put another slice on his hand and she performed the same trick.

"Can I try?" Lottie asked.

Kuul handed her a piece of apple.

"Just toss it," Skip said. "If you hold it wrong, we'll be driving back to town with a finger in the cooler."

Lottie laughed and started throwing pieces, one at a time to the three lucky burros. Ten minutes later they'd exhausted their supply. The two colts wandered away to inspect a promising looking mesquite, and momma trotted off as soon as the Mayan crunched up the empty bag.

Kuul looked skyward and sniffed the breeze. The air had assumed a wet, metallic smell. He held out an empty hand - palm up. A drop of rain bounced on his skin...then another, not heavy, but a harbinger. He glanced at Skip, shaking his head.

"Lottie, I think we're going to have to get Winonna and Webster and head back. We don't want to continue to the river if rain's coming. All these wide washes we've driven across can fill up with water in a matter of minutes."

"It's barely raining, maybe this is it," she protested.

"Let's hope so, but we still have to go," Skip said. "Maybe we can try later this afternoon if nothing develops or in the morning."

Following the burros had led them back up the road away from the van. He walked toward the overlook and Winonna was still out of sight, and now, Webster was missing too. Rain was pinging on the van and dark, wet spots began appearing on the road. A crack of thunder echoed from the cliffs to the east. Skip had a bad feeling and started running. He shouldn't have left them. The van door was open, and he glanced inside. Empty. He thought about running down the road, past and around the bend where he'd last seen Winonna. Instead, he ran up the overlook for a wider view. Kuul was behind him; Lottie, surprisingly, keeping up with him.

A yellow jeep was on the road at the bottom of the saddle, several hundred yards away. His friend with the cheap cowboy hat was pulling Winonna inside. Webster was there, looking up at him. He waved. Cowboy Hat ran around to the driver's seat after depositing the girl, and Webster got in the passenger side. In a cloud of dust, the jeep sped down into the canyon – toward the Colorado.

42

FAMILY TIES

"WE HAVE TO GET HER," LOTTIE WAILED, WATCHING THE DUST in the distance disappear. The rain was falling heavier, and her white hair was damp. It wouldn't be long before it was plastered to her face. Even with the rain, Skip could see she was crying.

She screamed again, "We have to get her. She doesn't know."

Skip looked to the hills as more thunder boomed. It was louder now, closer, rumbles rhythmically growing in intensity as they became roars. Purple-black clouds had blown over the top of the cliffs, replacing the lighter, gray ones. Trickles of water ran in the tire tracks. The first drips fell from his Stetson onto his back.

He was tired of being in the dark. He'd been too sympathetic and accepting of Lottie's story, too discounting of the warning bells and that sick feeling in the pit of his stomach when he knew it was past time to abort. Winonna at the bridge, Lilac at the Grand Canyon, and now Winonna again – he should have seen this coming. Webster wasn't who he claimed to be. He should have seen that too. Sky was right about him, but he'd let it play out instead of confronting him. This was supposed to be an easy tour, he cursed. *No more...Now was the time for truth.*

"We have to get her away from them! From him," she shouted hysterically, trying to run to the van, slipping on a wet plate of shale.

Skip caught her and held her shoulders, shaking her until she quieted and stopped fighting him. "Lottie, it's time you told us what this is all about. We want to help, but the truth...Lottie, the truth!" Anger was building inside him, more at himself than anyone else. The picture of how this was going to end flashed through his mind, and it wasn't Christmas card worthy.

A hand rested calmly on his shoulder.

"Kemo, the rain."

Skip looked into his friend's wet face. He turned back to Lottie, "Now, right now, or we're heading back to town."

"Let's at least get out of this storm," she answered.

They ran to the van, Kuul half carrying Lottie down the slick slope.

"I can talk while you drive," she urged Skip, once they were inside.

"Not until Kuul and I know what's going on."

She looked at both of them in turn, her eyes pleading, "Please, you can't tell anyone what I'm about to tell you. There's nothing you can gain from it. You have to promise!"

"We're not promising anything," Skip said.

Lottie knew she didn't have a choice. She had to get them moving. If that old man was in the jeep, which she was sure he was...they needed to get to Winonna. She took a deep breath, "Okay, you're not going to believe me, but you have to. We have to get to my daughter. None of this is her fault and she doesn't understand what she's done."

Skip and Kuul didn't say anything.

Lottie took another deep breath and let it out slowly.

"Bessie Hyde was my grandmother. She was pregnant, like so many have guessed over the years. That child was my mother. And, yes, she and my father did die in the plane crash. That was almost more than Nana Lou could bare. Louise was Bessie's middle name, and that's what she used when she reached California."

"And we are just supposed to accept that?" Kuul asked. "You aren't the first to claim she survived. They've all been proven false."

"Think!" she begged them. "How else would I know so much about them - you've wondered that yourselves? I've seen your glances back and forth. I can't prove it here, but, *PLEASE*, we have to follow my daughter. You don't understand who she's with and the danger she's in."

She was right about their not understanding. Skip wasn't ready to charge blindly into a situation he still didn't understand. Even if they accepted who she was, she hadn't explained what was going on. Empathy was one thing, knowledge another. Acting on the first without having the latter had ruined many an operation in his past. Who was in the van? Who was Webster? And why did Winonna seem to voluntarily join them?

"You still haven't told us what's going on," he said, making no motion to start the van. "Why'd Winonna go with them? She didn't look to be fighting for her life. The man with the cowboy hat had tried to kill her at Navajo bridge. You need to make sense of this for us."

"We don't have time! We need to GO!" Lottie cried, wringing her hands. "Webster's father believes he's Bessie's son. Not by Glen but by her first husband. He's bitter and mean and feels entitled to everything my grandmother left me. The younger man must be his grandson."

The story seemed incredulous to Skip. Not only did Bessie Hyde survive and get out of the canyon, but she also had two children. One of whom had died in the plane crash and another who had to be..."

"He'd have to be in his nineties," Kuul said. "You're asking us to believe a lot based on your word."

Lottie stared into his eyes without blinking, "Yes, I am."

"And Winonna's cooperation?" Skip asked.

"My guess is the old man, Austin Donald, is in that jeep and calling the shots. That's who I bumped into at El Tovar. Kuul wasn't there, but you were - you remember. He's either threatened her or told her so many lies she's confused, or both."

The thunder hadn't stopped, and the first bolt of lightning flashed in the rearview mirror. The rain was steady and heavier now. Down the hill he could see storm water running in the wash. Not too high yet, but if it was pouring on top of the plateau, much more water would soon be draining from side canyons into Diamond Creek and the Colorado. *They'd be driving right into a flash flood.* He looked atop the red walls and saw sheeting bands of dark rain. Any other circumstances and they'd already be on their way back.

"We have to go, *Please!*" Lottie cried. "Donald wants me. Winonna's just to make sure I follow. I can't think of what he'll do if we don't. He can have me, but we have to save her. She's innocent in all of this."

"Kemo, the girl is our responsibility."

Skip was trained to accept collateral damage, the loss of innocent life. You never risked yourself to prevent it. The operative was more important than the operation. Those rules were sacrosanct, drilled into him over and over. *That's who he'd been. Who'd he'd told Lilac he might still be.*

"Kemo."

Skip turned the key. The engine fired, and he drove down the hill toward whatever waited them at the river. Whoever Austin Donald was, he'd chosen a fitting place to end Lottie's story.

"We'll go as far as we can. Then we'll see," he said.

The rain slackened as he drove farther, but it wasn't the rain from the sky he was worried about. Every arroyo they crossed had more and more water draining off the mountains. The road got rougher the deeper into the canyon they went. The interstate they had started on became more like a neglected, county road. He pushed it, but couldn't go over twenty because of the ruts, fallen rocks, and deep puddles. A broken axle or blown tire would end the chase.

They entered the black schist of the deep inner gorge; soaring granite walls injected with pink veins of feldspar. Flecks of mica in the veins shone from water running over the cliffs. A quarter mile ahead, Diamond Creek intersected the road. They entered an open area, where the old Farley lodge had been, the roadway graded through fields of boulders on both sides of the van. A flash flood a few years past had washed the last remaining ruins away. Beyond, the canyon twisted and narrowed to little more than the width of the road.

Skip stopped the van.

"Keep going!" Lottie implored him.

"He can't," Kuul said, pointing to a deep ditch crossing the roadway several hundred yards away. It was filling with swift-moving water from the creek.

"But their jeep, they crossed it. We have to follow," Lottie argued.

"It has a higher clearance and that was earlier. The water would have been lower. It could be far worse farther in," Kuul answered.

Skip inched their way to within a hundred feet of the ditch. There was no way across, not now. "This is as far as the van goes," he said. "Kuul?"

The Mayan nodded, opened his door, and headed to the back of the van for their packs and whatever else he thought they might need.

"You're staying here," Skip told Lottie. "There's no way out for them. We're going on foot and whoever's left down there...we'll find them. Unless they get swept into the river," he added cruelly.

Lottie tried to slide the side door open, but Kuul was standing outside holding the handle so she couldn't.

"You're staying here," Skip repeated. "I don't even know if *we* can make it all the way to the river. After we leave, turn the van around and aim it back up the road. If that water keeps rising and jumps the bank...Go Back!" Another clap of thunder shook the van. "If you try crossing, you won't make it."

Lottie began to argue

"You're staying here!" he shouted angrily. "If I see you follow us, we all leave without her. Give us two hours, and if you haven't left because of high water, leave then. The best thing you could do for your daughter is to let the authorities know what's happened. Do-You-Understand?"

"Two hours," she said defiantly, checking her watch.

Skip stared at her hard. He saw panic on the surface but a deeper-seated determination in her eyes. He knew he shouldn't trust her. "For the record, I don't believe your story. But he's right," Skip said, motioning to Kuul who had walked ahead and was studying where to cross the ditch. "Your daughter is my responsibility."

43

WATERFALL

CROSSING THE DITCH BY FOOT HAD BEEN EASY. WHETHER IT would be that way coming back was doubtful. A few hundred yards farther in, the canyon narrowed to less than two hundred feet. The roadbed ran against the right side and the creek flowed in a graded channel to the left. In several places the two normally crisscrossed and a small amount of water, no more than a few feet wide, flowed across the roadway. That was normally; during the storm, the farther they hiked the more the roadbed disappeared.

Skip and Kuul paused on a knob of higher ground, where past floods had piled rocks against the granite wall. They needed a plan. Water was streaming over the entire canyon floor, topping their boots and halfway to their knees. No sign of the jeep, but they knew where it was headed, unless the Donalds had turned around and were coming back toward them. *No*, Lottie's feared old man, Cowboy Hat, and Webster would be waiting for them at the river.

"It looks like they're in a hurry, but we don't want to get ambushed in here," Skip said. "We need a plan."

"Is this the plan where the Indian goes first to draw fire? It's not my favorite."

"It's the other one. We split up but keep each other in sight. It's best if we stagger our approach, so give me a few minutes head start. I'll work down the left side; you go down the right. If the water forces us, we'll have to scramble up and wait it out. The movie star will just have to fend for herself. Don't take any chances."

"You first is a good plan. Did you take Lilac's advice?" Kuul asked.

Skip nodded, "It's in my pack, but I don't plan on using it."

•••

The yellow jeep stopped three bends ahead of Skip and Kuul.

"This is the spot you scouted?" Austin Donald asked, approvingly. "You did well for a change, grandson. Send the older woman to the river after you've finished the guides. Don't hurt her. Then stay here as a lookout."

"Why stay here? Why don't I bring her? This water is moving faster, and I don't want to be stuck here."

Donald didn't care if his grandson died in the flood. This was the end and whether Frank's boy made it out was immaterial to his plan. There wasn't a doubt in his deranged mind about the woman though; with or without Hyde, she would find a way to their destiny. All he needed from the boy was a little more time. The kid had a job to do and once he'd done it, he had no further use for him. Same for the smirking Earl, but with him he'd have to be more careful.

"I don't want any Indian ranger coming to rescue us down here - that's why. Just stay high and dry, we'll pick you up on the way out."

Donald knew the chances of anyone else coming this way in a storm were nil; the flood was a sign to him, a good sign. He could barely contain his glee at how things had gone so far. A lifetime of frustration, anger, and being treated as an inferior was coming to an end. He was going to get his revenge. Killing the smart-mouthed bitch beside him would be his first act, but not until his niece was at the river to witness it. She'd come, she couldn't help it, fate drew her there same as him.

Winonna watched Hyde scramble up a crack in the canyon wall beside a waterfall. Stormwater gushed over its lip before splashing into the rising stream where they were parked. Hyde had a rifle with him. It had scared her when he'd pulled it from its case. She'd thought this was about money and intimidation. She was beginning to realize how badly she'd misjudged this side of her family - if that's who they were. Before this stupid trip, she hadn't even heard of Bessie and Glen Hyde. She was still trying to reconcile the memories of her kind, elderly Nana Lou with Rhode's tale of the young, spunky, whitewater explorer. And with what Nana had done at the river, if Earl had told the truth, she could forget her career. If that story came out; she'd never be anything more than, *'that girl with the notorious family.'* It had made sense to just let her mother pay the old bastard off. That's what she'd thought back in the hotel room. Now she realized that this old man was insane. All he'd talked about in the jeep was 'getting even'. Not once had he mentioned the money.

"What's he going to do with that gun?" she questioned Webster.

Earl laughed as the old man slapped her across the face.

"Don't worry," he said, "He'll let Lottie pass. They have a date, she and my father."

"I'm done with this!" Winonna cried, wiping her mouth and seeing blood on her sleeve. "Let me out. You don't need me to convince her. She won't want this story told." She tried opening her door to jump out and the lock clicked.

"Child locks," Webster cackled.

"You still think her money is what this is all about? You stupid whore," Donald spat, not caring where it flew. His eyes were on fire and drool foamed from his mouth, like a mad dog. He suddenly began coughing and sucking for air, mumbling incoherently.

Earl turned, watching him closely. The old man seemed confused again. His body was shaking. Then he stopped and yelled wildly...

"You'll lose your whole fucking family in this hell gorge, in this river of death: your daughter - your granddaughter - all of them! I'll be the only one left, the one you should have kept. *ME!*"

Donald slumped back into his seat from his explosion. Earl almost pitied him. He knew who he'd been yelling at - his mother. The old man didn't plan on coming back.

Earl drove down the canyon toward the Colorado. Hyde was in position, and he knew Rhodes would be tracking them; the guide, or whoever he was, wouldn't give up...that had been clear on top of Hopi House. Earl needed to reach the river with enough time to take care of *his* business. From what he'd seen of Skip Rhodes and his Mayan pal, he gave Hyde, at best, a fifty-fifty chance of stopping them.

He felt water hitting the jeep's bumper and undercarriage. No longer could he avoid rocks in the road, they were hidden below the surface. This damn storm, it would ruin everything if it prevented Lottie from reaching the river. The old man's muddled confession to the starlet confirmed Earl's suspicions. He was insane. He'd heard him swearing at his mother before, as if she were alive. In his sick mind, it was her he wanted to hurt, not Lottie. It was Bessie he was proving something too, taking revenge on. He didn't care about the money; he never had. Earl would get the old man to the river, but like he'd said, it would end there...the way Earl planned.

. . .

Hyde's perch was behind a pair of thick bushes. On his scouting trip there hadn't been this much water going over the waterfall, only a trickle, but the heavy downpour made the spot even better. When the guides approached, they'd be focused on their footing, and with the noise from the water they'd never hear him. In a way that was too bad. After their fight on Hopi House, he would have liked Rhodes to know who had bested him before he died. That's how the old man operated.

Hyde was pleased to finally have his grandfather's approval. The old man threw compliments around like manhole covers. Making him proud was all he'd ever wanted growing up. Deep down, he'd always known that his father had been a disappointment. He had just never gotten the chance to prove himself. If he had, he'd be the old man's right-hand man, not snaky Earl. Taking care of business today would elevate Hyde in the family pecking order. He'd shoot the guides, capture the older woman, and, somehow, get to his grandfather and take care of his uncle.

Skip negotiated his way around a bend, avoiding the swiftest water by climbing over bigger rocks and boulders lodged against the canyon wall. Behind him, he could see Kuul doing the same on the other side. In the middle, Diamond Creek had overflowed the channel graded by the Hualapai and was rushing madly toward its rendezvous with the Colorado, still a half-mile away. He could wade across if he had to, but probably not in another ten minutes. Hopefully, Lottie was driving out of the canyon by now. The rain was letting up, but any wall of water coming their way was already on its way and wouldn't stop until it reached the river. As long as she made it back to the overlook, she would be fine.

He knew too much about Glen and Bessie's trip to accept her story at face value. They'd both drowned in the river, of that, he was sure. They couldn't have escaped the Grand Canyon from where history had last put them, which was well past here. Diamond Creek had been their last chance to walk away, and they'd gone farther. He'd never accepted the two had fought; they'd been working together too long and been totally depending on each other. And if they'd gotten out, that would make Glen her grandfather, the developer and movie mogul? If they'd both safely escaped, why keep everything a secret, why change their names? None of it made sense.

Ahead, the canyon pinched to the length of a Greyhound bus. He was amazed to see water shooting from a fissure in the wall. The spot was usually a weeping spring and peaceful grotto. He told his tours to look for it during their hike; it was a lovely, cool place to rest. They could sit and listen to the rhythm of the river just up ahead. Today, the Colorado was silenced by the roar of the waterfall and the churning creek.

He crouched behind a boulder, studying the top of the fall. If they had set up an ambush, this would be...*dust and pebbles struck his face!* A chunk of rock near his head exploded. A thud sounded against the wall behind him...another explosion rang against the front side of the boulder he was behind. Someone was shooting. He ducked just in time as another piece of rock evaporated.

Moving across the backside of the boulder, he reached in his pack for the pistol Lilac had insisted he start carrying - *thank you, sharp-shooting, yoga instructor.* The firing had stopped. He guessed the shooter was waiting for him to move past his hiding spot. With the rising water, he'd eventually have no choice. He looked back up the canyon for Kuul, who should be trailing on the same side as the shooter. The Mayan was nowhere in sight, he'd undoubtedly seen what was happening.

Hyde was pissed. The thorns on the damn bushes had been poking him, and he'd been repositioning himself when he saw the guide. He'd fired too fast and missed. *Patience,* he swore to himself. *Where was the Indian?* He'd probably been smart enough to head back to the reservation. At least he had the guide pinned down. He put himself in Rhode's shoes, trying to think what he'd do if someone had the drop on him. He wouldn't poke his head out again, at least not in the same place. If it was him, he'd move to the other end of that boulder to sneak a peek. Yeah, that's what he'd do. Hyde aimed his rifle there, head high. *Patience.* Just give me another shot, he grinned.

Skip counted to ten before peeking around the boulder's other edge. The shooter had to be near the top of the waterfall. He would fire a couple of rounds there to get him moving.

Gotcha. Hyde almost laughed as he saw the guide's face. He'd guessed right. He fixed the sight on the middle of the man's forehead and took a deep breath. *Hold the exhale and squeeze gently...* he pulled the trigger just as he was hit from behind. *Fuck*, a mountain lion or maybe a rockslide set loose by wet earth. The next thing he knew the damn Indian was knocking the rifle away, grabbing his arm, and picking him up by a shoulder. Hyde kicked him in the nuts, and he doubled over, letting him loose. He shoved the Indian's back, hoping the water would sweep him over the lip. The Indian stumbled but caught himself.

They squared off atop the waterfall, both fighting to stay upright against the rushing water. Hyde could feel his feet slipping, before they settled into the gravel bottom. The Indian had about steadied himself when a log heading for the fall whacked the back of his knee. Hyde reached for the jackknife tucked in his belt.

Skip saw Cowboy Hat pull his knife; he'd seen this movie before. Kuul was crouching in the middle of the stream but wobbling off-balance. He had to choose between grabbing a rock to brace himself or letting go to fight. Fighting meant probably going over the falls. Kuul used one hand to fend off the blade, but the attacker, surer on his feet, kept coming. Skip pointed Lilac's pistol and fired. He shot to Cowboy Hat's left, trying to scare him. The two men were close enough he was afraid of hitting Kuul.

The guide - Hyde glanced down and saw the gun. Rhodes was aiming at him. He was an easy target standing atop the waterfall. Their eyes met and he jumped to another rock as the man shot again. He reached the rock but landed awkwardly in the water, his feet slipping under him. He fell backwards into the rushing torrent, his arms and legs flailing like an upside-down insect.

The man screamed and reached for help. Kuul tried grabbing him, but the current swept him over the edge. It wasn't a long drop, but the waterfall twisted him, sending him down headfirst. Cowboy Hat hit a chunk of black granite at the bottom and the water turned red. The limp body was swept downstream finally wedging between rocks.

44

FLOTSAM

IT WAS ONE HELL OF A RIDE. THE JEEP SPLASHED AND BOUNCED down the raging creek; Earl had been too afraid of getting stuck to slow down. He sped around a sharp bend and the canyon suddenly grew wider, the water fanning out in its frenzied rush to join the equally angry Colorado. The roadway was invisible. All he could see was water, with rapids a hundred yards ahead. The jeep bounded into a ditch, water crashing against the bumper and splaying over the hood - it had to be the creek bed - heading straight toward the cascading river. To his right, Earl saw a rise to a beach and swerved. The jeep lurched and sprang out of the swiftly flowing water. As it bounced hard out of the creek and onto the sand, he felt a snap underneath. Somehow, he managed to drive the jeep onto the high end of the beach.

• • •

The old man leaned wobbly on a walker; the wheels and legs sinking into the sand. The three of them were huddled under a ramada. Earl was inspecting the undercarriage of the jeep. Donald, his eyes on fire, was aiming a pistol at Winonna. She was shaking, holding her head, whimpering.

The creek was out of its bank, backing up because of the rising river, and edging closer to the ramada by the minute. The Colorado's channel was narrower here, just a few hundred feet wide. Soaring walls of black schist rose all around them. Where Diamond Creek collided with the river, whitewater roared its objection at their intrusion. They were trapped in a deep crack quickly filling with water.

"What if this water keeps rising?" Winonna cried, not sure if she was more afraid of it or the old man.

"We go up there. The jeep's axle is broken," Earl said, pointing to a sandy trail leading up a huge dune at the edge of the beach.

"*NO!* We're staying by this fucking river," the old man snarled, waving his gun at his son. "We wait for that bitch; wait to end this. Here God Damnit! All of you." He swung the gun back at Winonna, "We all belong in there!" he yelled, gesturing toward the river.

"Why, why, why are you doing this?"

"So you can get to know your great-uncle." The old man laughed in her face. "*The whore bore me first. We're kin Lottie, you and I.*"

"You're insane. I'm not my mother!"

Donald ignored her, "She should have died in this river for running off with the fucking farmer and leaving me in that vile, stinking orphanage to be raped and abused. She picked your mother over me...and then the river took that bastard child. Justice, that's what that was. Now she's going to lose you too!"

Donald was screaming and waving the pistol. Rain had soaked his clothes and he tried wiping his face. He gathered what little strength he had and flung the walker aside. "When my dear mother gets here, your sweet *Nana Lou*, you'll both die! She'll beg for forgiveness, for abandoning me. And for when she came back and coldly decided to let me rot in that place. I didn't have to be like this, she could have chosen me. You'll all pay! I'll be the only one left of our sad lot."

Earl knew his father had to be stopped now. He was expecting his mother, Bessie, to show up. That reunion was what he was waiting for, that's what was playing out in his fevered, crazed mind. *Getting even*...the pain and hate were what kept him alive. But not Earl, he had been counting on this pay day.

His father continued ranting at the starlet - *his kin*. Earl slipped to the edge of the old man's vision; he was so absorbed with spewing his venom and damning his mother that he wasn't paying attention. He'd regret ignoring him. Earl reached for his gun hand. The old man moved quicker than he thought possible, taking a step back and raising the pistol. Earl froze, too far away to grab his arm.

"Fucking family," Donald said, keeping his gun leveled at his son. "He'd kill me if he could. See the fucking hate he has for me. Children, shit, they're just born to disappoint, there's no fixing them. I'd have been better off without them."

The old man's eyes lightened for a moment; the iciness seemed to disappear. He rubbed his temple, like he'd realized something important, something he'd never understood before. He glanced at Winonna and then stared at Earl, lowering the gun.

"Son...I..."

Earl jumped forward and Donald fired twice. His son staggered backwards and fell to the ground...dead; his eyes open, the spark of surprise and shock still fixed in his lifeless expression.

"My boys," Donald moaned.

Winonna started screaming and Donald grasped her arm, slapping her across the face, "They made me. Neither of them gave me a choice. This is the whore's fault, she made this happen!"

"Please, let me go. I won't tell."

"I tried reasoning with her, your grandmother, and your mother. They laughed at me and called me a liar. Told me to never bother them again."

"Just let me go, *please!*"

"*See this! Look at it!*" he yelled deliriously, pulling off a glove and shoving his stump of a thumb in her face. "This was their answer; this is how much she hated me. Your great-grandfather did it after I dared try to talk to my mother."

"You'll all pay!" he screamed, dragging her toward the river.

. . .

Skip and Kuul recovered Hyde's body and stashed it on a ledge out of the rising water's reach. They continued working their way down Diamond Creek toward the Colorado. Kuul soon crossed to Skip's side because the creek kept rising. Crossing closer to the river would be impossible due to the current. If there was another ambush, they'd have to deal with it together.

The feared wall of stormwater and debris hadn't happened, just a steady increase in the level and flow. The rain was a drizzle now. The purple clouds had passed and those that remained were a dull gray. The first rays of sun began probing the inner gorge. On any other day they would be on the lookout for rainbows.

Where the side canyon opened into the inner gorge, they left the creek on a trail that took them up onto a high dune of sand. The same trail would take them back to the beach, upstream from where Diamond Creek entered the Colorado. Hopefully, Webster would be expecting them to come down the flooded roadway. That's where he would have driven.

With the rushing water, the *pop-pops* weren't loud, but they were distinctive.

"Kemo! Those were shots!"

Skip charged down the sandy trail toward the beach. He was shielded from view by stands of arrow weed, grasses, and an out-of-place palm tree that had likely been deposited during a long-ago flood. The soft sand and slope of the dune made him take long steps, each foot sinking and sliding as it landed. He had planned to go slow and stop behind the palm tree to assess the situation. Once they hit the beach there would be no cover and he couldn't be sure Webster was the only threat. The ringing shots and Winonna's screams had changed his plan.

He ran, zigzagging onto the beach, quickly processing the scene to decide on his course of action. The flooded creek was to his left, inundating the road and the beach in that direction. The quiet stream had raged from its banks, furiously pouring into the larger Colorado. Webster was face down a few yards from the tree, no longer a threat, blood staining the sand under his chest. Standing near the confluence, only feet from the churning water and from being swept downstream, was an ancient, grizzled man holding Winonna. He saw Skip and tugged her closer to the water, jabbing a gun in her side to make her move. He screamed something, but the roar of the river kept Skip from hearing.

Kuul was behind him, and Skip motioned him right while he moved left. He kept the gun tucked in the back of his khakis, cold against his bare waist. A hundred feet of open beach separated him and the old man. He didn't want to needlessly antagonize him. From what he could tell, he'd already shot Webster. If he chose to shoot Winonna or push her in the river he couldn't stop him.

Skip calmly held his hands up, circling closer to him. Kuul was doing the same from the other direction. The old man kept talking as Skip inched forward, every other sentence capped by racking coughs. Skip could only hear snippets of the old man's weak voice over the river's howl.

"...is she...time...get even...bitch."

Winonna stopped struggling when she saw him, "Help me. He's crazy!"

Skip kept moving forward, separating from Kuul, hands still up, until he was twenty feet away. The Mayan was twice that far. The old man couldn't see both of them at the same time. His head pivoted back and forth, waving the pistol between them.

"Where's her grandmother, the fucking whore?"

"Buried at the Grand Canyon cemetery. Now just hold on a minute - no one else needs to die here. Who are you?"

The old man glared at him and coughed, wiping his mouth with the back of his gun hand, the other hand holding Winonna.

"Not her mother, her fucking grandmother."

Skip took another step.

"I'll throw her in if you come closer. Don't fucking test me. Same with that Indian. Why are you here, why didn't she come? She is supposed to come."

Donald was focused on the white man, but out the corner of his eye saw the Indian take another cautious step. He fired a shot at his feet. Kuul froze, held up his hands and gestured to show he wasn't coming any farther.

"*WHERE THE FUCK IS SHE?*" Donald screamed, pushing Winonna toward the floodwater. "I'll do it, swear to God I will! It's where they all belong!"

The old man was losing his grip, Skip saw. That made him beyond dangerous; it made him unpredictable. He had to know there was no way out for him. Even if he shot them all, he'd still be stuck here in a flood with a disabled vehicle.

"You don't want to do that."

Skip compared him to old pictures he'd seen of Bessie Hyde. According to Lottie, he believed he was her son. He had the same small build, the same dark, penetrating eyes, and thin mouth. But so did a million other people.

"Bessie's not coming," Skip said, guessing who he wanted and stalling for time.

The old man blinked and wiped his mouth again. He looked at Winonna as if he didn't recognize her. Confusion clouded his eyes.

"Don't screw with me!" Donald yelled. "Where is she? Bring her here," he said, frantically looking toward the sand dune, searching for his mother. His hold on Winonna slackened. "Is she up there? Did you leave her there?" He sounded like a small child lost in a busy Phoenix mall. "Are you there!" he cried toward the dune.

"She'll come down when you let her go."

"Don't make me kill her!" Donald screamed at the dune. "Why did you leave me? Was it for her? Here, take her. Come to me, please!"

He released Winonna and she ran to Kuul who had inched closer once the old man had been distracted.

Skip saw the veil lift and recognition reenter the old man's eyes. They turned bright, clear, and mean.

Donald glared at him and turned, pointing the gun at Winonna. "LIARS! She's not here. She won't come."

Kuul grabbed Winonna and threw her to the ground, shielding her with his big body. The old man laughed maniacally, and Skip charged him. Chances were he could take a bullet and still reach him. That would at least give Kuul enough time to pounce. The old man took a step back and aimed at Skip. Skip watched his trigger finger, ducked, and kept going.

Instead of firing, the old man looked away, back up the road. He'd been the only one facing that direction. The rental van was barreling down the middle of the flooded creek, racing toward them. Lottie was at the wheel, and Donald fired at the windshield, but it kept coming. The van flew up onto the beach out of the water, the engine revving, its wheels crashing hard in the wet sand and tires spinning before taking hold. Skip dove and the van just missed him. He rolled and rose to a knee.

Brake. Lottie, brake. For God's sake, "BRAKE! BRAKE!!"

Skip could just see her face over the wheel. She had a determined look and gave him a last, wistful glance, steering straight toward the old man by the river.

Kuul hurled Winonna away from the bouncing van and leapt after her. Picking her up, he threw her farther away. She had seen her mother and was fixated on her charge, unable to move, the horror of what was about to happen freezing her.

Donald had emptied his pistol into the van, cursing, still mindlessly pulling the trigger.

"LOTTIE, LOTTIE DON'T!" Skip yelled, up and running toward the old man, knowing she couldn't hear him and wouldn't stop. If he could get there and take him down, Lottie would have to stop or at least veer away.

From his blindside, Kuul tackled his friend, taking them both clear of the van's deadly path. "Kemo, she's not stopping, she's balancing her world. All you would have accomplished was having three persons sent to the Great Spirit instead of two."

"Bitch, Bitch, Bitch…Come on, I'm waiting. Come on!" Donald was yelling over and over, insanely just standing there, waiting.

Lottie never hesitated and the van plowed into the old man. Donald had seemed to hug it, his arms spread wide at the last, as they sailed airborne into the Colorado. The current captured it and turned it on its side. Water rushed into the shot-out windshield and Lottie disappeared as the van rolled upside down. Donald reappeared, moving underneath, stuck on the undercarriage. One leg was free, kicking at air, his screams silenced by the noise. The van struck something below water, shuddered, and threw him into the raging whitewater. He struggled at first, bobbing up and down, fighting the current, until exhausted he gave in, accepting the river's embrace.

Skip, Kuul, and the last survivor, Winonna, watched helplessly, hoping to see her mother, somehow, miraculously rise out of the waves. She never did. The river had accepted its gifts, reuniting generations of the doomed family that had become part of its lore. The river didn't care about personal histories, broken families, or old grudges; it only took what was offered. Time, eons and eons of time, was all that mattered to the river.

45

BESSIE AND GLEN

November 30, 1928

"**W**HAT DID YOU DO?" GLEN YELLED, WATCHING RAIN-IN-THE-Face glide into the current. He couldn't believe Bessie had shoved their scow into the river.

"I did it for us! Our family."

"You've doomed us."

"Don't you see? This river means to kill us!"

Bessie stared into Glen's furious face, his head swiveling back and forth between her and the scow. The short eddy they'd beached into was taking its time letting Rain go.

"Honey, darling...I'm pregnant! You can get us out of here. I know you can."

Glen's expression lightened momentarily. He grinned. She saw the blush of proud fatherhood. And then the old, determined look replaced his happiness.

"I will. I'll get us through."

He kissed Bessie on the cheek and dove into the cold water.

"NO! Not that way!" she screamed, watching him swim into the current after Rain-in-the-Face. *"GLEN, COME BACK! GLEN."*

She could barely hear her own pleading over the roar of the river. The rapids they'd pulled over to scout thundered at her, letting her know they'd won. This hadn't even been a fair fight. The river had been biding its time, toying with them. Just as it had ripped the land apart over millennia, the Colorado had torn her and her husband apart.

For an hour-long minute she felt Glen had a chance. The scow hadn't entered the main current and he was a great swimmer. The water was plenty rough, choppy, but not the crushing whitewater yet. She watched him pull powerfully forward with his steely arms, each surge getting him agonizingly closer. He was within twenty feet of the stern.

Rain-in-the-Face climbed the first large wave to its crest. Glen glanced back at her as he took another stroke. Bessie saw indecision. It was his point of no return. If he followed the scow into the bigger rapids and whitewater there'd be no coming back to her. He thrust a hand in the air, back at her. Was it a wave? He turned into the churning froth with another strong pull. Up he went toward the top. Glen crested and Bessie screamed as she lost sight of him.

She held her breath until he resurfaced, thrown out of the hole below the wave. The scow was still the same distance away but picking up speed.

Competing cross currents took Glen where they wanted, twisting and torquing his body. Ahead of him, Rain-in-the-Face bucked over a series of submerged boulders. In horror, Bessie saw her husband's body jolt and bounce as it ran the same rocks. But he was moving faster than the heavy scow. Without warning, the current drove him under again.

There he was! Up again! Ten feet from Rain! Bessie screamed as Glen was pulled down a third time. *Oh please God, let him come up and make it*, she prayed.

The scow was several hundred yards from her now. She scampered downstream over the rocky bank, trying to keep up, as far and as quickly as she could, but it was useless. The angry river carried it farther away. She reached a ledge overlooking the long drop of the rapids. Glen popped out of the froth. She could tell he was spent, his arms struggling. He and Rain were slotting straight toward the deadly fang rocks on the right. At the next wave, he went under again and stayed down.

All Bessie could do was watch from her perch. It seemed liked hours drug past, but it was only seconds. There, she saw him again. Five feet from Rain! Could he?

She watched her husband gather the last of his strength. He was flying up a huge twenty-foot wave. Rain-in-the-Face was just ahead, topping the crest. As Glen flew over the crest he threw his body forward, lunging for the scow. Her heart leapt as she saw his fingers reach the stern. His body rippled and twisted, one hand clinging to the edge, slipping...she threw her head in her hands and cried as the current tore him loose, throwing him away like a wet doll.

He was under again.

She watched as Rain-in-the-Face did as it always had, slip, slide, and bounce through the rapids. The rapids she'd refused to ride. It hit the fang rocks hard, but stayed in one piece and continued on, undaunted. Once, she thought she saw a hand rise from the foam and felt a brief glimmer of hope. But, if it was Glen, that was the last she saw of him.

Bessie sat on the ledge sobbing for a long time. It was her fault. If only she hadn't been so scared and stupid. On impulse, she'd eliminated their only way out. Her loving husband had paid the price trying to save them. He was right, she'd doomed them all.

She stood, screaming and cursing at the damn river that had taken everything. She used every swear word she'd heard Glen and his father use at the farm. She picked up the biggest rocks she could and threw them at the water until she was too exhausted to lift anymore. Then she sat and cried again.

Bessie didn't know whether she had fainted, fallen asleep, or been in shock. She came to lying on the ledge. It had been hours since she'd lost Glen. The sun was setting, casting the inner gorge into a deep, cold shadow. It was going to be a long night and she'd foolishly not taken any supplies from Rain. She checked her coat pockets, remembering she'd stashed a few doe dads from their last meal. They'd keep her from starving - for a few days, but they wouldn't keep her warm. The rest of the food, Glen's gun, their stove, her journal, the quilts, extra clothes - all of it was gone now, except for a few soggy biscuits and the sketchbook she always took ashore when they stopped.

She screamed again; this time angry at herself.

The steep walls of the canyon rose behind and in front of her as far as she could see. As if the impossible climb wasn't bad enough, the growing darkness seemed to mock any idea of escape. She gathered herself and stumbled back to where they'd beached the scow. Her only way out was upstream, back through the jumble and slide of rocks lining the river all the way to Diamond Creek. She knew it was miles of hard, probably impossible work.

Bessie rubbed her stomach, she couldn't feel movement yet, but the little bulge let her know she wasn't alone. If they made it through the night, she'd try saving them tomorrow. She climbed up the bank, away from the awful river, and found a patch of sand and dirt piled below several large rocks – partially buffered from the wind with just enough space to lay down.

The sun woke her. It was a beautiful morning. Streaks of light were marching down the black face of granite spotlighting parts of the canyon floor and river. She ate half a biscuit, staring downstream, unrealistically hoping to see Glen climbing over river rocks on his way back to her. She went to the river, tore off a piece of her shirt, using it to strain the muddy water. It was still brown and tasted awful, but it would keep them alive.

"Damn you!" she screamed at the rapids downstream; the rapids that had claimed her husband. "Damn, damn, damn you. You won't get us all."

She was so mad...at herself, at Glen, at the inanimate river, at the fix they were in, at everything. She finally relaxed by gently caressing her stomach and speaking to her child.

"I promise I won't go there again. From here on, we don't give in to it. We just keep going, one step at a time. We aren't going to die on this river. No, we won't."

Having no trail was hard. It took an hour to go several hundred yards, sometimes longer. Moving in a straight path was impossible. So was walking. She had to scamper up, down, and often backtrack, to work her way upstream. In a few places she was able to do better. Higher up the slope, rubble piled behind places where larger boulders had come to rest, leaving it less jumbled below.

By noontime she was so tired she began wondering if she could go on. *'One step at a time,'* she told herself. She stopped on a ledge to rest. She pulled out the half-eaten biscuit but decided to put it back. She could wait until evening. Lying down, she closed her eyes.

"Just for a minute, baby" she said, touching her belly.

A deep-throated, guttural cooing woke her. She knew it was an owl. Their barn in Idaho was home to a family of barn owls. The call came from higher up the rockslide. She shielded her eyes against the sun and searched. There! It was a Great Horned and it was sitting a hundred feet above her in a shallow cave. The owl was watching her and shrieked; it sounded like a bark. She imagined it beckoning her.

"Let's go see."

Bessie climbed toward where the owl had been. Halfway there the Great Horned flew away. She wasn't sure why she kept climbing; the sensible thing would be to save her energy and continue along the riverbank. When she reached the cave, it was only a shallow, crescent-shaped indent into a huge boulder. Twenty feet beyond it, the cliff face shot straight up. She sat panting, exhausted, in the mouth of the alcove, looking down at the river. Catching her breath, she studied the rubble to her left and right. She could just make out some sort of animal course. It was rough, but it paralleled the river, at least as far as the next bend. She didn't dare hope.

Following an animal path wasn't for the faint of heart. But it was better and quicker than down by the river. The path varied in width from mere inches to no more than two feet, snaking and dropping through fields of fallen rocks, yucca, and scrub cacti. Bessie stumbled and fell more than once from stepping on loose gravel, scraping and sticking herself each time. She made decent time and rounded a second bend, following the path as it passed through a slide of shale that had crumbled from high above. Slipping was a danger with every step.

Past the shale, she rounded a big boulder, stopping in her tracks. Standing a hundred feet away was a mother bighorn and her baby. The nervous ewe studied her, then high-stepped farther away on the path.

"If that momma can do it, so can I," Bessie said, rubbing her stomach, wanting to cheer the baby she carried.

She felt a renewed sense of purpose and pushed on.

They spent one more night on the path. It was a long, cold night. She huddled in another alcove and piled rocks at the entrance to buffer the wind. It worked, sort of. This high above the river, the wind blew harder; Bessie had never felt so chilled. *Why hadn't she at least thought to grab a blanket? Why?* Before falling asleep, she ate the rest of the biscuit, leaving one more. She was thirsty and thought about climbing down to the river, but was afraid of slipping and falling, and not finding the path again.

In the morning, she took a bite of the last biscuit and continued following the path. She had to be getting close to Diamond Creek. If she could just make it there...at least she'd have a chance of walking out to the rim. The railroad and people were up top, a real town. If nothing else, she could escape the damn river. The unnerving, incessant roaring was unshakeable. She knew it was angry at losing her.

Mid-morning, Bessie spotted the bighorn and its child again. Both were standing at the next bend in the canyon wall. Bessie was dead on her feet; she'd never been this drained before. Every joint ached and balked with each step, her feet rubbed raw in her boots. She knew she needed water; her mouth was so dry she could spit cotton. The mother ewe shook her short, ringed horns, beckoning her forward - *your baby, save your baby.* The ewe disappeared around the bend, her baby clumsily bounding after her.

Bessie kept stumbling forward - *one more step, one more step* - she rounded the bend. Ahead, she could see a side canyon cutting into the black cliff. She focused on the river below and recognized Diamond Creek rapids. She tried walking faster but couldn't. Her feet hurt so badly. She struggled around another bend and down below was the beach.

"We made it, baby! Momma got you back."

The beach sand felt so wonderful. She laid and rolled in it. Her mattress the past two nights had been solid rock with no soft quilts or bed springs. Each step they'd taken was on hard, cold rock. The soft sand was warm and inviting, a massage for her sore legs. And the water from Diamond Creek was cool and sweet, reinvigorating her as she gulped swallow after swallow. She was afraid to take her boots off, so she soaked them and her feet in the cold stream. That night, the two of them slept in the same dilapidated cabin she and Glen had carved their names in. Bessie traced her fingers over and over her husband's until she'd fallen asleep.

She awoke refreshed and excited. They weren't home yet, it was a long walk, but she expected they'd make it. She'd found two old whiskey bottles in the ruins and filled them with water. She ate the last of her biscuits and started up the old wagon road. The first several miles were easy, flat, and shady. The stream meandered with them.

Once the sun rose the air warmed. They'd left the brooding, black inner-gorge and the cool creek behind them. She passed the old Farley place where she'd hiked to with Glen. From there, the wagon trail wound through washes filled with rocks, climbing down and then up. Out of the washes, the trail rose steeply uphill. The sun beat down on her even though it was December. Her feet were on fire. The shrinking, wet leather only made them hurt more.

After hours of walking, she came to a stand of mesquite. *Shade! She so needed to rest!* Farther ahead, the trail climbed into a pass cutting through olive-green shale. A section of canyon wall had fallen or erupted, creating an overlook. She couldn't see the canyon floor past the point; she hoped the grade levelled out. Maybe it would - the walls of the canyon certainly spread wide from there on.

Resting in the spindly, mesquite shade, she emptied the first bottle of water. Clopping sounds thudded against the stone trailbed. Riding out of the wash ahead of her was a Hualapai on horseback. He reined to a stop when he saw her. She waved, but he didn't come forward. He surveyed the land in all directions, his gaze finally working its way back to her. Slowly, he rode toward her. It was hard to tell, but Bessie guessed he was young, younger than she. *Oh, thank God*, she thought.

She rubbed her stomach and smiled. *We made it, baby. We made it. Momma promised you we would. We weren't meant to die there.*

Tears were running down her cheeks. Bessie looked down the canyon toward the river. She pictured Glen, standing proudly on his platform, smiling, in his element, excited about what laid around the next bend. She hadn't had time to think how much she missed him, how her life was now a big unknown - *Oh Glen, my Glen, why couldn't you have stayed? The call of the river, that was why.* She imagined she could still hear it screaming for her.

She shouted, "You got yours. Wasn't that enough? Let me keep mine."

The river had all of time to wait.

EPILOGUE

"**I DON'T KNOW IF I CAN BELIEVE IT?**" LILAC SAID.

"You're not alone."

Skip stuck his legs under him and pushed the swing back.

A week had passed since the events at Diamond Creek. He had just finished telling her the full story. The hint of discovering a mysterious connection between the Chandlers and the Hydes had been enough to convince Lilac to join him for dinner at his cabin. Zula Ballsy had helped him fix the corn-husked tamales and ginger-crusted carrots. Sky had offered to bake a *humble* pie, but he told her Lilac wasn't the sweet type. He had a bottle of red wine in the fridge. That would do. They still had a lot to talk about.

"You need to oil this old thing," Lilac said. "A coat of paint wouldn't hurt either."

They'd finished eating and were on the porch, sitting on his rusty, metal glider. He knew her mind wasn't really on the squeaking swing.

She glanced at him from the side, "A Hualapai Ranger?"

He smiled. He'd already told her the story twice, albeit with each retelling she drew out new details.

"Kuul and I spent the night on the upper dune waiting for the water to recede. If we'd left earlier, we would have had to carry her. Winonna was calmer in the..."

"She probably spent the night curled up against you."

"She was closer to Kuul by then."

"Lucky Mayan."

"Right, anyway, at Bright Angel Pass we ran into a ranger driving down in a pickup. They knew we picked up a permit the day before and he wanted to check if we'd gotten out before the storm. We told him about Lottie and the old man, and that they'd find two dead bodies, one in the lower canyon and one at the beach. He radioed all that in. We didn't have a choice but to tell him what had happened; that Bessie lived and had two children, and that the dead man at the beach was her grandson - the whole nine yards. Kuul and I discussed it the night before and decided it was the right thing to do. Let the authorities figure it out, you know."

Lilac nodded. Skip had already covered how Winonna had been against it but been outvoted.

"It's the ranger's story I find incredible. What's the chance of him being the one who found you?"

"It's hard to swallow, that's for sure - only in Arizona. Like I said, he listened to what happened and why, stared at Winonna, and then we just sat there for ten minutes. You know how stoic these old Hualapai are. Finally, he says, *The spirits and the land showed her the way. They protected them and guided her away.*"

"The owl and bighorn," Lilac said.

"Kuul believes that once Glen was lost, *Tlaloc* balanced the score. *Tlaloc* is a Mayan God often represented in an owl-like costume. He was a lord of water and fertility. The mother ewe might have been a young *Ix Chel*, but he isn't as sure. Regardless of whether they were spirits, or animals that just happened to be in the right place, they led Bessie back to Diamond Creek."

"Spirits," Lilac mused. "Makes a better story."

"I'm going with animals. Now if it had been a toucan and crocodile..."

"The remarkable part is Bessie's running into the ranger's grandfather. He was a young wrangler and rounding up wild horses. Bessie was almost dead, her feet blistered and bleeding. They spent the next three nights at his camp. She tells him everything and actually sketched a picture of him that the ranger's grandfather kept framed above his stove. The grandfather said that after she'd slept and had enough food, she was overcome by grief and guilt over her dead husband. She was scared no one would believe her story and she'd be blamed for his death. On the third morning she's well enough to ride up to Peach Springs."

"Enter the intrepid Kolb brothers," Lilac grinned. "If nothing else, it's a great yarn."

"I wish I could use this chapter in my tours."

Skip was glad Lilac was relaxed and staying. He hadn't been sure what to expect...still wasn't.

"Bessie tries contacting Emery only to find out he's in Phoenix getting some medical treatment. But somehow, he got her message and wired Ellsworth in California who catches the next train east. When he arrives, she's still scared about what people will think. So, they cook up a scheme to send her to California under a different name. There wasn't a lot of ID checking in the 1920s."

"Not even social security cards and most women didn't have driver licenses," Lilac added. "Still..."

Skip smiled, "You have to admit that with Glen and Bessie never being found, his story *could* be true. It's possible."

"So why didn't this Hualapai ranger or his grandfather ever tell their tale?"

"I asked him. He said it was his grandfather's story, not his, and he died keeping her secret. If it had been a story important to his People he'd have passed it down, but it wasn't."

They glided in silence for several minutes. The sun had set and the light from inside the cabin didn't pass the steps of the porch. They were both thinking how to broach the subject of their future. Skip heard rustling in the dark and knew a mule deer or coyote or other creature was trekking to the creek for an evening drink. He'd watched them pass alongside his home before.

He wasn't unaware that Lilac was keeping an emotional distance since she'd arrived. She'd agreed to dinner and enjoyed a fantastic story, but she'd made it clear that was it - for now. He knew he had no choice, no right, but to give her space.

"It's sad and ironic," she said, finally breaking the silence.

"What?"

"They would have made it. The scow was recovered downstream, undamaged. All their provisions were inside. Rain-in-the-Face didn't break apart, flip, or sink. If she'd listened to Glen and stayed with it, they would have made it. They would have joined Lindbergh and Earhart as exploring heroes. Their dreams would have come true. Their flaw, if that ranger's grandfather was telling the truth, was they didn't trust and listen to each other."

"Especially Bessie," Skip said, sending the glider in motion with another kick.

The moon was shining through the trees around the cabin's clearing. They watched a pair of does prance across the opening. Maybe it had been a buck earlier, scouting the way. A breeze was picking up and he heard the wind rustling leaves. It was a cool October night, and he draped a serape across Lilac's shoulders. She wrapped it around them both.

She placed her palm on his cheek, turning his face toward her. The dim light from the cabin and the moon lit the amber specks in her brown eyes. Tiny drops of tears moistened her lashes.

"He should have understood her better. She was his partner. She believed in him, and he let her down. A man can't do that and pretend nothing's changed."

AUTHOR NOTES

TO BEGIN, THE 1956 AIRLINE DISASTER WAS REAL AND DID OCCUR over the Grand Canyon and directly led to the formation of the Federal Aviation Administration. With one exception, material related herein to that tragedy is accurate. That exception, of course, was none of the victims were related to Glen or Bessie Hyde.

Glen and Bessie, however, were real people. They did raft down the Green and Colorado Rivers from Wyoming to the Grand Canyon in the fall of 1928. Somewhere below Hermit's Camp, where they were last seen alive, something terrible happened. No one knows for sure what that was. What is known is that they disappeared. Likewise, the people they met along the way, at Lee's Ferry, Marble Canyon, Grand Canyon Village, and Hermit's Camp, and Adolph Sutro, were real and left records of their interactions with the Hydes. Most of those records were sketchy at best and some accounts changed over time – as stories tend to do. The only made-up character in the Bessie and Glen chapters of the book was Lou

Barker, who gave the Hydes a ride to El Tovar in Chapter Twenty-Nine; they did, however, hike up Kaibab Trail and walk along the road before being picked up by someone.

References to their lives before the trip are verifiable, but fictionally presented in this novel. Whether or not Bessie had a child, before meeting Glen, is debatable. The short, secret, unexplained marriage did happen.

The personal interactions between Glen and Bessie while on the river can never be truly known, except those told by Adolph Sutro. One way or another they went to their graves with those memories. The descriptions of those interactions in this novel are fictional, based on how two young, individualists, who were in love and setting out to conquer an unconquerable world together, might have acted under the circumstances, and upon what they told others along the way. Past Hermit's Camp there is no account of what occurred...or what didn't occur. Bessie kept a journal, but largely in her own shorthand and mostly only recording symbols for riffles, rapids, streams, and quiet water along with a few notations - according to Ellsworth Kolb's handmade copy of the last pages the brothers found in the scow. The original journal was lost in later years by Glen's sister. All that's known for sure is Rain-in-the-Face was found by the Kolb brothers, in sound shape, with their provisions and supplies aboard. Glen, Bessie, and her sketchbook were never recovered.

Personally, the author believes they were thrown from the platform and drowned...*but what if they weren't?*

ABOUT THE AUTHOR

PAUL JOHNSON IS A TOUR GUIDE AND AUTHOR WORKING IN Sedona, Arizona. Sedona is a small artsy town that gets upwards of five million visitors each year, all aspiring to balance their chakras, get lost in beautiful red rock canyons, and levitate over sacred vortexes. He has toured thousands of visitors to natural and cultural sites in Sedona, Grand Canyon, and various Native Nations. Paul shares stories, geologies, and histories to educate his guests about the Southwest's multicultural past and present, which often find their way into his books.

Whitewater Honeymoon is the second book in the *Sedona Chi Mystery series*. Skip Rhodes first adventure was in *Tale of the Broken Spoke*, available at most online retailers. Paul is currently working on the third book in the series, scheduled for release in 2023, which delves deeper into the character Kukulkan Baltazar and his Mayan heritage.

www.ingramcontent.com/pod-product-compliance
Lightning Source LLC
Chambersburg PA
CBHW011601210726
48287CB00012BC/2677

9 781956 203189